Privileges

Privileges

By

Scott Rachelle

1stBooks – rev. 11/02/00

To Kathy, for staying with me through all of this. To Rachel, for whom I would do it all again. To David, for showing the highest level of professional integrity and trust, despite what all the experts said.

PRIVILEGES

One

It was still dark when the alarm clock wailed. Rosalyn Hanley woke suddenly and reached for the shut-off. She started quickly, but slowed with the first twinge from her shoulder. Rose seemed to lose several decades in her sleep, but the years always flowed back with a vengeance when she awoke. Lately, even her sleep didn't feel as deep or refreshing. The arthritis reminded her quickly of her seventy two years. She knew she needn't hurry in silencing the alarm since Alvin, her husband, had died three years earlier. There wasn't anyone around to complain about the noisy buzzer. She looked at the window. The earliest blue hue of morning was beginning to reflect upwards from last night's half inch of snow. It was only five a.m.

She raised herself from the old bed slowly and swung her legs forward. Her knees stayed straight out for a second before she was able to coax her feet to the floor. God, she was stiff today. She wasn't sure if the arthritis was really worse than usual or if she was just anxious. The floor was ice cold. She felt around with her feet for her slippers, worked them over her gnarled toes, and inched to her feet, pushing hard on the side of her bed. She swore her hips cracked as she ratcheted herself up.

Rose picked up her glasses from the nightstand. Out of habit, she put them on. They certainly didn't help anymore. She could barely make out the large red numbers on the alarm clock. Feeling around the corner of the headboard, she found her cane. With a slightly shuffling gait, she made her way toward the bedroom door and felt for the light switch. She flicked it upward, filling the room with a soft, orange glow. She tried to make out the detail in the picture of herself and Alvin in Atlantic City. She knew the lines of the photograph by memory, he with that silly cap and she leaning toward him. Her lips were dark with red lipstick in the black-and-white photo. He was tall and natty. She closed one eye, then the other. No, she couldn't see

1

the detail. She could only remember it. She convinced herself again that she had made the right decision, and started down the hallway.

The fluorescent bulbs in the bathroom hummed, flickered, and popped on with a blue-green cast. She brushed her teeth, taking great care not to swallow any of the water. The nurses had been very explicit that she was to consume nothing--neither food, drink, nor water--after midnight last night. She rinsed the toothpaste, then spit out every last drop. She sighed, and decided she would bathe later. It was just too early right now. She would simply dress and wait for George, her son, in the living room. He would arrive in about half an hour.

The drive to Compton Memorial Hospital was uneventful. Rose worried that the roads would be slippery after the snow last night but the plows had been out already, clearing the way for the morning commuters. There was so much more traffic lately. Sometimes she missed the days when living in Yorkville meant being surrounded by farmland. Oh, yes, it was easier to drive to the Jewel or Dominic's for groceries, and it was nice to see all the young children playing, but she longed for the peace that had been traded so many years ago in the name of development.

Rose and George plodded into the hospital through the electric powered automatic doors. Their shoes crackled on the hard surface of the floor in the foyer, coated with sidewalk salt to prevent icing outside. She hated the salt, because it would stick to the rubber tip of her cane and make it unstable. They pounded some of the dark, slushy snow off of their shoes before making their way onto the soft carpet. Compton had remodeled only last year. She remembered the old linoleum tile floors that had yellowed and cracked from so many years of service. The colors were more muted and gentler now. She liked the new appearance of the place. Still, she became more anxious with each step into the hospital. They could change the appearance, they could change the doctors, but it was still Compton Hospital. Compton was where you went to die.

Rose sat down next to George in front of a simple gray desk tucked into a neat row of six admitting desks. The half-height walls that separated the desks jutted out about three feet, offering minimal privacy for each patient answering the admission questions. A woman with gray hair who appeared not much younger than herself typed Rose's answers into the computer. "Name. Address. Phone. Social security number. Date of birth. Religion. Next of kin." She hated that one. She felt a tingle at the thought of death. "Primary insurance. Secondary?" What a world this was. Health care was so expensive you needed two policies: One to cover the expensive care, one to cover the deductible and co-payment. It was confusing, but she was glad not to have to worry about the bills.

There were so many forms to sign. Claim forms. Forms that allowed the hospital to bill her insurance directly. Consent for surgery forms. Consent for admission. Consent for care. Rose signed them, and handed each one to George. He could scan them for her to see if there was anything meaningful printed on any of them. All she knew was that if she wanted the surgery to help her see she would need to sign all the forms, so she did.

The admitting secretary pushed a button on the computer, and a machine behind her made a clattering noise. A blue plastic card popped out, and the secretary attached it to Rose's paperwork with a clip. Another printer clicked away, and a small perforated card came out of it. The secretary peeled away a small strip of paper, threaded it into a plastic sleeve, and then attached the bracelet-sleeve around Rose's right wrist. It identified her by name, ID number, and doctor, although Rose couldn't read it because the type was too small and muddy. Then an attendant appeared from behind her with a wheelchair, and instructed Rose to sit in it.

They moved through the hallways like a small parade. The attendant pushed the wheelchair and George followed dutifully behind. Rose clung to her cane with one hand and held the plastic-bound medical record chart in her lap with the other. They whisked down the hallways passing doctors, nurses, and other wheelchair bound patients. Most were in hospital gowns. Many were attached to IV's or oxygen tanks. The sicker ones lay on litters. They passed one unfortunate looking fellow attached to several IV's, an oxygen tank, and a respirator. There were so many machines, tubes, and lines, that all George could see of the patient was a small crop of fine, thinning, white hair attached to pale, gray skin. He couldn't tell if the patient was a man or a woman. Rose shivered again. "Compton is where you go to die."

They passed through another set of electric doors and entered the Compton Ambulatory Surgery Center. The room was furnished with invitingly soft looking pine-framed chairs. This was quite a step from the harsh plastic airport chairs that used to be in the surgery waiting room. The entourage was greeted by a sharp young girl wearing a cranberry-colored scrub suit. The cotton shirt seemed smartly pressed, and the interlocking C-M-H logo of Compton Memorial Hospital was printed above the shirt pocket. The girl's brown hair was neat and short and she wore fine gold-framed glasses. "Good morning Mrs. Hanley," she greeted them with a smile. "You're here for cataract surgery for the right eye," she continued, reading from her surgery room schedule.

"That's right," Rose agreed.

"Are you able to walk?" Every patient came in with a wheelchair by policy, but few were truly handicapped.

"Yes."

"Then you can come with me into the changing room. We'll need to have you change your clothes. You can leave your purse with...is that your son?"

Rose nodded.

"You can leave your purse with your son. We'll put your cane in a locker if you prefer, or he can watch that, too."

Once changed, she entered the pre-operative holding room. There she was greeted by another young woman in a cranberry scrub suit. A curl of brown hair sneaked out from under a blue surgical bonnet, and she wore a yellow stethoscope around her neck. "Mrs. Hanley?" she greeted her. "I'm Janet Withers, and I'll be helping you prepare for surgery today. Please follow me." She led the older woman to a row of gurneys, and gestured toward one that was covered with a fresh, white sheet. There was a stepstool in front of it. "Let me help you onto this bed, please." With Janet's help, Rose crept onto the gurney. She sat down a little hard, and then swung her legs up. Janet Withers picked up the plastic-bound medical record. "You're here for cataract surgery this morning, is that correct?"

"Yes."

"Which eye?"

"My right eye."

"Did you have anything to eat or drink since midnight?"

"No."

"How are you feeling today, any medical problems?"

"Just my arthritis. I'm a little stiff this early in the morning."

The nurse smiled. "I understand. I have some medical questions to ask you. I know you've been through this with your doctor, but it's routine."

"Go ahead."

She read a long list of symptoms, none of which Rose suffered from right at this moment. As she read down the list of dreaded symptoms, Rose felt her anxiety growing. She was really going through this, in the hospital where you go to die.

The nurse wrote some notes in Rose's chart. "I just need to give you some drops to dilate your eye." She removed the red caps from two small bottles and placed one drop from each in Rose's right eye. The drops stung. At least Dr. Karp always warned her before he gave her drops. Rose reached up to wipe her eyes. "Sorry," said Nurse Janet. "Let me get you a Kleenex," and she walked away. She gave me eyedrops and didn't even bother to have a box of Kleenex nearby, thought Rose as her eyes watered. A minute later Janet returned. "Here you go." She dabbed the drops from her right cheek. The nurse turned, and before Rose could ask if George could come to stay with her, she was gone.

A few minutes passed and Rose was joined by a dark skinned man in a cranberry scrub suit. His dark hair was covered by a blue paper cap, and his forehead was greasy. He smiled with white teeth under a black moustache with random gray hairs. "Hello. I am Dr. Mahmood. I am the anesthesiologist who will be working with you today." He sat down next to Rose and picked up the chart.

"Anesthesiologist?" asked Rose. "Dr. Karp said that this would be done with local anesthetic. You're not going to put me to sleep, are you?" Now she was nervous. She didn't want to go to sleep in the hospital where you go to die.

"No, no, no," chattered Dr. Mahmood without looking up from the record. "You will not go to sleep. Dr. Karp will numb your eye with a shot." The thought of a shot in her eye frightened Rose. "You are here for cataract surgery?"

"Yes."

"Have you ever had problems with anesthetics before?"

"No."

"Do you take any medicines?" Mahmood proceeded to ask all of the questions that Nurse Janet Withers had already asked only moments ago. Dutifully, Rose answered them again. She didn't want to die.

"Very good," said Mahmood finally. He closed the chart with a slap and made eye contact with Rose for the first time since he had sat down. "Next I will start your IV. May I see your arm, please." Rose extended her left arm. Mahmood wrapped an inch thick band of yellow rubber around her upper arm and snapped it tightly closed.

"Ouch," said Rose meekly.

"I am sorry." Mahmood unwrapped a package of plastic tubing and inserted the large end into the bottom of a plastic bag full of sterile saline. He fiddled with the plastic tube. Rose's arm throbbed. Mahmood wiped Rose's forearm with a cold pad. She smelled the alcohol. "You will now feel a bee sting." He deftly slid the needle into her vein and threaded the plastic catheter forward. Releasing the tourniquet with a snap, he quickly attached the tubing to the IV catheter. "You did very well," said Mahmood without looking up as he taped the IV to Rose's arm. He smiled, and walked away.

Nurse Janet returned to give her more eyedrops. Rose asked if George could keep her company while she waited. "Of course," said Janet, "let me get him." Thank goodness, thought Rose. At least I won't have to go through this all by myself. In an instant, Janet returned with George in tow.

A few moments later, Dr. Karp strolled in. He, too, wore a cranberry scrub suit and a blue, fluffy bonnet over his hair. The only way Rose could recognize her doctor was by his prominent roundish nose, brushy brown moustache, and dark-rimmed glasses. He reached out a hand for her. "Good morning, Mrs. Hanley."

"Good morning, Dr. Karp."

Karp reached over to shake George's hand. "How are you today?"

"Pretty good, I guess," answered George. "I sure do hate to get up this early."

"I know," said Karp earnestly. "So do I. But if we don't get dibs on the first surgery slot on the schedule, we often have to wait for hours to follow the cases in front of us." He spoke in the plural, as was his habit, referring to his surgical team rather than himself alone.

"I hope you got a good night's rest," said Rose.

"You bet. You'll find that the waiting is the hardest part of the whole thing here. Try to relax, and we'll get you home as quick as we can." He picked up her chart and started writing, flipping pages, writing again, flipping pages. "Do you have any questions for me?"

Rose lay back on the gurney. "No," she said. "I don't think so."

Karp snapped the chart closed. "Okay. They'll be giving you some more drops, and then we'll see you next door." He

7

meant the Operating Room, but didn't like to refer to it that way with patients. Rose tried to relax. She felt the butterflies in her stomach.

Fifteen minutes later, after four courses of eyedrops and a lot of writing in her chart, another nurse wearing a cranberry scrub suit walked up to Rose. Beside the obligatory bonnet, she had a mask dangling around her neck. "I'm Leann," she introduced herself, "and I'll be the circulating nurse in the Operating Room today." Rose wasn't entirely sure what that meant. "I just have a few questions to go over with you before we move to the OR." Leann then began the same litany of questions regarding Rose's diagnosis, which eye would be operated, whether she'd had anything to eat or drink.

Finally, Leann wrote some notes in the chart and then replaced it on the gurney. "We'll go into the Operating Room now. Do you have any questions?"

"No."

George leaned over and gave her a little peck on the cheek. "Luck, Ma," he said. Rose smiled.

Leann unlocked the wheels of the gurney and pulled it forward. She turned it toward the electric doorway that led to the Operating Room Suite, then walked behind Rose's head and pushed the gurney in that direction. They passed Nurse Janet, who was checking another patient's blood pressure. "Good luck," she chirped. The doors to the OR Suite hummed open.

The hallway was brightly lit. Two nurses walked by carrying some large instruments. An orderly pushed a big bucket and mop into an operating room. Everyone buzzed by without paying any attention to the old woman on the gurney. Rose drew a deep breath.

The gurney turned toward the door to OR 4 and pushed it forward with a little thud. Rose could see the huge overhead surgical light hanging ominously above the operating table. The table was little more than a black vinyl pad attached to a heavy base by a scaffold of steel bars. At the head of the bed was the anesthesia machine, a tall mobile table with a chest of drawers attached by several umbilical hoses to the ceiling. Dr. Mahmood sat on a stool in front of the anesthesia machine and fiddled with a video monitor. Across from Mahmood and the anesthesia machine was a surgical microscope. It was all gray, and the eyepieces and optics hung from a long articulated arm. Thick black cables ran along the length of the arm, attached to foot pedals, control boxes, and a fiberoptic light source.

Along the far wall, another nurse was working with a table of instruments. Unlike the others, she wore a blue surgical gown over her cranberry scrubs. Everyone wore masks in the OR. The table she worked over was covered with blue paper that hung like a table cloth toward the floor. There were several other machines around the room, and a portable radio-tape player was plugged into a receptacle in the corner.

Leann maneuvered the gurney so that it was parallel to the operating table, then pushed them gently together. Mahmood reached for the IV bag hanging over Rose's head, failing to acknowledge the woman to whom it was attached.

"Okay, Mrs. Hanley," said Leann. "I need you to scoot to your left, onto the operating table. I can help you if you like, and it's all right to make lots of little moves."

Rose pushed herself up on her elbows and creaked her butt shallowly into the air. Her knees hurt. She pushed herself over the crack between the gurney and the table, just a few inches at a time. "A little further, please," Leann instructed. "A little more. That's good. Now, scoot up toward your head just a little. There, that's good."

The door creaked open. Rose averted her eyes and saw Dr. Karp bounce into the room. "Good morning," he greeted to all present, and picked up the chart once more. He flipped a few pages. In a moment, another man walked in, much older than Karp and wider. She thought she recognized him from the office as Dr. Karp's assistant. He said nothing and began arranging some instruments on a small table. Karp wrote in the chart, flipped it shut and walked over to her. "How are you?"

"A little nervous."

"That's to be expected. It would be odd if you weren't." His voice was reassuring. "Dr. Mahmood will give you some medicine to help take the edge off." He looked over towards the anesthesiologist.

"It will be a moment," responded Mahmood without looking up from the paperwork on his desk.

"It will be a minute or two," repeated Karp, who smiled under his mask, and turned toward the instruments being arranged by his assistant.

"Very good," said Mahmood finally. "I will give you some medicine in your vein. You may feel some burning. This will make you sleepy." True to his word, Rose felt burning in her left arm. Suddenly, her tongue felt thick. She smacked her lips.

"Are you feeling all right?" Dr. Karp appeared over her head.

"Yes, I think so," she answered groggily.

Karp turned toward Mahmood. "Okay?"

"Yes, I am ready when you are."

"Let's rock and roll."

"You may feel some more burning," said Mahmood. She felt it, but didn't care.

"Can I see the lenses," said Karp, suddenly across the room.

"Yes, Doctor," shouted the scrub nurse from down the hall. "They're on the mayo..." she was now in another building. Rose's eyelids were closed. Very sleepy. She sighed deeply, and hiccupped.

Karp looked at Mahmood. "Ready?"

"I think so."

Karp picked up one of two syringes from a nearby table and examined the label attached to it. It said "2% w/ epi," lidocaine with epinephrine, used for the local block of the nerve that activates the muscles of the eyelids. Gently, Karp turned Rose's head to the left and wiped her right cheek with an alcohol pad, just in front of the ear. "That will be a little cold," he said, still telling her what to expect, even though she was completely asleep and snoring from the Versed and Diprovan that Mahmood had injected through her IV. "Now you'll feel a little stick." He placed the needle, drew back on the syringe, and saw only bubbles form in the medication; there was no return of blood signifying an inadvertent placement of the needle into a vessel. Then he began injecting the medicine. "You'll feel a little stinging now." Rose snored. He advanced the needle and continued to inject, then withdrew it and quickly covered the injection site with a pad and replaced her head to a supine position, looking upwards.

The big man who had entered the room with Karp, Alonzo Morrissey, put his finger on the pad for Karp. Lon was twenty years Karp's senior, and had been with him for seven of those years. In the office he helped the doctor work up new patients, and at the hospital he assisted Karp in surgery. He was also an expert contact lens fitter, having learned the trade in the late 1950's before the advent of intraocular lenses. Back then there were no intraocular lenses, IOL's, used to focus vision following cataract surgery when the natural lens is removed. Patients depended on thick "cataract glasses" or wore contact lenses. Lon learned to fit, grind, and care for contact lenses. Years later he worked for a large optical concern that ran a shop across the street from Detroit General Hospital, where young Dr. Jerrold Karp was learning ophthalmology. They became friends, and Lon eventually joined Karp as a technician and jack-of-all-trades in the office.

Karp picked up the second syringe and examined the label. It said "Lido & Mar," which meant it contained a mixture of half Lidocaine and half Marcaine. The former was a fast acting local anesthetic with a relatively short duration. Marcaine took longer to kick in, but gave the patient freedom from discomfort for up to half a day.

"More cold," said Karp as he wiped the right lower eyelid with alcohol. "Another needle stick." He pushed the needle gently into the orbital space below the eye, using the index finger of his right hand to feel the location of the eyeball. "Nice anesthesia," he told Mahmood, as Rose didn't budge. This part was very painful for an alert patient, and Karp took advantage of

11

the short acting anesthesia and amnesia offered by the IV meds. "More burning," he said as he injected the anesthetic mixture. "That's the numbing medicine going in." Rose snored once more. "Very good," said Karp, as he quickly removed the needle. Lon tore open a packet containing an eye pad and handed it to Karp, who placed it quickly over the eye and put pressure over the injection site.

Lon reached for the eye pressure reducing cuff. It was a small rubber ball attached to a pump from a blood-pressure cuff. Using a strap, the ball was placed over the freshly anesthetized eye and blown up to a measured pressure with the pump. "Time," said Karp, indicating the start of a five-minute countdown to allow sufficient pressure reduction in the eye before the start of surgery.

"Eight oh-three," responded Lon.

"Okay," said Karp. As he stepped back and returned to the chart. He opened it up and flipped through the pages once more to double check that all the sheets that needed to be present were there and signed in ink by him. Cover sheet, yes. Diagnosis: Cataract, right eye. Procedure: Phacoemulsification with IOL, right eye. Signature, date. Orders sheet, signed and dated. History and physical, signed and dated. Lab, initialed. Discharge orders, signed and dated. Good. The chart was ready. He hated to have to sign papers after the surgery. By then his hands were puffy and warm from the rubber gloves and the talcum powder from them made his pen slippery. He glanced again at the manila chart from his office. The clinic note from the last visit recorded the vision as 20/200 in the right eye. Dense cataract, cornea OK. Retina healthy as visualized. He checked the IOL calcs, the mathematical calculations performed by his computer to choose the correct lens implant power based on the curvature of the patient's cornea and the length of the eye. Everything was consistent. Good. Time to wash up.

Karp walked out of the OR and turned to the large stainless steel sink under a window looking into the OR. Lon was already there with both hands and arms lathered with orange Betadine soap. Karp pushed the switch to start the water with his knee. It was designed that way so that once he was scrubbed he would not have to use his hands to turn off the water. Then he opened a sterile Betadine soaked scrub brush and started to lather himself up.

"Well, my boy, are you ready for the day?" asked Lon. They had four cases scheduled.

"Yeah, yeah, Lonnie. Four big cases. We ought to be out by, oh, say two p.m." They chuckled. Four IOL's in a privately owned surgery center could be completed within two hours. A really fast surgeon could do them even quicker. Karp knew that working in a hospital, where he had no control over the employees whatsoever, would take several hours more than that. They'd end up waiting between cases for more time than they'd spend operating.

They did not converse further. Lon knew that Karp's routine included going over the case mentally as he scrubbed. Karp closed his eyes and saw himself opening the conjunctiva, placing the incision in the white sclera, and then entering the anterior fluid filled chamber of the eye with a stab-incision. He saw the opening of the lens capsule, the prolapse of the lens nucleus, and its removal. Then he pictured the aspiration of the remaining lens material, extension of the wound, and placement of the IOL. He pictured the sutures in place, and closed the conj by cautery in his mind. He opened his eyes. Karp dropped the scrub brush and stepped on the foot pedal to coat his hands and arms once more with fresh Betadine soap. He turned to his right as he washed and saw that Lon was already in the OR drying and putting on his gown. Karp rinsed the soap off his arms, kicked the switch to turn off the water and dripped into the sink for a few moments.

Karp returned to the OR, and approached Edie, the hospital's scrub nurse, who handed him a blue sterile towel to dry his hands. Lon finished placing sterile drapes over the patient. Rose was now fully awake again. "You'll feel Mr. Morrissey covering you with some nice, clean covers," explained Karp as he dried his hands. "We have some oxygen blowing in your nose so you'll have plenty of good air to breathe while you're covered. Are you feeling okay?"

"Yes, I'm fine," came the muffled answer from under the drapes.

"Good. Try to hold real still and relax. I'll let you know before we do anything."

Edie draped the gown over Karp's arms, and Leann tied the strings behind him. It was a flimsy paper gown, gossamer in its thinness. "Low bid gown," said Karp, referring to the method of procurement used by hospitals to try to hold down costs. Stronger, absorbent gowns were reserved for wet, bloody belly surgery or orthopedic cases.

Edie held out a rubber glove, opening the edges so that Karp could slide his right hand in. Even though he was left handed, he gloved the right hand first by convention. Then Edie held out the left glove, and Karp opened the edge a little further with his now sterile right hand. He slid his left hand in, and as he did the glove tore. A large flap of yellow rubber hung down the dorsum of his hand. He shook his head. "Low bid glove. New left glove, please." Leann got a fresh package of rubber gloves from a cabinet, and Karp got the left one on with no breakage. "That ought to blow the profit margin," he commented.

Over the previous decade HCFA, the Health Care Finance Administration run by the government to dole out Medicare dollars, enacted fee cuts for ophthalmologists. Several other specialists saw cuts, too, but ophthalmologists had been hit hard and hit frequently. The main justification for this was the significant increase in Medicare dollars spent for cataract surgery.

Until the 1960's cataracts were removed only when they were extremely dense. Then surgical techniques improved dramatically. The operating microscope enhanced the surgeon's view, and the development of fine micro-sutures meant that the surgical wound could be closed more securely. Advances in the design and manufacture of IOL's meant that vision following surgery no longer required thick glasses or contacts. More and more patients wanted cataracts removed, and surgeons were able to provide better results with shorter healing times. The cataract surgery industry boomed and the cost to the system skyrocketed, so Medicare cut cataract surgeon's fees deeply. Now, only months after Bill Clinton's election to the Presidency, doctors and surgeons were worried. There was talk of severe cutbacks for all of medicine. Cost-cutting had become a way of life for people who had laughed at the ophthalmologists a few months earlier.

Jerry Karp was worried too, but he kept working to make his little solo practice successful. He had been with another doctor before in Oklahoma. His partner had started small and flourished during the golden years of the seventies and eighties, grossing millions of dollars for the thousands of cataract procedures he performed every year. He took on Karp to care for patients with other eye diseases and perform a small amount of cataract surgery. When the cutbacks came, though, he changed. Suddenly he wanted to do all the surgery. He moaned that he couldn't cover the payroll or the monthly mortgage on the ten thousand square foot office building he constructed to house the new practice. His wife's new Mercedes suggested otherwise, and Karp decided that a small practice that he could manage himself would be worth the considerable effort of moving and starting fresh.

Karp and his wife resettled in Aurora, Illinois, just forty minutes from Chicago's loop and located on the new corridor of growth west of the big city. The town was far enough away that it could not be considered a suburb; only a small number of Aurorans actually commuted to Chicago. On the other hand, it was close enough to civilization that they didn't have to feel isolated, like they did in Oklahoma.

Karp turned his attention to Rose Hanley's right eye. He picked up the fine speculum that held her eyelids open through the case. "How are you doing, Mrs. Hanley?" he asked.

"It's a little warm in here," came the muffled response from under several layers of sterile drapes.

"Turn up the air flow, please," directed Karp. "We'll turn up the air for you under the covers. That should make it feel better. Look up for me please," he instructed her. The eye made no movement. "Now look down. Right. Left. Good." There was nary a budge. He was happy with this block. "If you feel anything, let me know and we'll give you more numbing medicine, okay?"

"All right."

Karp moved the operating microscope in place. "Silk." Karp put out his left hand, and Edie handed him a needle driver holding 4-0 silk. He gently ran the needle underneath the superior rectus muscle and clamped it in position so that the eye wouldn't move when he pushed on it during surgery.

He handed the needle driver back, and Lon gave him a fine scissors. He made a small opening in the conjunctiva, only a few millimeters long, and then handed the scissors back. "Cautery." Karp ran an electric cautery device over the exposed white sclera to close the blood vessels in it and prevent bleeding.

"Sixty-nine," referred to the Beaver Surgical Blade Co. model 69 knife, which Karp used to make a partial thickness incision along the limbus, where the clear cornea merged with the white sclera of the eye. "Super blade," indicated the super-sharp single use blade that he used to enter the anterior chamber of the eye. A small trickle of watery aqueous fluid let him know he was there.

Just as he had rehearsed it before the scrub sink, Karp opened the lens capsule and removed the cataract through the tiny incision using the phacoemulsifier. This device softened the hard nucleus so that it could be aspirated from the eye. He used a smaller aspirator to suck out the small bits of lens material left behind by the first. He let out a deep sigh with the completion of this difficult part of the surgery, then lengthened the wound by a few millimeters so that he could glide the tiny lens implant--the

IOL--in place of the missing natural lens. Finally, he closed the incision with ultra fine nylon suture.

Karp examined his handiwork. The pupil was round and central. Behind it was the optically clear plastic intraocular lens implant, supported by the intact posterior capsule. He saw a sharp red reflection from the retina indicating clear ocular media. Good job, he thought.

"Mrs. Hanley?"

"Yes."

"The cataract is out and the implant is in. Everything looks terrific."

"That's great."

Lon pushed the microscope out of the way and removed the sterile covers from Rose's face. Karp taped a patch and metal shield over the eye to prevent Rose from rubbing it if it began to hurt later. "You did terrific," Karp told her.

"No, you did," she answered. "I didn't feel a thing."

Karp removed the mask from his face. He hated the thing because it made his nose run into his moustache. "I couldn't do it without your help," said Karp as he signed the IOL identification card that Rose would carry with her to designate the manufacturer, model, and power of the man-made lens inserted into her eye. "You can give lessons to my other patients to show them how to do this."

Rose smiled, proud of herself.

Mahmood smiled too, knowing Karp told that to all of his patients, no matter how much they flailed around under the drapes.

"Mr. Morrissey will see to it that you get to the recovery area while I tell George about your surgery. Remember to take it easy today and to take the antibiotic pills you were given. You'll also have a pain pill to use if it hurts..."

"Oh, it doesn't hurt," she interjected.

"I know, but if it does later, don't be afraid to use it. I'll see you in the office tomorrow at eight-thirty. Any questions?"

"No, you answered them for me."

"Very good." Karp placed a copy of the IOL label in his clinical chart for later reference. "We'll see you tomorrow." Jerry Karp then strode out of the room, a successful gladiator in the arena of cataract surgery.

After visiting with George and then with his next patient, Karp retired to the surgeon's lounge to wait for the second case to begin. The lounge was a small room next to the OR's, dimly lit by two table lamps and a flickering fluorescent tube overhead. There were two coffeemakers, one with decaf, and a half empty box of doughnuts on a table to his right. Straight ahead, the console T.V. glowed with CNN news reports most of the day. Across from the T.V. was an old sofa and two matching chairs. The dark coffee stains on the sofa matched the larger blot on the industrial-weave carpeting that covered the floor. This lounge was the only carpeted area in the entire OR suite. To Karp's left were two partially enclosed desks with telephones connected directly to the hospital's dictation department. These phones were used by the doctors to dictate operative notes for the medical records.

Karp pulled up a seat in front of one of the dictaphones and pressed the record button with his thumb. "This is Dr. Karp, K-A-R-P, dictating a procedure note on Rosalyn Hanley, H-A-N-L-E-Y. Today's date is February 15, 1993. Preoperative diagnosis, cataract right eye. Postop, same. Procedure performed, phacoemulsification with implantation of..." he checked the IOL identification sticker inside Rose's office chart. "...a Lenstech Model UV1745, plus nineteen point fifty diopter power intraocular lens, right eye." He went on, and carefully described the procedure in accurate detail. This was very important, as it would be the only record of exactly what had happened in the OR if there were ever a question in this regard. Of course, the only likely cause for this type of review would be the filing of malpractice litigation. Karp was reasonably confident that this was unlikely with Rose Hanley, but dictated with due caution nonetheless. He was compulsive about the accuracy of his medical records.

"...The eye was patched over Maxitrol ointment and a Fox Shield was placed over it for protection." Karp completed his report. "The patient was discharged home in good condition, having tolerated the procedure well without complication. She will return in twenty-four hours for followup. This is Karp, K-A-R-P, ending dictation on Hanley, H-A-N-L-E-Y, February 15, 1993." He pushed the LISten button with his index finger, and the tape recorder rewound a short distance and played back the last three seconds of his dictation. Satisfied with the completeness of the record, he hung up the handset.

Karp pushed away from the dictating station and walked over to the coffeemakers, where he poured himself a cup of decaf. As he chose a glazed doughnut from the box, Mahmood entered the lounge. "I need my sugar buzz," justified Karp, motioning with the doughnut. Of course, nobody else really cared, but he felt the need to justify the calories given the extra fifteen pounds he carried on his five foot eight inch frame.

As Karp sat down on the sofa, Mahmood poured a cup of coffee. Karp listened to a "Hollywood Minute" on CNN, half interested, and skimmed over the front page of yesterday's Tribune as he savored the frosted doughnut. "Did you hear about Bullock?" asked Mahmood, stirring a packet of Sweet'n'Low into his coffee. Adam Bullock was another anesthesiologist, one of a group of four employed by the hospital.

"No. What happened?"

"He was fired yesterday."

"What?" Karp could not think of any problems he'd had with Bullock. An unskilled anesthesiologist in a small hospital, even in a large one, soon developed a reputation. Surgeons would avoid him, not wanting to risk harm to their patients. "Why?"

Mahmood sat in the chair next to Karp. "Mr. Kilner calculated that the hospital did not need four anesthesiologists now." Daniel Kilner was the hospital's chief executive officer, who had taken over after Hank Greenley retired. He had a reputation as a cold businessman. "He determined that more nurse anesthetists could be hired at a cheaper wage."

"But didn't Bullock have a contract?"

"Of course, we all do." Mahmood snapped at a cruller. "All of the contracts give the hospital the right to release us with three weeks' notice, for any reason. Kilner told Bullock he could stay on for three weeks or just take the vacation time."

Karp smiled. "I'm sure he decided to keep working."

"Oh yeah. You bet."

"How'd he take it."

"Pretty well, I understand. His wife's upset, though."

"They just bought a new place in Naperville, didn't they?"

"Yeah, yeah. They put it on the market this morning."

"What's he going to do? Is anyone hiring?"

"He told me he's going to take some vacation time. Go skiing. He sent his resume in to a couple of locum tenens houses." Locum tenens relationships allow a practicing physician to take a long vacation and hire another doctor to cover his practice while he is away, preventing huge losses of cash flow. The work could be lucrative, although the locum tenens doctor usually had to share his fee with the agency that arranged the coverage. The hardest part about it, though, was the traveling. While it was interesting for a single doc or one just out of residency, it could be very difficult for a physician with a family.

Karp sipped his decaf. "Kilner did that from out of the blue?"

Mahmood nodded. "Last month he'd even hinted about hiring on a new man. It's all this talk about health care reform." His eyes narrowed. "All everyone thinks about is overhead, and for us that means manpower. I swear, I don't know how three of us are going to keep up with the volume...even with the nurse anesthetists."

Karp figured that meant he wouldn't be working with the MD's for anesthesia for much longer. The RN's were cheaper, and the MD's would be needed for cases that were more complex and potentially dangerous: Bellies, hearts, neuro cases. That's too bad, he thought. He liked the anesthesiologists and they treated his patients well. He didn't have to scrutinize every EKG and chest X-ray because he knew the anesthesiologists would pick up subtle problems. Karp sighed. He thought about that chocolate covered long john in the box. "Damn cold of Kilner," he mumbled.

Mahmood looked at CNN, and said nothing.

"Dr. Karp?" The metallic voice came into the lounge from the overhead speaker of the intercom system.

"Yes," he answered, without looking up from yesterday's sports section.

"They're ready for you in four."

"Thank you." Karp glanced at his watch. Nine forty five. "Fast turnaround," he said to Mahmood, noting a mere thirty five minutes to clean the OR and bring Mr. Johnson in.

"We'll see if they can move a little faster after the reforms kick in," said Mahmood.

"Why?" Karp grinned. "We'll all be government employees with lifetime jobs."

"Yeah, jobs for a lifetime," repeated Mahmood. "Like Bullock."

Karp and Mahmood left their nearly empty coffee cups on the table where they rested. Earl Johnson was already on the operating table, and Lon and Leann had begun hooking him up to the various monitors. Mahmood took over, and Lon brought the IOL's to Karp as he again reviewed the medical records for completeness and accuracy. Once Earl was adequately attached to the monitors, they again started the routine. Mahmood injected Diprovan into Earl's IV line, and within seconds he drifted off to a gentle sleep. Karp looked at Mahmood, who nodded and said, "He is ready."

Karp tore open an alcohol prep pad and cleaned the area of Earl's right cheek for the facial block. "You'll feel a little cold," he told his sleeping patient. "Now a needle stick and some burning." Karp accurately placed the needle, and Earl moaned and bucked. He injected the anesthetic, and Earl, still sleeping, grimaced and clearly moaned out the word "ouch."

"He could stand to be just a bit deeper," Karp advised his anesthesiologist.

Mahmood checked the patient's age and weight, and double checked his blood pressure, pulse rate, and heart monitor. Everything appeared to be in order, including the dose of Diprovan that he had already given Earl. He injected more into the IV line. He waited a moment, then nodded to Karp. "Okay."

Karp used a prep pad to clean the area of skin just under Earl's right eye. "A little cold again. Now a needle stick and some stinging." He then drove the needle into the orbit, past the equator of the eye, and turned it upward slightly to inject into the cone of muscles. As he pushed the needle into the orbit, Earl moaned again. "Jesus," said Karp, "I haven't even given him the anesthetic yet." He pushed on the syringe. As the medicine went in, Earl began thrashing his head from side to side. Lon reached down to help Karp steady the head as he finished placing the block. "Lovely," said Karp as he removed the needle and applied pressure to the globe. Lon helped him place the pressure cuff on the eye. "I'm glad that stuff has a good amnesic effect," he said to Mahmood. "You'd better try to keep him fairly deep through the case."

"Mr. Johnson," called Karp a few moments later, wanting to test the completeness of his nerve block. Johnson didn't answer, he just snored. Karp nodded and said, "Well, he sure looks sleepy now." He and Lon went out to scrub up.

"Mr. Johnson," called Karp after he placed the speculum to open his eye.

Earl responded with a dreamy, "Yeah?" followed by a gurgly snore.

"Keep him deep," reminded Karp. "Bridle suture," he requested. As Karp fixed the superior rectus muscle with his forceps, Earl groaned again. He ran the needle under the muscle,

22

and Earl tried to turn his head. Karp sighed. He knew this was going to be a tough case. He moved the microscope into place. "Scissors," he held out his hands for the instruments to begin the case. As he opened the conjunctiva, Earl groaned a tiny bit through a sleepy haze. Karp cauterized the blood vessels and entered the anterior chamber. Earl laid still. Karp went on working to remove the lens nucleus. It was especially hard, which meant that a little more time was needed for this step. Earl snored away. Finally, though, the nucleus was gone. Earl had not made a move nor uttered a sound since Karp had opened the conj. He took the irrigation and aspiration unit and inserted into the eye to remove the bits of retained lens cortex.

Midway through this maneuver, Earl woke up. His senses dulled by the IV medications, he had forgotten where he was and what was happening to him. He grunted and tried to look around, but saw nothing more than a bright, blue blur through the sterile drapes. "Mr. Johnson?" a voice called to him from the distance. He tried to answer, but his tongue was too thick. In fact his mouth was awfully dry. He was hot. He was covered. Where was he? He tried to look around. Nothing but blue. He felt a little tightness and tried to breathe deeply, but he couldn't, as the anesthetic was still a little deep. He was awake enough, though, to suddenly get scared.

He turned his head. He tried to cry out, but only made a little grunt. "Hold still, please," the voice called to him from nowhere. He tried to lift his hand, but it was tied down. He tried to turn his body, but couldn't. He was strapped in place, and he was terrified. He tried to move his head, to turn, to see something familiar. He couldn't. He tried again to breathe deeply, without much success. He grunted again.

"Mr. Johnson, relax please," said Karp. He had removed the aspiration tip from Earl's eye when he made the first jerking head movement. "It's Dr. Karp. The cataract is mostly out, we're moving right along. Try to relax." He jerked his head once more, then he fell back asleep, overcome by the systemic narcotics.

Karp surveyed his surgical field through the microscope. The pupil was still round and central. There was some lens cortex present on the left side and up above, near the incision. He concentrated on the posterior lens capsule. He saw it glisten against the microscope's light reflection. It was still intact. Good, we can proceed, he thought.

Karp replaced the handpiece tip and continued his aspiration of the lens material. A piece entered the vacuum port and was sucked away. Another piece at the top of the field wasn't so compliant. He sucked and sucked at it, controlling the suction power with the foot pedal. Finally, the cortex material came loose and seemed to fall toward the middle of the surgical field. Karp watched as it began to disappear into the port.

Just then, Earl Johnson woke up again. This time, he was agitated by disorientation immediately. He had to know where he was. Underwater? Dead? I'm not dead, he thought, and jerked his head hard to get a better look.

The soft red reflex of light through Earl's pupil disappeared from Karp's view through the microscope and was replaced by a white blur. He had his small finger and the edge of his palm resting against the side of Earl's face to make sure that any instrument inside the eye moved together with his patient, but the jerking movement was too much even for this safeguard. The tip of the handpiece plunged through the posterior lens capsule, and sucked out a large clump of stringy, gelatinous vitreous. Karp yanked the handpiece out, but he knew it was too late.

Earl groaned from under the covers. "Mr. Johnson, it's Dr. Karp. Try to relax. The cataract is out, and we're almost finished." That's where he was! In surgery. He relaxed a bit, and fell back to sleep.

Karp repositioned Earl's head under the microscope, and examined the situation. A gob of vitreous poked out through the incision at the edge of the cornea. "Vitrector, please," Karp said calmly. "At least there's no retained lens material," he noted mostly to himself as Leann and Edie worked to attach the vitrectomy handpiece to the machine. This handpiece not only aspirated material, but used a rotating blade at the port's entrance to cut away the fibrous matrix that made up the formed part of the vitreous. In this way, the material could be removed with minimal tugging against the retina. Too much traction might lead to a retinal detachment.

After ten minutes of vitrectomy, he reviewed the surgical field. He couldn't see any strands or chunks of vitreous. "Miochol," asked Karp. He injected this into the eye and watched the pupil constrict. He reformed the anterior chamber with Healon and asked for the anterior chamber IOL. This style of IOL, commonly used twenty years before, is supported in front of the iris and does not depend on an intact posterior capsule for proper support. He deftly slid it into position. Earl Johnson again awoke, and wriggled his head from side to side. "Good timing," said Karp quietly, as he now had no instruments in the eye. He then reminded his patient where he was. Mahmood asked if Karp wanted more IV meds. "No," he decided. "We're almost done." Earl settled down once more, and Karp closed the wound.

Finally he was able to remove Earl's sterile drapes. "You did terrific," said Karp. "The cataract is out and the implant is in. Everything went according to plan. You were a terrific patient."

"Thanks, doc," Earl answered. "I didn't feel a thing. I hope I didn't move too much."

"Oh, no," said Karp in his most reassuring tone. He tore off his paper gown. His back was wet with perspiration. "Not at all," he smiled through his mask.

PRIVILEGES

Two

Karp opened his locker to change out of the cranberry scrubs and into his street clothes. He stepped into a pair of navy Dockers, which he considered nice enough for OR days when he didn't see scheduled patients in the office. Since time at the hospital could linger long enough to make any schedule unworkable, he would just do paperwork and administrative tasks after cataract surgery. Karp put on a blue and red striped tie and turned toward the mirror to tie the knot. He rubbed the fold of extra tissue in his neck, and tried to decide if he had really gained enough weight to be developing a double chin. He pushed his glasses up the bridge of his nose for a better look. No, his wife, Valerie, was just prodding him a little too hard to lose weight, he decided. He turned back to the locker and slipped on his brown loafers, then reached up to take his wedding band and watch.

Karp closed the locker and went over to the mirror once more. He ran a comb through his now flattened brown hair. On OR days his hair was just unmanageable. The chiffon cap he wore in the OR somehow pushed it out of place and it would not look neat afterward no matter how he combed or fussed with it. He worked for a few moments, but left it tussled like a grammar school boy's mop. He next ran the comb through his neatly trimmed moustache for a few strokes. He loved that moustache, which he grew on a dare when Val suggested he'd look better with one. Convinced it would just look scraggly and thin, like the one he'd grown in college, he went ahead and was well pleased with the final result. He decided to keep the facial hair at last when his colleagues told him it made him look a little older. Karp was self-conscious about his baby faced look, especially now that he was getting a double chin. He was young. Only thirty-seven, he had finished college in just three years and gone on to medical school when he was twenty.

Karp checked his mailbox in the doctors' lounge for copies of lab reports and notices for unsigned charts, then made his way out to the parking lot. Although Karp had been a practicing physician for several years, he was still somehow amazed by the collection of automobiles to be found in the staff docs' lot. There were a couple of Cadillacs, a Jeep Cherokee, and some slacker even drove a Cutlass convertible. There were no fewer than three BMW's and two Lexus coupes. One of the gastroenterologists drove a new Nissan Z car, and Karp loved to park next to him. He knew that his own Dodge Stealth handled every bit as well as the Z and was only infinitesimally slower from a standing stop. At something less than half the price of the Z, Karp could still justify the luxury he had given himself in the Stealth, the first new car he'd ever owned.

He tossed the charts onto the microscopic back seat then slid gently into the front seat, careful not to tear the leather with his pager. The car started with a throaty roar. Karp loved the exhaust note. He backed out and headed away from the hospital. He had only three miles to drive to get to his office, and most of that was in a residential neighborhood. This was far more car than he really needed. He loved it.

By now, the snowfall from the night before had been well cleared away. The ice was nothing more than a very wet slush, having been melted by tons of salt spread by the Aurora road maintenance crews. Karp guided the Stealth over the Fox River and headed west, just a few blocks from the tiny downtown area. He drove up Galena Boulevard and entered a small complex of office condominiums across from Shipley High School. The Paramount Office Condos, owned by the same concern as the theater, were only a few years old and still quite clean. Karp liked the cozy little office he found vacant there, and with Val's help he was able to turn it into a workable place.

"Good morning," greeted Maureen, his office manager and receptionist. Except for Lon, who assisted Karp with patient care matters, Maureen was his only employee. She had been with Karp since he'd opened the practice. She was neat, organized, and had a calm, professional presence. Although she was overpaid for her position in a small practice, Karp felt that her experience and other qualities were well worth the extravagance.

"How did it go this morning?" she asked.

"Not bad. The average turn-around time was only a little more than half an hour today," answered Karp. "And they didn't screw up anybody's preop meds." He grinned as she rolled her eyes. "In all, I'd give them a B-plus. Any messages or emergencies?"

"There are two charts on your desk. No serious problems, one is coming in later this afternoon. Your wife called."

Karp walked through the door that led from the lobby into the hall and past her reception desk. He took in a deep breath. "Good call or bad call?"

"Value negative, I'd say. I think she wants to remind you to get home early for your meeting tonight in Chicago."

"Yes, yes," sighed Karp, "How could I forget?" He strolled by Lon's office and poked his head in. "Car run okay?" Lon drove an ancient green Chevy Citation that burned oil and didn't start easily. He had beaten Karp back to the office by only minutes.

"Like a dream, Doc. That old `Green Hornet' is a cream puff." He turned back to his papers. There were a few intraocular lenses on back order, and he was trying to organize the records so that he could be certain they would have the appropriate lenses for upcoming surgical patients.

Karp entered his own small office and dropped the charts on his usually neat desk. When he was in the office regularly, he was able to keep up with the paperwork and managed to minimize the disarray. If he was gone for a couple of days or spent too much time in the OR, however, the papers would pile up. Today he could see brown, so he knew the desktop wasn't far below the mail, bills, and charts requiring review or callbacks. He hung his overcoat on a brass coat rack in the corner and looked at the pile.

The first chart had the name of Betty Sheldon, a widow in her eighties who lived in a nursing home. She had dry eye syndrome, a chronic problem which resulted in irritated, red eyes. It was treated by liberal use of artificial teardrops, lubricants to ease the grittiness. There was no cure, and Betty didn't like to take her eyedrops. She would call several times each month complaining of eye pain. He would advise her to use the tears, she wouldn't, then she would call back saying her vision was getting dimmer. Karp would then offer to see her right away, only to find that her vision was stable and she was suffering from dry eyes. He figured he would be seeing her this afternoon. He sighed again, and chose instead to call Val.

"Hi, Hon. It's me. What's up?"

"I just wanted to make sure you get home early tonight so that we could get to Chicago on time. I know you hate these meetings."

She was right about that. "Don't worry, Val. I'll be home by four and we can leave straight away if you want. It's the last meeting and I'm looking forward to getting this over with."

"Now, Jerry, you know it hasn't been all that bad."

"Of course not. It's just that those people get under my skin so. I don't know who's worse, the social workers or the dysfunctional families in the group."

"It's just the whole process, Jerry. We're going to be okay and when it's all over it'll be worth it. Right?"

"Of course, Val. I'm sorry about last week."

"Me too. See you in a couple of hours."

"Love you."

"Bye."

The Karps had been discussing the group meetings that were part of their pre-adoption home study. They were unable to have children on their own, and had already tried means as aggressive as four cycles of IVF, in-vitro fertilization. Val even became pregnant once, but the pregnancy implanted in the thin tubes rather than in her womb, an ectopic pregnancy. After years of trying, her only pregnancy was terminated.

30

The Karps had looked into adoption several times. The costs were staggering, and the results weren't guaranteed. Val had a cousin who had spent several years on an adoption agency's waiting list, but this was for their third child. They heard about an agency that had a good record with adopting children from eastern Europe, Asia, and South America. After some soul searching and pocket digging, they agreed to take this route.

The requirements were not simple. The Karps had to file paperwork with the INS, Immigration and Naturalization Services, to bring the child into the country. They obtained notarized copies of their birth certificates and marriage certificate. The documentation seemed endless. In addition, they needed to have a home study performed by a licensed social worker. This required three visits to the Karps' home and counseling sessions on how to be good parents. Last of all, they needed to attend a six-week long group session which discussed parenthood, adoptions, and birth parents' rights.

The group sessions were led by their social worker, who advocated domestic open adoptions. Although such a result was unlikely, the Karp's feared the remote risk of a birth parent returning for their child one day, and they had no inclination to enter into an open adoption. They had some agitated discussions with the social workers and between themselves. The discussion one week before somehow turned into a pretty emotional fight. This was the reason for the mutual apologies, and for the relief with which both parties approached tonight's final meeting.

At least they were still talking, thought Jerry Karp as he picked up the second chart on his desk. The name was Beatrice St. Andrews, a seventy three year old black woman for whom he had performed cataract surgery three months previously. The case initially went well, but as he was preparing to place the IOL, Mrs. St. Andrews complained of the need to urinate. Karp tried particularly hard to hide his pique with the OR staff, since it was their job to see to it that she had urinated before coming into the OR in the first place. He suggested to her the need to wait just a little longer.

As he prepared the IOL, Mrs. St. Andrews pleaded, "Oh, Dr. Karp. I really have to go pee." Faced with no other reasonable option, Karp told her to go ahead and relieve her bladder there on the OR table. The circulating and scrub nurses glared at him from behind their masks, but he didn't budge. If they'd have to clean up the mess after the case, perhaps they would not forget to have the patient visit the toilet before the next one.

"Go ahead," advised Karp, "and pee here on the table. We can't lift you up for a bedpan until after the eye is closed. Can you wait another five minutes?"

"Oh, no, no. I can't wait another minute."

"Okay, then go ahead."

Karp expected her to wet herself and the table. He hadn't expected her to do it so violently. As she peed, she bore down, pushing the urine out as hard and fast as she could. This increased the pressure in the venous system of her body which was transmitted to the eye. The pressure forced the contents of the eye out. A large glob of formed vitreous burst through the posterior capsule and out through the wound. He tried to stop her, but it was too late. Karp completed the case by performing an extensive vitrectomy and placing an anterior chamber lens. After the case, he fumed out of the room, silently cursing the needless complication this patient had suffered.

Mrs. St. Andrews' vision didn't improve after the surgery. In fact, it got a little worse because of inflammation called cystoid macular edema, which occurs more commonly following vitrectomy. Mrs. St. Andrews became irritated with Karp, repeating to him at many postoperative visits how her friends all had undergone cataract surgery and saw so much better so quickly. She resented taking eyedrops to control the edema. The more Karp tried to explain the situation, the more irritated she seemed to become. At this point, Mrs. St. Andrews was not especially compliant with the medications. Karp didn't look forward to seeing her, and her feelings toward him were mutual.

He looked at the note on Mrs. St. Andrews' chart, which said that she had called complaining that her eye was red and irritated. So what else is new, he thought. Her eye had been red and irritated for the better part of three months. He pushed the intercom button on his desktop phone. "Maureen?"

"Yes?"

"Which of these nice ladies is coming in this afternoon, Mrs. St. Andrews or Mrs. Sheldon?"

"I'm sorry, I thought I wrote it out on the note," came the answer. "Mrs. Sheldon is coming in. I thought you might want to try to help Mrs. St. Andrews by telephone."

She was right about that. St. Andrews was the last person he wanted to see. "Thank you. I'll call her directly." He dialed her phone number and the phone rang twice.

"Hello?"

"Hello, Mrs. St. Andrews. This is Dr. Karp returning your call. What can I do for you today?" he asked in his most gentle voice.

"My eye seems red and it hurts a little."

"I see. Are you taking the white, milky drop?" He referred to Pred Forte, an antiinflammatory drop.

"Yes."

"How often?"

"Four times a day, just like I been for the last two months."

"Okay. How about the yellow top drop?" This was Timoptic, an antiglaucoma medication.

"Two times a day. I think I missed a drop last night."

"You need to use it regularly. We can't let the pressure get too high. That may be what's making the eye so uncomfortable."

"Well, maybe I need to use it more often."

Karp figured she probably used it once in the last few days, same as the Pred Forte. "Let's just try to get all the drops in for a while. That may help things feel better. If you think that the pain is worse or the vision is worse, you can come in and see me this afternoon."

"Oh, I can't do that. I got no ride." He wasn't disappointed. Neither one of them wanted to see each other.

"Okay. Let's stay with the drops, then. You still have the instructions I wrote out last time, don't you?"

"Yes."

"Good. I've got an appointment to see you next week, right?"

"Yes, on Tuesday."

"Tuesday will be fine. But if you think the vision or the pain is worse, I would prefer to see you right away, okay?"

"I don't think I need to come in today."

"That's fine," Karp kept an even tone in his voice. "Just call me so that we can get you in right away if you think things are worse."

"Okay. I'll let you know."

"Good," Karp forced a smile, enough so that he hoped it could be heard over the phone line. "We'll see you next week." Even though the whole peeing issue was not Karp's fault, he always felt bad when his patients weren't doing well. He hated for any of his patients to have discomfort or a less than perfect result. Despite his best efforts in the OR, Karp was faced with providing ongoing care for an uncomfortable and unhappy patient. It didn't seem to matter how much time he spent with her, how frequently he explained her situation, or that he offered her the best encouragement and support he could. Mrs. St. Andrews would simply not be satisfied, and made little effort with her eyedrops.

The telephone rang. It was Maureen on the intercom. "Mrs. Sheldon is here for you."

Karp entered the small examining room and Lon handed him the chart. Mrs. Sheldon had presented with a chief complaint of pain and blurred vision in both eyes. Her visual acuity with her current glasses was 20/40 in each eye. Her visual acuity had been 20/40 at each of her last three visits, and 20/50 at the one before that.

Karp sat down on a small black stool next to a frail, elderly woman with gray hair pulled back in a bun. Her wire frame glasses were resting on an adjacent table. Karp studied her

34

craggy, pale skin. "Good afternoon, Mrs. Sheldon. I see that you're concerned about your vision."

"I think my vision is worse, Doctor," she said in a serious tone.

"How long has it seemed that way?"

"Oh, several weeks. Since I saw you last."

"I see," responded Karp with a concerned tone. "Can I take a look with the microscope?"

Mrs. Sheldon didn't answer as he maneuvered the slit lamp microscope into position in front of her. This device was used to illuminate and magnify the patient's eyes for examination. Karp looked at her eyelids, lashes, and the conjunctival lining. There was some crusty buildup on the lashes, but no purulence or swelling. The cornea was clear. Her lenses had been removed years earlier, replaced with plastic IOL's that were well positioned. The eyes were otherwise clear and quiet. Karp placed a drop of yellow fluorescein dye and again looked at his patient's eyes. There was no staining or pooling. He looked at the tear film reflections. They broke up in a matter of seconds leaving dark, dry spots on the cornea.

Karp bade his patient to sit back, and he removed the slit lamp biomicroscope. Then he jotted down a few notes in the chart. Finally, he turned to the woman, old enough to be his grandmother. "Mrs. Sheldon, I have good news for you." He had always felt awkward referring to older patients by their first name; he thought it was disrespectful. "Your vision is excellent, completely unchanged from the last visit."

"What a relief," said the woman artificially. "What do you think is wrong, then?"

"How often are you using your eyedrops."

"Oh, all the time."

"How often is that," he grinned a little.

She grinned now, too. Karp knew that this exchange itself was the true reason for her visit today. "Oh, at least twice a day, I think."

"Well, now, there's the problem. Do you remember how we've discussed that your tear glands don't work as well as they used to?"

"Yes."

"That makes the eyes dry. When your eyes are dry, they can become very irritated. It can even blur your vision."

"And you think that this is the reason for my problem?"

"Yes, I do." He handed her a sample bottle of artificial tear drops. "I want you to use these artificial tears every two or three hours. You can use them more often if you need to."

"I'll do that," she promised. "I feel so much better now."

"Well, good," exclaimed Karp. "Maureen will get you checked out and see that you have a followup appointment scheduled." He helped her out of the tall chair, and led her to the doorway.

Lon met them a few steps out of the doorway and presented her his arm. "Let me help you," he offered.

Karp returned to his office and flicked on the computer resting on his desk. The screen flickered red and blue with a menu of programs. He selected his accounting software and sighed, knowing that the first few months of the year would be slow. Receipts were already down a little due to slow payments from Medicare and Blue Cross/Blue Shield. He looked at the balance in the account, and then wrote his regular monthly payments. There was office rent, the leases for the equipment and furniture in his office, and malpractice insurance. Next he turned to the stack of bills payable. He owed payments for pharmaceutical supplies and his telephone bill, including the yellow pages ad. This was followed by the electric bill, the gas bill, and postage. He'd taken some local optometrists out to dinner the month before, to schmooze and lobby for more surgical referrals. It was a cost of business. All at once the running digital total for the checkbook balance was dangerously low. Karp hadn't gotten to the mail yet, so he didn't know if they had received any payments against their billing. He sighed again, knowing that he would have to run payroll by the end of the week. He was thankful that the quarterly health insurance payment wasn't due for another six weeks.

Karp suddenly felt tired. He wasn't sure if he was dreading the adoption meeting, or if it was simply the knowledge that he was going to have a hard time making payroll this week. No, he wasn't tired. He was exhausted. He glanced at his wristwatch. It was three forty five. He was done for the day, he decided. Time to head home. We'll get to Chicago early and maybe have some dinner before the meeting.

PRIVILEGES

Three

Daniel Kilner was a talented and aggressive businessman. He had earned his M.B.A. from Colorado State University and taken a job as a Department Administrator at St. Elizabeth Hospital of Denver. Within two years he had been promoted to Administrative Vice-President of the hospital, where his long range planning and advice was instrumental in the success of their new cardiovascular unit. He was then offered the position of C.E.O. at Shawnee County Regional Medical Center, a two hundred bed facility in Wisconsin. He stayed there for three years, turning a small, failing overnight observation center for local general practitioners into a pugnacious, competitive institution for medium technology health care.

At the same time, Hank Greenley was trying to juggle hospital costs and diminishing reimbursement at Compton Memorial Hospital of Aurora, Illinois. He had already made Compton more competitive with nearby Chicago hospitals. He had recruited two cardiologists and built a first class Cardiac Care Unit. The antiquated Emergency Room was reconstructed and the part time ER medical staff was replaced with several full time docs trained in emergency medicine. Greenley predicted that HCFA, Medicare, and the political powers of medicine would increasingly push for outpatient facilities rather than inpatient hospital beds for the management of non-critical patients. To that end, he worked on the staged development of CMH's outpatient Medicine and Rehabilitation Center. He also integrated the Obstetrics and Gynecology Department there, so that the ob-gyn docs could stay closer to the hospital Labor and Delivery Suite. Along with the new ER, he developed space for a separate but adjacent Urgent Care Center which could be utilized to see less critical patients outside of the ER facility at a reduced cost.

The next stage of Greenley's development was the refurbishing of the OR suites. Old, outdated machinery and furnishings were removed and replaced with new state of the art equipment. An Outpatient Surgery Center was developed as a free standing building, connected to the OR suite by a hallway umbilicus. This way, the facilities could share common equipment and storage space and still be maintained as separate entities so that, should HCFA require a free-standing facility for surgery, CMH would be prepared.

Greenley thought this was a brilliant long term plan, but the hospital staff was not in unison with him. As the federal mandate for outpatient care weakened, the unnecessary expense of having constructed the OR suite in "two parts" became a battle cry. Other Greenley detractors used a similar argument to question the rationale for having split the Urgent Care Center away from the ER. They argued that Emergency Care now required double staffing. The real point of contention, though, was that Greenley had planned to erect a medical office building on campus. This would help to centralize medical care for Aurora and maintain a community identity. The problem was that most of the staff physicians already owned their offices. Some had large buildings and rented out space. The shift to on-site offices meant that there would be a sudden glut of professional space in a town of limited size, driving down property values. The established docs were very reluctant to consider the new building.

The failure of the office building-outpatient center concept was viewed as a vote of no-confidence for Greenley. Compton's old reputation as the "place you go to die" resurfaced, and Greenley was said to be the cause. In a bitter administrative coup, the Medical Executive Committee voted to recommend he be fired. Greenley agreed to stay on as a figurehead until the new C.E.O. was in place, but he clearly wielded no power within the hospital. He secretly thought that the Development Fund was involved in his ouster. In the meantime, no new physicians were to be recruited, the last four having been Karp in ophthalmology, Adam Bullock in anesthesia, a urologist named Bruce Carver, and Melora Peltier, an obstetrician-gynecologist.

The process of recruiting and hiring Kilner to CMH was unusual. Kilner and the other candidates for the position were interviewed by the medical staff en masse, where the physicians were invited to ask any questions they desired. The quizzing was very specific and pointed: "When might you vote against the wishes of the medical staff?"

"What growth plans do you advocate for the next ten years?"

"How would you recruit new physicians?"

Kilner was a well trained diplomat, never letting the inquiries stymie him and never directly answering them either. He projected open mindedness and a willingness to work along with the doctors, and in a short time the match was made. Kilner was hired, and Hank Greenley quietly left Compton Memorial Hospital after ten years of hard work.

The telephone on Kilner's desk rang with a double chirp, signifying a call from within the administrative suite. He looked up from the report he had been working on. The call was from his secretary, Vicki Downs. "Mr. Kilner, I just wanted to remind you of your meeting with Dr. White."

Kilner looked at his watch. It was three thirty. His meeting was scheduled for five p.m. in Chicago. Weather and traffic promised at least an hours' drive, and he had to stop for his mail. "Thank you, Vicki. I'll finish up and be on my way shortly."

Kilner made a few more calculations and transcribed some numbers into the spreadsheet on his computer, then saved the file and turned off the machine. He pushed away from his desk and went to the small private restroom attached to his office to straighten up. With a flourish, he unbuttoned his shirt sleeves, rolled them up, then washed his hands and his face. His features were gentle with few lines on his face. He examined his five o'clock shadow, and though it was not especially noticeable, he decided that it made him look tired, vulnerable. He wanted no vulnerability in this meeting, so he used a small electric razor that he kept in the drawer and splashed on a light rinse of Drakkar.

41

He rebuttoned the sleeves on his white shirt, which still held the press from the dry cleaner, and reknotted his red patterned silk tie. The gray coat that matched his suit pants was hanging neatly on the back of the door, and he slipped it on. He took one more glance in the mirror. His slight features had begun to fill in over the past few years. He still played tennis on the weekends, but he had no time for it anymore during the busy weeks. He noticed a slight bulge beginning at his waste. Must be the hospital food, he reasoned, knowing that even the "lighter" fare in the cafeteria tended to be a bit greasy. I need to make a note of that, he thought, deciding to address the hospital's menu with the dietary department.

Kilner considered his first year at CMH to be a great conquest. Although the patient out-migration problem proved to be more challenging than he had initially thought, the trend was slowing. This evening would prove to be very interesting. He was about to meet with the physician who had singlehandedly developed the largest referral based ophthalmology practice in the midwest. That man, Dr. White, also happened to be in competition with Kilner's own CMH ophthalmology division. Kilner was smug in that White had called him to meet. His conceit was tempered in the knowledge that White was known never to involve himself in activities that did not stand to benefit himself, his clinic, or his financial standing. In addition, he had no respect for other doctors, or for ophthalmologists who didn't work for him. He was known to hate administrators, who he felt were parasites. Kilner wasn't sure how tonight's meeting would go, but he was excited about it.

Kilner exited the restroom and took a seat at his desk. He surveyed the paperwork there to be certain no sensitive documents would be left out overnight. There were some building plans, an HMO provider contract proposal, and some departmental financial figures. He organized the financials, placed them in a manila folder, and set them in a desk drawer. He locked the desk, then checked the time. It was three forty. He picked up another manila file from his credenza. The label on it read, "Karp, Jerrold M., M.D." He placed the file in his briefcase and snapped it shut. It was time to get on the road.

Dan Kilner left the hospital and unlocked his Lexus SC400. The leather seats crackled as he slid into the car, placing the briefcase on the front seat next to him. It started briskly with a slight flick of the key, despite the chilling weather. He gently backed out of his reserved space in the doctor's lot and headed the maroon car through downtown Aurora and then east, toward the Fox Valley Mall.

Just before he reached the Mall, there was a smaller strip of shops on the right side of the road, Fox River Place. It had a Stop-N-Go convenience store, a dry cleaner, a Subway sandwich shop, two empty storefronts, and the Mail Center. Kilner, a non-smoker, opened the ashtray on the Lexus' console beside him. In it was a small, unmarked key. He slid it out of the ashtray and shut off the car. Inside the Mail Center, he proceeded to a large bank of locked post office boxes. Following the numbers on the boxes, he quickly came upon one marked `1020' which was just below his eye level. He inserted his key into the mailbox and opened it. In it were six legal size envelopes. Each had been mailed to a company called DF, Inc. and each was addressed to a different department within the company. Kilner slid the envelopes out of the box and glanced at the address labels, mentally noting the departments to which the letters had been sent. After this, he placed them into his coat pocket, closed the mailbox, and locked it.

The Chicago Institute of Ophthalmology, CIO, was located in a large office building in Schaumberg. Their corporate business offices were here, along with a clinic and an ambulatory surgery center with four operating rooms. They had fifteen ophthalmologists on staff who kept the OR's busy five days per week, and there had been talk about expanding hours to include Saturday mornings for elective radial keratotomy cases. The seven year old orange brick edifice was smartly finished with tinted glass windows looking in upon a huge lobby whose fifteen foot ceilings made it appear even more cavernous than it really was. The spacious parking lot included a circular drive adjacent to the sliding glass door entry, all of which was covered by a tall carport to protect patients from the weather. Finely cropped shrubs and tall evergreen trees decorated the area, and the lot was bounded at tasteful intervals by tall deciduous trees, now bare of leaves for the cold winter. The building's design, inside and out, had been overseen and approved by Dr. Billy White.

Dr. White was, in every sense of the word, the master of the Chicago Institute of Ophthalmology. His formal title was Chief Surgeon and Medical Director, but no detail--medical, business, or personal--escaped his full attention. All of the administrators and doctors there answered directly to him.

The practice had actually been started by Billy's father, Dr. Aaron Weiss. Aaron's father, a tailor, had come to the United States from Germany as a young father of three. Aaron Weiss' two brothers were intelligent, but had no interest in further schooling. One had been offered a job in the garment industry by his uncle Sherman Weiss in New York. He quickly rose to the top of the company, but had a falling out with his uncle and started his own company. The other brother took a job selling Chevrolets. He eventually came to own the largest Chevrolet and Cadillac dealerships in Chicago.

Aaron Weiss was headed for a career in medicine from the day he entered college. His father had worked long hours and saved for many years to allow at least one of his boys this great honor. He saw to it that Aaron, his favorite, would have no profession less than a physician. After eight years of diligent study at the University of Chicago and Northwestern University School of Medicine, Aaron was chosen to complete his residency in ophthalmology.

Dr. Weiss was a gifted surgeon and his warm rapport with his patients soon became well known throughout Chicago. While modern cataract surgery was in its infancy, Aaron had a reputation for the gentleness of his procedures. His patients' visual outcomes were quite good, even without the benefit of intraocular lenses or operating microscopes. At that time, surgery was the method of choice for treating glaucoma as well. Aaron Weiss was nationally recognized for the work that he had done in refining surgical techniques of his era for glaucoma patients. Finding himself burdened with more patients than he was able to treat on his own, Weiss took on a partner, and the Chicago Institute of Ophthalmology was born.

Aaron had two sons, William and Benjamin. Both boys were brilliant students. Blessed with the good fortune of being able to attend the finest preparatory schools, both rose to the top of their classes and attended Northwestern University. Ben continued his studies in chemistry and physics, and earned a teaching position at the University of Michigan, and eventually, Stanford University. William, like his father, attended the Northwestern University School of Medicine. Aaron loved both of his sons, but always had a special place in his heart for William, who would be a doctor like himself.

Despite his love for William, the young man and his father bickered. Aaron spent many long hours caring for his patients, and William responded by treating the man like a stranger, nurturing resentment for his absentee father. By his third year in college, the two argued terribly and regularly. A frequent topic of argument was William's decision to court non-Jewish women. In fact, the younger Weiss did this for one reason: As a means to distance himself from Aaron. It was then that William Weiss performed an act that wounded his father for the rest of his life. William Weiss had his name legally changed to White, and became known by his colleagues as Billy. This was done to segregate himself from his heritage as a Jew, and as the son of Aaron Weiss.

Dr. Billy White was accepted as an ophthalmology resident by the Northwestern University School of Medicine Department of Ophthalmology. He was a prized addition to the Department as he graduated medical school in the top five percent of his class. The fact that he was the son of a respected ophthalmologist helped him secure the position as well. He went on to become Chief Resident, and proved that his skills as a surgeon were equal to his father's. They wanted Billy White to be among the few residents invited to join the University's Department of Ophthalmology following his residency. Much to their disappointment, he refused the honor.

Although wounded, Aaron Weiss still loved his physician son. They settled their arguments, the elder ophthalmologist realizing that continued hostility would be futile. Dr. Weiss wished to be a part of his son's life and a part of the lives of his grandchildren to be. He invited Billy to join the Chicago Institute of Ophthalmology. Within three years Billy White was a full partner. Two years after that, his surgical prowess had earned him the right to challenge his father for the position of Medical Director. As there had never been a formal declaration for the position in the past, Aaron Weiss chose to allow his son this honor. He hoped that this would forever dispel the anger his son bore toward him by allowing the boy to show his superiority.

Billy White developed a network of referring optometrists. Doctors of optometry, OD's, are trained to measure and dispense glasses. In the 1960's and 1970's there were relatively few ophthalmologists compared to OD's, and the MD's perceived no need to solicit surgical referrals. In the decades that followed, the ranks of ophthalmologists swelled. MD's cozy with O.D.'s reaped a harvest of surgical referrals and led exceptionally comfortable lives as polished surgeons. Those who resisted these associations were banished to live on the scraps of surgery cultivated by their own smaller practices. Amid this political rivalry, the ranks of the ophthalmologists were effectively split. The old guard resented the success and the excess of the new networked ocular surgeons.

Aaron Weiss was a member of this old guard. Billy White never let him forget it. Although the old man's surgical skills were on a par with the best, Billy White, M.D. never allowed a single suboptimal surgical result to be overlooked by the physicians of the CIO, particularly when the patient had been operated by Dr. Weiss. They met biweekly to discuss problem patients, and every meeting was sure to include several of Dr. Weiss' cases. Of course, there was no mention that Dr. Weiss's patient population was older and sicker than the other doctors' patients, nor that his patients were frequently referred as difficult cases by other ophthalmologists. With time, it was made clear that Dr. Weiss was the least competent of the physicians at CIO.

On September 14, 1989, Dr. Aaron Weiss was fired as a physician by the CIO. The motion was presented to the CIO partners by the Medical Director, Dr. Billy White. Although the vote was carried out by secret ballot, the voting was unanimous.

On September 14, 1989, Dr. Aaron Weiss retired from ophthalmology and from medicine. On November 8, 1989, Dr. Aaron Weiss died of a heart attack. Billy canceled half a day of surgery, six cases, to attend the funeral. He returned to work at one p.m. rather than attend the minion.

A maroon Lexus piloted by Dan Kilner pulled into the CIO parking lot just around five thirty. He entered the lobby and hung his overcoat on a convenient rack, then approached the oversized mahogony reception desk. A neat young woman whose smiling face was framed by dark hair greeted him there. Her blue eyes shone, even this late in the day, matching her dark blue blazer. She sat at the desk accompanied by a young blonde woman at the check-out window dressed in a similar outfit, prepared to assist patients requiring a follow up appointment. "Mr. Kilner?" she asked.

"Yes." He smiled, impressed that she was prepared for him and presumed to know him even though they had never before met. "Nice to see you, sir. Please have a seat right over there." She gestured to a corner of the lobby. "Dr. White is seeing his last patients and will be right with you. I'll let him know that you're here." She amplified her smile a notch.

"Thank you," said Kilner as he turned back to the lobby and sat down. Within ten minutes he was bade to enter the hallway leading to the inner offices by one of the assistants. Kilner was impressed by the tasteful yet unpretentious style of the whole office. There were a few bright watercolors hanging from the walls of the hallways, which were painted in light pastels. The lighting was indirect and subdued throughout the complex to minimize the discomfort of patients whose pupils were dilated for examination. At the end of the hallway they arrived at Dr. White's office suite. His private secretary greeted them with a smile. "Dr. White will be just a few moments."

At once, the door to Dr. White's inner office opened. He was not a tall man, at about five-nine. His curly, dark hair showed streaks of gray and was thinning a bit from his forehead. He had a paunchy belly which rested within a well tailored, pressed white shirt with gray stripes. His pants were also crisply pressed and tailored, his shoes freshly shined. He wore a perfect white lab coat with his name embroidered over the pocket. In his left hand was a manila medical record file, and a pair of reading glasses perched tenuously on his greasy nose. His brown eyes peered over the top edge of the readers. He extended his right hand to Kilner. "Mr. Kilner, thank you for accepting my invitation to meet here."

They shook hands as Kilner rose from his chair. White had a firm, warm handshake. His palm was somewhat moist, and Kilner presumed that he had just washed his hands. "Nice to meet you, Dr. White."

White briskly turned toward his office. "Please, come in. Sit down." He gestured toward two dark red leather chairs side by side in front of his huge mahogany desk. The wood matched the furniture in the lobby in color and grain. White plopped himself into an oversized chair behind the desk. The chair whooshed as air in the cushion blew out from the sudden weight thrust upon it. White tipped his chin up to examine the charts he held in his left hand through the readers. He frowned, and placed the records roughly on the desk in front of him with a dramatic plop. He stripped the reading glasses from his face and flipped them across the desk where they came to rest on the pile of charts, then leaned back in his chair and looked Kilner over.

White decided that Kilner was a pisher, a kid. He was one of the fast track MBA's that got into the hospital business just a little too late to really make it big. He would still do all right, he decided, as he appreciated the fine looking suit and conservative red patterned tie that Kilner wore. Still, he would do so only by making the right decisions. Difficult decisions. He would need to be cagy to survive health care reform in his little hospital with a bad reputation. "Did my assistants get a chance to show you our little facility?"

"I would hardly call the CIO little," flattered Kilner. "You have the largest ophthalmology practice in the state."

White smiled. "Actually, we're the nation's largest outside of California and Florida. We do a lot of surgery here. All of my associates are nationally recognized."

"You run the midwest's most respected ophthalmic referral center and you're not directly affiliated with a teaching institution."

White was flattered. He didn't respond.

"And you do more surgery here than any four of your competitors combined."

White grinned. Kilner had done some homework. "We are very busy. Beyond that," he stressed, "all of our surgeons are the best. All of our patients expect the best."

Kilner sat back in his chair, working hard to look comfortable. He hated arrogant physicians, and he thought that White was one of the most arrogant physicians he had ever met.

"You know that we don't do much marketing here," White continued. "We rather frown on that."

Kilner wrinkled his eyebrows and lowered his chin. "I know that you have a very active program recruiting referrals from optometrists. I'd call that marketing."

"In a sense, I suppose so." He sat forward and placed his left hand palm up on the desk. "Please, call me Billy."

Kilner nodded.

"We are of the old school here," he continued. "I dislike the entrepreneurial approach of television and radio ads. We're not selling cars here, we're providing health care."

There was an awkward silence. White sat back in the chair once more and rubbed his chin for dramatic effect. He wanted Kilner to be uncomfortable. In fact, he relished it. "We have a problem, here, Mr. Kilner, with one of your surgeons. Dr. Karp." He paused.

Kilner wanted to tell this slick operator to kiss his ass and leave. He concentrated on looking intent.

"You know, Dan, we track a lot of variables here on our computer databases. Patient demographics, visual outcomes, complications. We want to know exactly how we're doing." White pressed his fingertips together. His movements were smoothly choreographed. "I've been following our surgical trends for some time. We noticed a drop off of surgical patients from Aurora. This started about the time that Karp came here."

Kilner was impressed. He knew that Karp was doing a small number of cases, but he didn't realize that this would visibly affect White or CIO. He made a mental note to congratulate the hospital's marketing department on their successful efforts with Dr. Karp.

"That piqued my interest, frankly. You know, Dan, I've been considering adding a satellite office in Aurora."

Now Kilner was genuinely interested. "No. I didn't know that."

"CIO has had an excellent relationship with the O.D.'s in Aurora for some time. I thought that this would be an excellent way for us to improve the level of care out there."

And to augment your volume of surgical patients, added Kilner silently.

"You know, Dan, I've seen a lot of patients who've had cataract surgery elsewhere over the years. Some have had excellent surgery, others, well, you know. Still, I think it's important to respect one's colleagues."

Kilner nodded. "Of course."

"Lately, I've had the opportunity to see several of Dr. Karp's post-op results. I must tell you that I've never seen as consistently troubling results as I have from Dr. Karp."

Kilner concentrated intensely to keep from showing his indignance at this implication. He nodded.

White gestured toward the stack of records on his desk. "Here are the charts of four of Dr. Karp's post-ops. The first," he picked up a chart and opened it, "is a seventy two year old gentleman who had cataract surgery a year and a half ago. He has been back to see Dr. Karp innumerable times, but despite this his eye is red and vision blurred." He looked up from the chart. "He had untreated cystoid macular edema. We treated this and his vision and comfort level improved dramatically. His lens implant was badly dislocated." He exchanged the chart he held for the next one on the pile. "This nice lady had cataract surgery four months ago, but her vision never improved. The acuity is not correctable beyond 20/40, and her pupil was badly damaged by the surgery." He set this chart down, too. "There are two more examples. I don't see any reason to belabor this right now."

"Nor I," said Kilner gently. "Have you discussed this with Karp?"

"I don't see that there is anything to be gained by wasting my time with this incompetent young man. I doubt that he would admit his ineptitude to me if he is unable to recognize it in himself."

Arrogant son of a bitch, thought Kilner.

"I am even more concerned when a butcher like this calls himself an `expert' in cataract surgery in his ads. You know, Dan, I have worked for years to be an expert cataract surgeon. A true expert need not waste his money advertising the fact. His patients will do it for him at no charge."

And the OD's with whom you legally split fees by co-managing your surgical patients will do a pretty good job, too, thought Kilner. "What are you getting at, Billy?"

White clasped his hands together and leaned forward on the desk. "Well, Dan, at the very least I think that a QA review, quality assurance, should be done for Dr. Karp's work. Candidly, I'm surprised your routine QA didn't pick up these deficiencies. He needs some remedial work."

"And if they don't reach the same conclusion as you?"

"Well, it's a bit premature to make such a judgement, I'd say. I am very troubled by all this. I feel compelled to report these actions to the State Medical Board, Dan. They may consider pulling his license."

Kilner nodded. "Why are you telling me all of this privately?"

It was playing out just as White had planned. "Mr. Kilner, I'm certain that you share the concerns many of my colleagues have expressed regarding Compton Memorial Hospital's reputation. The physicians there are, if I may be blunt, known not to be very good."

"I've heard that said." He felt his pulse quicken. White was good at knowing just which buttons to push.

"I suspect that the CMH staff and Medical Board would prefer to avoid a messy public airing of these unfortunate results. Whether or not Dr. Karp is found culpable for his mistakes, it will not serve the Hospital's best interests, will it?"

"The legitimate findings of a QA review should only stand to enhance the Hospital's best interests, Doctor."

"That is true. But if the public perceives that the Hospital's professional backs were turned...well, I can only estimate how that might negatively impact your reputation. Right or wrong, you understand."

Kilner understood.

"You know," White continued, "I'd really rather that we not be competitors. That is why I called you here tonight."

"Go on."

"As I said, CIO is considering opening a satellite office in Aurora. I'm certain that a significant proportion of our Aurora patients find driving to this office a hardship and would prefer to stay closer to home. In these cases, not all mind you, but in these cases, I think it would be preferable to offer the option of having surgery at Compton."

"So you're suggesting," said Kilner slowly, "that it would be better for us to have some of CIO's surgery than all of Dr. Karp's."

"Mr. Kilner, even in a slow month I see far more Aurora residents than Dr. Karp. Such a relationship would more than likely result in an increase in your surgical volume." He paused for the effect. "You understand, though, that the only way I or any of the CIO doctors would consider applying for staff privileges at Compton would be if we could be certain that such an affiliation would not reflect badly upon us. The QA process there would have to be exhaustive."

Kilner responded slowly. "I think I understand."

"The alternative," said White, "would be up to the State Medical Board. Of course, any discussion I would have with them would be done in the best interest of the community, and of these patients. It would be maintained in the strictest of confidence under the law."

"As would this conversation?"

"Of course. My only concern is for the patients of Aurora."

"Of course." They paused again. Kilner needed to stall. He needed to think.

Billy White loved victory. He could tell that this horse shit MBA was now spinning through alternative ends to the scenario he had just presented. For a moment, Billy was disappointed. This had been too easy. "I have a patient in the recovery room who needs a discharge examination. Excuse me, if you will, to allow me to assist this nice lady on her way."

"Of course."

Billy White stood and slowly exited the office. Kilner looked around. There was a wall of photos of White that showed him shaking hands with celebrities. Some were local celebrities, like Ryne Sandberg, whose mother's cataract Billy had treated, or Scottie Pippin, who visited with Billy following a minor injury in a ball game. There were politicians, like the Governor of Illinois and C. Everett Koop, the former Surgeon General. Most of the celebrities were ophthalmic ones, though; world renowned physicians with whom Billy had lectured at various courses around the world. Dr. Fyodorov, for one, the Russian father of radial keratotomy surgery, and Dr. Ridley, the British ophthalmologist who implanted the first intraocular lens. Billy White was a famous and renowned man. It would be quite a coup to add his likes to the staff roster at CMH.

Who was Karp, after all, thought Kilner. He and his former employer in Oklahoma had left on abysmal terms. Greenley and the Compton recruiting committee weren't even able to use the man as a reference for Karp. Maybe he was incompetent. An inept physician on staff reflected very poorly on everyone. At least he hadn't recruited Karp himself, he thought. Maybe a Karp-for-White trade wasn't such a bad deal for CMH.

Still, Kilner wasn't certain that recruiting White onto the CMH staff, if you could call this recruiting, would be enough to justify the professional hell through which they would have to drag Karp. There had to be more. White would have to make a greater commitment to CMH; a personal one. Kilner would need to know that White wouldn't just pull out of Aurora and abandon CMH as soon as the OD's were comfortably referring patients to him.

There was always the Development Fund. It would tie White and CIO to Kilner himself. White's willingness to work with the Fund would be a sign of strong commitment to CMH and Aurora. The Fund had always worked well for the Aurora docs. Why not White?

Why not White? For one thing, White wasn't an Aurora doc. If things didn't work out he could always just pull up stakes and settle conveniently back in his CIO digs. For another, the current Fund members had to vote on a new recruit before asking him to join. On the other hand, most of the CMH docs had referred to Billy before Karp came on staff anyway. The dollars

White brought in to the Fund could help underwrite the expenses that Karp's litigation would cost CMH.

Karp would simply have to take the heat. He would be given to White as a sacrifice in exchange for Fund cash. In the end, though, White, CIO, and CMH would all emerge as victors. Only Karp would be a loser. Karp, he concluded, was already a loser. In life, money is the measure of success. In surgery, volume is the measure of money.

When Billy White returned to his office, he found Dan Kilner comfortably gazing out of the picture window. It was coated with a two-way mirror so that Billy could look out over Schaumberg, but Schaumberg could not spy in on him. The view was one of suburban arboreal beauty. There was a full moon tonight, and it reflected from the snowfall of the night before with a phosphorescent glow. The world was blue and soft and lovely.

Kilner turned and walked toward White with a newfound calm. He had clearly come to a decision. His ease was evidence that he had reached the right decision. "Dr. White, I see your point and concur with your distress regarding Dr. Karp." White smiled. "I think that a QA review is in line here."

"I'm glad you recognize the gravity of this situation. I presume, Dan, that our discussion tonight will be held in confidence. I would be uncomfortable if it were made public knowledge that CIO was planning an Aurora satellite. I have competitors who might take advantage of that kind of information."

"That bothers me as well," said Kilner, as he leaned toward White and place his hands palm down on the desk. This caught White off guard. "Our discussion is confidential?"

"Entirely. It never took place." He slapped the four charts on the desk. "We only discussed patient histories tonight."

"Good. Let me tell you about a system at CMH that ensures freedom from competition. It has worked flawlessly for decades, and allows CMH docs to flourish despite the Hospital's marginal reputation, of which you are so familiar."

55

White was all ears.
"It's called our Development Fund."

Four

The dentist sat in his chair and read the New England Journal of Medicine. It was an article on the response of AIDS patients to a new combination of antibiotics. It was a terrible disease, AIDS, he thought. He saw a lot of AIDS patients here. Of course, there was precious little that he, a dentist, could do for them but add them to the list of patients to be seen by the medical doctor.

What an asshole he is, thought the dentist. He swaggers in this place one day a week with his pink, bald head, his neatly trimmed beard, and his brightly polished black shoes. He sputters and reads the patients records, then he hands out a few miserable pills as if he'd paid for them himself. Most of their patients suffered from infections, for which they needed antibiotics. They also needed pain killers. These people suffered from severe pain. Who wouldn't be in pain in a rathole like this? Sure, a few were addicted, but it took the edge off of living in this sewer. He even indulged himself in the occasional barbiturate or benzodiazipine when he could spare a few. For just a few moments with those glorious medications, he could ignore the scent of the urine, the feces, the sweat. He didn't have to hear the noise of the music, the fighting, the laughter, the threats.

But he was careful not to depend too strongly on medications. He needed to keep his mind clear and his tongue sharp. It was his wits, his training, and his intelligence that protected him here. It was his clean record and minimal contact with the others that allowed him to maintain his special privileges. His job in the infirmary was clean work, not physically intensive. He had access to medical journals, books and newspapers. He treated patients with simple diseases: cuts and bruises, infections, diarrhea. He managed a lot of gonorrhea. When patients didn't improve, they were added to the physician list.

He thought often of the practice he'd left behind to come here. It wasn't a large operation, but it was busy. He had three hygienists working for him. He could discern the tiniest cavity on the X-rays, and could perform a root canal as slick as you like it. His hands were good, and he made good money. He worked hard in his practice. He saw hundreds of patients in a week. They'd sit in his chair, lie back, and close their eyes. They'd open their mouths, and he would adjust the light to examine them. He would use the mirror, the probes, the picks. He would need to move in close, close for a better look. He could always smell their breath. Warm, musky, humid. He would look at the teeth, the mucous membranes of the mouth. He would also see their lips, their skin, their neck. He could smell their perfumes, their personal scents. He loved taking care of the women. The young, well groomed ones, with sweet smells and soft skin.

It was a tradeoff, he reasoned. He'd traded the sweet smelling lovely women for his patients here. That was a trade down. But he also traded dentistry for medicine. Oh, he knew that he couldn't perform surgery and dealt with only a few basic drugs. Still, he was practicing medicine. Like the arrogant doctors. He ordered blood counts, chest X-rays, electrocardiograms. He knew when a patient was sick, goddammit, even if there was nothing he could do about it but wait for the insolent, pink cheeked, bastard doctor to come on Thursday. The instruments were old. The table was rickety. There was only one gurney and two rusted beds. The medication cabinet was triple locked, and he had to document every aspirin he dispensed. Aspirin, for Christ sake. His assistants were incompetent. They were dishonest, stealing medications when he had his back turned. He had to be careful, he knew he'd be blamed.

In a few weeks, of course, it would all be different.

Jerry Karp worked rapidly and smoothly on his computer. He opened his surgical database and identified each of the cataract patients who had required vitrectomy. Karp had the computer subtotal the procedures by month, calculating the total number of surgeries and the rate of vitrectomy. Finally, he created a graph of the data to use as a visual aid.

Maureen had been standing in front of Karp's desk for almost a full minute. He was concentrating on the computer, oblivious to all else. Karp was an intense worker. He paid attention to every detail of a patient: their gait, their speech patterns, their skin color, their hygiene. When he looked at a patient's eyes during conversation he was looking for physical characteristics such as color, symmetry, fixation, eyelid shape, even the intensity of the light reflections. It tended to spill over into his everyday life. Maureen had never told him about her lazy eye, but he made reference to it in idle conversation one day.

"How did you know my right eye doesn't see well?" she had asked.

"You wear hyperopic glasses, magnifiers. The light reflection from your right pupil is slightly off center. You always fixate directly with your left eye," he answered. "I suspect you had surgery as a child, because your right eye is always just the tiniest bit redder than your left, especially when you're tired. It's well healed, and I don't think that it's cosmetically noticeable." Maureen knew that when Karp was involved with something, he immersed himself. He had been especially involved since this meeting was arranged.

Mr. Kilner had called him the day before. She gathered from Karp's tone of conversation that the time for this meeting had been prearranged. Karp was not invited, he was instructed to appear. The meeting had something to do with Karp's surgical patients. It wasn't so much what Karp had said as the way he had said it. Quiet. Deadpan, serious. His face was a little pale. Maureen had never seen Karp quite that shaken.

"Did you need me, Doctor?" she finally asked.

"Yes," he said without looking up from the computer screen. He reached over to the printer and tore off the list of cataract patients' names. He wheeled the chair around to hand it to Maureen. "When you get a chance, I need you to begin pulling these charts. They're our postop cataract patients."

She looked at the list. There had to be a hundred fifty names there. "Do you need me to go through the records?"

"Thanks, no," he answered. "I'm not entirely sure what data I'm going to need, and the information may be in several different places. I'll go through them myself."

She looked at the list again. "There are a lot of names here. You're sure you don't need help?"

"Positive," he smiled. "This is no big deal. I'm going to waste a little time preparing information and then we'll get back to life as we know it." Life as they knew it was going to be difficult enough. He had deposited just enough money to get through the month, and the accounts receivable was sufficient to last a while longer, but Karp was still concerned about the practice's cash flow. The last thing he needed now was to have his surgery challenged.

Billy White had, in fact, done exactly that. Karp's phone call from Kilner was brief and pointed. Kilner said that White had seen several of Karp's patients and described horrendous post-operative results. Karp's reaction to these charges was initially emotional. Did some of his patients experience late complications? Was there infection, retinal detachment? Kilner had no details. Well, then, Karp had asked, who were the patients? He could pull the charts, review the records, and respond to the challenge directly. Kilner said that he didn't have the patients' names. He simply wanted to meet with Karp to discuss the situation. He was told to be present at the specified time.

Karp asked Kilner if he was aware of rumors that White was opening a satellite office in Aurora. Yes, Kilner said, he was. He insisted that the rumors had nothing to do with this meeting. The only detail Kilner would let on was that there was a question about the rate of vitrectomy for Karp's cataract patients.

Karp knew that the vitrectomy rate for his patients was higher than he would like. He was still learning phacoemulsification techniques, to be sure. Of course, a case with vitreous loss that was well managed would often result with good vision. He knew that his patients, in general, did about as well as anyone's. He reviewed his own surgical results at the close of each year. His last review showed that the rate for 20/40 vision or better was ninety five percent, and that was an acceptable result. His telephone chirped. It was Maureen on the intercom. "Dr. Karp?"

Karp clicked on the speaker phone. "Yes?"

"It's twenty minutes till five. You wanted me to let you know in time for you to get to your meeting."

Karp looked at his watch. He didn't realize how late it was. He knew that he would still need to perform a more detailed medical record review later, but this would be a good start. "Thanks, Maureen. I should be finished shortly. I don't suppose this meeting will begin much before I get there."

Karp drove the Stealth rapidly through town. He wasn't looking forward to this. The whole issue of Billy White making a fuss over Karp's surgery was absurd. The more he thought about it, the angrier he got. How could a nationally recognized doc make such a big deal over a competitor as piddling as himself? Surely the son of a bitch had better things to do with his time. If he was opening a satellite office, White would eclipse Karp's patient volume in a matter of weeks based on his reputation alone. All the marketing Karp could do wouldn't change that. He turned the Stealth into the doc's parking lot a little too fast, sliding for a second on an icy patch. The steering responded before he collided with anything, and Karp cursed himself.

He parked and walked quickly to the hospital's side entrance. This door was well away from the main entry, just near the physician's lounge. There, Karp hung his overcoat. He ducked into the rest room to check his hair and overall appearance. He was sweating already. Something told him this was not going to be comfortable. He collected his papers and crossed the hall from the staff lounge over to the administrative offices.

At the end of the administrative corridor was Dan Kilner's office. The door to Kilner's domain was closed. "Good afternoon, Dr. Karp," said Vicki, recognizing him immediately. "You can go right in. They're waiting for you."

Karp continued into the office, and Vicki rose to follow him. She would be taking notes in the meeting. Karp felt that was not a good sign.

Seated at the round table in the administrator's plush office were several people. Karp felt immediately intimidated. This wasn't going to be the informal meeting that Kilner had described over the phone. Kilner rose and extended his right hand. "Thanks for coming, Jerry," he said. "Have a seat. I'm sure you know most everyone here." He was wrong. Karp knew everyone there. "This is Dr. Kingston, chairman of your department." He motioned toward John Kingston, III, M.D., an otolaryngologist who lived kitty corner to Karp's own backyard. Kingston was the chairman of the department of EENT, or eyes, ears, nose, and throat, which combined the relatively small surgical specialties of otolaryngology and ophthalmology at Compton. He was young to be a department chairman, not yet forty. His face was long and birdlike, and his cheeks were pocked with craters from a particularly bad case of acne that had made his adolescence difficult. The chairmanship was more or less a formality which changed hands every year to the doctor who was able to give the least convincing argument as to why he should not be chairman. It meant going to a lot of meetings and took time away from family.

"This is Dr. Porchette. He is the chairman of the Quality Assurance Committee," continued Kilner. Karp knew Porchette as well. When he had applied for privileges at Compton, he checked off the appropriate boxes on the eye surgery list provided. Temporal artery biopsy, a simple procedure performed to obtain a sample of the forehead artery, was not on that list, and Karp hadn't thought to add it. He only performed the procedure once every year or so. Because he had not been granted privileges for it initially, he had to provide evidence that he was adequately trained before Dr. Porchette.

Karp had performed over two dozen temporal artery biopsies as a resident. Fortunately, he had kept his log of surgical patients since that time, and he had only to cull the database to obtain a list of patient names and surgical results. Dr. Calvin "Kip" Porchette needed to look over this information in order to determine whether he was qualified to perform the procedure. Karp brought it to Porchette's office as requested, and was then made to sit and wait for forty five minutes while Dr. Porchette completed his patient schedule. Finally, he was invited into Porchette's office.

He was not yet fifty years old, no taller than Karp, with thinning black hair combed straight back. There was a tall, messy pile of charts and a second pile of X-rays on the orthopedic surgeon's desk. He was dressed impeccably, as he could well afford to. Porchette and his partners had the only orthopedic practice in town and were very well set financially. Karp sat down before Porchette, who grunted toward him without looking up from the chart he was reviewing.

Finally, Porchette glanced at Karp. "Why do you want to do temporal artery biopsies?" he asked, implying that someone other than Karp would be better or more interested in the procedure. Karp explained his qualifications and how he occasionally treated patients who had indications for the surgery. Porchette looked at the printed list of patients for whom Karp had done the procedure. He tossed the list on his desk with a quick flick, like he might toss a section of newspaper after he was finished with it. "You've done a lot of these?"

Porchette had, only seconds ago, reviewed the names of every patient on whom he had done the surgery. "Twenty eight," he answered. "Most of them as a second year resident."

There was silence for a few moments. "Fine," said Porchette, like Solomon. "Do the biopsy." The disdain in his voice was only thinly shaded.

Porchette now looked up at Karp through the same dark framed reading glasses that he had worn on the day he granted Karp the right to perform temporal artery biopsies at Compton Memorial Hospital eight months before. It was the only temporal artery biopsy Karp had performed there, and was, in fact, the only temporal artery biopsy performed at Compton in the previous two years. Porchette was annoyed that he had been made to waste time approving Karp for the procedure, when it had been Karp's ignorance to omit the surgery from his initial request for privileges. He had suspected Karp was a fuck up from then. Leave it to Greenley, he thought, to hire a fuck up ophthalmologist. He could not bring himself to greet Karp verbally, instead nodding toward the eye doctor following his introduction.

"Nice to see you, Dr. Porchette," said Karp in the most sincere tone he could muster.

Kilner motioned toward the man sitting to Porchette's right. "This is Dr. Harmon. He is President of the hospital staff." Orville Harmon was in his sixties. Six foot two, white haired, and paternal in countenance, he was elected President of the hospital staff two years previously. His duties required him to reign over the functions of the Medical Executive Committee, or MEC. This was the doctors' group that guided the medical activities of the hospital. The administrators' equivalent of the MEC was the Executive Board, which was chaired by the Chief Executive Officer of the hospital, Dan Kilner. Of course the President and the CEO attended both meetings.

"Good to see you, Jerry," said Harmon.

"Thank you, Dr. Harmon."

"Of course, you know Vicki, my secretary," said Kilner. She had taken the empty seat next to Harmon. They nodded toward each other.

"And, finally, there is Sheryl," Kilner motioned to the woman sitting next to Vicki. Sheryl Barden was thirty four years old with mousy hair pulled back in a tight bun. Her simple skirt and coat outfit was maroon, accented by a loose white blouse. She wore little makeup and only a modest wedding band. She began her career at Compton Memorial six years previously as an administrative intern, just out of the University of Chicago. Sheryl was the only member of Hank Greenley's administrative team who still worked at CMH. The rest had quit or were terminated shortly after Greenley left.

All at once, Karp felt haunted by the ghost of Hank Greenley. Kilner, clearly in charge of the meeting, was Greenley's successor. Porchette and Harmon had actively worked to have Greenley fired. Kingston, while not as aggressive as the other two doctors, had circulated a letter of no confidence among the members of the department to be presented at the MEC meeting. Karp, having no axe to grind with Greenley, was the only person who had refused to sign it. Karp wondered if his relationship with Hank would work against him tonight. He sat down in the last vacant chair at the round table and folded his hands as comfortably as he could before himself.

"Well, Jerry," Kilner began, "let me try to explain what brought all of this about." Karp watched him intently, making certain not to lose eye contact. Kilner matched his effort. "I received a call from another doctor earlier this week. It was someone who said he had seen several of your patients...specifically, your cataract patients. He noted a number of complications."

"How many patients of mine did he see?" interrupted Karp.

"Uh, four, I believe."

"I see. And how many uncomplicated cases did he see?"

"He only mentioned the four patients."

"That would make sense. I guess those patients happy with their results wouldn't have a reason to seek a second opinion elsewhere."

Kilner wrinkled his brow. Karp wasn't being as conciliatory as he wanted. "He was concerned not only by the number of patients, Jerry, but by the severity of complications."

"I can understand that. Who were the patients, Dan? I'd like to review their records for you, or offer them to the QA Committee for their own review."

"I don't know their names."

Karp sat back in his chair. He brought his still clasped hands up to his chin. "So Billy White called you about four unhappy patients whose names you don't have. This is the basis for a meeting with several committee and department chairmen?" His tone was quiet and businesslike.

"We just want to get a handle on what's going on, Jerry," said Kingston in a smiling monotone. "We're not accusing anyone of anything." His voice was dreamy, disinterested.

Not yet, thought Karp. Suddenly he didn't trust the new hospital administrator. "Did any of these patients complain to anyone in this room? To the hospital? If I were so incompetent, I find it hard to believe that I have yet to be threatened with a malpractice suit." Jerry Karp had never been sued.

"As a matter of fact," said Sheryl quietly and slowly, "we haven't received any complaints yet. The doctor involved intimated that we would hear from these patients soon, however." Her eyes blazed.

He could no longer hold his hands together, he had to move. Karp unclasped his white-knuckled fist from his chin, and made pains to move his hands slowly to the armrests of the chair. He blinked his eyes consciously as he said, "How convenient." He pursed his lips and nodded. "Four patients have all seen Dr. White for a second opinion. He expresses his concerns about me, and at the same time," Karp looked around the room. There was little effort by the others to maintain eye contact. He continued, "At the same time, he is planning to open a competing office here in Aurora."

"We know that Dr. White is coming this way," answered Kilner directly. "Regardless of his plans, we need to address the issue of his complaints."

"He has made some serious allegations about you," added Porchette.

"I hope you can...appreciate my frustration," punctuated Karp, "when I am asked to respond to serious allegations without the benefit of knowing which patients I am alleged to have mistreated."

"I'll try to get the details to you as soon as I have them available," Sheryl responded in a softly diplomatic voice.

"We really need some information about the surgeries, about any complications you're aware of," said Kingston.

Fine, thought Karp. They were fishing for an admission of guilt. "How do you mean?" he asked.

"We would like to respond to these claims of deficiencies right from the start," answered Kilner. "We want to be able to say that we've researched the threat and found no flaws." Kilner sounded well rehearsed.

"Well," Karp responded finally, "were there any QA fallouts?" He referred to the Quality Assurance process, which reviews all surgical cases and hospital admissions for adverse events. These events signal medical quality shortcomings. Karp knew the answer to this question. There had been none.

"Obviously, I checked your file before this meeting," said Porchette. "There have been no fallouts."

Karp made a note of that response. Kilner had already mentioned to him that the rate of vitrectomy was a concern that White had expressed. Karp knew that vitrectomy was one of the QA fallouts for cataract patients at Compton, and he had never been questioned about a single case. He knew that this meant the vitrectomies had been evaluated and found to be appropriate.

Armed with this information, Karp thought about his response to the question at hand: Was he aware of any deficiencies? Vitrectomy was the deficiency on the table, and he was aware of it. "Certainly I have experienced complications in my surgeries. Every surgeon does."

"We realize that, Jerry," said Porchette, trying to mask his irritation. "Are there any recurring complications?"

"The only complication whose frequency I am not happy with is vitrectomy."

"We're not all ophthalmologists, Jerry. What exactly is a vitrectomy?"

"The cataract is like a peanut in a shell. In cataract surgery, we cut a hole in the shell, the capsule, and use the ultrasonic phacoemulsifier to pulverize and liquefy the peanut, the cataract. The back of the shell is left intact, and we refer to that as the posterior capsule of the lens." Karp continued his explanation, "If the posterior capsule ruptures or is torn in the course of the surgery, the material behind it can present itself in the surgical field. That material is a fibro-viscous gel called vitreous.

"It's important that vitreous gel not be allowed to herniate forward. If it is incarcerated in the surgical wound, it can lead to infection. The vitreous is naturally attached to the retina, the inner part of the eye. Vitreous traction against the retina can cause retinal tears and detachments, and can induce swelling in the retina called cystoid macular edema. Any of these conditions can induce serious vision loss.

"When the vitreous comes forward, it must be gently removed. That process is called vitrectomy. Years ago, vitrectomy was performed with a scissors. Now, we use a machine called the vitrector, which cuts the vitreous and aspirates it out of the eye with minimal traction. It's cleaner and gentler. The visual results are much better this way."

"What is your rate of vitrectomy?" asked Kilner.

"In the first four years of my practice, I did ten to eighteen cataracts per quarter. That's about one a week," he stressed. "The vitrectomy rate fluctuated from ten to twenty percent. Since the overall number of surgeries I performed was small, a vitrectomy or two resulted in a high rate. Now my vitrectomy rate is less. It's bobbed between five and fifteen percent, but generally held at ten percent or less per quarter.

Dr. Porchette looked up from the notes he was taking. "So your rate of vitrectomy is about ten percent," he repeated.

"Yes," answered Karp. "But the rate varies with the number of surgeries I do. If I have one vitrectomy and do only four cases in one month, the monthly rate seems very high." He felt it was important to put this calculation in perspective. "By comparison," he continued, "someone like Billy White does about twenty five cases per week. That's ten or twenty times as many as I do. Cataract surgery is a finesse procedure, and the more cases you do, the better you are."

"But your vitrectomy rate is ten percent," stressed Dr. Kingston.

"Yes, that's right."

"What would be considered an average vitrectomy rate, a normal rate?" asked Dr. Harmon, who had been relatively quiet.

"I must be honest with you," answered Karp. "I don't know."

"What?" asked Kilner.

"I don't know," Karp reiterated. "Compton doesn't exactly have a dedicated ophthalmology library. I checked my reference files, and the papers I have don't address that issue directly. I have a textbook published years ago when I was a resident, and the text itself was probably based on older research. That textbook refers to ten percent or less as desirable." He stressed, "I think that this number is not acceptable today."

"What do you think is a respectable vitrectomy rate?" asked Kingston.

"The fewer vitrectomies you perform," answered Karp, "the better. Every eye surgeon's goal is a rate of zero." He paused. "I keep a database of my surgeries," he continued. "In that database I record complications along with other pertinent data. When I was a resident, I assisted the staff docs with their surgeries. It's a natural part of the learning process." The others nodded agreement. "I worked with several doctors during that period of three years," added Karp. "Some were better surgeons

69

than others. I calculated the average rate of vitrectomy of all the staff docs where I trained. Their combined rate was seven and a half percent. That," he concluded, "is what I would consider a reasonable rate of vitrectomy."

"And you have yet to attain that goal," pointed out Porchette.

"No, sir," responded Karp. "That is not correct. For four of the last eight quarters, my vitrectomy rate has been between zero and five percent. For the other four quarters, ten to fourteen percent. The exact number fluctuates widely depending on the number of procedures that I perform in a given month."

There was a pause in the discussion. Karp watched as Sheryl Barden and Vicki made a few notes on the papers in front of them. "There's one other point that we haven't discussed," added Karp after a moment. "This point is critical in the evaluation of cataract surgery, and we haven't even touched on it."

"And what is that?" asked Kilner, annoyed.

"The goal of successful cataract surgery is not simply the avoidance of vitrectomy or other complications." He paused. There was no comment from anyone. He could hardly believe it. "The purpose of cataract surgery is to improve vision."

"That's obvious," said Dr. Kingston.

"Yes, I agree," said Karp. "And no one has asked about the visual results of my patients."

"Go on," instructed Porchette, looking up over his reading glasses.

"My patients without other eye diseases achieve 20/40 vision or better over ninety five percent of the time. Most surgeons consider 20/40 or better to be acceptable vision as this will allow legal driving vision and excellent reading vision."

"Okay," said Kingston. "Does that include all of your patients?"

"No," answered Karp. "Only those without other vision threatening conditions."

"What about the overall results? For all patients?" asked Porchette.

"I'm still calculating that result," Karp responded. "There are a lot of charts for me to pull on short notice. The result seems to be that between eighty five and ninety percent of all my patients achieve 20/40 or better. On the other hand," he pointed out, "I do a lot of work with people who have retinal disorders. I see people with macular degeneration and diabetes, both diseases that can affect the retina and diminish vision. A lot of the cataract surgeries I do are for these people. Their best possible result is often far less than 20/40 vision."

"So about half of your patients are part of this group," repeated Barden.

"That's right."

"And how does that compare with other ophthalmologists?" asked Porchette.

"I don't know the details of my colleagues' practices," Karp answered. "I suspect that they see fewer patients with these problems. They refer most of the retina patients away...some of them even to me."

"How do these results compare with generally accepted norms?" asked Kingston.

"I have no idea how many people who undergo cataract surgery nationwide have other eye diseases. There are studies published which report visual results following cataract surgery for patients without other eye disease. About ninety three to ninety four percent of these patients achieve 20/40 or better."

Karp paused again. Barden and Vicki continued to take notes. No one in the room commented. "So you see," Karp repeated for all to hear, "my patients achieve the same or better visual results as nationally accepted norms."

"Does that include the vitrectomy patients?" asked Kilner.

"Yes."

"Do you have documents that can back this up?" Kilner went on.

"Yes. There are several studies in my files."

"Could you get copies of them to us?" requested Kingston.

71

"Certainly. I'll send them to you along with a report stating the overall results of my patients once I've finished the chart review," offered Karp. There was another uncomfortable pause.

"That's good," said Kilner, finally smiling. "The articles will be a great deal of help." Despite his smile, Karp couldn't help but hear irritation in his voice. "Does anyone else have any questions?"

"Jerry," asked Porchette, "have you taken any continuing education courses on cataract surgery?"

"Yes, of course, along with other topics."

"Would you consider obtaining further training?"

"I attend several conferences every year," he answered. "There is the annual Academy meeting, and I make it a point to attend as many conferences nearby as I can. I'd have no problem with that."

"No, Jerry," said Porchette. "Would you be willing to do some intensive retraining? A fellowship, perhaps?"

Karp was incensed. A fellowship meant taking a year or two away from his practice and a huge cut in pay. His practice would surely suffer in the shadow of Billy White's new satellite office. Karp had a home and mortgage and was trying to complete his adoption. There were also his debts from medical school, not to mention a significant sum loaned to him by the hospital to help start up his practice. In addition to all that, Karp knew that he had done nothing wrong. He hadn't committed malpractice. His patients' visual results were more than acceptable. Karp breathed hard and swallowed. He took great effort to avoid showing hostility although he was really hot. "I don't feel, Dr. Porchette, that there is a need for fellowship training here. We're talking about degrees of refinement. It's not as if I've been sued for malpractice." Karp never raised his voice or altered his tone, but he punctuated the last statement specifically for Dr. Porchette.

Porchette's group had recently been sued. His youngest associate, Dr. Marcus, had performed a hip replacement for a man in his fifties with arthritis. In the process he inadvertently tied off the patient's femoral artery, the main vessel that feeds the leg. The error went undiscovered while the patient laid in the hospital with intense pain. Eventually the stress proved too much for him, and he suffered a heart attack and died. The surgical misadventure was discovered at autopsy. Aurora was a small town and the details of the case had been published in the local newspaper. Rumor had it that Marcus and Porchette's group were preparing to settle out of court for a substantial sum of money.

Marcus had killed a man, but he was still working. He hadn't been subjected to this type of QA scrutiny. Karp had neither taken a life nor been the subject of a suit. Porchette had a lot of balls, he thought, to suggest a year of fellowship training. Karp maintained unblinking eye contact with him.

"Okay," said Kilner finally. "Anyone else?" There was no response. "Very well. Jerry, we appreciate your help. Obviously this is just an informal meeting. We have no plans to take any action."

Karp nodded, not altogether reassured.

"I look forward to receiving the papers that you've mentioned," added Kilner. "You can send them to me and I'll see to it that the others here get copies. Is that all right with everyone?" It was. Kilner stood and offered his hand toward Karp. "That should do it then. Thanks for cooperating."

"No problem," said Karp. "I'm here to help in any way that I can."

"That makes a big difference for us, believe me," said Barden.

Karp stood up from the table and bade a farewell to the group. No one else moved. Fine, he thought. They're going to discuss my answers when I leave. He headed for the door, which Kilner quietly closed behind him.

PRIVILEGES

Five

It was a lovely, warm afternoon in May. Karp had decided to take Lon and Maureen out to lunch. The sweet spring air renewed them as they walked back to Lon's dusty green Citation; he hadn't had time to get it washed in several weeks and the late winter grime clung to it. The dried slush and faded green paint made the car look as if it had battle camouflage. A thick black stripe worked its way up over the tailpipe, indicating the stain of burned oil. Only the windows and headlights were cleaned well so that Lon could see where he was going. They decided to take the Green Hornet to lunch since it was the only four-door that any of the group owned. Maureen had a two-door Honda Civic, and the Stealth would never carry more than two adults comfortably. They got in the car and Lon pumped the gas to prime the engine. He turned the key, the starter strained, and the high mileage engine fired with a chug and a pop. It ran a little rough at first but quickly settled down as oil deposited in two of the cylinders burned away.

They had enjoyed a pleasant lunch, talking of various plans they had for the upcoming Easter holiday. Maureen was having her father and her daughter's family over to her home for the day. The Morrisseys intended to fly to Virginia for a visit with their children. Jerry and Val were to spend a quiet weekend alone. They were now on the agency's short list of parents waiting for children. They needed to stay close to home in case their long awaited phone call were to come.

Clean fresh air blew into the open windows, making Karp and Maureen a little sleepy after their lunch. Lon pulled into the Paramount office complex, and eased the Citation into its reserved spot next to Karp's white Stealth. In contrast to the Green Hornet, the Stealth was pristine. Karp had it washed at least every other week when it was too cold for him to do it himself. The low slung sportster was backed into its parking spot, poised to race out.

They entered the office and each of the three went immediately to their stations. Karp settled in to his green leatherette chair. He faced his computer monitor and pulled up the paper he was working on before lunch. It was a short article he was preparing on the use of prism glasses for evaluating computer-processed angiograms in stereo. It seemed as if he was writing for only a few moments when the intercom buzzed. "Dr. Karp?" It was Maureen.

"Yes?"

"Lon has some patients ready for you."

Karp looked at his watch. It was one thirty. "Okay. I'll be right there." He saved the document in the computer and went to the clinic exam rooms.

Mrs. Hanley was his first patient. She had undergone cataract surgery with lens implantation a few months previously and had excellent visual rehabilitation. With a minimal spectacle lens the vision was 20/20. Her other eye still had a cataract, though. She had wanted to wait to have surgery on that eye until the worst of the winter weather had passed, and apparently was in today to discuss this option. He entered the exam room. "How are you, today?" he asked.

"Oh, the eye you operated on is doing very well. I'm real happy with it."

"Good. How about the other eye?"

"Well, you know it's still pretty fuzzy."

Karp guided Mrs. Hanley to the slit lamp biomicroscope so that he could examine her eyes. The right eye, the one he'd operated, had healed well. There was no inflammation and the lens implant was in excellent position. The capsular bag that held it in place was clear and intact as it should be. He looked at the left eye. The lens was deeply yellowed and translucent, not clear and transparent as it should be. She had a moderate nuclear sclerotic cataract.

"Well, Mrs. Hanley, I agree that you have a pretty significant cataract in the left eye. You did well with the cataract surgery in the right eye and I see no reason that you should expect to have problems with the left, but obviously there are risks to any surgery we do." She nodded. "If the vision in the left eye isn't bothering you, I wouldn't push you to have the surgery. On the other hand, if your vision is a problem, I wouldn't hesitate to recommend the surgery. The decision is really up to you."

"Well," she thought for a moment. "The vision in my good eye is so much better now. Sometimes I feel like I need to close my bad eye to see without glare." She decided. "I think I would like to go ahead with the surgery for the left eye."

"Okay," said Karp, who brought Rose to Lon's office, then added a few notes to the record. He excused himself and put her chart in the rack for Lon.

Karp looked at the records for his next patients. Geneen Oakman was a twenty four year old with diabetes according to her history. Her chief complaint was "large pupil." Interesting, thought Karp. He opened the door to the lobby and called for Ms. Oakman. She was about five foot three with long, stringy blonde hair that Karp didn't think was a natural color. Her face was pale despite a little rouge and some too bright lipstick. She wore tight but dirty jeans and a calico shirt covered by a well worn black leather jacket. She walked by Karp leaving a scent of old cigarettes. Karp got the sensation that Ms. Oakman probably did not take good care of her diabetes. They entered the examining room and Karp introduced himself. "Tell me what brings you in to see us today?"

"I noticed that my left eye looked darker than the right one. Lately other people have been noticing it, too." Karp looked, and nodded. Her left pupil was "blown," it was at least seven millimeters in diameter, fully dilated. "I got worried. I figured it might be due to the diabetes."

"I see. How long would you say this has been going on altogether?"

"I don't know. A while I guess."

Karp took a short breath and tried to hide his annoyance. He hated having to ask the same question more than once. "How long do you think that might be? A few weeks or a few months?"

She thought for a second. "I guess it's been a few months," she said in a manner that showed that she didn't care if it had been two months or two years. Now he was certain she didn't take good care of her diabetes.

"Has your vision been affected?"

"Oh, yes," she answered. "The left eye's been blurry for about the same length of time."

Blurred vision for months, he repeated in his mind. "I see. How long have you had the diabetes?"

"Since I was three."

Jesus, thought Karp. Twenty one years of diabetes, and she waited months to come in after she noticed the vision drop in her eye. He wrote down the history.

"Okay, then," he said. "Let's check your vision." He handed her the occluder and instructed her to cover the left eye first. "Can you read that?"

"No way. It's just a light." It was the 20/40 line.

Karp ran the chart up a few lines. "How about this one?"

"I think the first one's a D." She paused, squinted. "F? O. Is the last one a T?" That was 20/70 with two wrong.

"Go ahead and cover the other eye. What can you see?"

"Not a thing."

Karp ran the chart up to the big E. "Now?"

She squinted. "Nothing. Is there a letter there?"

Karp held up two fingers about two feet in front of her nose. "How many fingers do you see?"

"Mmm," she struggled. "I can't tell."

Karp opened his hand and waved it in front of her face. "What am I doing now?"

"You're waving your hand."

Great, he thought, hand movements vision. He moved the slit lamp into place and evaluated the right eye first. The cornea was clear. The iris showed no abnormal blood vessels. At least the right eye is salvageable, Karp hoped. He looked at the left

78

eye. The cornea was a little hazy and the iris appeared to be plastered too far forward, butting against the cornea. It was painted with fat blood vessels, branching along the body of the iris and diving around the pupil. The abnormal vessels pulled the iris widely open, which explained the abnormally large pupil that Geneen had noticed. The blood vessels had likely grown around the circumference of the iris as well, resulting in dramatically elevated eye pressure. This condition, neovascular glaucoma, is difficult to treat, often leading to blindness.

Karp measured the intraocular pressure. It was normal in the right eye, eighteen millimeters of mercury, but elevated in the left eye at thirty two. He noted the pressures in the record and placed dilating drops in the right eye. They wouldn't be needed in the left.

"Doctor Karp?" Maureen called for him as he walked down the hall. "Your wife is on line one."

"Thanks." Karp ducked back into his office and closed the door. "Hi, Hon," he said as he picked up the receiver. "What's up?"

"I just got the mail. We got more papers from the adoption agency."

"More papers? What for?"

"We need to get visas and permission to travel through eastern Europe. Even with the fall of the Soviet Union, they have restrictions on Americans."

"Okay."

"We also have to file forms with them so that they can arrange child placements."

Karp sighed. "I guess I can handle a few more forms. As long as I don't have to send them any more money."

There was no response.

"Okay, how much?" he asked.

"Three thousand. It's the agency fee for the placement service."

The practice was starting to get busy again, but payments from insurance companies always lagged behind business by a good month or two. He'd not taken a paycheck for himself for the last two months to help maintain the cash flow, and this meant he had been supplementing the household cash from their savings. He tried to buoy his spirits by recognizing that they were coming out of the annual slow period. "Okay," he said finally. "Just write them a check. I'll stop at the bank tonight and see to it that it's covered."

"I already did."

Karp was not surprised. As important as it was to him, he knew how much this meant to Val. The adoption was the foremost topic of discussion for them, even though the process hadn't budged for several months. Val talked about the trip they'd take to bring the child home, the new furniture she'd buy for the baby's room, the wallpaper she wanted to get. Whatever it took to complete this adoption, Karp figured, he'd do. He'd been in debt for so long from his student loans that a couple thousand dollars more one way or the other wouldn't make that much difference. He'd just pay everyone a little more slowly. As long as the business picked up, they'd be okay. "No problem, Val. How long did they say it would be before we'd start to get information on available kids?"

"A week or two once they get these forms."

"Which you already copied and sent along with the check."

"Right."

Lon poked his head in the room. He showed Karp two fingers, meaning he had two patients ready in the examining rooms. "Gotta go," he said. "Lon's got a couple for me."

"We'll go out and celebrate tonight, all right?"

Karp thought about how overdrawn their checking account was at the moment. "Tell you what...let's just celebrate quietly at home instead."

"If you say so." She was disappointed, but decided not to press the issue. Jerry always gets so anxious about money, she thought.

Karp returned to Geneen Oakman, the diabetic. He dimmed the room lights and focused the ophthalmoscope light on his patient's right eye, the better of the two eyes. On the optic nerve was a large network of fine vessels, neovascularization on the disc. These vessels can leak and bleed and eventually lead to the development of retinal detachment and blindness. He then looked at the left eye. The neovascularization was even more extensive here, working along the vascular arcades toward the center of the retina. There were also small pockets of hemorrhage in the vitreous cavity obscuring the view of the very back of the eye.

Karp hung the ophthalmoscope back on its hook and scratched some quick notes in the patient record. Finally he sighed, turned toward his patient, and clasped his hands in his lap. "Ms. Oakman," he said, "your eyes show signs of advanced injury from the diabetes." He explained the association of vascular damage with diabetes, and discussed with her how this resulted in new vessel growth. He also explained how the new vessels had caused the asymmetric pupil and the glaucoma. She listened quietly, nodding occasionally. "We need to be very aggressive with both eyes at this point," he said. "We need to use the laser for the left eye to try to induce the new vessels to regress. In the right eye, we'll be aiming for new vessel regression and we'll try to prevent the glaucoma from occurring. Do you have any questions?" She did not. "I must be honest with you," he added, "the disease in your left eye is extremely advanced. I'm afraid that the chances of returning useful vision to the left eye are rather slim. My goal is to do the best I can with the left eye, but to do everything possible to preserve the right eye. Does that make sense?"

"Yes. I guess so." She paused. "How about if I get the diabetes under, you know, better control?"

"Well, of course that's a good thing. You are a young person, and I think that's in your best interest. As far as the eyes go, the damage is already there. Tight diabetic control may not make a difference for your eyes now."

She nodded, but said nothing. Her eyes watered a bit. Karp wondered how many times Geneen had similar discussions with her internist over the past decades. He knew how difficult it was to convince a young person that poor health habits can lead to ill consequences, and he figured that this was the first time Geneen had actually realized the result of her disease. It was such a waste.

"Lon will be back in a few minutes. We have a videotape for you to watch that explains the laser treatments in detail. Afterward, we'll make arrangements for the laser treatments. I'll also want to get photos of your retinas. Okay?"

She nodded again.

He left the room. Lon and Maureen were waiting. He turned to Lon first. "She needs fundus photos and then she can review the videotape on PRP." He referred to panretinal photocoagulation, the laser procedure he would perform. "See if we can arrange the first laser treatment for tomorrow." Lon nodded as he jotted down notes on a small pad to keep track of the plan.

"Doctor Karp," Maureen interrupted. "Dr. Harmon is on line one for you."

"Harmon?" said Karp, thinking out loud. What could he want? He nodded. He hoped that this was good news. He realized that it had to do with the Medical Executive Committee and his cataract surgery. Karp hadn't heard anything more about the issue since his conference with Harmon, Kilner, and the others. He'd provided the documentation that they'd requested and hoped this was sufficient to complete the internal review. Now preoccupied, he ignored the patient in the second examining lane and returned to his office, closing the door behind him. He did so without another word, and Lon and Maureen shared a glance over their glasses. They, too, hoped this would be a more social conversation than the alternative might promise.

"Dr. Harmon? Karp here," he answered the phone as he was still lowering himself into the chair.

"Jerry, I appreciate the interruption into your day. I didn't take you from a patient, did I?" His voice was gentle, slow, and polite.

"It's no intrusion. What can I do for you?" Karp didn't like the polished, deliberate tone in Harmon's voice. He couldn't remember another staff doc ever apologizing for interrupting him, especially an administrative doc like Harmon. He felt his pulse begin to race.

"Jerry," he answered, using Karp's first name. He sounded patronizing, Karp thought. "Jerry, I just came from an emergency meeting of the MEC." Emergency meeting? What constituted an emergency meeting, Karp wondered. The MEC members were all practicing physicians with scheduled patients and surgeries. For this many docs to cancel schedules would require a situation of grave importance. Karp felt a tightness in his neck. "We received additional information regarding the situation we'd discussed several weeks ago, regarding your cataract surgery."

"Additional information?" Karp tried to relax. This was not going well, and he wanted to maintain his composure and thought processes. He had to sound sharp.

"We received a formal letter of complaint from Dr. White. He's made several allegations regarding your surgical skills, as you know."

"Yes, I know. We've discussed that."

"Of course. The letter was very specific, though, and we'd discussed it at the last MEC meeting." The last meeting? That would have been weeks ago, thought Karp. If this was so important, why hadn't I been told about it? He fumbled on his desk to find a piece of note paper. Taking a pen from his coat pocket he wrote: "Letter fr White--weeks?" Harmon sighed gently as he continued. It made him sound more sincere. "We tabled a decision on the matter until the tape was received."

Karp wrote the word as he spoke it: "Tape?"

"Yes, Jerry. Dr. White sent us a videotape demonstrating several of your patients. I must say that the tape was a very

83

dramatic representation of your surgeries." Karp felt a stab in his chest. He knew what was coming next. They hadn't even extended him the courtesy to review the letter or see the tape to defend himself. He still didn't know which patients were involved. This was crazy. He kept writing notes, and saw how shaky his penmanship had become. He struggled to breathe slowly, to maintain composure and present a rational exterior. This was not good. "This is difficult for me to say, Jerry, but the MEC is very concerned about your surgical skills. We think there's a serious problem here. You do understand what I'm saying?"

"I think I do, Doctor." Karp spoke remarkably slowly, with measured words. "You can appreciate, I'm sure, that I am quite concerned about not having had an opportunity to review the letter, see the tape, or offer a defense before the MEC."

"Certainly, Jerry, I understand." Karp was starting to get irritated by Harmon's continued use of his first name. "There will be plenty of time for all that. Still, you need to be aware of the...difficult position in which we've been placed. The MEC has a...problem with you doing surgery at the hospital just now."

Karp would need to prepare a formal defense, and he would have to find a good lawyer. His practice was teetering on the edge of financial stability. The adoption would be going through soon, or so he hoped, and that would be expensive. Without surgery to generate income he would be through in a matter of months.

"The way I see it, Jerry, we have two options here. Those options are," Harmon continued, "to either suspend your privileges or to have you voluntarily withdraw them."

"This is a final decision? Dr. Harmon, I've yet to be able to defend myself."

"I'm sorry, Jerry. I didn't make myself clear. The MEC is going to perform a thorough, objective, outside review of your surgery. The action we're discussing now is a temporary matter, pending the outcome of this review."

Karp wrote some more notes. "You know, sir, that if I cannot perform surgery my practice is going to suffer great distress. Per our contract, I have privileges only at Compton." In return for the money borrowed to him, their contract stipulated that he would practice only at Compton Memorial Hospital.

"I know. You need to recognize our position and fully understand the consequences of this decision."

"I think I understand your position very clearly, Doctor."

"Good. Here is the point, then. If you withdraw your privileges voluntarily pending the outcome of this review, we do not need to make a report to the Databank yet. On the other hand, if we suspend your privileges we will need to report it. That's a very significant distinction."

The National Practitioner Databank was set up within the federal government Medicare system. It maintained files on all medical practitioners to report adverse actions taken against them. If a doc was sued for malpractice, convicted of a significant crime--especially those related to drugs--or if his privileges were altered, a report was filed with the Databank. A negative report in the Databank was a significant hurdle to overcome before any professional review. Karp knew he must avoid an outcome like this at any cost.

"I see what you're saying, Dr. Harmon. We're just talking about cataract surgery here, right?"

"At this point, that's correct."

"At this point?" asked Karp, taking more notes.

"Jerry, we're going to need to review all of your surgeries. Our concerns are broad based."

"Has Dr. White made allegations about other procedures?" He knew that White's practice was specialized and limited to cataract surgery only. He wanted to know if anyone else was involved.

"No, only cataract. But the scope of the problem is such that the MEC is going to request a review of all of your work."

85

"So we're talking about my agreeing not to perform cataract surgery at Compton until this review is done?" Karp needed to hear this again.

"That's right, Jerry. No cataract surgery."

"What kind of time frame are we looking at?"

"Mr. Kilner will be making arrangements for the review process immediately. I hope it will be a matter of weeks, but of course I can't make any promises."

"So you need for me to agree not to perform cataract surgery for a few weeks."

"That's right. Our only alternative is a suspension."

"I don't want to have to deal with a Databank report. I'm certain we'll be able to have a positive outcome." He hoped he was convincing Harmon better that he had convinced himself. "As long as we can move this along quickly and positively, I can agree to hold off on cataract surgery."

"I think this is a wise decision, Jerry. Your cooperation here will be a big help."

"You know that I do have several patients scheduled for surgery in the next two or three weeks."

"Those surgeries will have to be canceled. They can see another doctor."

Sure, thought Karp. How about Dr. White? "Or they can be postponed." Cataract surgery is never, or almost never, an emergency.

"That would be your choice. We cannot have you doing any cataract surgery at the hospital until this issue is settled."

"Fine." I'll deal with that, he thought. "Now, I need to know the names of the patients involved so that I can review the records."

"I'm sorry, Jerry, I don't have that information here. We'll get that to you soon."

Soon? So far, they hadn't exactly been scrupulous about keeping him informed. "Dr. Harmon, I need to know the names of these patients right away. I also need to know the full extent of the allegations against me. I want to see the letter and the video from Dr. White."

"I'll talk to Mr. Kilner. Let's see if we can have this information available to you within the week."

"Dr. Harmon, can we see about having this information available to me by tomorrow? We're talking about my career, and I'd like to prepare a response. I need to know which patients are involved in this."

"I'll see what I can do. Thank you for cooperating with us."

Dan Kilner nodded to Vicki as he walked past her desk and into his office. He was trying very hard, but unsuccessfully, to hide his anger. He'd talked to Billy White about the Karp situation months ago and had received the long promised videotape only two days before. Kilner wanted to have dealt with Karp at the MEC meeting in March or April, but by now they'd missed both of those meetings and he'd had to expend a great effort to arrange an emergency meeting. Fortunately, that meeting went pretty much as Kilner had orchestrated it. To White's credit, the videotape delivered the punch that he had promised. Kilner knew nothing about the details of cataract surgery nor what the results should look like, but White had created and edited the tape personally, and the eyes looked terrible. When White described the patients' histories and findings, Karp seemed to be the most incompetent surgeon in Illinois.

There was another issue at hand, though. Despite their tacit agreement, White never requested an application for privileges. White's tremendous reputation locally and nationally was Kilner's justification for serving Karp before the QA board. Instead, requests for privileges were placed by Herb Genello, one of White's young protege IOL surgeons, and Elaine Stutz, a glaucoma specialist. Kilner wanted White.

Kilner neatly hung his blue jacket and meticulously rolled his sleeves up. He washed his hands and face, and splashed on a bit of Drakkar. He took a deep breath and resolved himself to present more opposition to Genello and Stutz's applications, just out of principle. He sat down at his desk and made a note in his organizer to discuss the issue with Dr. Porchette before the next Credentials Committee meeting.

Next, Kilner turned toward the credenza behind him. He had left his leather briefcase on it. In it were records for the Development Fund on computer disks. He opened the blue plastic diskette case and removed one whose label read simply "DF." He placed it in the computer and opened the files after properly entering his password. A large spreadsheet appeared. It detailed the activities and balances of several bank accounts that held considerable sums of money. It also showed the names of every doctor who made monthly payments into the fund and how much was paid by each.

The idea for the Development Fund was developed in 1953 by Alvin Wooster, who was Compton's administrator at that time. Then, as now, CMH was the only hospital in Aurora. Then, as now, CMH fought competition by hospitals just out of town. Cottage Hospital in Geneva, now little more than a small Emergency Room and a few beds, vied with CMH for Aurorans' health care. Rush-Presbyterian, the University Hospital, and even Northwestern University Hospital of Chicago were always "the place" to go for health care, and most of the docs in Naperville and Chicago's western suburbs were on staff at the big city's infirmaries.

Wooster not only understood the concepts of marketing, but appreciated how they could be fully applied to the health care industry. He arranged public forums and support groups, and he appointed hospital staff members to appear at these meetings. They needed to maintain a high public profile and provide the best care available despite Compton's relatively small market. To do this meant aggressive growth, addition of new departments, equipment, and highly trained staff. This was paid for partly from hospital funds and partly from donations.

However, the hospital's financial base was limited. To augment the funds at hand, Wooster invented the Development Fund.

Initially the Fund was open to all Aurora docs. For a regular monthly fee, the docs were invited to participate in the hospital's marketing programs. Eventually, only doctors with a full time practice in Aurora were invited to join. A heightened sense of community and collegiality formed, and this led to an unwritten rule that those involved in the Development Fund would refer patients only to others in the Fund, effectively shutting out carpetbagging Chicago docs with part-time offices in the area. Wooster met individually with the Fund's physicians once or twice a year in a private room at Harrigan's pub over drinks or at the Aurora Country Club for a meeting and a round of golf.

After Medicare was instituted in the sixties, more federal attention than ever was placed on the medical profession. Compton's legal counsel reviewed the Development Fund structure and advised Wooster that the program could be interpreted as collusion. He recommended that they discontinue it and instead have the docs make their donations directly to the hospital. With some consternation, the Development Fund officially disappeared. Unofficially, though, it continued without change. Rather than operate in the open, the docs chose to continue to make regular monthly payments in secret. Wooster collected the money and directed the Fund's use. He had done well, and the docs generally let him work with the capital as he saw fit. Over time, Wooster's Fund related contacts with them became increasingly infrequent.

By the time Wooster retired, the Fund was a self sufficient business. It was used to recruit new physicians in underserved specialties, but it was never used to recruit competing physicians in specialties already served by Fund members. This way, a single dominant practice in each of the medical specialties developed. By the late nineteen eighties, there were five otolaryngologists in Aurora. Three of them, from the same group practice, accounted for over ninety five percent of the ENT procedures performed at Compton. There was essentially one orthopedic practice, that of Dr. Porchette and his partners. Two others worked in Aurora a few days a week, but they never built up a reliable patient base and rarely operated at Compton. Similar patterns were seen in urology, ob-gyn, dermatology, psychiatry, family practice, cardiology, internal medicine, and pediatrics. Although the physicians retained their own practices, they operated as a large, connected multi-specialty group. Interlopers were not welcome.

The sums paid into the Development Fund grew substantially over the years. Hank Greenley, the CEO before Kilner, found himself unable to spend the money being paid in even with his aggressive plans for growth. Increasingly uncomfortable with the large sum of money that had grown, he split the money into smaller aliquots and hid it in various accounts at several different banks. He used some of it to augment his own income, taking "bonuses" for himself along the way.

Kilner hoped eventually to make the bond between Aurora's physicians more formal. Threats of federal health care reform convinced him that small solo practices would soon be a thing of the past. His goal was to somehow unite the city's doctors more formally and then abandon the Development Fund. He was nervous at first about the Fund's illegal background. On the other hand, it had worked for over three decades to bond the separate practices into one working unit, and that was part of his long term plan anyway. In the meantime, there remained a comfortable cushion of cash from which he was able to generously finance his new Lexus and reduce his home mortgage. The Development Fund would remain intact.

The dentist sat quietly and calmly in his chair at the end of the table. It was a long table in the hearing room, which was carpeted and pleasantly decorated. There was a small potted rubber tree plant in one corner, and a large picture window facing out over the yard. Sunlight beamed brightly in through the window. Most inmates rarely saw beyond the gray cinder block wall topped with coiled razor wire that surrounded the yard. One of the guards' nests was just visible at the corner of the wall. About three hundred yards beyond was another chain link fence, electrified, also topped with razor wire. Beyond that was freedom. U.S. Highway 14 ran along the edge of the prison grounds. From the hearing room, he could see the occasional car or truck pass the prison in the distance. Freedom. Freedom to return the many favors that had brought him here in the first place.

"I see that you have been working in the infirmary as a physician's aide," noted the social worker. Her hours were long, and the work taxing. Her dark hair was streaked with gray, and she looked through reading glasses that hung on the tip of her nose. She was heavy set and unmarried.

Bitch, thought the dentist. What kind of question is that? "That's right," he said quietly, with only the gentlest smile on his face. He measured it carefully to demonstrate limited pride in his ability to function usefully within the prison's society, but not excessively to imply arrogance. He maintained direct eye contact with her, although she did not look up from the papers in his file. He blinked, to be certain that no one else in the room thought he was staring. She looked up at him finally, and he blinked again.

"If you were to be granted parole, what type of work do you think you will do?" she asked finally.

"Well, ma'am, I know that I will not be practicing as a dentist." He looked downward at his hands folded peacefully in his lap. "My license is suspended, and I don't expect reinstatement." Fucking bastards. He looked at her again. "I understand that the parole officer may have some contacts for me. I'd like to stay in the medical field if I can, perhaps starting out as an orderly or working in hospital maintenance. I can cook, so that may be a foot in the door." He wanted to show that he had higher aspirations, but reasonable ones. "Perhaps, after a time, I might be able to get work as an aide." He made it a point

91

not to say `physician's assistant.' He knew the bastards at the State Board would never reinstate his dental license and probably wouldn't grant him a PA license, either. He had other plans anyway. "I've been doing a lot of reading," he added, as if that would make a difference. Bastards. He smiled again.

"What about your inner thoughts, your drives?" asked the psychiatrist. "How do you feel about all this?"

He looked at the psychiatrist's long, dark hair. It hung in a pony tail, just touching the back of the wheelchair to which he was confined following a diving accident in high school. He wore a loose blue shirt that looked not very different from the inmates' cheap blue cotton uniforms. A red and blue striped tie hung down, but the top shirt button was left open. This made the tie hang limply around his neck. The dentist found this strangely appropriate. Fuck you, you little asshole, he thought. That's how I feel about it, you prick. Why don't I just wheel your skinny, wasted pile of flesh down to the cellblock? Some of my friends would haul your bony, limp ass onto the floor and fuck some sense into you. "As you know from our sessions," he said meekly, "I recognize the urges that controlled me before, so it's easier for me to control them. I no longer feel compelled to act out." He pursed his lips, as if thinking more deeply about his answer. In fact, his answer was well prepared in advance. "I've done a lot of soul searching," he added finally, expecting to impress the chaplain. "And I've also done some private meditation. I feel more at peace. It's important for me to understand what I've done. I know that I can function more acceptably now. I also realize that I will need to continue working on those urges, continue my therapy, if I am to function on the outside." No doctor wants to lose his patient.

"You have been well behaved," noted the warden. "You expressed some thoughts about violent behavior to your family during and after the trial. What about those threats?"

They're not threats, you cocksucker, he thought. "I was distraught, confused," he paused, then, "upset. I was wrong. What I did was wrong, and my reactions were wrong. I was

92

driven by strong compulsions before." He drew his lips together, looked to the side and sighed audibly, making his best effort to express remorse. "Months ago, I would have been worried about acting out on those violent thoughts. I know that I'll need to be monitored. I also know that Melora has a restraining order in effect against me." He made eye contact with the warden. Without your goddamned guards, you'd get your sweaty, fat head crushed in a minute, he thought. "It would be extremely foolish of me to try to make contact with her or the kids now." He caught his breath when he mentioned his kids. He missed them terribly. He loved them. He'd make Melora hurt for what she'd done, make her bleed. He needed to be with his kids again, he'd do anything to be with them. "That's the price I have to pay for what I did."

"You make reference to `what you did,' to your `actions' and `urges.' You never use the word `crime.' Do you fully understand what you've done and why you're here?" It was the social worker again.

Cunt, he thought. "I am guilty of child molestation," he said as a matter of fact, maintaining eye contact with her. He blinked. "I had sexual contact with both my son and my daughter, and it was wrong. I felt compulsion to do it, but it was behavior unacceptable to society. I recognize that my incarceration is only part of my debt to the community, and that, if I am granted parole, I will be obligated to maintain my therapy so that I never again succumb to this dark urge." Fuck you, he thought.

When Karp finally emerged from his office, he was pale and silent. While he hadn't said a word, both Lon and Maureen knew exactly what had transpired. They shared a quick glance between each other to confirm the unspeakable, then returned to their respective jobs. Without conversation, Karp went into one of the two lanes, flicking the chart out of the basket on the door. He reviewed the notes, and examined his patient.

93

Karp continued to manage his patients without much interference by higher functioning thoughts. He provided the care that he knew by rote was appropriate for each individual. If he encountered a really tricky case, he determined, he would have them return in a couple of days for followup evaluation when his attention for detailed reasoning returned. About an hour into the patients, there was another odd call for him from the hospital.

"Who is it now?" Karp asked, quietly enough that the patients in the lobby couldn't hear.

"Amy West, from the marketing department," answered Maureen, as confused as Karp.

He sighed. "What more do they want out of me? Blood?" The question was rhetorical. Maureen was distraught. Lon tried to help keep Karp's humor up.

"Maybe they want you to develop a new cataract surgery seminar for the other doctors in town."

Even Karp had to smile. "Yeah. You bet. Okay, I'll take it in my office. Try to keep the patients occupied, Lon."

"I'll slow down my workups."

"That's the idea. Be constructive." He disappeared into his office, closed the door, and lifted the telephone from its cradle. "Karp here."

"Hi, Dr. Karp. I'm sorry to interrupt you."

He'd heard that apology once before this day, and didn't find it particularly comforting. "What's up?"

"Well," she hesitated, looking for the right words. Karp had helped the marketing people arrange seminars to try and increase the locals' awareness of CMH. Karp translated her hesitation to signify bad news. "Well, I wanted to let you know about a problem that's come up."

"Yes?"

"We've had several patient complaints in the last few days. Complaints about you."

"I see."

94

"These were all patients for whom you'd done cataract surgery."

Karp was not surprised at all. "Really."

"It's just that this situation is so...unusual. All four calls came in yesterday and today. I'm a little worried."

"So am I. What troubles you?" Karp was trying hard to maintain his composure. He again felt his blood pressure soar from the adrenalin rush. He was so angry he could feel the warmth of his own breath at his nostrils.

"To be honest, Dr. Karp, this type of complaint is very unusual. They have all called to let the hospital know that your surgery ruined their eyes. That's the specific word that three of them used: ruined."

"That's a pretty serious charge." He sensed that Amy was legitimately concerned for him. She might still be on his side.

"It is. But these patients have other things in common. They were all seen by Dr. White at the Chicago Institute of Ophthalmology, and all were sent to him by Dr. Demmel." Demmel was an optometrist who had sent patients to Karp for cataract surgery. He had previously referred most of his surgery to White. White probably hoped that one or two of these patients might sue Karp. Whether the suit had any merit made no difference, since the negative publicity would affect Karp's practice either way.

"That is quite a fluke," said Karp. "What do you make of it?"

"Dr. Karp, I'm worried about these allegations against you. I had no choice but to report these complaints to the MEC, to Mr. Kilner and Dr. Harmon. I wanted to make sure you know what's going on, because Dr. White may be involved in other activities against you. He's been known to do this sort of thing before."

She didn't know that the MEC was already involved, and she didn't appear to know that Harmon and Kilner were deeply entrenched in this. Most curious, though, was her statement about White having done this before. "What do you mean?"

"Don't you know about Dr. Bookner?"

"No. Who is he?"

"Have you ever seen any of the Bookner Eye Center offices around town? There was one in Naperville once."

Karp did remember seeing the old, closed office in a strip mall. There was a huge neon eyeball logo over it. The Bookner Eye Center sign had long been the target of vandals' projectiles. Karp couldn't help thinking that, in its prime, this was a rather gaudy facade for an ophthalmologist. He didn't realize that there had been other offices like it in Chicago. "Yes, I know of that office."

"Dr. Bookner had quite an extensive network in Chicago until about five years ago. He was charged with Medicare fraud."

"So now he's in jail?"

"No. He was acquitted of all charges. The court case was in all the papers and on television. I'm surprised you don't know of it."

"At the time," he reminded her, "I was living in another state. I'm sure it was big local news, but it wasn't national."

"I guess so," she answered. "Anyway, even though Dr. Bookner was eventually acquitted, he developed an awful reputation. Nobody referred to him anymore. Patients didn't want to let him do their surgery. He had to close all the offices but one."

"So he's still around?"

"Yes, but it's a much smaller operation. Everyone remembers the pictures of him being led into court in handcuffs. The acquittal was buried in the back of the newspapers."

"So what did White have to do with all this?"

"Officially, the Medicare audit and review were standard practice. Dr. White's involvement was strictly off the record."

"Of course." Karp could guess the rest.

"It's rumored that Dr. White alerted the local Medicare office of the fraud. He told them that Dr. Bookner was billing for procedures he'd never performed. Dr. White has a lot of powerful friends."

"I've never met the man," said Karp, "but the more I hear of Dr. White, the less I like him."

"I just wanted you to know so that you could prepare yourself. You've been very cooperative with me and I'd hate to see you get in any trouble."

Karp sighed and leaned back in his chair. He stared at the ceiling. "I appreciate that. I'll do the best I can." He thought a moment. "Do you happen to have the names of those four patients handy? I'm sure I'll get all the details soon enough, but it would help me to review their charts."

"Of course, doctor. I have them right here." There was a pause as she organized the papers on her desk. "They are: Susan Gruen, Colleen Davis, Helen Beam, and Leonard Bouchian. Are any of those names familiar?"

Helen Beam had unremarkable cataract surgery. The procedure flew along and he was just about to insert the IOL, when the capsule just ruptured. It wasn't a little tear, either, but a massive rip through the flimsy structure. A big gob of vitreous came forward, and Karp cleaned it up with the vitrectomy machine. He placed an anterior chamber IOL with no difficulty, completed the case, and lifted the drape off his patient. As he routinely did, he then told her that everything went well and that the cataract was out and the implant in. Instead of sighing, smiling, or asking some questions, Mrs. Beam burst into tears. "I felt the whole surgery!" she cried. "You lied to me! You lied! You said you'd use anesthesia and you didn't. It hurt the entire time."

This took Karp by surprise. She'd been given the standard retrobulbar injection of long and short acting local anesthetic. Like all of his patients, she'd received IV sedation before the injection, so that she could gently doze through the unpleasant shot. The anesthetist was concerned that she was too deep, in fact, because she stopped breathing for a short time. Following this, though, Mrs. Beam had no signs of anything less than perfect anesthesia. She was unable to move her eyeball in any direction, nor did she complain of discomfort during the procedure. The anesthesia record showed no spikes of blood pressure or racing heart rates which would indicate pain.

Still, she swore that Karp had given her no anesthesia whatever. She bellowed in the OR, and she wailed in the postop lounge. She broke down and cried again the next day when she came to the office, too. Karp went over the anesthesia and the surgery with her, but she persisted in her story. Eventually, her vision was 20/25 and the eye was quiet. Karp sent her back to Dr. Demmel for glasses and asked her to return in six months for followup. "I'll never come back here," she spat. "You are a bastard, and you did surgery on me without anesthesia."

Karp also remembered Mr. Bouchian. He had cataract surgery complicated by early rupture of the capsule when the patient began flailing around on the table. He completed a vitrectomyand lens insertion and closed the eye. The next morning, Mr. Bouchian had a choroidal hemorrhage, bleeding under the vascular layer deep in the eye. Although a small choroidal can look bad, they usually resolve without any further treatment. Such was Mr. Bouchian's case. His final vision was 20/25, and he was pleased with his care. He returned a few months later with decreasing vision, and Karp diagnosed cystoid macular edema. Karp treated this with eyedrops, and it resolved in short order. He had seen Bouchian a few more times, and he had maintained excellent visual acuity with no further complications.

"Yes, a couple of them are familiar," he answered. "As far as I know, everyone was doing well when they left to see Dr. Demmel, but I'll go back and review the records anyway."

"Okay," she said. "I'm sorry to have to be involved in this."

"There's nothing either of us can do about it now. I'll just deal with it."

Karp hung up and returned to his patients. Without introduction or explanation, Karp asked Maureen to look through the schedule book to see which patients were scheduled for cataract surgery in the near future. He wanted her to gather those charts and leave them on his desk. "I'll have to change their surgery dates," he said. "Also, I'll need to review the charts for these patients." He handed her a slip with the names of the four patients that Amy West had told him about, and returned to lane one to complete the examination of a patient with glaucoma.

Despite the anxiety that each silently felt, they managed to complete the afternoon smoothly, ending around four thirty. After the last patient checked out, Karp finally came back from his office. "I'm sure you both have a good idea about what's happening," he said to his employees. "Dr. Harmon called earlier. The hospital has decided to review my surgical results, and until the review is complete I won't be doing cataract surgery." He paused, waiting for any immediate questions or comments. "Now, this is only going to be temporary, because we all know that the cataract surgery results we've achieved are good. Right?"

Maureen nodded. Lon said, "Of course."

"Our patients' visions are well within standard range. This will be inconvenient for us until the review process is over, but it's important to remember that it will be a temporary problem only." There was no comment from Lon or Maureen. "For now, it'll be business as usual but we'll just put off cataract surgeries until this mess is cleared up."

"How long should that be, may I ask?" asked Lon.

Karp sighed. "God knows. They promised it would be soon, so I expect it will take a couple of weeks." He thought about it, and amended his first impression, "No, make that months. I don't know. We'll just have to weather this storm." He shrugged. "Any other questions for now?"

There were none. They all just sort of looked at each other, wishing this weren't happening. Like Karp, they tried to maintain a facade of confidence. The telephone rang, breaking the awkward silence. "Dr. Karp's office, how may I help you?" A pause, then, "Just a moment." She clicked the caller onto hold and turned back toward Karp and Lon. "It's a Rick Leach, personal business?"

"That would be my lawyer," said Karp, as he turned back toward his office. "I suspect I'll be a while. Feel free to lock up and call it a day. And what a day it's been." With that, he disappeared into his office, closing the door behind him.

Six

The videotape player clicked into gear and the motor hummed as it began its second run of the tape. The first time Karp watched the video without stopping it, taking only scant notes. He'd waited a long time for the opportunity to watch this program and he wanted to evaluate it with the closest scrutiny.

Somehow, every time he'd called Kilner or Harmon they were too busy. He couldn't see the tape just yet, they'd tell him. They also seemed to develop selective amnesia, as neither one could recall the names of the four patients whose cases were demonstrated on the tape. Karp never let on that he'd already gotten the names from Amy West. Only after Rick Leach had called and demanded that Karp be allowed to review the tape immediately did they agree that it could be done. Leach advised Karp that this was not a good sign.

"The first case," intoned the narrator, "is that of Mr. L.B," which referred to Mr. Bouchian. The narrating voice, Karp presumed, was that of Billy White. On the screen, a huge eye blinked. It was injected, its conjunctival vessels engorged. There was another blink. An intraocular lens was visible behind the transparent cornea. Aside from the injection, this clearly resembled Mr. Bouchian's eye the last time Karp had seen it. "This is a seventy five year old white male who was initially treated by Dr. Karp some two years previously. The patient underwent complicated cataract surgery with anterior chamber IOL placement." Karp noted that on his legal pad. Aside from the presence of an anterior chamber IOL rather than a posterior chamber one, the statement regarding complicated surgery was presumptuous. The great red eye blinked again. "Despite many visits to Dr. Karp following the surgery, this patient experienced a stormy postoperative course. He complained of eye pain and redness for many months, for which Dr. Karp provided no treatment. At the time of his initial visit to me, this was the

101

appearance of the eye. The vision was 20/70, and there was marked anterior uveitis."

Karp referred to the chart. Mr. Bouchian's postoperative course was a bit drawn out, as it had taken three weeks for the choroidal hemorrhage to fully clear. Following this, though, the vision responded well. Six weeks postoperatively, he saw 20/25. Karp next saw this patient two months later, after he had developed cystoid macular edema, which Karp had treated with eyedrops. Within four weeks later the vision was again 20/20. Karp's last visit with this patient was five months ago. The vision was 20/20, the eye was white and quiet. He jotted all of this information down on the legal pad along with Dr. White's history, which was clearly contradicted by the medical record.

The video switched to the posterior pole of the eye, a view of the retina through a hand held lens. The optic nerve appeared normal. "This view of the retina shows obvious optic nerve swelling and cystoid macular edema." Karp wrote down more notes. The macula wasn't even well visualized on the video, and with its poor resolution, calling macular edema was a real stretch. The history and exam findings of this report were inaccurate or exaggerated to cast Karp as having provided inadequate care.

The retina view on the tape dissolved into another external shot. "This is the same eye three weeks later," White continued, "following initiation of appropriate treatment by our retina specialist at the Chicago Institute of Ophthalmology. Notice that the eye is less inflamed and more comfortable. The vision is 20/20." The video faded out, then returned with another eye filling the video screen. This eye, too, was somewhat injected and red. The pupil was distorted, the top of it elongated with the upper edge of an IOL pushing forward through it.

"This is patient C.D., a seventy five year old woman who had undergone cataract surgery with lens placement by Dr. Karp three months prior to this examination." The eye blinked, as if on cue. "The patient reports a stormy post-operative course wherein the visual acuity never improved."

Karp paged through Mrs. Davis' chart. The surgery was uneventful and the IOL was in good position. One week after surgery, the patient's vision had improved from 20/100 to 20/50. Three weeks after that she was 20/30, her vision somewhat limited by macular degeneration, an unrelated condition of the retina common to the elderly. Karp had noted several times that the patient was vigorously rubbing her operated eye. Karp warned her not to do that, and recommended lubricants instead. He also told her daughter, who accompanied Mrs. Davis, of the risks associated with such severe eye rubbing. She could damage the cornea or even reopen the surgical wound. He gave them several samples of artificial tear lubricants and sent them back to Dr. Demmel for new glasses.

"At this point, the visual acuity is 20/100. This poorly placed posterior chamber IOL is clearly visible distorting the pupil." White had conveniently ignored the fact that the IOL was evidently well placed before. He also ignored the fact that this patient was rubbing her eye, which would have dislodged the IOL. "The eye is chronically inflamed with evidence of cystoid macular edema." No kidding, Karp thought. She rubbed her eye so hard that her IOL was scraping the delicate iris.

The image dissolved into a less magnified view of the eye through a surgical microscope. A forcep was in the eye, grasping the edge of the IOL. With a single fluid motion, the IOL was whisked out of the surgical opening. "The poorly placed IOL was removed by Dr. Genello at the Chicago Institute of Ophthalmology Surgery Center." Karp felt pressure in his neck. His heart rate increased. In one sentence, the bastard denigrated Karp's surgery, misrepresented the facts of the case, and reminded the docs at Compton that White would continue to steal Aurora eye cases, performing them in his own ASC. The image dissolved, and a new IOL could be seen sliding into the eye. "It was replaced with a new posterior chamber IOL, competently inserted in the ciliary sulcus." The image dissolved back to a view of the eye at the slit lamp, presumably postoperatively. "Despite the careful completion of this difficult procedure, some problems with cystoid edema and dry eye symptoms persist. The vision at this point remains 20/50." The picture faded to black for a short, yet dramatic pause. Unbelievable, thought Karp. He was brilliant in his manipulation of the facts.

The picture returned to show another patient's eye with an anterior chamber IOL. "This patient is S.G., a seventy two year old woman who had undergone a cataract procedure with complications and anterior chamber lens placement by Dr. Karp one year prior to this evaluation." Karp referred to his notes on Susan Gruen. Her cataract surgery had gone smoothly until midway into the aspiration of the cortical lens material. A small tear developed in the inferior edge of the lens capsule. There was no vitreous herniating anteriorly, so he carefully completed the aspiration of the lens material and placed the IOL. The pupil was round and central, and Karp completed the surgery without difficulty.

"The patient returned to Dr. Karp on numerous occasions after the surgery complaining of pain and poor vision." The chart showed that the patient was seen routinely four times in the first five weeks after surgery. The eye was quiet, comfortable, and had 20/30 vision. She returned to see Dr. Demmel for her glasses. Three months after surgery she returned to see Karp after she fell at home, striking her head. She said that her vision had been fine up to this point, but that it was blurred after the fall. In fact, the vision was 20/25 and there was no sign of injury. She returned two months later complaining of flashes of light and floating objects in her line of vision. These symptoms can occur with tears or detachments of the retina, a problem that Karp was especially worried about following her fall. The vision remained 20/25, and there was no sign of retinal pathology. He reassured her and saw her again three months later to be safe. The vision was stable, the eye was quiet, and there was no retinal detachment. The patient's only complaint at the time of her last visit with Karp was blurred vision in the other eye from cataract, but by now it was late autumn and she wanted to hold off on surgery until spring. She never returned to Karp's office.

"The vision is now 20/70, and the eye is chronically inflamed." Despite the narrative, the eye did not appear red. "The IOL is poorly placed and there is cystoid edema." There was a dissolve to another surgical view, with the IOL being removed. "Dr. Genello removed this IOL in an attempt to relieve the long-term pain and blurred vision that this patient had experienced, and replaced it with a state-of-the-art posterior chamber IOL." The video dissolved back to another clinic shot. The eye now had a posterior chamber lens implant. It blinked at the camera. "Post operatively, the best vision was 20/50 from chronic cystoid macular edema."

Very interesting, Karp noted. That makes two patients whose vision was good in his office, but were then seen by Billy White and were told to undergo IOL exchange surgery. The video made no mention of alternatives to surgery offered to try to improve the visual complaints. Instead, patients were reoperated and experienced poor visual results. Could it be that White was recommending surgery when less aggressive medical management might have been equally or more successful? He wondered if anyone else watching this video would care enough to consider this possibility. White was a well respected surgeon and, after all, White was not under review here.

The video dissolved once more to another patient's eye. A finger held the eyelid open, showing a rather large peripheral iridectomy which gave the appearance of a second pupil. Karp recognized this as Helen Beam's eye. He remembered the large iridectomy. "This is H.B., a seventy seven year old woman who underwent difficult cataract surgery with anterior chamber lens implantation in this eye three months previously by Dr. Karp. Again, the vision never improved in the eye despite several visits after the surgery." Karp referred to the medical record. Preoperative vision: 20/70. Post operative vision: 20/25. "The vision is now 20/200. More serious, however, is the problem of IOL induced glaucoma. The lens implant was so poorly placed that this patient experienced severe, intractable elevated intraocular pressure that was unresponsive to medications."

Karp looked at the chart. Before surgery the pressure was twenty five millimeters of mercury in both eyes. Normal pressure is twenty one or less, however a solid diagnosis of glaucoma should include more than just elevated pressure. High eye pressure damages the optic nerve, and the records showed no evidence of such damage in either eye. After the surgery, at each of her visits with Karp prior to returning to Dr. Demmel for glasses, her eye pressure remained between sixteen and twenty. Two weeks after this, Demmel returned her to Karp's office questioning the pressures. In fact, the pressure had gone up to thirty two in the operated eye, and to thirty six in the other eye. The nerves were still normal. Obviously, both eyes were affected, not just the operative eye. White had conveniently neglected to mention that.

The video dissolved into yet another view of surgery, with IOL replacement. "Dr. Genello replaced the poorly positioned anterior chamber IOL with a posterior chamber model. Despite this, the pressure remains high and the prognosis for this eye is guarded." White made no comments about the fellow eye. As the video faded to black, he commented, "These cases raise serious question about the surgical skills and clinical management of these patients." The screen stayed black for a moment, then switched to snow from blank tape.

Karp packed the charts neatly into his briefcase and stood slowly in order to maintain his composure. He switched off the TV and left the room, entering Dan Kilner's administrative suite. "Is there anything else I can do for you?" Vicki asked sweetly. Karp knew that she was being extra kind because he would be reporting her conduct to Rick Leach. "The videotape refers to the patients only by their initials for reasons of anonymity," she continued. "Do you need the patients' full names?"

"No, thank you. I already have them," Karp answered without slowing or turning toward her. He wanted not to have to explain his answer. Karp continued down the corridor, through the dark, linoleum floored hallway to the doctors' lounge. His plan was to check his mailbox for any documents he needed to return to his office, and then to leave Compton Memorial Hospital for the day. Three of his colleagues, two family practitioners and an internist, were sitting at the round table next to the wall of mailboxes. They were sifting through their own mail, drinking coffee, and talking. "'Morning," said Karp automatically as he drifted toward his mailbox.

The three looked his way. Their conversation stopped abruptly. "Uh, hi," one answered.

"How are you Jerry?" asked another, without averting his eyes from the lab report he was reading.

"Fine," he answered blandly. He knew that there would be no more discussions of patient matters, business, or social issues as long as he was in the room. Compton was not a large institution, and Karp knew that rumors about him had spread throughout the hospital. He opened his mailbox and extracted a large sheaf of papers.

One of the three docs at the table tossed his empty coffee cup in the trash, stood, and snatched his stethoscope from the table. He ambled out of the room without a word.

Karp began sorting the papers from his mailbox. There were some departmental meeting notices, which he threw in the trash. He also found several information notes in the box, along with lab reports and a few old admission slips. As he was about to flip one of the informative notes in the trash, a bold-faced header caught his eye. "Chicago Institute of Ophthalmology plans to open Aurora office." The two page stapled document was titled "Administrative Report." It was one of the house organ papers that Kilner had instituted after taking over from Greenley. Kilner shared his long range plans with the medical staff regularly in the Report.

Chicago Institute of Ophthalmology plans to open Aurora office.

I have been in contact with Dr. William White of the Chicago Institute of Ophthalmology. CIO has been considering opening a satellite office in Aurora for some time, and I want to be sure that this is done keeping the best interests of Aurora patients in mind. Dr. White, who has previously made presentations at our continuing education conferences, expressed an interest in joining our medical staff so that appropriate surgical cases may be performed here. We have met several times since February, and I look forward to establishing a relationship that will result in a win-win situation for all parties.

Karp just stared at the statement for a while, then read it again. The sons of bitches are in a conspiracy, he thought, and they aren't even trying to conceal it. Karp shook his head slowly and placed the Administrative Report alongside the ER documents and operative notes in his briefcase. He snapped it gently closed, and lifted it from the table. He made his way to the doorway without another word to the other docs, who were openly uncomfortable with his presence there. He wasn't in the mood to talk to anyone.

Once more in his office, Karp dropped into his chair and opened the briefcase to refile the patient charts. "So, how'd it go, old man?" It was Lon. Karp hadn't even heard him walk in. He was sitting in the chair across from Karp.

"It was a treat, Lon. This should be no big deal," he answered facetiously. "There's nothing mentioned in the tape that doesn't exaggerate, distort, or outright contradict the truth of the patients' cases. The whole thing makes me out to be as incompetent as a first year resident. Defense should be a piece of cake."

"I suspected it would be that bad. What are you going to do?"

Karp sat far back in his chair. He put his arms out and interlaced his fingers behind his head. "What can I do? I'm going to prepare the best defense against these ridiculous charges that I can possibly muster. I can only hope that enough of the MEC members will examine all of the legitimate facts in this case. I'll put myself into the hands of the system that was designed to protect me as well as my patients."

Lon shook his head. "I don't know, Jerry. Was the system really designed to protect you?"

Karp squinted and sat forward. "Of course it was. From the day you are accepted to medical school, the system works in order to see you succeed unless you are a menace. No one wants to admit that they made a mistake by hiring an inept doc. Even guys who get sued over and over are only required to take a few remedial courses and can then return to practice."

"Jerry, you're probably right about how docs protected their ranks in the past. I'm not so sure it's like that anymore."

"How so?"

Lon had been around the hospital as much as Karp. He hung around the nurses' station and lounges, and was privy to some of the rumors that doctors never heard. "I don't know for certain, but I get the sense that organized medicine, the old boys' network that's been around forever, is more interested in looking out for themselves than for the new faces. The complaints against you are all contrived, and you know it. Those jackals Demmel and White were poisoning your patients' minds. It's all this Health Care Reform shit that's coming down. I'm telling you, these guys are worried that they're going to lose their piece of the pie, and they're used to making big money. The government is designing a brand new health care system, and the old guard doesn't give a shit about you."

Karp heaved a sigh and put his feet up on his desk. "That's great news, Lonnie, 'cause if you're right...I'm screwed." Lon said nothing, just looked at him. "If I beat this rap, it's sure to cost me what's left of my life's savings in legal fees. I'm certain it will take a long time, and without surgery, this practice won't survive. Even if I'm acquitted, the perception of ineptitude is out there and the practice suffers. If I lose my case, I'm out in the cold immediately."

"Well, Doc, that's great," Lon answered.

Karp paused and looked at the ceiling. Lon was a good friend and confidant. If for no reason other than to assure Lon of the fact, Karp studied the ceiling for guidance and concluded, "Look, Lon. This situation sucks. No doubt about it. But," he looked straight in his friend's eye, "no matter what it takes, I'm going to get through this, and we'll all survive. I've got too much invested in this." He smiled. "Hell, I've got everything invested in this. We're going to get through this, and we're not going anywhere. None of us. It's just a matter of belt tightening, gut checks, and the confidence that comes from knowing that we've done no wrong."

Lon grinned back at his friend. "That's the kind of talk I want to hear from you, old man. Don't let these bastards get to you." He stood. "I've got work to do. One of us has to keep this practice running." With that, he left Karp alone.

"Dr. Karp?" It was Maureen on the intercom. "Mr. Leach is here to see you."

Karp came out to greet Rick Leach personally. He struck Karp as looking young for his profession. Slim and unassuming, he was dressed in a neat but by no means tailored gray suit and white shirt. His hair was conservatively short and freshly combed to one side. He carried a monstrous brown briefcase. Karp extended his right hand. "Thanks for coming out, Rick."

Leach's handshake was firm. "No problem, Doc."

"Let's sit down in my office. I've gathered together the documents you asked me to arrange."

They proceeded to Karp's office and he bade Leach to sit in one of the chairs that faced the small desk that was covered with various documents, charts, and long lines of computer printouts. He cleared off an area near Leach by lifting a stack of documents and placing them rather unceremoniously in a pile behind his own chair. "Sorry the place is such a mess," he explained. "I've been inundated with paperwork lately."

Leach smiled. "I'm pleased to know that you're doing your homework."

Karp settled into his chair.

"Did you get to see the infamous videotape?" asked the attorney.

"Yes. Infamous is a good description."

"Tell me about it."

"Billy White narrates the tape. The patient histories as presented are patently untrue."

Leach took notes on a yellow legal pad as they talked. "How so?"

Karp presented two of the cases and pointed out the false statements about damage to the eye.

"Okay," he noted the discrepancies on his pad. "So White presented historical facts on his video that differ from your recollection of the case. Do you have documentation of your side of the story?"

"Of course. The patient's clinical records clearly state their concerns at each visit contrary to White's statements."

"Good. What else can you tell me about the tape?"

"He never came out and said I was incompetent, but he implied it over and over. He made statements like, 'complicated surgery,' or 'our specialist initiated appropriate treatment,' suggesting that my care was not appropriate."

"Okay. How did the patients do? Did any go blind?"

"One maintained excellent acuity after CIO management of his macular edema. Two patients underwent IOL exchange, removal of the lens that I had placed. Both had reasonable vision; 20/50 or so. Both had chronic inflammation, which could honestly be attributed to the second surgery."

"Or the first?" asked Leach.

"These patients were seeing well when they left my office to see the OD, Demmel. Obviously, they had some late inflammation and vision problems. IOL exchange isn't always the method of choice to treat this problem."

"And that method is...?"

111

"One might try a course of anti-inflammatory medications to control the symptoms. If this relieves the problem without surgery, you've saved the patient a lot of aggravation."

"And lost the opportunity to imprint upon them the fact that their first surgeon was inept."

"You said it, not me." Karp folded his arms on his chest and sat back in his seat.

Leach took all this down. "Can you prove that the second surgery was unnecessary?"

"Not without a good look at the entire medical record from CIO. I'd also be interested to know what kind of informed consent these people were given. Were they advised that further surgery could be risky? Did White tell them about alternatives to surgery, such as eyedrops?"

Leach nodded. "You mentioned the results on three of the patients. How did the fourth do?"

Karp sighed and sat forward, placing his elbows on the desk. "Not so well. She'd had slightly elevated eye pressure in both eyes before surgery. Afterward, she did well with good vision and a quiet eye. A few weeks later, Demmel asked me to see her because the pressure was up in both eyes. I began to treat that and ordered followup testing, and she went to see Dr. White at CIO. He recommended the IOL be removed, and implied that the IOL was the cause of the pressure. Following surgery, the pressure is still high and the eye isn't doing well."

"Did your surgery induce the pressure problem?"

Karp thought for a moment. "Cataract surgery in one eye would not affect the pressure in both eyes, and this woman has problems with both eyes. I don't think the surgery caused her problem," he concluded. "Still, White is the expert."

"And he's biased." Leach looked closely at Karp. "He didn't mention that the pressure was bilaterally elevated?"

"No. He said nothing about the other eye."

Leach noted that. "It's an important omission."

Karp closed his eyes. "Only if anyone in a position to act upon that omission cares."

"You're starting to sound paranoid about this, Doctor."

"Paranoid? Who wouldn't feel paranoid? Look at this." He handed the attorney his copy of the Administrative Report outlining Kilner's attention to White and CIO. He read it carefully.

"What do you think this means?"

"You tell me. The hospital recruits me to come here to compete against CIO and White. Next, Kilner and White are working out a `win-win' proposal to work together, and suddenly Billy White is the main witness to Dan Kilner's prosecution of my surgical skill." He shook his head. "You can't convince me that these guys aren't somehow working together on this."

Rick Leach folded his hands on top of his legal pad. "What would Compton Memorial Hospital have to gain? Why would they do this to you?"

"I don't know. I owe them a lot of money."

"Just how much do you owe them?"

"About a hundred fifty thousand dollars."

Leach shook his head. "A pittance to a busy hospital. Go on."

Karp shrugged. "It may be a pittance to them, but it's a ton of dough to me. Anyway, if White is so good, what's to keep Kilner from putting him on staff and letting him just grind me out of business by demonstrating his superior skills? Why does he need to destroy me? Even if the money is small potatoes to the hospital, why just give it up, when allowing me to continue to work there means that they'll get it back eventually? It doesn't make sense."

"You're right, Jerry. Tell me, just who do you think is the bad guy here, White or Kilner?"

Karp chuckled. "Why not both? White is just plain greedy. I think Kilner's taking the path of least resistance. Maybe White suggested that he'd induce some of these patients to sue me for malpractice and name the hospital as co-defendant, and Kilner wants to avoid that. I don't know, I can only guess."

Leach rubbed the bridge of his nose. He considered how to proceed with the conversation. "What do you know about Ben Bookner?"

"Dr. Bookner, of the Bookner Eye Centers? I didn't live around here when he had his legal problems, but I know that Billy White was instrumental in the proceedings against him."

Leach nodded. "That's pretty accurate. I didn't represent Ben, but I was his patient. I was impressed by his facility, his professionalism, and his care."

Karp nodded.

"Ben Bookner was accused by Medicare officials of padding his books with unnecessary and unperformed medical procedures. The federal government can be most intimidating."

"I understand that he was indicted, handcuffed, the whole nine yards."

"That's right. Officially, the charges were a result of Medicare auditing."

"But that's not what really happened, is it?"

"No. It seems that Dr. White has connections to several politicians. It is speculated," Leach stressed, "that White showed copies of patients' bills to his federal friends. Someone then ordered a detailed audit of Bookner's activities."

"I thought that Bookner was acquitted."

"He was. But the audit, the indictment, the charges, the court case all took a long time. It was almost two years before the acquittal. The indictment was big news. Nobody cares that he was innocent. Everyone remembers him as the doctor carried away in handcuffs."

"But Bookner is still around. He's not in jail, and he's not bankrupt."

Leach leaned forward and spoke slowly to emphasize his point. "Don't ignore the long range consequences of a public trial. Ben is still around, but he's got to fight to stay in business. Patients don't trust him anymore and managed care providers don't want to contract with him. He's got a bad reputation, even though it's not deserved. Other doctors don't refer patients to him. His wife and he were separated for a while. They're back together, but it almost cost him his family. It did cost him his reputation, his life's savings, and to a large extent, his spirit. Dr. Bookner does not enjoy his profession very much anymore."

"So the point is," concluded Karp, "not to take this public."

"Not altogether," Leach went on. "If you have a good case, and if you can be the aggressor, you may want to go public. But," he admonished, "if you take on someone like White, or even Kilner, this will be a drawn out affair. The legal fees will be considerable, and no respectable attorney will take a case like this on contingency."

Karp nodded. He knew what that meant. "What would make this a good case?"

"The type of litigation you're suggesting would be a restraint of trade case. To proceed, you need to exhaust the due process of the hospital's bylaws. The court won't interfere with a professional medical quality assurance process."

"Fine. We're dealing with that. That means I have to go through the review process fully."

"Right. Presuming you fail the outside review, you will appeal the MEC's decision. That means you plead your case and call witnesses before an appellate board made up of the hospital's administrator, the president of the MEC, and an arbitrator chosen by the hospital. That arbitrator is usually an attorney, though not the hospital's counsel."

Karp motioned with his palms up. "So my appeal would be before Kilner, Harmon, and some lawyer that they get to choose?"

"That's right."

He snickered. "Not a very impartial jury."

"True. They need to demonstrate that the actions taken against you are appropriate for the situation...that any reasonably acting hospital review board would instigate similar sanctions in similar circumstances."

"To do otherwise would be the basis of a restraint case," concluded Karp.

"Only part way," Leach corrected him. "There are other points that you must prove. The actions taken against you need to have violated your right of due process or the sanctions should be grossly out of proportion or otherwise agredious. You'll need to prove that you have endured financial hardship because of those actions."

"That will be simple enough."

"You also need to be able to convince the court that the parties involved in this case colluded to act against you. Your Administrative Report is a first step, but by no means proves collaboration between the parties. This is often the hardest point to prove in court." Leach emphasized the conclusion, "These individuals may be acting in concert. The hard part is proving it."

Karp nodded. "I understand. So what do we do now?"

"At this point, I would suggest that we do everything in our power to avoid such a confrontation. It would be in your best interest for you to pass the outside review unscathed and forget lawsuits."

Karp looked past his attorney at the back wall of his office. If only it were that easy, he thought.

"Have you completed your review of the cataract surgeries?" asked Leach.

"Still working on it," was the answer. He gave Leach a thin stack of papers stapled together at the top. "It's sort of a work in progress. I'm trying to research the cases from every angle: Preoperative conditions, postop complications, visual acuity, eye pressures, everything I can think of."

"Are there any problems? Any deficiencies we need to be aware of? You need to be very introspective here, Jerry. Is your surgery up to snuff?"

"There is no doubt about the vitrectomies. I've not argued that from the beginning."

"Right."

116

"I've looked extensively through my papers and books, and the most specific references I can find suggest that the rate should be less than five percent. My rate is ten percent."

"Where does that leave us?"

"I am still on my learning curve. Most experienced surgeons agree that you need to do about fifteen hundred cataract procedures before you've mastered the skills. I've done about six hundred, including my residency. I'm getting better."

"But are you good enough?"

"I haven't been able to find any documentation that clearly delineates what makes a `bad' cataract surgeon. Most papers refer to visual results that should be achieved in these patients."

"And how do you compare?"

"The generally accepted visual outcome for cataract surgery is to achieve visual acuity of 20/40 or better ninety five percent of the time in patients with no other preexisting eye disease. My patients who meet that requirement achieve 20/40 vision ninety seven percent of the time."

"That sounds pretty good."

"I also did some research to see how patients who undergo vitrectomy compare, as far as final vision and other parameters. Of course, their outcomes aren't as good as patients who don't undergo vitrectomy. Still, 20/40 should be achieved around three quarters of the time. My patients reached that goal ninety percent of the time."

"That's very good, isn't it?"

"Yes and no. Remember that the sample size--the number of patients who've had vitrectomy--is very small. There's only a little over one hundred sixty patients to begin with. Even with a rate of ten percent, that's a little over a dozen eyes. I'm not sure that the results are statistically significant."

Leach studied the document. "This isn't a publication you're presenting, Jerry. This research looks good to me. It should help your case a great deal." He placed the papers in a pile, organized them, and filed them in his briefcase. "Can you find someone else who can look at your charts and give us another opinion about this, preferably one that will support you?"

"I talked to a doc I know in Minneapolis, Preston Keith. He trained at Detroit General and was on staff there for a short time. He agreed to review all of my surgical reports and results. He also said that he'd look over any specific charts that I send him."

"Good. Have you gotten any results yet?"

"I express mailed him copies of all the op notes and the complete records on the four cases cited by Dr. White. I got a FAX from him just this morning." He fished out a short document from another pile on his desk and handed it to Leach. "Here's a copy. It's brief, but it says that the op notes look all right. He agrees with what I've been saying all along, that the vitrectomy rate is high but obviously improving."

Leach read the two page letter. He pointed at a passage in the last paragraph. "And he says right here that it would be unconscionable for a hospital to restrict your privileges based on the allegations made against you. This is terrific. He said he'd look over other full charts?"

"Yes. Pres said he'd do that if the review went badly, to give us a second opinion if we need it."

Leach filed the letter from Keith with the others in his briefcase. "It's clear to me that you've got this situation about as well in hand as you can at this point. Do you know who this outside reviewer is going to be?"

"Not yet. John Kingston is the HEENT Division Chairman, and he's handling this. He promised to let me know who the guy is going to be to make sure that there's no conflict of interest."

"That's all right. Just remember, Compton docs and administrators have already broken promises they've made you. Let me know if they try to pull a fast one here."

"Don't worry."

"How are you holding up otherwise?"

"Okay, I guess."

"I mean it, Jerry. How are you doing? How's your wife taking all this? I know it can be rough."

"Val's hanging in there," he finally answered. "She's pretty much consumed by the adoption process." He paused. "I'm basically okay," he went on. "I'm not sleeping well at night, and I find myself dragging through the day."

"That's a common response to this kind of stress." The lawyer smiled, "You know I'm usually on the other side for these proceedings. I try a fair number of malpractice cases," he pointed out, "arguing against a doctor's credibility and competence."

"I know."

"How is the adoption going?" asked Leach.

Karp breathed heavily. His voice was quiet. "It's going forward. The problem is that it's so expensive. We've already committed considerable sums to this, but business is down and now, with all due respect, I'm going to be generating some significant legal fees."

"I'll try to be as gentle with that as I can. I'm sure you have a lot of patients who don't know how they're going to pay their medical bills."

"A few, but most have insurance."

Leach smiled and folded his briefcase. "Is there anything else for now?"

Karp shook his head. "Not that I can think of."

"Okay." The attorney stood and offered his right hand. "Let's stay in touch by phone. Call me when you hear from anyone on this, and send me copies of all documents that you receive."

"Don't worry. I will." Karp led his counselor to the front office and saw him to the door. Once Leach had gone, he turned to go back to his office. Maureen said nothing as he walked by her, but tried to give Karp a supportive smile. As he walked past Lon's office, Karp added, "We'll get through this."

"Damn right," returned Lon as Karp closed his door.

Karp sat down and stared into space for a few moments, wishing that the whole thing would just go away. He was tired of reviewing the same charts over and over for picky details. He was tired of juggling his books and his personal finances. He wished he could get back to his job, to concentrate on being a doctor. He sighed, and tried to do a little reading. There was a recent copy of Ophthalmology Times on a corner of his very cluttered desk. In it were a couple of articles on various aspects of cataract surgery. There was a story describing new strategies for investments in light of the low interest rates, and a photodocumentary case on a congenital retinal anomaly. Karp skimmed over the magazine, absorbing very little of it.

The back of the magazine had several pages of classified ads. There were practices and equipment for sale, services offered for angiogram processing, laser repairs, and so on. Karp always read the classifieds listing job opportunities to check for docs in the Chicago area looking for new associates. He liked to know just how busy his competitors were, and he kept up on new subspecialists being recruited into the area.

One ad caught Karp's eye. It said, "Chicago area. Recruiting a general ophthalmologist with subspecialty interest-- retina preferred. Work with a thriving anterior segment practice. Over one thousand cataracts and seven hundred radial keratotmies per year in practice. New associate to provide medical and subspecialty care only. Argon and Yag lasers in office. Progressive salary and benefits. Write Oph Times Box 614." The services listed were exactly what he was doing now that he was barred from cataract surgery. He thought about it, and decided that some additional work might help his shaky financial situation. At the very least, he wanted to know who was hiring. He wondered if it was that bastard, White. He had nothing to lose.

Karp turned toward his computer and accessed the word processing software. He started his letter. "Dear Sir: I am writing in reference to your advertisement in Ophthalmology Times. I am currently in private solo practice in Aurora. Although I have been doing cataract and anterior segment surgery, I am interested in medical retina and laser procedures. I am comfortable interpreting angiograms and performing macular laser procedures." He paused to think about how to address the next issue. "The recently proposed changes in our health care system have been distressing to me." They'd been distressing to every doc he knew. "I no longer find cataract surgery enjoyable," an understatement, "and I would prefer to focus my professional efforts on retinal problems and medical eyecare." Either that, or I'll be forced to do it anyway.

"As I am currently in the area, I am particularly interested in the position you have advertised. I would enjoy meeting with you to discuss our mutual interests. At the very least, our proximity may offer us the chance to work together on a trial basis with minimal financial risk to either party." Karp wasn't too keen on giving up all of the advantages of running his own practice. Besides, he still held out hope that the problem at Compton could eventually be resolved. "Please contact me at your earliest convenience. Enclosed is a copy of my curriculum vitae. Sincerely, Jerrold Karp, M.D."

PRIVILEGES

Seven

The room was lit only by flickering kaleidoscope colors from the television. One moment the walls reflected blue, the next red, then again white. Specter shadows danced all around. The blinds were drawn, and little light escaped this dim world. The sound was turned very low, just a whisper of noise accompanying the video program. Every few seconds the image snapped to a new one, with a short connection of black screen separating the pictures. Karp "surfed" the video channels for hours without stopping at one for more than a glimpse. The clock on the wall behind him ticked unnoticed, then rang once. It was three thirty, Karp knew, because the last chime was three a.m.

He ran up the forty channels, past the news and weather channels, over CNN and around ESPN's rerun of last night's Astros-Mets game. He paused there for a minute, but bored quickly. He knew the Astros would win, and he didn't care much for either team anyway. The American Movie Channel was playing *The Flight of the Phoenix* with Jimmy Stewart rebuilding a crashed World War II bomber in the desert. He continued to the Discovery Channel. There was a show about insects. A spider was building a web. It squirted a line of sticky fluid and formed the corners of the web with its feet. It was interesting and Karp liked nature shows. Besides, he'd seen *The Flight of the Phoenix* at least three times. He hoped that the spiders would catch his interest long enough for him to stop thinking. If he could relax, he might fall asleep. He needed sleep.

"What are you doing?" Karp jumped, and almost fell off the sofa. It was Val.

"Sorry, honey," he answered quietly. He wasn't sure why he was keeping his voice down. There was no one in the house but the two of them. She squinted at him, covering her eyes against the light of the television. "I thought I'd kept the sound low enough not to wake you."

"It wasn't the sound. I rolled over and found you not there." She sighed, and crossed her arms. "Is this going to be a regular occurrence now?" she asked.

It was the fifth night in a week that Karp had awakened before four a.m. He'd be exhausted by early evening, but tried to stay up until their usual bedtime of eleven. They'd crawl in bed, watch the news and Karp would drift off to sleep. Every night, all too soon, he would waken. Sometimes it came with a startle when the dreams got to him, and sometimes he'd just start thinking about things and wake up slowly. He'd stare at the ceiling, fluff the pillow, check the alarm clock. He rarely fell back to sleep, and he'd try to get out of bed quietly to let Val rest.

This was hard on Val, too. She understood the magnitude of the charges against her husband and she hated how it had affected him. Both of their tempers had become short. They snapped at each other over the most trivial subjects. Last night it was because Jerry had left an empty glass in the sink rather than put it in the dishwasher. He'd just become so empty minded lately. He was constantly fixed on work.

Karp rarely went outdoors anymore except to wash the Stealth and cut the grass. The neighbors, John Kingston and his wife, wouldn't make eye contact with him. Val noticed that their social life had come to a fast stop. They were no longer invited to dinner with their physician friends. The wives often went shopping together in the past, and the men had card games a few times a year. No one called the Karps anymore. Except for dinner with the Morrisseys or with Maureen and her husband, Jerry and Val rarely went out.

They were also stressed out about the adoption. The agency had sent pictures of children for them to review. As the situation at the office dragged on, Jerry Karp became more pensive. He was very worried about money.

Karp hadn't paid the leases on his equipment for over two months. One company called, and he put them off saying it was a clerical error that he'd rectify. The others were simply sending him late payment notices and adding penalty charges to his bill.

He hated to do it, but it was his only option. Lon and Maureen had to be paid. He had gone without a paycheck himself now for three months. There was no place else to cut corners.

Karp still hadn't heard from Compton about the outside review. They promised to move the process along, but there'd been no word for weeks. Karp was sure Kilner was stalling intentionally just to make him sweat. Rick Leach told him that was nonsense. The delay benefitted neither party. Karp tried not to be so paranoid, but he had a hard time controlling his thoughts. He had a harder time sleeping.

"I'm sorry, Hon," Karp answered. "If I could fall back asleep, it would please me more than I can tell you." He sat up, dropping the spare blanket that covered him. His hair poked out in every direction, and he wore only a pair of undershorts. He looked a mess. He nodded toward the TV screen. "Sometimes watching this will occupy my mind enough to let me go back to sleep."

She sighed. "Well, I'm going back to bed." She turned and walked back up the stairs. "I hope this ends sometime soon."

"No more than I do, Dear. Believe me." He covered himself and stared at the TV. A spider was eating a bug that was caught in its web. The narrator said something about the spider's venom, but Karp wasn't paying attention. He repositioned himself on the sofa, trying to find a comfortable position. He needed to get some sleep. This morning he would be driving into Chicago for a job interview, and he had to look fresh and alert.

When Karp first heard from Dr. Alex Boren, he was taken by surprise. "Who are you?" he asked.

"Alex Boren. You sent me your curriculum vitae." It took a moment, but Karp remembered. It was the classified ad he'd responded to from Ophthalmology Times...the guy looking for an associate interested in retina diseases. It suddenly occurred to Karp that he'd heard of Boren before: He was the guy who advertised on TV and radio. "This is Alex Boren. If you're looking for an alternative to a life of glasses or contact lenses, call me for a consultation. You've nothing to lose...except your glasses." Boren did radial keratotomy, RK. He'd done thousands of them before anyone else in Chicago considered the surgery to be anything more than butchery. "Slash for cash" is what the others called RK, at least until Medicare fee cuts forced them to look elsewhere for income. Now everyone did RK.

Boren's practice was called the Heartland Eye Group. They had two offices in Chicago, one in Deerfield and the other in Lisle. Boren was a general ophthalmologist, although his practice consisted mainly of doing cataract surgery and RK procedures. He had lasers in the office as well as a fundus camera for doing angiography, but he mostly sent these out to subspecialists. Boren was the only ophthalmologist in the Heartland Eye Group. He had hired three optometrists to help him see patients in the clinic, and was now looking for an ophthalmologist so that he could concentrate solely on doing surgery. The new MD would handle the difficult clinic cases rather than Boren or the OD's. It was to be understood, though, that the new doctor would not be doing cataract or RK surgery. This would be Boren's responsibility alone. Karp knew why Boren was having a hard time filling this position: Most ophthalmologists looking for a job don't want to give up anterior segment surgery. Even though Karp did only a few cases a month, the cataract procedures accounted for nearly two thirds of his billing. If a doc committed himself to this kind of situation, he'd be giving up any chance of making a significant living.

Now Karp was nervous. He couldn't sleep, and he wasn't sure how he should approach the issue of Billy White and his privileges at Compton Hospital. What if Boren already knew? Obviously, White wasn't keeping this a secret. The ophthalmic community was not big, and rumors passed quickly through the city. He dare not lie to Boren, because that would surely sour their relationship. On the other hand, it wasn't exactly a great coup to tell your potential employer that your hospital privileges were suspended.

Karp felt cold all of a sudden, and shivered under the blanket. He tried to concentrate on the spider crawling across the inside of the TV tube. He yawned, and closed his eyes for a moment. He watched the television a little more, vacillating between interest in the creatures on the screen and wanting to run the channels again. Wasn't there a rerun of *The Avengers* on USA Cable at three thirty last night? No, he decided to stick with the spiders for a little longer. All at once he saw two spiders, so he closed his eyes again and just concentrated on the whispered narration. "The bite of the black widow is only rarely fatal to humans. In this case, the spider injected the venom in her victim's abdomen..." He snored, and slept for almost an hour.

Dan Kilner walked quickly toward the administrative suite. He was angry and kept the brisk pace to try to calm himself. This whole matter was taking far too long, and he decided that he was going to call Billy White this very morning to put some pressure on him. As he marched past the gift shop, he passed two nurses who had stopped there to pick up a candy bar before their work shifts started. "Good morning, Mr. Kilner," said one as he passed.

"Morning," he answered with an automatic smile, as he continued on without breaking stride.

He'd just left a meeting with the Operating Room Committee over breakfast. It ended promptly at eight, and as he left the conference room next to the cafeteria, he was stopped by John Kingston, who was in charge of Karp's review. "Dan," Kingston had asked, "can I talk to you for a minute?"

"Sure." He always wanted to be available to the staff physicians. "What's up?"

"It's about Jerry Karp," answered Kingston quietly. The matter was still closed to those outside of the QA committee and the MEC. "I'm concerned about the time that's passed since we last talked about this. We were supposed to have someone to review his charts by now."

"That's right," he motioned with his index finger. "I was going to get back to you on that. In Wisconsin, we used to use a very good consulting firm on these medico-legal issues."

"That's what you said, Dan, but I hadn't heard back from you. I'm sure this is killing Karp, not knowing what's going on and not being able to operate."

Kilner rubbed his chin. "You're probably right, John." In fact, he'd told Billy White about the review right after the emergency meeting of the MEC. They would be using the MedCo Corporation to review Karp's surgeries. MedCo hired specialists from every branch of medicine to review records and provide expert witness testimony. Usually they worked for malpractice attorneys, but they also provided "objective" reviewers in cases like this. White said that was fine, and told Kilner that he knew of an ophthalmologist who occasionally worked with MedCo. He asked Kilner to stall the process until after he could meet with this fellow at the American Society of Cataract and Refractive Surgery meeting. Kilner figured that White was going to exert some of his considerable political strength to assure an outcome favorable to himself. As John Kingston noted, several weeks had gone by with no call from Billy White.

"I'm sorry. I dropped the ball on this. Can you have your secretary call me this afternoon? I'll contact MedCo and initiate some activity this morning." He nodded for emphasis, "I agree we have to get moving on this."

He meant that, too. White was paying in to the Development Fund for himself, Genello, and Stutz, but none of them were actually doing surgery at Compton. With Karp out of the OR too, Compton was losing money.

"Have you contacted Karp's former partner in Oklahoma?" asked Kilner, trying to change the subject away from MedCo.

"Yes," Kingston nodded. "He didn't want to discuss Karp at all until after he had time to confer with his legal counsel."

"What does that mean?"

He shrugged. "I wasn't sure at first, but then I got this letter." He pulled a sheet of paper from a file folder he was carrying. "Dear Dr. Kingston," he read aloud, "I had the opportunity to discuss the issues you raised regarding Dr. Karp's surgical skills with my legal counsel. I was advised to tell you that this matter is confidential between myself and Dr. Karp, pursuant to Oklahoma Statutes...and then he gives some numbers."

Kilner looked at the letter. "It appears that he has some unflattering things to say about Dr. Karp, but doesn't want to put them in writing."

"That would be my guess, too," said Kingston, sounding disappointed. Kilner figured that Kingston might want to see his neighbor cleared of the charges. "He must be afraid that Karp would sue him for slander."

"His own QA records probably aren't complete or accurate enough," agreed Kilner. He thought for a moment. "Why don't you call this guy back. Ask him what all this means," he motioned toward the letter.

"And then what?"

"Ask him to tell you personally about his concerns over Karp's surgery. Tell him that it will be off the record and that you won't press for a written statement or any details. You just want to know about his surgical skills, using broad strokes of the brush."

"But without a written report, there's no validity to those statements, and no way to enter them into the formal hearing."

Kilner shook his head. "That's not true. You can provide this letter and a report of your conversation with the man. You can tell the MEC what he told you."

"That's hearsay," Kingston protested. "It's not admissible."

"It's up to the MEC to decide what's pertinent in this case, and I think that they'd like to know what Dr. Karp's former employer thought about him. I'll be willing to bet," he concluded, "that this guy's statements will only support the impartial review that we perform."

Kingston understood the importance of establishing a pattern. He nodded. "Okay. I'll give him a call."

"Good." Kilner touched Kingston's shoulder. "I'll get on MedCo." He excused himself, and left the conference room, working hard to mask his anger at White for having wasted so much time.

Now, as he entered his own office suite, he worked to focus his emotions. He was about to instruct Vicki to get Dr. White on the phone, but before he could, she greeted him. "Good morning, Mr. Kilner. There are some telephone messages for you on your desk. Dr. White asked that you contact him this morning."

"Thank you, Vicki. Can you get him on the phone for me?" He entered his office without stopping to wait for the answer. Before he sat down, he extracted the Karp file from his credenza. He reviewed the documentation in the file, and found his memo regarding MedCo. They'd recommended a fellow named Vincent Porter from New Mexico to perform the review.

"Mr. Kilner, Dr. White is on line three for you," informed Vicki on the intercom.

Kilner lifted the handset. "Dr. White? Dan Kilner here."

"Just a moment," answered a female voice. "Dr. White will be right with you." Before Kilner could answer, the voice clicked off and music-on-hold played an instrumental version of the Beatles' A Day in the Life. It was a strange sort of power game doctors played, to see who could keep a caller on hold longer.

"This is Dr. White," came the response a few moments later. He sounded testy.

"Dan Kilner here, Dr. White. I was returning your call from this morning."

"Yes, yes," said White, perturbed. "I wanted to let you know that I spoke with Dr. Porter at the ASCRS meeting. There should be no problem with his review of Jerry Karp."

It's damn well about time, thought Kilner. "Good. I'll see to it that his people at MedCo are contacted today." Before White could hang up, Kilner added, "Dr. White, we need to talk about CIO and Compton Hospital."

"What of it?" He was clearly annoyed now, and there was no attempt to hide it.

"None of the applications for CIO staff--yours, Dr. Genello's, or Dr. Stutz's--are complete. We need to have all of the documents in the files so that we may proceed with the credentialing mechanism for you." White didn't respond. "I am very much looking forward to having you all on our medical staff."

"I'll talk to Genello and Stutz. They'll be operating at CMH. We haven't got the satellite office open yet."

"I see." Kilner tried to sound cheery and interested. "Can we assist you in locating the site?"

"We have a place," he answered. "They'll start staffing it when the equipment is up and running."

"I hope that you'll be using CMH facilities for surgery, too. Your patients think the world of you, and we're very excited here about working together with you."

"We'll have to see, Dan. Genello and Stutz will be staffing the Aurora satellite, and they'll be dealing with the Aurora patients. I'll see to it that they complete their applications. Everything else," he stressed `else,' "is in order, is it not?" He referred to the payments into the Development Fund.

"By all means," Kilner answered. "It's just that we want to begin working with your surgical patients here. That is a part of the plan."

There was a pause. White said something to someone nearby, which was garbled over the phone line. "Right, right," he finally answered distractedly. "We'll get on with it. Let me know what happens with Karp. That's very important to me."

"You have my word. Thanks for your time, Doctor." They hung up. God, thought Kilner. White was an arrogant son of a bitch.

131

Karp pulled the Stealth briskly off the interstate and onto the exit ramp for Lisle. He never slowed the car on the ramp, at least until he approached the stop light. The fat, speed-rated tires gripped the road surely as he whipped around the curve. He had to control himself from speeding on the toll road to avoid a ticket. Since cops didn't watch the ramps, he amused himself by speeding down them.

He drove about a mile until he passed the Dominick's market. On the next block was an unassuming orange brick medical office building run by Jewish Medical Center of Chicago. The JMC logo was the only signage large enough to be legible from the roadway. Karp pulled into the lot and parked.

Dr. Alex Boren's office suite took up the entire third floor. The lobby was tastefully decorated with a pastel carpet and green walls. There was no artwork hanging, although several professionally mounted newspaper articles featuring Dr. Boren dotted the walls in large frames. You could pretty much follow Boren's career by reading them. Just after he completed his residency he donated some time to a cataract mission in India, performing hundreds of surgeries for the native population at no charge. Following this there was another cataract article featuring the advances of small incision surgery. A Sun-Times story discussed RK surgery. There was a clipping from Chicago Magazine penned by a writer who had undergone the surgery himself. It discussed RK in the first person, and heaped great praise on Dr. Boren. This was followed by another journal article on Boren's cataract procedure, an article he authored on Yag laser treatments, and on and on and on. It was an impressive "bragging wall," thought Karp.

He approached the reception desk. There were two receptionists, both on the telephone. He could see past the desk through a glass partition that there were several technicians buzzing around the examining lanes. The lobby was filled with patients. Finally, one of the receptionists got off the phone. "Hello," she smiled at him. "Are you here to check in?"

"I'm Dr. Karp. I'm here to see Dr. Boren."

132

"Oh, yes, Doctor. We're expecting you. Please come in."

Karp took a quick glance around. He could count seven lanes. Three patients were watching a videotape that explained the indications for Yag laser surgery and its inherent risks. A technician was helping an old lady with a walker make her way into one of the lanes. "Right this way," instructed the receptionist. "I'll show you to Dr. Boren's office."

They walked around the reception area through another doorway. This room was brightly lit with overhead fluorescent lamps. There were rows upon rows of manila file charts for Dr. Boren's patients. Beyond this room was another hallway with several offices attached. The largest, by far, was Alex Boren's.

His personal office, while generous, was by no means excessive. The furniture struck Karp as appearing cheap more than anything else, as if they'd been purchased second hand. The desk was plain: Not simple or unadorned, but rather sparse in appearance. The chair behind it was not leather covered, but instead had a shabby material finish with tattered edges. The guest chairs did not match Boren's, and didn't appear to go with the decor. The walls were a bit gritty, in need of a coat of fresh paint. There were unrelated photos on the wall, one of Wrigley Field in black and white taken several decades ago, another of Salvador Dali. A couple pieces of modern art were hung on another wall, along with a poster showing various models of Porsche automobiles. Karp realized he liked Boren already. If he enjoyed baseball and fast cars, they had something in common. Karp also noticed the NordicTrac in one corner of the room.

"You can have a seat right here." The receptionist motioned toward a small round table that filled most of the office. "Dr. Boren is with patients, but I'll tell him that you're here."

"Thank you." Karp sat down. He felt miserable. He still had mixed feelings about merging their practices, but he knew that he could not tolerate the continued hemorrhage of cash required to maintain his office. He was also exhausted from his sleepless night.

"Welcome," said Dr. Boren as he entered the room with a bounce. "Al Boren." He extended his right hand. It was tanned, and his fingernails were neatly manicured.

"Jerry Karp. Glad to meet you." Karp shook hands, noting that Dr. Boren was no taller than he despite the impression he made of being larger than life. He wore a light blue scrub suit, unusual for a man in an office practice thought Karp. It contrasted well with the bronze tan. His hair was tightly curled, and his green eyes sparkled. His smile was clean and white. He wore a thin gold chain on his left wrist. His body was well proportioned. It was clear that he actually used the NordicTrac.

Boren sat down next to Karp at the round table. Karp was impressed, because another man might have chosen his own chair behind the desk as a power play. "Did you get to see the office yet?" asked Boren.

"No, actually, I just arrived."

Boren placed his hands on the table top. "Well, we've got lots of patients to see today, so we'll talk for a while, then you can get a tour of our office. We've got a full compliment of equipment and our own surgery center with two OR's."

Karp smiled. It wasn't as if he would be using the OR's, he thought. "You've also got lasers and a fundus camera, I gather."

"Right. Up to now, I've been sending the angios out to one of the retina docs in town. He reads them for me gratis in return for any lasers or surgical pathology he finds in them." Boren grinned a toothy smile. "He won't be happy to know that you're here to keep that work in house." Boren sat back. "I'll be honest with you: I've been fighting against our administrator about this whole issue of hiring on another ophthalmologist."

Karp noted that he said nothing about partnership.

"I really didn't want another doc on board." He sat forward toward Karp. "I just don't want to share the surgery. I love doing cataracts and RK's."

"Well, I see no conflict there," said Karp. "I don't do RK, and I don't enjoy cataract."

Boren nodded. "That's one of the things that set your letter and CV apart from the others' for me. Most other guys like to do cataracts." He narrowed his eyes. "Why don't you?"

"Cataract surgery is the single most intense thing I do as a physician. When I operate cataracts, my entire being is drawn to that little piece of the anatomy. The pressure is huge." He shrugged, "I just don't enjoy the stress."

"Fair enough," he sat back in his chair.

"Add to that," Karp went on, "the fact that cataract surgery has been singled out for fee cuts. I just don't see that cataract surgery is going to be nearly as profitable in the future."

"So it will be even harder to make ends meet," concluded Boren, baiting the argument.

"It'll be hard to make ends meet no matter what. That means that every ophthalmologist in the country is going to kick, fight, and scratch that much harder to increase his surgical volume. There's already advertising, marketing, and kickbacks to OD's for referrals."

"Kickbacks?" Boren knew this was illegal.

"Let's face it, that's all that co-management really is." Karp referred to the practice of legally splitting a portion of the surgery fee that is apportioned to post-operative care with a referring optometrist. The MD does surgery and the OD provides post-op care. In reality, very few patients need much care after they are discharged from the MD-surgeon. "If I'm going to have to face that kind of competition," continued Karp, "I'd rather do it for something that I enjoy. I just don't enjoy cataract surgery."

Boren nodded, apparently convinced by Karp's answer. "So that's why you want to concentrate on office-based care and retinal lasers?"

"Right. The problem is that my current small office practice won't support itself without cataract surgery. Combining our resources will give me someone I can trust to work with my cataract patients and provide another referral source for my retina work."

135

"And allow both of us to offer more complete eye care services for third party contractors," finished Boren.

Karp nodded. "Exactly."

Boren sat back and smiled. "Dr. Boren?" A young blonde haired woman, also well tanned and with a luscious figure, opened the door. Karp couldn't help but admire how well the white uniform complimented her. "I'm sorry to interrupt, but we have five patients waiting."

He stood. "Terrific!" Boren genuinely loved being busy in the office. It meant positive cash flow. "Karen, while I see those patients, would you show Dr. Karp our office?"

"Of course," she smiled.

"I'll meet you back here when you're done," he said, and he bounded out of the room leaving Karp with Karen.

Karp tried to look extremely interested as the technician walked him around the office. She introduced him to several of the employees as they went. Karp counted at least two dozen. He tried to think about how many cataracts would need to be operated to cover that kind of payroll.

She showed him eight examining lanes. Several had patients in them, and they entered one which was empty. The chair was tattered and clunky, but it worked. The slit lamp was an old Haag-Streit model, a tall, black monster whose optics Karp considered inferior to the Zeiss brand. The indirect ophthalmoscope in the room must have been twenty years old. Its headband was coming apart, wrapped in adhesive tape to hold it together. Karp hoped that this room was empty because it had the worst assemblage of equipment in the suite. "Are all the lanes like this one?" he asked.

Karen flashed a lovely smile. "Unfortunately, yes. The equipment works, but it isn't much to look at. Dr. Boren keeps promising new lanes, but, well, fee cuts..."

Karp suspected that Boren's Porsche wasn't nearly as old as that indirect scope. They went on down to the other end of the office suite, toward the ASC. There were two modest OR's with anesthesia equipment, heart monitors, phaco units and operating microscopes.

Karen and Karp started back toward Boren's office. The closed door to one of the lanes popped open. "Dr. Karp?" It was Boren's voice from within the lane. "Perfect timing. Can you join me here for a moment?"

They entered the examining room. There was an older patient, a big woman, sitting in the chair. The room was dark, but she looked pale, with stringy gray hair. Her husband, a tall, thin man, sat in the chair just to the side of the door. Dr. Boren was on a stool, reviewing the patient's chart. Karp stood just behind him, and Karen had to wait in the doorway. Karp checked out the equipment quickly. The indirect didn't look any better than the beat up one in the other lane.

"This is Mrs. Hardy," said Boren without looking up from the chart. "She is a seventy-three year old diabetic woman who had uneventful cataract surgery four weeks ago. Her vision never improved beyond 20/70, though. I was wondering if you'd take a quick look at her retina and tell me what you think."

"Of course," said Karp.

Boren looked at the old woman. "Mrs. Hardy, this is Dr. Karp," he said. "He is visiting our office today from Aurora, and he is a retina specialist. Would you mind letting him have a look at your eye so that we can get his expert opinion?"

"I guess not," she answered.

Boren stood to allow Karp to get in closer. He moved the slit lamp into position and reached down to switch it on, but fumbled for the knob of the device so strange to him. Karp's hands were warm, his palms moist. He was unnerved about this part of his interview. He finally found the button that turned on the light, and concentrated on the task before him. "Do you have a ninety diopter lens?" he asked, referring to the magnifying lens he would require to examine the details of the retina.

Boren handed him a small, flat carrying case. Karp popped it open and extracted the fat, quarter sized device. "This will be a bit unpleasant," he warned the patient, "because the light is very bright." He positioned the lamp so that it shined directly into her pupil. He quickly glanced at the anterior segment of the eye, noting the cornea's clarity and the well positioned IOL. The capsule was clear with only a very small, symmetric round opening. It was a lovely postop cataract eye, he thought.

He positioned the small lens before the patient's eye and drew the retina into focus. The margins of the optic nerve appeared sharp, and the cup was appropriately small. The meat of the nerve was nicely pink, and the vessels were of normal caliber. There were no hemorrhages. Next, he looked at the macula, the point of central focus on the retina. It was pallid and thickened. There were little swollen pockets and numerous red dots, hemorrhages and microaneurysms signifying damage to the blood vessels there. "There is a moderate degree of retinal edema," noted Karp. "About two-plus cystoid changes," he graded the damage.

In addition to the hemorrhages and the microaneurysms, there were many small, well circumscribed yellow blotches. "Two plus hard exudates..." he continued. "And one to two plus cotton wool spots." He glanced again at the nerve, to be certain that there was no evidence of new vessels, the more severe kind of proliferative diabetic retinopathy like his own patient, Geneen Oakman, had. There were none. "The nerve looks good. No NVD," he said. He removed the lens and told the patient she could sit back. "I'd say that the macular edema easily accounts for the level of vision," he concluded. "I'd recommend a fluorescein angiogram, though, so that we can tell how much of the swelling is from diabetic microvasculopathy rather than postop cystoid edema. The former can be treated with laser; the other would need intensive steroid treatment."

"I agree entirely," said Boren. "Dr. Karp wants to do a special test," he told the patient, "to help us find out why your retina is so puffy. That will help us decide how to make it better. Is that okay?"

The patient nodded.

"Good. Rita," he referred to his technician, "would you take Mrs. Hardy next door for a fluorescein?" He left the room.

Karen guided Karp back toward Boren's office. "He'll be back here shortly," she finally said. "He's so busy, he's always running around like this." She left Karp alone with the photos and posters and cheap furniture. He looked at the Porsche print, and smiled. He knew that Boren was going to get the angiogram anyway.

Eventually, he returned. "I'm impressed," he said. "You did a good job with Mrs. Hardy. Thanks."

"No problem."

"Is there anything else that I need to know?"

It was a perfect and obvious invitation. "Well, there is something."

"Yes?"

He thought again about just how to say it. "There's a little more to the reason that I'm getting away from cataract surgery." He went on and filled in Boren about CMH, the review, and Billy White. He told him about the satellite office, White's letter, and the memo about CIO and CMH. Boren took it all in, nodding, and adding nothing.

When Karp finished, Boren said, "Tell me, Jerry. Is there anything truly wrong with your cataract surgery? Be honest with me."

"It's like I said. The rate of vitrectomy is too high. But I've done a comprehensive review of all my patients. The vitrectomies are an issue, but the rest of this..." He just shook his head.

Boren ran his hands through his curled hair. "I've got to tell you, Jerry," he said. "I'd heard rumors about all this. Billy White is very proud of how he's put you out of business, and he's gone out of his way to tell everyone he possibly can."

Karp just blinked. He'd suspected as much, and found it to be no surprise.

"Let me show you something." He got up and picked up a chart from the mess on his desk. He opened it, and extracted a hand written letter. "This is from a patient who I'd operated for cataract a few years ago. She had a terrific 20/20 result and wanted the second eye done, but she'd joined an HMO and needed a second opinion before they'd approve the case. Read this."

"Dear Dr. Boren," the letter read. "I went to Dr. White at the Chicago Institute of Ophthalmology for the second opinion on my cataract surgery. Many of my friends are patients of his, and he was highly recommended. Dr. White asked me who took out the first cataract, and I told him that it was you. Then he examined my eye with several instruments.

"He put pictures of my eye on a television, and kept saying things like, 'What terrible surgery,' and 'Butchery.' Finally he told me that you had ruined my first eye, and that I was lucky to have any vision at all. He said that the second cataract was ready to come out, and that he would be willing to do it because he knew that he could do a better job than you.

"I told Dr. White that my vision in the eye that you had operated was perfect and that I had no problems with your surgery or your treatment. I told him that he should fill out the second opinion forms as I'd asked if he felt the cataract was ready for surgery, and that if he insisted on doing the surgery himself I would report him to the HMO.

"I am very pleased with your care, but I wanted you to know about the things that your colleague said about you. Sincerely, Arlene Schuster."

"Wow," said Karp finally. "He pulled the same trick on you."

Boren nodded. "Do you know about Ben Bookner?"

"Yes."

"I used to work with him. We split up before the indictments, but I can tell you that Bookner is a good doc. He didn't deserve all that."

"No one does," said Karp knowingly.

"There are others."

"Others?"

140

"I know of another doc at Rush-Pres who went through a similar review process instigated by Billy White. I've heard more stories. They all passed the reviews, though."

Karp grimaced. "Sure. Their hospitals had nothing to gain by screwing their own medical staff."

"Probably so. Do you think that you're going to get screwed?"

"Let's just say I don't get a warm, fuzzy feeling from the QA Committee. It's another reason that I don't want to do cataract surgery anymore, even if I do pass the review."

Boren crossed his arms on his chest. "You're serious, then. No cataracts. You spent three years of residency learning to do that surgery, you know."

"I do. At best, Dr. Boren..."

"Al."

"...Al, at best I'm ambivalent. One minute I swear I never want to touch an IOL again. The next...well, the next minute I miss it."

Boren said nothing.

"The point is, that if I can make a living without having to worry about cataract surgery, life will be just as pleasant as far as I'm concerned."

There was another pause. "What do you think the QA Committee will recommend for you?"

He shook his head. "Honest to God, I don't know. Maybe a period of retraining. Maybe something more."

"What if you offer to take some training on your own. Observe surgery. Manage pre- and post-op patients. Do you think that will help?"

"It couldn't hurt."

Boren leaned toward Karp. "I do about twenty cases a day six days per month. If they want you to observe, say, a hundred cases..."

"We could do it in a matter of weeks."

"Exactly. Then you can clear your name. Whether you want to do cataract surgery or not."

Karp didn't hesitate. "When can we start?"

"My next surgery day is Wednesday. Plan to be here about eight. Now, what are we going to do about having you work here?"

"Why don't I come to your offices two days per week? That way, I can earn some extra money--and I can use the extra money."

"No doubt."

"It will give us some time to get to know each other. We can make sure our practice styles are compatible. After a few months' trial we can formalize the relationship and merge the practices."

Boren didn't think about it for very long. "I like it. In the meantime, what have you been doing about your patients who require cataract surgery?"

Karp shrugged. "Putting them off. Since we're working together, I can refer them over here. It will help justify my time in your OR." It wouldn't hurt either, thought Karp, if you decided to watch me do a case or two at some point.

Boren smiled. "It's a deal, then." They shook on it. "Jerry," said Boren, "Billy White is an evil man. I'm glad you have the balls to stand up to him. I'll do what I can to support you."

"I appreciate it, Al. This means a lot to me."

John Kingston was irritated, but it was not his manner to demonstrate it outwardly. He held the telephone receiver away from his ear because the recorded message played too loud. It was now the fourth time he had to listen to it as it sang the praises of Dr. Donald James "D. J." Fitch. The tape lauded Dr. Fitch's experience with small-incision cataract surgery and radial keratotomy. It went on about his training, his experience, and the thousands of patients who owe their excellent vision to the skilled hands of Dr. D. J. Fitch. The tape ran about four minutes in length. Exactly two sentences were allotted to information about D. J.'s associate, who also apparently did refractive surgery.

Kingston tried to make his time waiting for D. J. Fitch as useful as he could. He reviewed charts, signed preoperative history and physicals, and looked over some lab reports. One of his nurses brought him a second cup of coffee, and set it down on his desk. "Can I get you anything else?" she asked.

"No," said Kingston, and he smiled blankly at her.

There was a click on the phone line. "Hello?"

"Dr. Fitch?" Kingston sat up straight in his chair.

"Yes," came the slow drawl.

Finally, thought Kingston. "Dr. Fitch, thank you for taking my call."

"Uh huh." Fitch clearly was not happy about talking to Kingston again.

"I'm sorry to bother you again, sir. I had the opportunity to review your letter about Dr. Karp with our hospital administrator. We were a bit disappointed."

"Uh huh."

"Doctor, I know that you were advised not to send us any information about Dr. Karp. Could you just tell me, informally, if you had any concerns about his surgical skills."

D. J. thought about this for a moment. He hated Karp, and everything for which he stood. They had done their residencies at the same hospital although they were separated by about ten years. Fitch asked several of the docs at Detroit General about Karp before he brought him on to work in Altus. They had nothing but praise for his skills as a surgeon and his acumen as a physician. He was bright, pleasant, and had good results.

The problems started in the spring of their first year together. Fitch was a strong fundamentalist Christian. He had his entire office staff attend a seminar on Christian living, and he asked Karp to come along. Afterwards, Karp was incensed. He reminded Fitch that requiring such a meeting for employees was a violation of civil rights. Fitch told him that attendance wasn't required, but Karp found out that every employee who had ever

143

refused to go had been fired within months. The arrogant little Jew threatened to contact the ACLU.

Fitch kept Karp on a short leash after that. He had noticed that Karp's rate of vitrectomy in cataract surgery was high. He watched a few of his cases, walking into the OR in the middle of the case and peering over his shoulder. One day he told Karp that he had decided to do all of the cataract surgery from that day forward in the practice. He was the boss. Karp was an employee, no more than the others. He knew that he'd never share his practice with a Jew, but that wasn't the point. Fitch was the better cataract surgeon, and he deserved to do all of the surgery.

Karp went crazy. He called a lawyer, went over their contract. He started looking for other places to work, eventually resettling in Aurora. Fitch hired on another associate. He was pleased enough to be free of Karp, but now this Kingston fellow kept calling and asking about him.

Of course Karp wasn't a good surgeon; not near as good as he was, anyway. Fitch talked with his own lawyer about Karp and was advised that any QA issues were privileged information and could not be shared without a court order. Since Fitch had no formal QA protocol or review of Karp, he was best advised not to respond to the request at all.

"Dr. Fitch?" Kingston asked again.

"This discussion," he said slowly with a twangy, nasal accent, "is not a matter of record, am I correct?"

"That's right, Doctor. I just want to know your impression of Dr. Karp as a surgeon. Any QA information you have about him would be privileged. However, you were his senior associate for three years. I presume you saw his surgery, and that you provide continuing care for his former patients."

"I do."

"I would just be interested in your personal opinion of him."

He paused again, and decided that these off the cuff comments couldn't harm him. "All right, Dr. Kingston. I'll tell you. Dr. Karp is not a good surgeon. He is slow and heavy handed. He managed to get his patients out of trouble in the clinic, but I always thought that it would be better for him to...reconsider his skills as a surgeon."

Kingston wrote down notes quickly. "I see. Were there any specific problem areas?"

"As I said, I was concerned about Dr. Karp's skills as a cataract surgeon."

"Yes, sir. I mean, did you have any specific concerns regarding that surgery? Was there anything in particular that Dr. Karp did poorly?"

Fitch thought about that one. He definitely did not want that obnoxious little bastard to threaten to sue him again. Altus was a small town and the publicity could be damaging. "I'm sorry, Doctor. I'm afraid I can't elaborate any further."

"Well, did he ever blind a patient? Was he ever sued?"

"No, he was never sued. Some of his patients had suboptimal results, but I can't provide any specifics. That's just my...personal opinion."

Kingston took down his answer. "I see."

Before Kingston could ask another question, Fitch interrupted. "Dr. Kingston, I know you're very busy. I'm afraid I must return to my own clinic patients."

"I understand. Thank you for your time, Doctor."

The dentist waited calmly for the elevator. Although the work he performed now was menial, this was certainly not the worst of it. His attorney had helped him get this job along with some references from the prison infirmary. That fat doctor proved to be useful to him after all. A job in the hospital laundry was better than washing dishes in a restaurant or doing auto maintenance. He knew that it would only be temporary anyway.

Most of his day was spent piling bags of dirty laundry into the huge, hot washing machines. The linens, towels, and scrub suits had to be washed in scalding hot water because they were always contaminated with bodily fluids: Blood, urine, feces, pus. They had to be cleaned and decontaminated. After the wash cycle, the materials were transferred into huge dryers. Between the hot water in the washers and the gas powered dryers, the room was always hellish. Summers in Atlanta proved to be especially bad, as the humidity seeped right through the concrete walls in the dark, forgotten bowels of the hospital complex.

After the laundry was cleaned and dried, the items were folded and stacked on carts to be brought to the appropriate parts of the hospital. All the employees of the laundry were required to haul the heavy carts, but the men usually took the heavier ones and spent more time with this while the women took longer shifts in the hot laundry room. There was no splitting up the work with the dirty clothes, though. Everyone put on special protective clothing to prevent exposure to infections like HIV, and emptied the stinking wretched-on linens into the wash machines.

He enjoyed pushing the carts around the hospital. He got to see more faces, familiar and not, and liked the freedom of movement around the building. He had spent the last four years without that freedom. After work, he had to take the bus back to a halfway house. If he was not signed in to the house by six every night, he would have to face his parole officer the next day to account for the time. Too many late arrivals would mean revocation of his parole. He could not allow that. He had too many important plans. This was all temporary.

It was now nearly four p.m. This would be his last trip to the OR with fresh scrub suits for the next day. He was maneuvering two racks at one time; pushing one, pulling the other. The late afternoon was calm in the OR since the majority of the surgical cases had already been completed. The changing rooms would be vacant.

"Afternoon, Doc," said the black OR nurse at the front desk as he entered the OR suite. Most everyone knew that he was a dentist, and the nickname just sort of stuck with him. When his mood was bad, it irritated him: A reminder of how much he had accomplished before and how little was left of it. Today, though, he didn't care.

"Hi, Marge. Busy day?"

"Not really." She looked back at her newspaper, to ignore him. It wasn't as if he were important enough to converse with at length.

He nodded toward the women's dressing room. "Anyone in there?"

"No," she said, without looking up. "They're pretty much gone for the day. Dr. Healy is doing an emergency lap in three. They'll be in there for an hour more at least."

"Thanks." He knocked on the door; it was protocol. "Laundry." There was no answer. He opened the door and wheeled in one of the two carts. There were bloody scrubs all over. Many were in the hamper bags set around the locker room, but several were on the floor around the hampers, thrown and missed. Still others lie on the floor where they had been removed. Pigs, he thought. They carry on as if they are clean and special, but they are pigs. All of them. He wheeled the cart toward a corner of the room where the fresh scrubs were piled, catching a wheel from time to time on clothes on the floor. He kicked a scrub shirt away. It wasn't his job to remove the dirty clothes. Housekeeping dealt with that. At least there was some job in this place more menial than his own.

The dentist then moved the second cart up to the men's dressing room. He knocked again, "Laundry." There was no answer. Just as with the other cart, he wheeled it into place and removed the empty cart. Just as in the women's locker room, dirty scrubs were thrown about.

Before he left the room, he went over to a small metal table in the other corner of the room. He took a small piece of paper out of his shirt pocket and unfolded it, reviewing the numbers he had written on it days ago. He carried it with him at all times, waiting for the right time to place the call. He didn't have long distance access at the halfway house. He picked up the phone and dialed the operator.

"Switchboard," she said.

"Hello, this is Dr. Healy. I need to place a long distance call to Philadelphia, the American Society of Obstetrics and Gynecology."

"Do you have the number."

"Let me check," he said, glancing over his shoulder to be certain no one was coming in the room. "Yes, here it is. It's 215-783-4910."

"Thank you. I'll place the call."

The phone clicked to silence as the operator put him on hold. He waited, and it clicked back with a ringing tone. "American Society of Obstetrics and Gynecology, may I help you?"

"Yes, this is Dr. Alan Healy calling from Emory University in Atlanta. I'm trying to locate another doctor who worked in Atlanta several years ago and then relocated. I was hoping you might be able to help me."

"Just a moment, I'll connect you with our membership office."

She put him on hold, and a moment later there was another voice. "Membership."

He explained his request once more.

"Of course, Dr. Healy. What is the doctor's name?"

"Dr. Melora Peltier. P-E-L-T-I-E-R. I'm sorry, I don't know what state she moved to."

"That's all right, sir. Let me check our directory for you." There was a brief silence. "Here it is, sir. Do you have a pencil and paper?"

"Yes, go ahead."

"Dr. Melora Peltier. Her address is 4799 Everly Boulevard, Aurora, Illinois, 60506. Her telephone number is listed as 708-532-7141. Does that help?"

"Yes, it does. A great deal. Thank you for your assistance."

"Not at all, sir."

Eight

It was a muggy summer afternoon as Karp negotiated the Stealth up Interstate Eighty-eight. Traffic was thin, but it was the middle of the day. The air conditioner was working hard to keep the cockpit cool, and Karp let the cruise control pull the vehicle at a steady sixty three: Fast enough to get back to Aurora with time to finish his work, but not so fast as to invite a speeding citation. Lon was belted in the passenger seat next to him, gripping the door handle with his right hand. Lon rode to Boren's offices with Karp since his old Citation wasn't up to the task of a true daily commute. Karp tended to run the little white rocket pretty fast, and Lon was concerned that his friend's mind was preoccupied.

Karp was now working with Alex Boren on a full time basis. After six weeks of part time work, Boren knew that he could trust Karp to act as a member of his network. He never argued about pulling call or managing the postop complications that inevitably occurred in a practice this busy. Although Boren hadn't been sure whether he wanted another ophthalmologist on staff initially, he was pleased with Karp's skill and judgement. He worked well with the patients, the staff, and the optoms. In addition, by having another MD on the premises, Boren didn't have to pay as close attention to the clinic patients. Karp took care of that, leaving Boren to concentrate on surgery and running the business.

Dr. Porter had visited CMH several weeks earlier. The entire review took about three days. Porter spent most of the first two days reviewing the hospital's records pertaining to Karp's surgery and lasers. He provided Karp with a list of twenty five patients' names and had him pull the charts and copy the clinic notes for in-depth analysis. Karp invited Porter to his office several times to review the entire medical records, but Porter refused, stating that he only needed to see the clinic notes.

When Porter's review was finally made available to Karp, it was the most disappointing event in his professional life. Every case that was reviewed was faulted regarding preop workup, performance of the procedure, or postop care. The sixty eight page document was damning. It was clear that the MEC would revoke Karp's privileges based on this. A hearing before the MEC was scheduled to give Karp the opportunity to present evidence in his favor and to answer the charges against him.

The hearing was scheduled for this evening, and Karp had taken the afternoon off from seeing patients with Boren so that he could complete his preparations and ready his response. He had already reviewed the cases ad nauseum with Boren and discussed each subtlety with Dr. Keith in Minnesota. He prepared his own rebuttal rather than depending solely on the report from his friends. A new paper published in the Archives of Ophthalmology helped his case. It summarized the results of hundreds of previously published reports on the accepted results following cataract surgery. This paper bolstered the conclusion that Karp's surgical results were within established norms, particularly regarding visual acuity, with the single exception of the rate of vitrectomy. He hoped that this reference would increase the chances of a good outcome following tonight's hearing, but it was obvious that Porter's review was difficult to refute.

There were more worries for Karp beyond his legal defense. He and Val were moving forward with the adoption. They had been presented photographs of several children, and fell in love with a little boy named Mikhail. He was eleven months old and lived in a small orphanage in Ukraine, just outside Kiev. Karp promised Val that, after all they'd been through, he still wanted to complete the adoption. He wasn't sure how they'd be able to pay the fees, but he'd manage somehow. The more quickly and the more positively things worked out for him with Compton, the better the results would be for his family and for their finances.

Karp's finances were a disaster. Having put off the right to do cataract surgery, he was now left with a heavily indebted practice and no means to generate cash. He'd gone on for months without paying the leases on the equipment, using what cash reserves that remained for Lon and Maureen's payroll. Except for the small paycheck for his work with Boren, Karp hadn't paid himself for many months. His student loans had been thrown into arrears, and he paid the rent and utilities with cash advances on his credit cards. He received calls from one creditor or another almost daily.

Karp pressed Boren to hire him on a full-time basis. They negotiated on the terms that surrounded Boren's formal takeover of Karp's Aurora practice, but Billy White had left the little solo practice a worthless, indebted venture. Karp agreed to have Boren take over without compensation of any kind to himself. Boren would get what few assets remained and pay off the leases on any equipment he wanted. Everything else would be sent back to the lease holders. Karp held his ground, though, on one point: He insisted that both Maureen and Lon would be retained as employees of the Heartland Eye Group. He was adamant that neither lose their jobs because of him.

Karp paid the final highway toll before the Aurora exit, then launched the Stealth forward with a solid stomp on the accelerator. "Gonna sell it anyway," he said to Lon, referring to his unorthodox driving method. Lon gripped the door handle a little tighter. Karp sped up the ramp as if leaving pit row in Daytona, then slowed for a gentle stop at the light at the top of the hill. He made a right, and drove down Lake Street. They passed the K-Mart, Perkin's pancake house, the muffler shop, and the stores along the main drag. He turned right on Galena, and returned to the Paramount offices.

Once there, Karp headed silently to his office. Maureen just watched quietly as he walked by, then turned toward Lon who shrugged. Karp was re-editing his final defense position paper and preparing the oral presentation he would give. He had been working for about half an hour, checking over his manuscripts for typos and factual accuracy, when the phone rang. "Dr. Karp." It was Maureen.

"Yes?"

"There's someone here to see you. It's a Mr. Wells, from the State Medical Board."

Karp closed his eyes, then rocked his head in a circle, as if to work out a muscle strain in his neck. "Fine. I'll be right there." He turned toward the stacks of cataract patient charts that had apparently been moved permanently to the back wall of his office. He and Maureen had stopped bothering to refile the charts long ago. He went toward one particularly small pile which contained only four charts. Karp knew those particular cases so well that he really didn't need the records anymore. He picked them up, and walked toward his lobby.

Paul Wells, sitting on the other side of the door, could not see Karp or Maureen. She looked at her employer with plaintive eyes. What is going on, she wanted to ask. Karp, of course, couldn't answer out loud. He opened the door while he examined the business card Wells had given Maureen. It had his name and his position, Examiner, State Medical Board of Illinois, printed in raised black letters. The seal of the State of Illinois was also on the card. "Mr. Wells," said Karp, as he walked into the little lobby.

"Thank you for seeing me, Doctor," said Wells. He stood and shook hands with Karp. Wells was an older man, easily in his late fifties. His thick hair was dark with broad streaks of gray. It was combed along his forehead as if he had just been to a stylist. The man was nearly six feet tall, and his hefty build suggested both that he had eaten well and that he maintained his physical conditioning. He wore a sharp gray suit with a bright red tie. His shoes were black and neatly polished, but by no means expensive. His thick lips spread into a friendly smile. "I'm sorry to bother you today."

"It's no bother, sir. Would you come this way with me?" He led the examiner to the consultation room. They entered and closed the door. Lon, who had been waiting around the corner but still outside of Karp's office, walked up to Maureen.

"What in the world is going on now?" she asked him.

He closed his eyes. "I have no idea, but you can be sure that the State Board is not here to congratulate Karp on his fine years of service as a physician."

Maureen shook her head. There was nothing more to say.

The two men sat down, facing each other. "Doctor," continued Wells, "I know how intrusive this business can be. Let me start by telling you what I do in general. I am a field examiner for the Board. It's my job to gather basic information and documentation. I have no part in determining whether there's a problem or not."

Karp nodded. "Okay."

"I'm not a physician," he went on. "Actually, I used to be the Kane County Sheriff." He smiled, "That was many years ago. Now, I'm retired. I just do this to stay active. I don't have a medical background."

Karp smiled. He tried to look entertained by Wells' story; anything but intimidated. "I see."

Wells sat back in his chair. "Well, then, as long as you understand that, then you'll see why you have to help me a bit with the jargon and technical aspects here."

"Certainly."

Wells reached into his worn leather briefcase. He pulled out a yellow legal pad and some papers. He quickly slipped the papers under the first sheet of the legal pad, then extracted a pen from his coat pocket. "Let me start by getting some simple background information from you."

"Sure," Karp answered. "I got my medical degree from the University of Wisconsin Medical School in nineteen eighty four. I performed my internship and resident training in ophthalmology at Detroit General Hospital."

Wells quickly noted the facts that Karp had passed on. "And you've been here since then?"

"No, I practiced with a Dr. Fitch in Altus, Oklahoma for several years before settling here. I can get you a copy of my curriculum vitae if you like. That will give you all the particulars of my professional training."

153

"That would be a great help."

Karp picked up the telephone and dialed Maureen's interoffice number. "Can you prepare a copy of my C.V. for Mr. Wells? Thanks."

"Okay, then. I should probably tell you why I'm here."

"You're investigating the four cases that Dr. White documented as having received questionable medical care," Karp answered for him.

Wells looked puzzled. He picked up the first sheet of his legal pad and examined the documents he had placed under it. "That's right," he responded slowly. "That information is, uh, confidential. I'm not allowed to discuss with you the source of the allegations, whether it's from a patient or anyone else."

"That's all right," said Karp. "I know that Dr. White sent you a letter. It told about four patients who had undergone cataract surgery by me, implying that their care was below standards."

Wells again referred to his paperwork. "Did Dr. White discuss this with you?"

Karp smiled. "Not directly." He leaned forward in his chair, offering a pose that expressed complete openness. "Dr. White has gone to great lengths to publicize these allegations." Karp reasoned that discussing the Compton situation with Wells would demonstrate he had nothing to hide, that he was being fully cooperative. He told Wells about the hospital's review, though he discreetly left out the results of that review by Dr. Porter. He pointed out that White proposed opening a satellite office in Aurora, for which Karp would be the main competition. He also told him that three of the four patients involved had sent letters to Karp ordering him to release copies of their records to attorneys, presumably to be evaluated for malpractice cases.

"Have their been any cases of malpractice filed?"

Karp shook his head. "None. Not one."

Wells raised his eyebrows. "Really? That's good. I would expect that if there were any wrongdoing, at least one case would be filed. If not more." He laughed. "You know those lawyers: All they need to do is smell blood."

Karp laughed, too, just a little. The statute of limitations hadn't run out on these cases yet. He went on to tell Wells that he was working with Alex Boren, and that under his supervision he was already performing duties that could be considered part of his retraining program.

"I'm impressed," Wells commented. "It seems to me that you're approaching this with a very mature attitude."

"Look," said Karp. "I just want to be sure my patients get the best care I can possibly offer them. If there's any deficiency here, I'll do everything I can to improve it."

"Thank you, Doctor. Your attitude is very refreshing in my line of business." Wells sounded sincere. "I'm not much of a lawyer, but it sounds as if you may have a case for a restraint of trade suit against this Dr. White. Have you discussed this at all with your lawyer?"

"Yes, some. These types of suits are very difficult to prove. Besides, if I go public with all this, right or wrong, I look bad. In fact, we all look bad: Me, White, the whole profession. I'd really rather avoid that. I mean, even if I did win, people will just associate me with the whole awful mess." He shook his head. "I don't need it, Dr. Boren doesn't need it. All that I want to do is to clear my name, remedy any real deficiencies, and get on with my life."

"That's commendable, Doctor. I'll need to ask you a little bit about the cases." He referred again to the papers he held. "Let me check the names," he said.

Karp knew them by heart. "Gruen, Davis, Beam, and Bouchian," he said.

Wells examined his form. "That's right."

Once again, without needing to refer to the charts, Karp told the medical histories of his four patients. He discussed the vitrectomies, the postop situations, the final visual acuities. He went on and shared the overall rate of vitrectomy and compared his visual results with those of accepted published standards. He referred to the paper he would be presenting at the meeting tonight, and asked if the examiner would like written copies of this information. He nodded, and Karp said that he would provide the appropriate documents before he left. He answered a few questions that Wells asked for clarification, mostly to describe the technical terms and procedures that Karp used in his testimony.

"Well, then, it seems pretty clear that this White fellow has inflated these claims against you."

Karp didn't want to appear arrogant. "Mr. Wells, I don't want to say that my surgery needs no improvement. Honestly, what doctor doesn't strive to be better and better? I do agree that this was...overstated by Dr. White. He's gone to great lengths to create trouble for me that is vastly out of proportion to any real threat I might pose. The simple truth is that I represent the only obstruction to the Chicago Institute of Ophthalmology's ability to lock up the eye surgery market in Aurora. Everything else has been embellished by Dr. White to discredit me for his own gain."

Wells nodded. He reviewed the two pages of notes that he had written as Karp talked. "I can't draw any final conclusions here, but I think that the State Board reviewers will close this case quickly based on these notes."

"Good."

"There's just one more thing I need to do today, and, please, accept my apologies for this." He reached into his briefcase and extracted another document, folded in three, and handed it to Karp. "I need to have the original records of these four patients to return to Springfield. The reviewers there need to look over the actual charts."

Karp looked over the document. It read, "INVESTIGATIVE SUBPOENA DUCES TECUM. We hereby command you to summon Jerrold Karp, M.D., 1047 Paramount Dr., Aurora, IL 60506 or other responsible individual having custody and control of records..." He didn't need to go further. It was signed and notarized with an embossed seal, and listed the names of the four patients that Karp and Wells had just discussed.

"You won't mind if I call my lawyer to discuss this?" he said finally.

"Not at all, Doctor. I understand your concern. We have no choice in this matter, and we need to review the charts."

"I understand," he said. "I just want to discuss the subpoena with my counsel."

Wells nodded.

"I have no intention of disobeying the subpoena, either. I just want to advise him."

"Go right ahead. You'll probably need to make copies of the charts for yourself anyway. I can wait here."

Karp excused himself, taking the four charts with him. He handed them to Maureen.

"Here's the C.V. you asked for," she said, presenting him with the papers.

"Thanks," he answered. "Would you please copy everything in these charts and make duplicate records?"

"Everything?" she asked.

Karp nodded. "Every bill, every statement, every lab test, every clinic note, every letter," he instructed her. "Complete and absolute duplicates of everything in all four records." He turned and went back to his office and dialed Rick Leach's phone number. He knew it by heart.

"Doctor. I presume you're preparing for the big presentation tonight." He sounded exceptionally upbeat for a man who knew his client was about to receive a sound thrashing. Karp figured this was part of Leach's role as cheerleader.

"I was, Rick. I thought I should advise you that there's more excitement here today."

"Really?"

"I have a visitor. Mr. Paul Wells, from the State Medical Board's office."

"He's an examiner, right?"

"Correct."

"I think I know this fellow. Older, big guy?"

"That's right."

"He used to be a sheriff, or something. He does this gopher work for the Board now."

"That's pretty much what he told me."

"Well, Jerry, we knew this would happen. We discussed it after we saw Billy White's letter to the hospital. What's up?"

"We discussed the four cases and the nature of the situation with White."

"Good. So you cooperated with his questioning?"

"Fully, I think. The only thing I left out was how the hospital's impartial reviewer crucified me."

"Good. That's still privileged information. What else is there?"

"He served me with a subpoena for the records on the four cases. I presume that I have no choice but to turn them over."

"That's right. Make copies of everything in the charts. You keep the copies, hand the originals over to him. Be sure to be pleasant about it."

Karp understood. "We're in the process now. Wells seemed decent enough. He said that, given the circumstances surrounding White's involvement, he didn't think that I'd encounter any difficulty with the Board."

"Jerry, there's been no breach of the standard of care, and your records document that. It's Wells' job to be comforting, reassuring. If he can get you to feel all warm and fuzzy with him, you're going to be less likely to withhold information. His job is to get information. He cannot influence the outcome of this review. He just turns over the evidence. I don't want you to stay up at night worrying about this review, but only because it won't alter the outcome. Don't get lulled into a false sense of security. He'll say whatever he has to in order to get you to talk with him."

Karp sighed. "Okay, I understand."

"Just make sure you don't lie to him."

"Don't worry."

"Anything else?"

"No."

"Okay. I'll see you tonight at six thirty." Leach would be allowed to accompany Karp to the MEC meeting, but this was

158

nothing more than a favor to Karp. Orville Harmon had made it clear that Leach was not invited to speak at the meeting or question any of the participants. His only role was to offer instructions for Karp if needed. If he was too obtrusive, Harmon warned, he would be invited to leave. Despite his limited role, Leach figured that it would be best for him to go along simply as moral support. He'd probably be his only friend.

"See you then," Karp answered.

He walked over to Maureen, who was busy at the copier. Lon was helping her, collating the papers. "When you're through with the copies, just give the originals to Mr. Wells."

"The originals?" Maureen had worked in medical offices for years, and she knew that a physician would never give up the originals.

"That's right. This time, he gets the originals, we get the copies. It's only temporary, they'll return them. Okay?"

"Whatever you want," she said with a smile. It was increasingly difficult to maintain composure here, she thought.

Karp returned to Wells in the consultation room. "There's no problem. Maureen is working on the records for you now. Is there anything else I can do for you?"

Wells had already put his papers away in the briefcase. "I don't think so, Dr. Karp. I want to thank you again for your candor today."

"Not at all." They shook hands. "When will I know the results of the Board's review?"

"I can't say for sure. They'll probably go over your records some time in the next few weeks. If they need any more information they'll either contact you directly or have me get in touch. Please, don't worry about this affair. I'm certain it will be nothing more than an inconvenience."

"I hope so," Karp said with sincerity. "Let me show you to the lobby. Maureen will bring you the charts when she's done with them."

Wells returned to the front lobby, and Karp went back to his office. Rather than return to the charts right away, he went to the bathroom. He looked at himself in the mirror. His face was pale, his eyes red. He was tired. His sleep was still fitful and irregular. He couldn't remember the last time he felt fully relaxed. He needed a vacation, he thought, but there was no room in his tight budget for that now. He sighed, and went back to his nearly finished presentation.

All at once, the telephone rang again. Damn, he thought, I don't need all these interruptions. He looked at his watch, and realized that he had been working without a break for over two hours. "Dr. Karp, it's Dr. Carver for you, on line one."

"Carver? Who is Dr. Carver?" he asked to no one in particular.

"I think he is a urologist," answered Maureen using the intercom.

Karp thought for a moment. "What in the world could he want?" he wondered out loud. It was unlikely that a urologist would have a referral for an ophthalmologist, and, anyway, nobody in Aurora referred patients to Karp anymore. He picked up the telephone. "Karp here."

"Hi, Jerry. Bruce Carver. How've you been?"

"Not bad, Bruce," answered Karp, perplexed. "What can I do for you?"

"Well, this is kind of difficult..." he paused. "Uh, I guess there's no discreet way to ask, but, uh, I've heard that you've been having some...problems with Compton Hospital."

He wondered how much Carver knew. "You could say that."

"I'm sorry. I know this is...embarrassing. Let me explain: I've already been through this."

"You have?"

Carver laughed out loud. "You mean you haven't heard?" He laughed again. "I'm sorry, I know it isn't funny, but I thought everyone associated with the hospital...no, everyone in Aurora...I thought everyone knows. My practice was killed. Decimated. For nothing."

"No, Bruce. I didn't know. What happened?"

"We were recruited at about the same time, right?"

"Of course. We were introduced to the hospital staff at the same meeting."

"I went to work with Jason Gramercy."

"Right. He's been here for years. He was too busy, needed some help."

"Actually," Carver corrected, "he'd been in Aurora for decades. He was so busy that he'd be booked months in advance. There was enough business for him and two others. I was recruited fresh out of residency, and we got along for about six months."

"Don't tell me. After that, he decided that he really didn't want to give up the surgery to you, right?"

"Exactly. His wife, Nancy, worked in the office. She wanted Jason to stay in charge of everything. She was always around to second guess me, contradicting me over medical management of patients. Add to that the fact that the son of a bitch didn't want to take call anymore, and well, I figured I'd be better off on my own."

"I went through pretty much the same situation in Oklahoma," sympathized Karp. "But that didn't cause you to lose privileges, did it?"

"No. I opened a small office on the other side of town. I figured that I'd do okay if I could see half the number of patients I was able to with Gramercy. After all, I wouldn't have to turn over my surgery to him."

"Right. So what happened?"

"The trouble started about a year after I opened the solo office, just after Kilner came to Compton. He called me and told me that there were some reports of problems with my surgery."

"Were there?"

"Not with simple prostate resections or common cases. I did have a couple of complicated radical cancer resections, but they were very difficult patients: Old nursing home guys who'd ignored their disease until it was advanced. The surgeries were difficult, the tumors were huge, and they bled like crazy. One ended up in the Unit."

161

Karp began to see the details fill in. "So they called for a review, and gave you a hard time about your surgical privileges."

"That's right. I fought them every step of the way, but I was guilty from the day the accusations were made. There was nothing I could do."

"Did anyone file suit against you?"

"No. A lot of people had records reviewed by attorneys, and some are still within the statute of limitations, but I haven't been sued yet."

Karp knew exactly how this man felt. It was strange, but he found some reassurance in hearing this story. "What happened?"

"That's why I'm calling you. Do you know where I am?"

"Isn't your office down Galena Boulevard?"

Carver chuckled out loud. "No, not for a while. I'm in New Orleans, doing a fellowship."

"Jesus," said Karp out loud. "They really did you in."

"Make no mistake about it. They're out for blood...your blood. They called in some guy from a company called MedCo to review my surgery."

Karp nodded. "They did that to me, too."

"He sliced me to bits. Made it look like I couldn't tie my shoes without fucking up."

"I know what you mean."

"The MEC voted to suspend my surgical privileges. I fought them with an appeal, but the hospital chose the location, the judge who moderated the proceedings, and the course of the hearing. I had no chance. The decision was upheld, and the state courts want nothing to do with the case. My attorney tells me I don't have enough evidence to support a restraint of trade charge."

Karp nodded again, though Carver couldn't see it. "God, Bruce, that story is exactly what's happening to me. Practically every detail is the same. What is going on here?"

"I don't know," he answered. "I don't know. That's why I called, Jerry. I wanted you to know what happened to me, and to understand what they're going to do to you."

Karp didn't respond. He didn't know what to say.

"Jerry, I have a suggestion for you."

"What's that?"

"The MEC is going to vote to suspend your privileges. You know that, right?"

"That seems apparent, I guess."

"It is. They will do it. It really doesn't matter how well you defend your case before them, they will vote to suspend your privileges. Consider a deal." As he made the statement, he let out a little sigh, having gotten a great load off of his mind.

"Deal?"

"Right. Your recourse to the suspension is an appeal, but I already told you how that works. You can't win on appeal, and I don't think you want to go to court, right?"

"Agreed."

"Then have your lawyer talk to them about a deal. See if they'll let you voluntarily withdraw your surgery privileges in return for an agreement to undergo a course of retraining. Trust me, you're going to have to retrain anyway."

"What advantage does that give me?" Karp asked. If he withdrew surgery privileges and retrained, he'd have to close his practice. It was by no means a victory for Karp.

"Jerry, if they suspend your privileges, that's going to be reported to the Databank. It'll follow you for the rest of your life. You'll have to leave to retrain, and in the meantime your practice will die. No one is going to see you after the MEC does this, no one. You won't see surgical patients, you won't see medical patients, you won't see referrals, you won't get calls from the ER. You'll just sit, and you'll go broke."

"That's what happened to you?"

"You bet. I lost my house, I lost my cars. We filed bankruptcy. We lost our life savings, and I came damn close to losing my wife. She had to go back to work to support us. Jerry, we lost everything." As he finished this statement, his voice became weak. Carver was deflated. This was the message he wanted Karp to understand.

Karp took in a deep breath and heaved a loud sigh. "Bruce, I'm not sure how that's going to help me. My lawyer told me that it still has to be reported to the Databank if I withdraw privileges in the wake of an investigation."

"That's true, but you'll be better off this way. When your right to do surgery is yanked and you lose your defense at appeal, it looks much worse. I had a hard time getting a fellowship with this shit on my record. The staff here told me it would have been better if I had `recognized my shortcomings.'" There was a pause. "It sucks, Jerry. I know just how you feel. It ain't getting any better for you for a while, either."

"Bruce, why is this happening?"

"It's like I said. They want you out."

"Yes, I know. I guess that your hassle with Gramercy started your problems. In my case, Billy White wants to take over my share of the cataract market in Aurora. I don't see what the hospital has to gain."

"I don't know either, Jerry. I think Porchette just had it out for me. He was the chairman of the QA Committee."

"Sure, he's working on my flogging, too. But why would the MEC go along with him? In the end, the hospital looks bad for having hired us in the first place. Compton Memorial doesn't exactly have the finest reputation."

"That's for sure."

"I just don't get it. Why do they want to harm our reputations just to make us leave? There's got to be something more in this for the hospital."

Carver didn't answer right away. "Jerry, let me tell you something I've heard about Compton. I don't know for a fact that any of this is true, but I heard the Gramercy's talking a couple of times when I still worked with them."

"Yes?"

"Nancy Gramercy was complaining once about all the money they had to pay in to the hospital."

"You mean she didn't want Jason to pay his hospital dues? They're only a couple hundred dollars a year."

"No," said Carver, "it wasn't just dues. She talked about some kind of fund they were paying to support."

Karp didn't understand. "Fund? You mean donations to their building fund?"

"No, Jerry, not the building fund. She implied that they paid into some slush fund that the hospital uses to recruit docs and buy equipment. She said that it was a damn lot of money 'just to stay in practice.' When she said that, Jason got pretty upset and told her not to bring it up."

Hospitals are always squirreling away money for one project or another, thought Karp. "That seems pretty innocuous, Bruce. I think she was just tight with what she perceived to be her dough."

"That could be, Jerry. I'm not sure there isn't more to it, though. Let me ask you this: Now that I'm gone, how many urologists are there in Aurora?"

That was easy. "One. Gramercy."

"Right. How many orthopods are there?"

"Five. Porchette's group."

"Right," agreed Carver. "But they all work together."

"Yes, they're partners."

"One group of orthopedic surgeons. How many otolaryngologists are there in town?"

Karp saw the pattern now. "Three, but they all work for one group. What are you getting at, that the physicians at Compton Memorial Hospital are colluding to keep competition out of town, and they pay the hospital to be part of the deal?"

"You said it, Jerry, not me."

"Sure," argued Karp, "but what about other specialties, like internal medicine. There are several internists."

"Yes, indeed. But all the subspecialties--gastroenterology, pulmonary medicine, endocrinology--they're all represented by guys who practice with the Aurora Medical Specialists. They also have the greatest number of practicing internists in town. Look at ob-gyn: There are three guys working in one group who see at least eighty-five percent of the deliveries and gyn surgery

165

in town. There are a couple other gynecologists, but they're hardly busy." He let Karp think about that for a minute. "You name the specialty. There is either no competition to the one practice in town, or the other doc is part time, nearly retired, or starving."

It was a wild concept, Karp thought. "So many people would be involved," he thought out loud. "I can't believe they'd all be able to keep this a secret. What you're suggesting has got to be Medicare fraud." He considered the repercussions. "No," he concluded, "I can't believe that there's such a great conspiracy. Aurora just isn't big enough to justify it, and Compton has little to gain. They're the only hospital in town already, for Chrissake."

"And nobody else has even suggested building a competing facility even though Compton has a terrible reputation. I guess," Carver intimated, "they'd just rather stick with Compton. Hmmm."

Karp considered this theory a little more.

"Look, it's just a speculation," said Carver. I don't have any proof other than Nancy Gramercy's casual remark and her husband's response. I'd have no way to prove it."

"Man, if you could..." proposed Karp.

"If I could, I'd still be doing a fellowship and you'd still be an inch away from losing your privileges. Nobody is going to corroborate this. The others would just deny it, and the whistle blower would be out looking for a new place to practice medicine."

"Possibly with a history of suspended privileges in Aurora," added Karp.

"Look, I've gotta go. I need to do post-op rounds. I just wanted to help you realize what you're facing."

"Oh, you have," he said with a dejected tone.

"Sorry, friend. You'll need to work out some long term plans. Good luck with the MEC."

"It sounds like luck has nothing to do with it."

166

The dentist hated riding the bus. It reeked of burned diesel fuel, not to mention the nauseating scent of unshowered human sweat. The hot and humid Atlanta afternoon sun made the bus ride an event that could be most unpleasant. He got off the bus while he was still downtown, not far from the hospital. He had been in the halfway house for some time now, and he had earned a slightly greater degree of freedom. He always returned with a checked out book, and the caretakers at the house were pleased that he was spending time at the library reading, learning, and improving himself. They were careful to send someone there a couple of times to check up on him. The charges for which he had been jailed would follow him forever, and the parole officer insisted that he be monitored. He had done nothing wrong, though, and he had no intention of violating his parole. He had plans.

He crossed the street, cursing the traffic. He felt dirty from the stuffy air in the laundry, and he looked forward to getting back home for a shower. He longed for a cool beer, but alcohol was not allowed in the halfway house. As much as he would love the drink, he had no intention of returning to prison.

He entered the library and felt the cool rush of air as the automatic door opened with a buzzing electric whoosh. He used the handicapped entrance even though he was fully capable of opening the other door. There were several people at the checkout desk as he walked by. A college-age girl was helping them check out books, and he slowed to admire her blond hair and lovely, young breasts. He hurried toward the back of the hall.

He passed the card catalog drawers where a few individuals were looking up references. There was also a bank of six computers across from the cabinets, used for finding books. T electronic database was very user friendly. He had oper himself only a few weeks ago in order to look u referencing methods of obtaining new personal id There were several very useful books listed in the had to order one of them from another branch

167

pointed out that the most important pieces of ID to possess were a Social Security card and drivers' license. Once you had these in a new name you could travel throughout the country, even apply for a legal passport, and no one would have to know your original given name. The problem, of course, was that a forged Social Security card or drivers' license would be worthless. You have to obtain a legitimate Social Security card and drivers' license in a new name. That's what brought the dentist back to the library.

At the far edge of the main room, just beyond the card catalogs and computers, he made his way to the microfilm viewers. There were eight, and only two were in use. Few library visitors found a need for these machines. They kept old documents like newspapers and magazines on long reels of microfilm to avoid risk of damage or loss. The dentist looked up the year nineteen-fifty nine. He had read through the Atlanta Constitution for several years already, but had yet to find the information he needed.

He lifted the pink plastic reel from its cradle and sat down in front of one of the projection viewers. He wound the microfilm around the cogs that fed it through the machine, enlarging the images on a screen. The film threaded onto the takeup spool and ran quickly to about a third of the way through the reel. He slowed the advancing black and white images and peered at the date: March sixteenth, nineteen fifty nine. He ran the film a little further forward. He had to leave last time after he had gotten as far as March twenty-first.

He glanced at the old newspaper. First his eye scanned the front page. There was news of the day regarding American relations with the Soviet Union and national stories. No local stories, no auto accidents. Next he looked at the small box with the paper's table of contents. The obituaries were on page seven. He ran the reel forward, counting the black bars that separated the pages. On page seven, he found the obits. There was a long list of names of elderly people who had died that week. A prominent businessman, two "negro" women, a nursing home resident. Nothing here that he needed.

He ran the paper ahead until he could see the narrow print of the classified ads. He slowed the reel, knowing that the next day's paper would soon follow. There was the masthead and main headline. He stopped the film, and scanned the front page for news of interest, then ran forward to the obits. Again, he found several older individuals. There was also a notice for "Infant Sayers." He zoomed the projected newspaper page up for a closer look at the article. "Baby Girl Sayers, beloved daughter of Albert and Doreen Sayers died at seven thirteen in the morning on March twenty third of complications following birth at St. Elizabeth Hospital of Atlanta. Services will be held..." This would not do for him, as the baby was a girl and she died in the same county in which she was born. He needed a young male who had died in a county other than that of his birth. When the two events happened in the same legal municipality, the birth and death certificates would be cross-referenced. If the child died of some disease after being transferred to the big city from a rural town or if the death were from an auto accident, there was a good possibility that the two counties would not share the birth and death certificates. This was the situation he would require in order to obtain a certified copy of the dead child's birth certificate without raising suspicion.

He ran the newspaper ahead to another date. Nothing here for him. He continued the process, checking over several weeks' newspapers. Finally he found an obituary entry that he knew would be valuable. "Lawrence J. Evans: Lawrence J. Evans, age 2, died at eleven fourteen in the evening on April sixteenth at Atlanta Children's Hospital, of complications of leukemia. He is survived by his parents, James and Dolores Evans, and a brother, Dwaine. Services will be held at the First Calvary Church of Savannah."

This gave him a great deal of useful information. First, the unfortunate young man was very close to his own age. Second, the fact that he was in Children's Hospital meant that he was probably ill for some time. It is unlikely that his parents had time or interest in applying for a Social Security number for their son. Finally, he might have been born in Savannah, the place where he was to be buried in the family plot. In addition to the family history he already had from the newspaper, he knew that the hospital registration form in the patient's chart would be invaluable. From that he could get the exact date of birth, address, and data on the parents.

He pulled a small piece of paper from his shirt pocket, and a black Bic pen. He took down the details from the newspaper. He thought for a moment about whether he wanted to keep looking for more potential ID candidates, and decided against it. It was getting late, and he would have to check in to the halfway house shortly. It was going to be difficult enough to get to the Chatham County courthouse in Savannah for a copy of this young man's birth certificate without a car and without raising suspicions. He'd probably have to take a day off of work, and that would be some doing all by itself. He looked forward to spending some time in Aurora, Illinois, getting to know his children again.

Karp and Leach waited in a small classroom adjacent to the meeting hall across from the cafeteria. The committee members wanted to finish their other business of the evening before proceeding with Karp's case. They expected the discussion following his statement would take some time. Vicki Downs had told them it would be about ten minutes.

That was twenty minutes ago, and Karp was starting to get a little edgy. He had no fear of speaking in public and had prepared this presentation to the finest detail. He had a large stack of documents for the MEC members to review and follow along with as he spoke. Although they told him he could take as much time as he wished, he planned for a twenty to thirty minute presentation. The longer he took, the less interested his audience was likely to be. Most of them had probably already made up their minds based on the documents in his file.

As Karp paced, Leach sensed his client's jitters. He worried that Karp's own frustration might work against him. If this happened in the meeting, there was little that he could do to help. It had been made very clear to him that he was a guest tonight. If he tried to cross examine the other doctors or if he tried to steer the course of the meeting in any way, both he and Karp would be asked to leave.

"Do you have any plans after the meeting?" Leach asked, trying to get Karp to think about anything other than the delay.

"Yes, sir, I do. I am meeting my wife and another couple, and I am going to try to raise my blood alcohol level well above the legal limit."

Leach grinned. "Now, you're not going to be needing me later in the evening, Jerry, are you?"

"No, Rick. Once I am well on my way to intoxication, I will be handing the car keys over to my wife. It isn't as if I'll need to be alert to hear the outcome of this meeting, which is, after all, preordained."

"Now, you don't know that for a fact." The two had discussed Carver's call earlier. "That whole story about the MEC working in concert against you and your friend sounds a bit...well, paranoid."

"Rick, by definition, you are not paranoid if people really are out to get you."

The two men laughed, enjoying the comic relief. All at once, Vicki appeared at the doorway. "Dr. Karp. They're ready for you next door."

Karp picked up the large folding cardboard poster to which he had mounted several photographs to use as visual aids. He decided that a slide presentation would be too difficult and formal. Leach slung his considerable briefcase over his shoulder by its thick strap, and helped Karp by picking up the stack of handouts. He divided the pile in half, handing some to Vicki.

"Each member of the meeting will need a copy of this," he said, directing her to assist in passing out the documents.

They entered the big room and met dense silence. Dan Kilner and Dr. Porchette stood up at the head of the table on the other side of the room. Kilner gestured to a pair of empty seats to Karp's right, about halfway along the large ring of tables. "Why don't you and Mr. Leach have a seat," he directed. Karp placed the large cardboard display on the floor behind him and opened his own highlighted copy of the handout in front of himself. When he was appropriately organized, he looked over at Kilner. He presumed the man sitting next to him and Porchette was Dr. Porter, the man who had performed the fatal review of Karp's work. He realized that they had flown Porter in to be present at this meeting to redirect any statements that Karp made in his own defense.

"Are you all right?" asked Leach quietly. He wanted to make sure Karp was ready for the considerable job that lay before him. If he felt uneasy, the attorney would ask for a recess even though it would be frowned upon by the MEC.

"Rick, I'm fine. Guaranteed."

"All right, then," said Dr. Harmon. "I think we can proceed. Most all of us here know Dr. Karp. For the record, I want to re-introduce Dr. Porter, seated next to Mr. Kilner and Dr. Porchette. As you know, Dr. Porter performed a review of Dr. Karp's surgical and laser patients' records. Dr. Karp is here this evening to respond to that review." He paused to allow Vicki to make the appropriate notes for the minutes, and to permit any questions. There were none. "Seated next to Dr. Karp is Mr. Richard Leach, Dr. Karp's legal counsel. Mr. Leach is here this evening as a guest of this committee, and he is aware that his comments are not invited as part of the record at this time." Harmon spoke very slowly and distinctly, intoning his most paternal sound. "That is correct, Mr. Leach, is it not?"

"Yes, sir."

"Very well. Dr. Karp?"

Nine

The automatic door opened with an electric buzz and a whoosh, and Karp and Leach walked into the cool evening air. They made their way to the parking lot without conversation. Karp stopped in front of his white Stealth. Leach's blue Cadillac was parked two spots further over. "I'll call you as soon as I hear something," he promised.

"I'll be waiting. Don't expect a response tonight. I have a feeling that they're going to be working in there for a while. They may not call you until tomorrow."

Karp smiled as he piled his stack of papers into the hatchback of the car. "If they call too early," he said, they're going to get my answering machine because I'm going to be out." He slammed the door closed with a thud. "If they call too late," he added, "they're still going to have to leave a message. I intend to be in a stupor. This is more excitement than I can take."

Leach continued over to his car and fumbled with the doorlock. "Just don't go out driving, Jerry. I don't want to get a call from you at the Kane County Jail."

"Don't worry. I'll be with friends." He slid into the car and took a deep breath of the leather upholstery's perfume. It was refreshing after the stuffy, humid air in the auditorium. He eased himself into the seat back, letting the bolsters hug him gently. He felt the wetness on his back, and realized just how nervous he must have been while making the presentation. He inserted the key in the ignition, but just held onto the thick, padded steering wheel with both hands for a moment and closed his eyes. How very much has changed, he thought, since I bought this car. It doesn't take much time to sink from the high of a successful business to the low I feel just now.

He turned the key, eventually, and the engine roared to life. He goosed the gas pedal a couple of times just to listen to the cylinders firing. It gave him a sense of power knowing that he controlled this dynamic little car, and that power was welcome relief for the impotence that enveloped him. He switched on the headlights and watched the warm orange glow of the dashboard. The tach jumped as he played with the throttle. The bank of instruments to his right made the vehicle seem like it had a fighter plane's cockpit. He reached over and moved the shifter into gear, pulling out of the parking place and humming toward the street. The traffic was light, but steady. A lot of ER patients are going to have a long wait tonight, he thought, with all of the medical staff in that meeting.

One of the smaller storefronts at the Galena Crossing shopping center belonged to Harrigan's Pub, a quaint little tavern that served good food and great beers. It was surely a watering hole, as many of the locals ate and drank there regularly. The bartender kept Whitbread's ale on tap, along with Moosehead, Labatt's, and several more pedestrian domestic labels. The bottle beer selection was even more diverse, and the burgers were large, tasty, and well priced. The Friday night fish fry was so popular that the wait for a table could be as long as two hours.

Tonight, there would be no such delay. It was late for the dinner hour and only a few tables were filled with parties lingering after their meals. There were four men sitting at the bar watching a night Cubs road game on WGN. They were losing, three to two, and Harry Carey was doing his best to inject a little enthusiasm into what was turning into a standard, disappointing Cubs ballgame. Karp walked into the dark little pub, and passed several of the tables in the front dining room until he came upon the bar. There, seated on one of the stools, was his friend Lon Morrissey. Karp pulled up a stool next to him. "Good evening, Lonnie," he said as he signalled the bartender. "Whitbread's," he said without giving Lon a chance to answer his greeting. He demonstrated with both hands and instructed, "A tall one, please."

The bartender nodded and started to fill a large glass with the golden brew. The natural carbonation formed a frothy head as the dark beer flowed along the side of the tilted glass. Karp felt his mouth water. "How'd it go?" asked Lon.

Karp pointed at his chest with his right thumb. "I did a great job." He paused. "The rest of them had probably already made up their minds. I might as well have come in and read off the front page of the newspaper tonight." The bartender gently placed Karp's long awaited beer before him. He picked up the glass, studied its contents under the dim light of the bar, and finally took a long draw off the top. The barley and the bitter hops were soothing in his mouth. His parched throat hummed approval. "I think that this is the high point of the night so far," he added. After a pause, he concluded, "I don't know. I think my defense was legitimate, realistic, and based in fact. I just don't trust the others to share that decision. I'll have to wait and see."

The Cubs' center fielder bobbled a fly ball and dropped it. The others at the bar groaned, a ritual for Cubs fans. Morrissey shook his head and peeled his eyes away from the television. He didn't know which was worse, watching the Cubs or his friend's pained face. "Is that what Rick Leach said?"

Karp took another long draw of the Whitbread's. "No. He said I did a great job and that I should relax. He thinks they're trying to come up with some alternative to yanking my privileges." He pulled down some more beer. "I wish I could share his optimism."

Lon sipped his own Miller Genuine Draft. "I wish I knew what to say. I just don't see why they want to hurt you so badly."

"Well, God knows, they're not going to get the money I owe them if they screw me. There'll be no way for me to pay them back." He finally noticed that the rest of their party was not there. "Where are the girls?" he asked.

"We weren't sure when your meeting would be over. They went to the Fox Valley Mall to do some shopping. They figured you'd need a beer or two to relax, and they didn't want to be here right away if you were going to be too depressed."

Karp grinned and sipped his drink. There wasn't much left in the glass. "Well, they were wrong. I'm going to need more than a beer or two tonight." The bartender gestured toward his empty glass, and Karp nodded for another.

"They're going to get here about eight. If you're hungry, they said we should eat now."

Karp finished off his first glass. "I'll be hungry in just a bit. For now, I believe I'll have another beer. I won't be sharp enough to drive, so you can run me home in the Stealth and have the girls follow, or Val can drive. I just want to stop thinking about all the shit in my life for awhile."

Lon sipped at his drink again and watched a couple of pitches. "Well, Jerry, if you want to set work aside tonight, can I bring up one final issue first?"

"As long as it doesn't have to do with Compton Memorial Hospital or Billy White, let's get it over with."

"No, it's not Compton or White." He paused, and figured there was no way to sugar coat this. "Jerry, you need to know that I'm looking for another job."

Karp sipped at his beer, a little less aggressively this time. "I'm not at all surprised, Lon," he said gently. This was true. Although he had been able to assure both Lon and Maureen would keep their jobs when they merged with Boren, he was not in a position to guarantee their wages. Both had taken pay cuts, and Karp knew it would be only a matter of time until his employees quit for better wages. "To be honest, I'm amazed you stuck it out this long."

"Well, I haven't found anything just yet. You know, the job market isn't all that open for a man in his mid-fifties. Everyone wants to hire a kid at part-time wages and no benefits."

Karp turned and looked his friend in the eye. "Honest to God, Lon, if there's anything I can do to help you find a position, just tell me. I'm so sorry about everything that's happened here. I don't want you or your family to hurt needlessly over my...failure."

Lon shook his head. "Jerry, it's not your fault goddammit, and I want you to stop talking that way. The only difference between what they've put you through and an old fashioned witch hunt is the bonfire. I just can't make it on the pay right now."

"I know, I know. Listen, can I write you a letter of recommendation? You're a skilled man, and I know there's someplace out there for you."

"It probably wouldn't hurt. I'm not looking around here, you know."

Karp watched the pitcher smoke one by the batter. He didn't even care who was playing tonight, and he was a loyal Cubs fan. "Afraid that my reputation will pass on with you?" he asked.

"No, it's not that." He sipped his beer. "I'm hungry, man. Let's get something to eat." Karp nodded, and Lon grabbed a menu. "No, we want to move out to Virginia. The kids have settled there, and it would be nice to be a little closer to them."

Karp nodded again. "Makes sense." He looked at a menu, too. "I wish it were Friday. I love the fish fry. Any reasonable opportunities yet?"

"Well, I've got a couple of feelers out. We may move out there before I've found something. The kids said they'd put us up, and it'll make it easier for me to find a job out there."

"And, it'll help you get out of this atmosphere of impending doom. What does Angela think of all this?"

"She can't wait to get closer to the kids. We're both gonna miss you guys, though."

Karp put the menu down. "Ah, hell, Lon. Once this crap blows over, we'll get together for a vacation with you out east." He glanced at the TV. "Or you guys can come back here and we'll go to Wrigley for a game one weekend. Like I said, I don't blame you for trying to move on."

"And I," added Lon, "do not blame you. I mean it."

The two men clinked glasses and toasted each other silently with a sip of beer. "Still, I do feel guilty," said Karp.

Jerry Karp sat in the passenger seat of the Stealth as Val drove them slowly home. She disliked driving the car at night because it sat so low to the ground that oncoming headlights were blinding. Tonight, she was in a particularly bad mood. Jerry was downright drunk. He had exhibited no sign of slowing the beer consumption as the night went on. He remained quiet in Harrigan's, and seemed to be falling asleep at the table.

Karp wanted to drive, but knew well enough that he should not. Instead, he just sat silently in the passenger seat allowing the scenery to float by the window. The couple remained silent. He wasn't sure that he could speak without tripping over his tongue. It was past midnight, and he hoped to just crawl into bed and get some sleep without incident...as if either sleep or absence of an incident would be possible tonight.

Val drove slowly up the street and steered the Stealth toward the garage. Karp preferred to back in and drive straight out, but Val found this maneuver difficult. He didn't argue. She cut the engine, and he opened the door.

He had a little trouble heaving himself to his feet from the low slung automobile, but he managed. Slowly, with great attention to the matter of moving his legs, he ambled toward the door. Val was already there, and she pushed the button to close the garage door. She quickly walked through the kitchen, toward the stairs, and padded up to the bedroom. His own movements were more fluid, lubricated by the alcohol. He worked through the kitchen, but stopped at the telephone answering machine. The red LED blinked that there was a message. He grinned stuporously, suspecting that he knew who'd left it. He wanted to know what they had to say. He pushed the button, and the message cassette whirred as it rewound itself. It snapped to a stop, and the machine clicked into the play mode. There was an electronic beep, followed by the message. "Jerry, this is Dr. Harmon." *They are castrating my title and surname from me,* Karp observed. "Mr. Kilner and I stopped by your house this evening at about ten o'clock. We wanted to discuss the outcome of this evening's MEC meeting with you, but, of course, you weren't home. You may call me at home, or I will..." Karp pushed the `stop' button. There was no need to go further. If the conclusion of the meeting had been positive, Harmon would have told him so in the message. The fact that both men had come to his home personally was all the information he needed to draw his own conclusion. He sighed, feeling depressed and liberated. He had been freed from the gnawing sense that this was hanging over him. Despite the awful result, he was relieved enough to know that he'd never have to face this group again to discuss the issue of his surgical skills. He turned the answering machine off and slowly made his way to the stairs. He wouldn't say anything to Val, he decided, unless she asked. He knew she wouldn't.

PRIVILEGES

Ten

The dentist worked his way around the hospital with a cart of laundry for the sixth floor inpatient ward. It was a medical-surgical ward, and they went through an inordinate number of sheets and blankets. It seemed that someone was always spilling some bodily fluid up on six-east. As the elevator door opened he could smell the combination of disinfectant phenol and human feces. He found it revolting, and moved his nose a little closer to the freshly cleaned linens. He was glad that this would not be part of his daily routine for very long.

He moved the cart over toward the nurses' station, then just beyond, to the door marked "Clean Utility." He removed the nearly empty linen cart from the room, then pushed the fresh rack into it. There was a wall phone hanging in one corner. He picked up the handset, dialed nine, and waited for the outside dial tone. Then he dialed the number for Atlanta Children's Hospital, which he had memorized from the phone book this morning.

"Atlanta Children's Hospital."

"Medical Records, please."

"I'll connect you." With a click, he was on hold.

"Medical Records."

"Hello. This is Dr. Davidson at Memorial Hospital. I need to speak with someone about reviewing an old medical record."

"I can help you, sir. What is the patient's name?"

"Lawrence J. Evans. He was treated at Children's back in the fifties for leukemia and died. I'm seeing his brother now for lymphoma, and I wanted to review the records to see if there are any other similarities between the siblings."

"Just a moment, sir. I'm checking the computer. Yes, sir, here it is. The record is in archives on microfilm. I'll need to copy it to paper. May I send it to your office?"

"As a matter of fact, my assistant will be running your way later this afternoon. Would it be a problem for me to have him pick it up personally?"

"Not at all, sir. Just ask for Sharon. I'll have it ready in an hour."

"Thanks." He hung up. With a chance to look at the dead kid's medical record, he'd soon have more than enough biographical data to go to Savannah for a certified copy of the birth certificate. Then, he would leave Georgia for good.

Jerry Karp felt like shit. His hangover wasn't the only problem. The throbbing in his head came also from the knowledge that his career was hobbled. He still couldn't reach Harmon, who hadn't arrived in his office yet. He found it ironic that those who called him a bad doctor weren't able to start work before the crack of ten. The secretary said that Harmon did not carry a pager, and could not be reached until later in the morning. Karp would have to wait.

Lon did not bring up the subject, although he figured that Karp would tell him as soon as the call came through. He was worried that Boren might outright fire Karp if he lost his hospital privileges, even though Karp told Lon that wouldn't happen. Karp trusted Boren, for he knew that the money he was being paid represented only a small fraction of the cash he was generating for the practice. As long as Karp could turn a profit for Boren, he'd have a job. Lon wasn't too sure.

Karp moved slowly as he slogged through his patient schedule. It would have been nice to have a light day after all the energy he'd spent the night before, but he knew that would be a lot to ask. Boren had kept Karp's schedule light leading up to the MEC meeting. The next few days would be payback time. The list seemed to go on and on. There were almost ten lasers for him to do today in addition to the regular patient load.

He looked at the chart before him, realizing he'd already read the cover sheet twice and still couldn't recall much about the patient. He shook his head to clear the cobwebs. The patient was Avery Prater, a fifty two year old diabetic with complaints of diminished vision at near. His last eye exam was five years previously. He was on oral hypoglycemics rather than insulin, and was otherwise in good health.

Karp entered the dimly lit exam room and introduced himself. Although he'd already read the notes that Lon had put on the chart regarding Prater's chief complaint, he asked again. "What brings you in to see us today?"

Prater looked at least ten years older than fifty two. His skin was pale, like a man who didn't get out much. He was thin, and bald, although he wore a toupee. Karp couldn't help but notice the toup, because it was simply awful. It covered his head like a plate of colored angel hair pasta. The strands were combed so tightly that they could never be real hair, and it stood out so thick on his temples that Karp thought there was enough space to reach his hand up underneath the wig from the side if he tried. He wore oversize glasses in a wire frame. The lenses were tinted amber, but much too dark for indoor wear. "I've been having some trouble seeing at work," said Prater, his teeth ivory white. Karp figured that they must be caps. He smelled tobacco on the man's breath, and knew that a smoker could never have teeth that white. "I work on a computer, and I can't see the screen well with these bifocals."

Karp examined the glasses, then looked at the lens prescription on his exam sheet. "I would imagine your neck gets a little tired when you look through the bifocal for your computer," he suggested.

"That's right. And now the darn things don't work for reading fine print."

Karp nodded. "Let's see if we can't fix that up for you." He moved the slit lamp into place. "I also want to get a good look at your eyes." He gestured for Prater to position himself in the chinrest for his exam. "You know that diabetes is not simply a disease of blood sugar, it's also a disease of blood vessels. It's important to get a dilated eye examination annually."

"Okay," he said. Karp moved the light back and forth, examining the various layers of his patient's eye. There was a little cataract, nothing exceptional or visually significant. He moved the slit lamp out of the way, and put on the indirect ophthalmoscope to peer deep into Prater's eyes. There were a few small hemorrhages from the diabetes, but no exudates, no retinal edema, and no sign of new vessel growth.

Karp explained diabetic retinopathy to his patient, and again stressed the need for annual followup visits. "As far as the glasses," he went on, "I'm going to suggest that you consider getting a separate pair for working on the computer. By backing off on your near correction, we can give you a focus depth that will be more comfortable and keep you from having to tilt your head like a contortionist. You'll still want your standard bifocal for driving, reading, and other everyday tasks."

"There's no way to get one set of glasses for everything?" He sounded disappointed.

"Unfortunately, the answer is no. If we use a trifocal or a continuously variable bifocal lens, you're still going to have to tilt your head unnaturally to see at intermediate distances." He wrote out two prescriptions for glasses, labeling one for the computer, and handed them to his patient. "Give these a try. I think you'll be very happy once you get used to them."

Prater looked over the slips of paper. "I see," he said. "You added half of my reading prescription to the distance strength for the computer glasses. That would focus them at about a half meter, then?"

"More or less. Do you know optics?"

"Some. I used to work for the Air Force. I designed most of their computer systems around the country. I do private consulting now, though, because I hate working with those military assholes. They think they know everything, you know?"

Karp nodded. "I'm familiar with the type."

"I've done some work for various medical offices around Chicago, Doc. I noticed that your office staff uses a few computers."

Karp wasn't really familiar with the systems they used. He'd had other priorities. "We've got some, yes."

"I might be able to help you organize your systems. Do you think I could get a chance to quote your business office on my services?"

Karp wasn't the one to ask. "You can check with Tanya, at the front desk. She'll get you to meet with our administrator, Mr. Alder. I can tell you, though, that the boss doesn't really like spending a lot of money on upgrades unless he's convinced it will help generate cash flow. Computers don't generate billing here, the doctors do."

"Oh, I understand. Listen, I write a lot of my own software and programs. Like I said, I did a good deal of work with Defense...I helped them generate some of their guidance systems and their security systems on various bases." He laughed. "Once the idiots forgot their own passwords, and I had to break into my own software. It wasn't easy, I'll tell you. Anyway, I've got some real interesting programs that I can show you." He reached into his shirt pocket and extracted a business card. He handed it to Karp. "Give me a call anytime. I can help you speed up your machine, and maybe show you a few things to help your productivity."

Karp examined the card. Prater Digital was the corporate name he used. "Avery Prater; Digital Systems Design, Software Development, Hardware Support."

"I'll hang on to the card," said Karp, as he placed it in his shirt pocket. "I do have a PC that might need a little tweaking. I'll also tell Mr. Alder about you. I can't make any promises about the company, though." He wanted to be nice to his patient, and tried to sound interested.

"Thanks, doc. That's all I ask. I'm starting this business from the ground up, and you never can tell where you might find a new client. Why, just last week, I had the chance to quote a Chicago bank. You'd be surprised how outdated their hardware and software were. I showed them how easily an employee could get in and steal funds electronically."

"Dr. Karp?" The door opened a crack, and he saw one of the technicians poke her head in the room. "There's a Dr. Harmon for you on line three."

Karp appreciated the interruption. He found Prater's story interesting, but he was already behind in his schedule and frankly didn't care if Prater had designed the security system for the U.S. Treasury. "I'm sorry, Mr. Prater, can you excuse me? I need to get this call."

"Sure, Doc, sure." They shook hands, and Karp directed him to the checkout desk. There were three patients ready for him in rooms. They'll just have to wait, he thought. I have to collect my bad news.

"Good morning, Jerry," said Harmon on the phone.

God, I hate it when he calls me by my first name, thought the ophthalmologist.

"I'm sorry Mr. Kilner and I missed you last night. We stopped by your home to tell you about the meeting."

"I was out," said Karp.

"I see. Jerry this is very difficult for me. The MEC voted last night to uphold the recommendations of the QA Committee. It was decided that your cataract and anterior segment surgery privileges be suspended."

"I see." There was an awkward silence, as if Harmon were waiting for Karp to express anger or surprise. Quite the contrary, this was the result that he fully expected.

"It was decided that you should maintain privileges to perform laser procedures. However, you should know that the MEC members felt that there is room for you to improve these skills as well. We recommended that all of your laser procedures be done under the continued close scrutiny of the QA Committee."

"I understand." Karp's voice remained flat, although he was genuinely surprised that they hadn't yanked all of his privileges.

Again, Harmon paused for Karp's response. "You should know that there was a great deal of discussion about how we

186

should handle things from here. You have many friends on staff at the hospital."

Karp had no response at all. He wasn't so sure about his friends at Compton Memorial.

"We felt that it might be appropriate to reconsider the situation after you undergo a period of retraining, Jerry. Dr. Porter made some very helpful recommendations to the committee in this regard."

"I'll be interested in seeing those suggestions, Orville." Karp decided that he would call the senior staff doctor by his first name. "I'll be talking to my attorney soon, of course. I think you should know that I don't wish to pursue an appellate hearing on this matter."

"Really?" It was Harmon who was surprised.

Of course not, thought Karp. The result would be no different from the MEC recommendation. "I was hoping that we might be able to come to a mutually beneficial conclusion here."

"I see."

"I hoped that we might come to an agreement about retraining if I agree to voluntarily withdraw my privileges. I really don't want to have the suspension on my record in the Databank."

Harmon thought for a moment. "I see your point. You realize, Jerry, that we would still be obligated to report to the Databank that the withdrawal came as a result of this review. The record cannot be wiped clean."

"That may be so, but it would certainly be preferable to a suspension. Don't you agree?"

"Yes, I do. Have you talked to your attorney about this?"

"We've discussed it in general terms. We had hoped that the end result of the MEC meeting would be different."

"Certainly."

Karp waited for a response.

"Well, Jerry, I'll talk to Mr. Kilner. Let's get together on this after we've explored this option further."

"I look forward to that, Orville."

There was another pause on the line. Karp figured that Harmon didn't like being referred to by his first name. "Jerry, I'm truly sorry that this had to end this way."

"As am I."

As they hung up, Harmon was able to speak without having Karp listen in. "I'm glad I'm not you, Jerrold Karp," he uttered.

"Mr. Kilner?" It was Vicki on the intercom. "Dr. White is on the line for you."

He picked up the phone. "Billy? Thanks for calling me back."

"Yes, yes. You called last night?"

Kilner played his best poker face. In truth, he wanted to strangle the arrogant son of a bitch. "Yes, Dr. White. I wanted to let you know about the MEC meeting."

"MEC?" It was as if White didn't know at all what Kilner was talking about.

"Yes," Kilner smiled. "The Medical Executive Committee. Dr. Karp's privileges were on our agenda last night."

"Yes?" He was irritated by the time being wasted on this phone call.

"The MEC voted to suspend his cataract surgery privileges, just as Dr. Porter recommended."

"It only makes sense, Dan. What of it?"

"I wanted to make sure that the CIO doctors were aware of this, Billy. I was hoping that we would now begin to see Drs. Genello and Stutz here for surgery."

"Our satellite office in Aurora opens next week. We need to start seeing patients there, Dan, and then we'll be operating at your hospital."

"Good, Billy, good. I was hoping, too, that you might reconsider applying to be on our staff yourself."

"We've discussed this, Dan." He didn't try to hide his irritation. "Genello and Stutz will be working at the Aurora office, and they will be doing surgery at Compton. I really don't have time to commute that far."

"I understand, Dr. White. Your reputation in Aurora is well known. We think a lot of your work."

"Thank you, Mr. Kilner. Is there anything else that I can do for you?"

He thought for a minute. "I have some concerns about how this affects our Development Fund."

White said nothing.

"Our efforts with Dr. Karp depleted the Fund significantly." Again, White had no response. "I'm sure that you'll agree that freedom from competition can help build a practice, Dr. White." Again, no response. "We may need to review our Development Fund situation."

"You mean more money."

"I want to assure our staff of your commitment to Compton Memorial Hospital's long term position. The federal health care reform plans have me worried. I know that Dr. Karp understands what I mean."

"Get to the point, Mr. Kilner."

"Long term viability is the key, Dr. White. We want your full commitment, that's all. When the surgical volume is at the level we had discussed, I don't see why we couldn't renegotiate down."

"How much, Mr. Kilner?"

"Twice as much until surgeries begin. Then we'll split the difference until the volume reaches the levels we had agreed upon. Then, back down to baseline."

"Double?"

"Yes."

It was a pittance, reasoned White. A small portion of the cost of establishing a new practice. In the new world of health care reform, increasing volume and market share would be all important. White had honed his skills in crippling his competitors, and this meshed well with the hospital. "Fine. This is just temporary, though, correct?"

"You have my word."

"Very well. I agree to your request." As he hung up, he shook his head. He felt pity for Karp. The Compton Memorial Hospital privileges would soon be the least of his concerns. White had spoken with a former classmate of his from Northwestern who was now with the Illinois State Department of Health and Welfare. His recommendations for Karp's medical license would finish the young doctor's ability to practice. Karp would no longer represent any form of competition for Billy White.

By the time Karp got to Suburpia, the hoagie shop near Boren's office, Lon had already ordered lunch for both of them. He'd ordered two Italian subs, easy on the oil and the mayo. The sandwiches were coming, and there were two tall colas on the table. Lon hoped that his friend would be hungry.

Karp ambled in, walking slowly but without wavering. There seemed to be no energy in his movement, and he did not smile.

"How's it going, pal?" Lon gestured for Karp to sit across from him.

"It's going, man, not much more than that." He took a tall sip of the cola, swallowed it, and licked his lips. "The sugar is good," he said.

"Too much last night?"

He shook his head. "Not enough. I'm just sleepwalking today."

Lon understood. "How did Boren take it?"

He drank some more soda. "Well, as a matter of fact. He was pleased that I managed to salvage my laser procedures and assured me that I would be able to continue to work here while I..." he shook his head. "...address this further."

Lon drank some soda. "That's good, pal, that's good. I'm glad he's giving you some support."

"I tell you, it seems as though he's the only comrade I have in medicine anymore."

"How about Val? Does she know?"

A teenaged girl set down two sandwiches on the table without a word, and turned back toward the counter. "Great service," Karp said nodding in her direction. "As a matter of fact, she does. I called her after I talked to Rick Leach."

Lon grinned.

"Yes, I told the lawyer before my wife. He had suggestions about my next move. She would only be disappointed."

"Was that all?"

"Well, she's doing okay, Lon. This is pretty rough on her, too, you know."

Lon bit into the sandwich. "Of course it is," he said between chews. "She cares." He nodded toward Karp's plate. "Eat. You need it."

Karp sighed. "I suppose I should. Anyway, I wasn't the only one who had a phone call this morning."

Lon gave a quizzed look.

"The agency called. The adoption is on."

"What do you mean?"

"I mean," Karp worked on a bit of sandwich between words, "the paperwork is all finished. We're looking at a two to three week wait for visas and we're cleared to go to Moldova to meet our new son."

"That's tremendous," he grinned.

"Well," Karp went on, "we're not both going to go. I can't afford it." He swallowed and laughed. "Hell, I can't even afford for one of us to go. This is going to suck up what little space we have left on the credit cards. As long as I'm working, though, I'm going to finish this process."

"For God's sake, who could blame you?"

Karp shrugged. "I haven't even gotten a bill from Leach yet, and I can only guess how much the legal fees are going to run. If I stay out of bankruptcy court it will be a goddamn miracle."

"So, tell me about the baby."

"He's eleven months old, in excellent health. His birth mom wasn't able to support him. She had four other children, and that's a real hardship for a single parent in eastern Europe."

"I can imagine."

"He's the cutest thing," said Karp, sounding already like a proud papa. "His hair is fine and blond. His eyes are bright." Karp's shone, too as he spoke. "He can grow up to be anything he wants, Lon, as long as he's not in the field of medicine." Just thinking about his profession wiped the smile from Karp's face.

They worked on the sandwiches a little more. "Jerry, I'm glad that Boren and Val are giving you some support. You know that there are people who still believe in you."

Karp smiled. "That may be, but few things will age a man as fast as being put through this kind of psychological abuse."

"But you are on the way up again. That's what's important."

"I agree."

"Jerry, there's something I need to tell you."

"Oh, Jesus, Lon, what's happened now?"

He sat back in the chair and slapped the table top gently with his hands. "Jerry, it's like this: About three weeks ago I sat down to a meeting with Dr. Boren. I think he's concerned about the cost of my health insurance benefits, but he said he felt that I wasn't needed on a full time basis."

"What?"

"I'm a part time employee, now. That means I get no health insurance, no vacation time, no paid leave, no benefits. He did promise to keep me on staff here, but I need insurance. I need the pay. I already took a hell of a pay cut."

Karp nodded. "I know you did." He looked at the half eaten submarine sandwich. "Geez, there goes my appetite again."

Lon held his palms up toward Karp. "Jerry, I don't blame you. For that matter, Boren's just being a reasonable business man."

"For crying out loud, Lon. Truly, I'm sorry that my misfortune has had to impact so hard on you."

He shook his head. "It's not your fault. I've talked with my kids, and we're going to move out in a couple of weeks. I'm giving Boren my two weeks' notice this afternoon."

"Have you got a job out there?"

"Not yet. But I will. It's hard to interview from this distance."

"What can I do to help you, Lon?"

"Not a damn thing. Keep your head screwed on straight and keep fighting. I'll be fine. I'll miss you, but I'll be fine. And so will you."

Karp nodded, but fought a tear. He and Lon had been together for too long, had been too close as friends not to be upset. It was still one more indignity he would have to face. "So, what are you doing with your furniture, your apartment?"

"We're taking some of our stuff, selling the rest. The apartment is sort of a problem, because we have a lease that runs for the next two months, but I'll just have to forfeit the security deposit, I guess. As for the Green Hornet, well, I'll probably take a gun and shoot it. There's no way that oil burner is going to make it all the way to the east coast. I'll just have to worry about wheels when I get there."

"If I can give you a few bucks, Lon..."

"Yeah right. The man who's this close to the brink." He shook his head slowly. "I'll be fine. Eat your sandwich, goddammit."

With a full stomach and a little less achy head, Karp returned to the office. As he headed toward the examining rooms, one of the receptionists called him aside. "Dr. Karp, there's someone here to see you."

"A patient?"

"No. It's someone named Paul Wells. He says he's here from the State Medical Board."

"Jesus Christ, what now?" muttered Karp aloud. "Sorry," he continued, catching himself. He didn't want to take out his frustration on his co-workers. "Of course I'll see him. I'll be right there." He opened the doorway to the main lobby. "Mr. Wells?"

The examiner rose from his chair and approached Karp. "Dr. Karp. Thank you for seeing me."

"You know I'm always available to help you with this situation," he answered. This mess, he thought.

"Yes, I do. Is there someplace private where we might talk."

Karp didn't like the implication of the request. He felt his pulse begin to race. "Right this way," he gestured toward an open exam room. "I hope there aren't any new problems, Mr. Wells."

"Well, Doctor, I'm sorry to have to bring you this information, but you must understand that this is my job. I don't make the decisions, just gather data and carry messages back and forth."

Karp swallowed hard. "And that message is...?"

Wells reached into his jacket pocket and removed an envelope, which he handed to Karp. "The State Medical Board has suspended your license pending a hearing."

Karp felt his chest tighten. He lost his breath for a moment, and struggled to keep from passing out. His temples pounded, his eyes watered, and his heart raced. It was only a moment, but it seemed like forever. He finally regained his composure from the adrenaline rush and breathed hard twice, able only to spit out the words, "Hearing? When?"

"I'm sorry Dr. Karp, honestly. I've only seen this happen before twice, and I must say that the charts you gave me did not alone justify this kind of action in my experience. There has got to be something more in your file. Are you certain that you've never had a malpractice case filed against you?"

He worked hard to control his anger. "Don't you think I'd know if I was being sued?" he wanted to scream. Instead, he squeaked out, "Yes, I'm certain. Never been sued." He felt an iron band tighten around his forehead. Stress headache. He'd never had one, but he was certain this was what one felt like.

Wells shook his head. "They'll only suspend your license if there's evidence of gross incompetence that places the public at risk of serious consequences. I can't imagine cataract surgery, even grossly inadequate cataract surgery, placing patients at that level of risk." He shook his head again, thinking aloud. "No, there's got to be something more." Karp could have no rational response to this one-sided conversation. "Anyway, they'll contact you in the next few weeks regarding the date of your hearing before the Board. I am not in a position to advise you formally of how you should proceed," he said, but he felt bad for the young physician so he added, "but I'd recommend that you get in touch with your legal counsel right away. This type of action is not a good sign."

Karp could only muster a nod in response.

"In the meantime, you must not practice medicine or surgery until the hearing. You may not treat patients or prescribe medications. To do so would be a violation of law and would result in prosecution, even if you were subsequently granted your license at a later date. Do you understand that?"

Karp nodded again, slowly. He understood also that it meant he had no job, no income, no savings, considerable debt, and an upcoming adoption.

Wells stood. "I'm sorry, Dr. Karp," he repeated, and excused himself from the room. Mechanically, Karp stood and accompanied the man to the doorway. Wells stopped him, and gestured for Karp to stay behind. He would find his own way out. Slowly, with a rhythmic pace, he made his way to the front lobby and continued out of the office.

Karp just stood there, still and pale. His sweaty hands trembled. His entire life had been spent training for his career, his entire adult existence had been ruled by the superseding call of medicine. Whenever a choice had been required, his career had come first. And now, after all of this, his career was over. Even if he were able to reverse this decision, the stigma would follow him for the rest of his life.

Karp moved slowly toward the doctors' office. He passed Lon on the way. "What is it? What happened?" he asked. Karp said nothing. He just proceeded to the office. He needed to think. Somehow, he needed to find a way to save all that he knew he would soon lose.

Rick Leach pored through the vast files that referred to his client, Jerrold Karp, M.D. Leach was no physician, but he had been involved in enough medical malpractice cases to recognize the difference between gross incompetence and the errors of judgement or skill suggested by these documents. There just wasn't enough here to explain why the man had been hung out to dry. Why should the State Medical Board come down so hard on him? There had to be more to this case.

Leach's intercom buzzed. "Dr. Karp is here for you."

He entered the large anteroom and found his client seated by himself, staring out the large picture window behind the receptionist, head in hands. His hair was blown every which way, badly in need of a combing. His glasses perched on the tip of his nose, about to fall off. His complexion was pale. He still had his necktie on, although it was loose, hanging limp on his shirt. There were sweat stains under his arms, and he looked a little heavier than usual. "Dr. Karp."

Karp jumped when he heard his name. He quickly stood and shook his lawyer's hand.

"Come this way. Can I get you something to drink? Coffee, a coke?"

"Hemlock?" They each uttered a nervous chuckle. "No, thanks. I'd probably just spend the rest of the afternoon needing to visit the john, and I'm going to have to battle rush hour traffic to get back to Aurora."

Leach was genuinely worried about Karp. He looked awful, and sounded beaten. "How are you doing?" He wanted to know if the physician recognized his own debilitated state.

Karp looked at Leach over his glasses. "I'll tell you the truth, Rick, I've been a lot better. This hasn't been a real good day for me, you know?"

"I do," he said, with his best reassuring tone. "I just want to make sure you're going to get through this thing in one piece."

Karp smiled slightly. "I guess the jury's still out on that one."

They entered Leach's private office. It was a respectable size, at least twenty feet square, Karp observed. The decor was conservative affluence. He had a mahogany desk, heavy and dark, but not ornate. There was a maritime flavor to the adornments in the room, with an oil painting of a seascape, a small model of the Cutty Sark, and a large brass ship's bell. Karp wondered if Leach was a boater or if this was just for appearance sake.

"Tell me again what transpired today, just so that we're both up to speed."

"I talked to you this morning after I spoke with Orville Harmon. The MEC voted to suspend my cataract surgery privileges, but I managed to preserve laser and other procedures."

"Right. I still think that's a good sign. It showed that even their expert had to concede several points on your behalf. You also said that Harmon seemed open to the suggestion of you agreeing to withdraw privileges."

"He said he'd have to talk to Kilner, but he didn't nix the idea outright."

Leach nodded. "I phoned him just after lunch, but he wouldn't take the call. I suspect that word got to him about your license."

"Terrific. They don't waste any time with that, do they?"

"It's the nature of the beast, Jerry. They have to protect the public interest."

"The public interest?" Karp parroted. "How dangerous can a cataract surgeon be? I averaged no better than four cases a month, and even if I fucked up ten percent, that means about five eyes a year. For one thing, I didn't fuck up that many eyes. For another, the problem was already being dealt with at the local level. I haven't done a cataract in months. Why in hell couldn't they hold off on yanking my license until after a hearing?" His voice got louder and louder with each sentence. "What was the goddamn rush?" Leach let Karp finish rambling, then gave him time to reestablish his composure. "It's okay," he apologized, "I'm better now."

Leach shook his head gently, gesturing that Karp shouldn't think about it. "Did the examiner, Mr...."

"Wells."

"Mr. Wells, did he say anything about why the Board took the action they did?"

"No, not that I can remember. I was pretty much shell-shocked when I met with him, so I can't say that I recall a lot of our conversation." He looked up in the air, trying to reconstruct the meeting with Wells. "He said something about there being more information at the Board's disposal than just the charts I had provided. He didn't elaborate, though, so I don't know what information he had."

"Could it have been the video from Billy White? Or something from the hospital?"

Karp shrugged. "It could have been anything, I guess. Aren't the hospital's actions considered confidential at this point?"

"Technically, yes. If they were subpoenaed, there would be nothing stopping them from providing that data to the Board."

"Great. That means the State Board could have been influenced by anything in that bogus file from Compton. Fitch's private conversation with John Kingston. Dr. Porter's bullshit review. Billy White's exaggerated claims of my incompetence."

"Don't get excited, now, Jerry. I've already filed a motion with the Board requesting copies of everything in their possession. We should know what's going on within a week."

"A week. That's terrific. Meanwhile, my wife and I are this close to adopting a little boy. Without cash for the adoption fees, we have to put the thing on hold." He snorted. "Val wasn't all too pleased when I told her about our little setback. She wasn't sure that they would let us push the travel date back. They're ready for us now. I haven't the savings, and I've just lost my job."

Leach didn't know what to say. So often when he'd dealt with physicians, they were very well off. They had large savings accounts and investment portfolios. Those who had been in practice for years had managed to save significant sums of money. Karp came from a different generation. He was one of a growing number of doctors who were deeply indebted. "Jerry, is there anything that I can do for you?"

Karp was taken by surprise. He thought for a moment, trying to be certain he understood his lawyer. "Do you mean financial help?"

Leach nodded. "Understand, this is not something that I regularly offer to my clients. I just...it's that these charges against you are so inflated. I can't help but think that we'll be able to turn this around, given enough time. If I can do something to help you get through, I'd...I want you to know that I think this is unfair."

Karp looked hard at Leach, and realized that he had a true friend. Leach empathized with Karp in much the same way Karp empathized with Lon Morrissey. "Thanks, Rick. I really do appreciate the offer, and I know that it's legitimate. My money problems extend beyond the depth and breadth that a loan, even a hefty one, might be able to help." He sat forward in his chair. "As a matter of fact, at some point this afternoon I need to talk to you about filing for bankruptcy."

Leach nodded. Karp knew what he faced. "We'll explore that later, if you want."

Karp sat back in his chair. Nothing was going to come easy today. "Let's say we find out that our case is strongly defensible. How long is it going to take to reverse the ruling?"

"Best case, Jerry, we'll get an early hearing date. The letter you got today states that the hearing will be granted in less than ninety days. If there are no bombshells in the package from the Board, I'll petition for an immediate hearing. Still..." He paused.

"Yes?"

"Well, if this is all they have," he patted Karp's file, "even with Billy White's video and letters, I just don't see why they did this. I have a friend at another firm, a fellow who used to be a general practitioner. He later went to law school, and then took a position with the Medical Board about ten years ago. Now he's in a private law practice. I discussed your case with him informally, and he can't see why your license was pulled. He's convinced that there is something more to the case against you."

Karp shook his head. "If there is, I don't know what it could be. You have everything that the hospital does, and you know the patients as well as I do. There have been no malpractice cases filed. I don't know what more they can have."

"I'll certainly be interested to find out. As far as worst case scenario," Leach continued, "this could take months to sort out. If the decision at your hearing is unfavorable, you'll have to file a suit in civil court."

"Which will also take several months to be heard," continued Karp.

"Possibly years," responded Leach. "Also, the court system grants wide latitude to the Medical Board. Unless there has been gross misconduct on the Board's part, the court will not want to overturn the decision."

"So this whole thing could be a hell of an uphill battle."

"Could be."

Karp felt himself pushed back into his chair. "Oh, I'm very optimistic about this."

"I know it may be hard, but I want you not to obsess about negative outcomes. I suspect that there is a simple explanation: Some biased document, a highly emotional letter from a patient, something unexpected that has convinced them to take this action. I'm going to remain encouraged that we'll be able to turn this around for you."

Karp nodded, and stared past Leach. Leach saw that Karp's eyelids were swollen and discolored.

"How does Dr. Boren stand on this?" asked Leach.

Karp's eyes brightened just a little. "Actually, he's still very supportive. He told me that he had no argument with my work and that he would pass that information on to any interested party. He could have outright fired me. Instead, he put me on an extended leave of absence until this is rectified. I couldn't say for a moment that he was unfair to me." He sighed, "If I do get this straightened out, I wouldn't hesitate to work with him again."

"Good. How about your wife?"

"Like I said, she'd been doing well up until today. This curveball from the Medical Board really hit hard. It's seriously jeopardized the adoption, and neither one of us was prepared for that."

"It's not much consolation, Jerry, but tell her that we're working on this thing as aggressively as we can. If everyone can be a little patient, you may be able to save the adoption."

Karp nodded.

Leach looked at the substantial stack of paper before him. "Is there anything else I can do for you right now?"

"Two things. First, I really was serious before about exploring bankruptcy. I don't know how I can salvage my finances even if this takes only a couple of weeks. Perhaps we should begin looking into the paperwork."

"Jerry, that isn't really my line of work. I have a partner here in the firm who does this sort of thing. Should I have him get in touch with you?"

"Yes."

He wrote down a note to himself. "I'll have him phone you at home this evening. You'll probably need to prepare some statements for him with the names of your creditors and the amounts you owe to each. In the meantime, don't use your credit cards until you can work out a plan with him."

"Understood."

"What else?"

Karp looked at the floor. "I'm a little embarrassed to ask, but..."

"Yes?"

"What are the chances that this is going to go public. I mean, how much do I have to worry about walking outside and being accosted by the Channel Nine Newsteam? I can see the newspaper story already: `Local Doctor Loses License After Blinding Patients.'"

"I can't tell you. Certainly, if you are approached by the press, give them the `no comment' response and refer them to me. It's my job to deal with them. The hospital is bound by law to respect the confidentiality of this matter, so they aren't going to go to the press. I've never heard of the State Board doing so, unless you fail to respond to their requests or try to open another practice somewhere."

"Okay."

"Don't do any of those things. It's unlikely that publicity will become an issue."

"I guess I don't trust Billy White. Something tells me that he's the common link in all of this, and I don't for a moment believe he is above calling the press anonymously if it means more pain for me."

Leach smiled. "Remember, we're going to avoid paranoia."

The smile was infectious. "I don't trust Billy White."

"I don't blame you. If something does happen, just let me know."

"Immediately."

Karp got back to Aurora by six forty five. Rush hour traffic was especially bad, and he sat bumper to bumper for an eternity. He was awestruck by the fact that traffic in all lanes could come to a complete stop. Even if there were a collision that blocked two lanes, he reasoned, surely traffic would continue to move along at a slower pace. How could every vehicle cease to move altogether? He had plenty to think about in the car, and he was actually pleased that the crappy traffic could wrestle his attention away from more pressing matters for a few moments.

The evening sun was still bright as Karp came to his own driveway. He reached up and triggered the automatic garage door opener, and positioned the Stealth to back into the right side of the garage. As he did, he saw that Val's Cougar had the trunk open. He couldn't imagine that she had been shopping. His chest tightened yet again. He shut off the car and hyperventilated a few times, as he felt his head start to pound. He was afraid he might be getting a migraine.

He opened the car door and swung his legs over the high ledge of the rocker panel. As he walked toward the door, he went around the Cougar to check the trunk. There were a couple of suitcases and several loose pairs of shoes, purses, and jackets. He felt dizzy, because he knew what this meant. He wanted just to get back in the Stealth and sit there, cuddled by the soft leather seats. He wanted a beer. He did not want to open the door and hear what Val had to tell him. He had no choice, though.

Karp entered his home and looked around cautiously. The entry from the garage went through the laundry room to the kitchen. From there he could see into the living room. He heard footsteps upstairs. "Val?" he said quietly, willing her to respond from the living room. "I'm home." There was no answer. He took a deep breath, concentrating as hard as he could to relax. He walked through the kitchen, past the chili peppers and Gorman prints that decorated the place with a southwestern accent, and made his way to the stairs leading up to the bedrooms. "Val? I'm home," he repeated quietly.

"I'm upstairs," she answered coolly.

Karp worked his way slowly up the steps. At the top, the master bedroom light was on, casting long shadows into the hallway. Val was not to be seen, but he heard her rustling in the closets. There was a small suitcase on the bed, its lid open, showing piles of underwear within. There was a clunk from the closet, as Val closed a drawer. She walked out at a businesslike pace, ignoring her husband entirely as she carried a load of panty hose to the suitcase, neatly placing them among her other clothes. She then stood up straight and examined the full bag for sufficient tidiness, resting her hands on her hips. At last, she purposefully closed the bag and latched it. She picked it up in her right hand, making a little heaving noise and walked toward Karp. She made no suggestion that she intended to speak to him.

"You're, uh, going somewhere?" he observed.

"I need some time," was her answer. She continued past him and started down the stairway.

"Time," he repeated.

She said nothing and continued down the stairs, turned, and made for the garage where she would add this bag to the collection in the Cougar's trunk.

Karp walked over to the closets. Val's was nearly empty. Most of her clothes were gone. Only some sweaters and winter dresses remained. That's comforting, he thought: At least she's planning to come back before Christmas. He moved on, entering his own closet. It was just as he had left it that morning. He shook his head, removed his necktie, and hung it on the rack. All at once he heard Val's footsteps coming up the stairs. As she entered their bedroom, carrying an empty tote bag, he stopped her at the bedside. "Val," he said gently, "I think we need to talk."

She walked by him and started collecting her earrings, necklaces, and jewelry, in order to place them in the tote bag. "Oh do we? About what?"

"Well, for starters, I thought you might want to fill me in on your travel plans."

She snorted, and stopped stuffing the tote bag, making no effort to mask her disgust. "How did your meeting go with Rick Leach?"

"No magic or surprises, if that's what you mean," he answered flatly, working hard not to make things worse by sounding sarcastic.

"Well, there's no magic here, either. I talked to the agency, and they said we had forty eight hours to decide whether we want to proceed or not. This problem isn't going to be cleared up in two days, is it?"

Karp looked at the floor. "No. It isn't."

Val started to pack again. "Well, then, I need some time to think about things. I've lost quite a bit in the last few hours. Your career is finished, our reputation is ruined. The neighbors barely acknowledge me anymore, and I'm tired of being embarrassed to walk around in my own home town. This bullshit has been dragging on for the better part of a year. You barely sleep at night. Now, we've lost any real chance of having a child. Even if you can straighten this out, we're inevitably going to lose our home." She stood up and looked through him with laser vision. "Have I left anything out?" she said icily.

He tried to think of the right answer. There wasn't any. "I guess not," he answered quietly, meeting her stare with his own.

"Fine. I'm going to Detroit for a few weeks. I talked to my parents, and I'll be staying with them. If a miracle occurs, well...that will take a miracle, won't it? If not, we'll just have to see, Jerry. We'll just have to see."

She went back to her tasks. Karp saw her point. He didn't like being Jerry Karp anymore, either, and he couldn't argue with Val if she didn't want to be around him. He knew that she would be unhappy in the extreme when the adoption had to be halted. What more could he add?

He went back to his closet, took off his work clothes, and settled into a pair of gym shorts and a large tee shirt, one comfortable enough to cover his considerable girth. He wore slippers on his sockless feet. This wasn't going to be a very entertaining evening, and he saw no reason to dress well.

He left Val to continue packing, and went downstairs. It had been a long and unpleasant day. He was tired and thirsty, and he wanted very much to turn off the noise in his brain. Karp went directly to the refrigerator and extracted a green and gold can of Genesee Cream Ale. He popped the top and poured the golden liquid into a tall ceramic stein. Snapping the video on, he deflated into his recliner and zapped up the cable channels to twenty three, which broadcast WGN. The Cubs were getting ready to start a game with Atlanta. It seemed a fitting end to a futile day, preparing to watch the Cubbies lose to a juggernaut Braves team.

Somewhere into the third inning and the fourth Genny Cream Ale, Val walked toward the living room, stopping only at the entry way. "I'm leaving," she said.

I know that, he thought in a stupor. "I wish I could change your mind," he said without getting up. He knew that he couldn't change her mind, and saw no reason to expend the energy trying to move.

"Maybe we can still work things out, Jerry. I'm sorry."

Everyone is sorry, he thought. Harmon is sorry. Leach is sorry. Val is sorry. Of all of us, though, I'm the sorriest of the lot. "I hope we can," he said, resisting the urge to lift his stein of beer at just that moment to toast everyone's sorrow. Otis Nixon fired a liner into the gap, driving in two runs. This was not going to be a good night for the Cubbies either.

Val turned. "I'll call you in a couple of days. Try not to drink yourself into a coma." Her footsteps crackled on the clean linoleum floor, and the door to the garage closed with finality.

He heard the Cougar fire up, then rev down as she put it into gear. The engine noise tailed off as the car drove smoothly down the driveway and into the street. There was no other sound from the house with the exception of the ball game on the television. Harry Caray pointed out the Nixon's name, backwards, was Noxin. Karp sipped on the Cream Ale. Well before the Cubs lost six to two, he had fallen asleep in the recliner, alone in his home, and as far as he was concerned, alone in the world.

Eleven

From his sleep, Karp heard the telephone ring. He wasn't sure if it was part of some muddy dream or if it was the real thing. He roused slowly and felt a throbbing in his forehead. The room was dark, lit only by the strobe of the television. A rerun of Night Court was on. The ball game had ended some time earlier. The telephone rang for the fourth time as he reached for it, and the annoying bellow of the bell ceased as he lifted the handset from the cradle. He glanced at his watch. It was nine forty five. "Hello?"

"Hi. Is this Dr. Karp?" It was a female voice. Karp didn't recognize it. She called him by his title. His first thought was that it was the ER or answering service. Didn't they all know that he wasn't working anymore? Didn't everyone know? "Yes." He had learned long ago to answer the first few questions with only one word when he was awakened by the phone. The caller couldn't be certain by his voice how deeply asleep he'd been so that his medical orders were less likely to be questioned.

"It's Melora Peltier. I hope I'm not interrupting anything."

Melora Peltier. Who in the world was that? A nurse wouldn't introduce herself by name. He began to run through the names of the patients he'd seen recently. Peltier, Peltier. Her voice was too young for a cataract patient. Not diabetic, he was certain of that. An RK patient, perhaps. "No," he stalled for time to think. "You're not interrupting. What can I do for you?"

"I'm not sure just how to start, Jerry, but I had a professional question for you."

Professional question. She was a doctor. Yes, that's it, Dr. Peltier, the ob-gyn doc. She started in Aurora about the same time that he had. She'd joined a practice with another female doc. What kind of question could she have for me, he wondered. Gynecology and ophthalmology have little in common, unless she had a pregnant woman with eclampsia and eye signs. He wouldn't be of much value to her tonight. No license to practice.

"No problem," he said cautiously. John Larroquette bellowed something suggestive on the television. "Hold on a second," he said, as he set down the receiver and hunted around his recliner for the remote. He moved aside a half empty bag of potato chips, another of Dorito's, and several empty cans of Genny. He found it, and snapped on the Mute button. "There, that's better," he added, noting that his movements were still slowed. He should have been awake by now. It was clear that he was still intoxicated from the beer. He picked up the phone again. "What's up?"

"Jerry, I'd heard that...well that you were having some problems at the hospital."

There were plenty of rumors at CMH, he thought. "You could say that," he said, wondering where this was leading.

"I'm sorry. I know this is probably very difficult for you. I just needed some advice. I got a call today from Kip Porchette. He's on the QA Committee, you know."

He smiled. "Yes, I do."

"He told me that there was a quality assurance issue raised by one of the other gynecologists in the hospital, and that I was under review."

Karp didn't respond.

"I heard that this was how your problems started and I was hoping that you might be able to give me some advice. I don't know what to do."

She sounded genuinely worried. Karp sensed fear in her voice. Bastards, he thought. They couldn't even wait for the ink to dry on my death certificate before they started dissecting another one. "I may not be a lot of help," he said finally. "I wasn't especially successful."

"I'm sorry. I'd appreciate knowing what to expect."

He certainly had nothing to lose. "Okay. What can I tell you?"

"Would you mind if I came over? My mom is here to watch my kids, so I have a little time. If you're free."

He looked at the mess in the living room, then ran his fingers through his greasy, uncombed hair. "Could you give me about half an hour to get straightened up? It's been a rough day." He figured the extra time would also help him metabolize some of the alcohol.

"Yes," she sighed, relieved. "I really appreciate this."

Karp went about cleaning the living room. Val kept the house spotless, and he had only needed a few inebriated hours to make this mess. He removed the empty beer cans, looked at the half eaten bag of potato chips and thought about saving them, then thought better of it. He decided that the living room was neat enough. He'd better take care of himself.

He dragged himself up the stairs, nearly tripping on the third step. Once in the bedroom, he undressed and started up the shower. He stepped in and let the hot running water slap him awake. He mostly just stood there, letting his nerve endings get stimulated by the warmth.

The stream of consciousness that played in his mind was agitating. It frustrated, and even frightened him. He thought about how he had started his career, and how so much of the politics of medicine had changed. He had poured years of his life into the system, and those years flowed away like the dirty shower water that spun around his feet. He fumed at the fact that Billy White, in concert with Harmon and Kilner, had so aggressively maligned him. That was never part of the bargain with the system, with organized medicine. Once you entered the club, you were supposed to be a member for life.

This lifelong brotherhood began in medical school. They were reluctant to fail a student without giving him a liberal opportunity to relearn the material and pass the course at a later date. There were study sessions, tutors, and, when needed, repeated courses during the summer break. Medical schools don't like to see their students, presumably the best and brightest from which to choose, fail out. To do so would suggest that the rigorous admissions process was flawed.

Even as a clinical medical student, if hands-on incompetence is uncovered, instructors work with an individual to polish their skills rather than suggest he abandon medicine. One student in Karp's class exhibited real difficulties mastering such clinical skills. He made a medication error once that nearly cost a child in the pediatrics ward her life. The counselors and preceptors offered private teaching sessions and tightly overseen clinical responsibilities. The student graduated with the rest of his class, went into general practice, and soon killed a diabetic woman with an overdose of insulin. Before the malpractice case was tried, he took his own life.

Karp had seen many cases where other ophthalmologists' surgical skills were questionable. While his own surgery needed some polish, he knew several patients who had been operated elsewhere with poor results and poorer looking surgical outcomes. His work wasn't as bad as many cases he'd seen. It was always clear that a physician should never impugn another's skills. It risked malpractice litigation. Everyone has their share of disaster stories. You never know who is going to see your train wrecks, and you don't want them defaming you. This whole episode left a sour taste in Karp's mouth.

Satisfied that he was reasonably cleaned up, he shut off the shower and toweled himself off. Instead of getting fully dressed, he decided to throw on a pair of scrubs. The surgeon's uniform would add credence to his diminished status as a physician. He brushed his hair, choosing to let it dry naturally without a blow dryer. He was too tired and disinterested to use the machine just now.

No sooner had Karp finished preparing himself than the doorbell rang. She was early. He took one last, hard look in the mirror and decided that the shower had done a good job to help him work off the alcohol. His eyes weren't quite as red or as dull, and his mouth not nearly so dry. He sauntered down the stairs to the front door.

On his front porch, Melora Peltier stood in a pair of jeans and a checked long sleeve shirt. The evening was cool, and this served her needs without a jacket. She was heavy set, but by no means fat. She had a lovely figure with full, round breasts. Her face was gentle with soft lines and a creamy complexion. Karp decided that she could be gorgeous if she dropped thirty pounds. Hers was not so much a sexually exciting appearance, but rather an inviting girl-next-door pleasantness. Still, her hands were fine, her fingernails neatly manicured and coated with simple, clear polish. Her lips were full, ruby red without makeup. Her only indulgence was a bit of eye shadow and mascara to highlight the contrast between her blue eyes and fine strawberry hair. She wore a thin gold necklace and a matching bracelet, a simple ladies' Timex, and no wedding band. "Hi, Jerry. Thanks for seeing me tonight."

He gestured for her to come in. "No problem, Melora. I'm sure you're a little anxious about all this."

Her faint smile faded. "If half of what I've heard about you is true, I'm terrified. I don't need this just now."

Karp chuckled. "And there's a good time to be crucified?" They walked to the living room. Karp offered his recliner to his guest. "Can I get you something to drink? A Coke, beer, wine?"

She shook her head.

"Something stronger?" He smiled.

"Not yet. Maybe later."

He thought about another beer, but reconciled himself to the fact that he had just sobered up. It could wait. A Coke would be good, but he figured that Melora wanted to talk first.

"I guess I should tell you what has happened to me at Compton," she said. The subject matter for the evening was shameful. "There are basically two ob-gyn practices here in Aurora."

"Right. You're with..." Melora's partner's name escaped him at the moment.

"Jane Valvano."

"Right. She's been practicing here for about ten years as I recall."

"Yes. She was the first woman ob-gyn doc in Kane County. The other practice is the Women's Medical Group." She grimaced as she said the name.

"Dave Simons, Mark Hanson, and Gil Blaine are with that group. They're known around the medical community as the `Three Amigos' because they've known each other since med school."

She snorted in disdain. "Medical school, residency, and practice. They're practically a little white upper class Boys' Club."

"And between them they see three quarters of the ob-gyn pathology in town."

She shook her head to correct him. "More than that. Much more. They have the full sanction and support of the hospital and the staff docs." She leaned forward to let him in on a secret. "Most of the other docs in town don't like women physicians."

"No," said Karp in mock surprise.

She sat back and grinned. "So you have seen what our colleagues are like, I gather."

"Oh yes. Please, go on."

"Well," she continued, "about three weeks ago I got a call from Kip Porchette. It seems that Gil Blaine saw one of my patients who'd had a hysterectomy, and he felt that my surgery wasn't up to snuff. Called the incision `sloppy,' the operative note `second rate,' and so on. The patient had a three week history of hemorrhage. It would have been malpractice not to remove the uterus."

"I'll take your word for it. I'm no gynecologist."

"Anyway, she developed a postoperative abscess. She saw Blaine on referral from her internist."

Karp closed his eyes and sat back. He could already fill in the rest of the story.

"Blaine said that I'd obviously butchered her. `Dropped the ball,' he said. For God's sake, Jerry, how am I supposed to diagnose an infection when the woman is afebrile, nontender, discharged home, and doesn't come back to see me? What am I, a mindreader?"

"Well, by golly, you're just not Gil Blaine."

She was so angry she could barely continue. "Well, Blaine complains to Porchette, and Porchette recommends a review of my surgery. Dan Kilner called me in, and now they're bringing in a third party who is supposed to be unbiased to review me."

"Someone from a company called MedCo, no doubt."

"So what I've heard about you is true," she said, her breathy voice more hushed.

"Yes. It is." Karp proceeded to tell her the story of Billy White's allegations of surgical misconduct, and of Kilner and Harmon's war on his practice. Melora spoke little, nodding and emitting little sighs of disbelief. Karp told her how his practice had suffered, and how Al Boren took him in. "If it hadn't been for him," Karp said, "I'd have been dead long ago." He advised her of the State Medical Board's action, and how that meant he couldn't work anywhere in Illinois for the moment. "Without that job," he said quietly, "my life is shattered. It's cost us our adoption, and now Val left me, too." He shook his head. "I can't say I blame her," he added quietly. "She's lost everything she had. I'm staring bankruptcy right in the eye. If this isn't over soon I'll lose everything that's left." He saw a tear well in Melora's eye.

"My God," she whispered. "How can they do this to you?"

"I don't know, exactly," he answered to no one in particular. He stared straight ahead, toward the fireplace. "I've been through all this for six months now, though it feels like six years. Doctors just don't do this to each other."

"What can I do?" she asked. "How can I protect myself?"

Karp snapped back to the present tense. He clasped his hands together and leaned toward her. He smelled her perfume, a light, sweet scent. He decided that he noticed it only because it was different from Val's. He ignored it, but was somehow drawn to her blue eyes. It had been some time since he and Val had been intimate, and he found the vision of this young woman appealing in a visceral way. "You have to know, to be certain: Is there anything truly wrong with your surgery? Any unexplained or excessive complications? Any unusually bad results? Anything that can be construed as malpractice?"

She thought for a moment. "You know, Jerry, every physician has difficult patients. I'm no different."

He nodded. "I understand. Is there a pattern of problems or anything out of the ordinary? Believe me, this MedCo doc will find out."

She considered for a moment. "I don't know. I don't think so, anyway. I have to go back through the records and look."

"Exactly," Karp pointed out. "Look at all of your surgical records. Search out all of the complications you can think of. Major ones, minor ones. Any maneuver that you made that was out of the ordinary. Any unusual findings, unexpected outcomes, odd pathology findings. Don't stop with your surgical cases, either. Review your ob cases. They will. Review your outcomes, the frequency of complicated deliveries, everything."

Melora was deflated. She sat back in the chair, pressed her legs together. "So much work to do."

Karp could not help but feel a physical attraction. He wasn't sure exactly why. The alcohol? Her vulnerability? His frustration from several cold months with Val? Perhaps it was just the fact that, for a few welcome moments, he was able to take his mind off of his own misery and focus on someone else. "I've found myself with...uh, some time on my hands. If you need help..."

"No," she said softly. "I think I ought to do the work myself." She stared off, thinking about the great task before her.

"I can't argue with you," said Karp. "The more certain you are of the facts and of your innocence, the better able you'll be to defend yourself. It's the only way I managed to salvage my laser privileges. Until they yanked my license, anyway."

"I don't need this. Don't need it now, that's for sure." Her voice was breathless again.

"Is there something else going on?"

She didn't answer.

"Are you being sued?" No response. "God, that won't help your case a bit."

"No, Jerry," she sighed. "No, that's not it." She looked him in the eye. "Jerry, if I tell you something very private, can you keep it to yourself?"

"Of course." Who was he going to tell?

"Jerry, you know I'm divorced, right?"

He shrugged. "I guess I haven't seen you with anyone, but I honestly hadn't given it much concern."

"I understand," she said, although she felt as if it were common knowledge. "Gaven, my ex, he's in prison."

"Really?" That got Karp's attention.

"God," she went on, "this is awful. I'm so embarrassed."

"Why?" asked Karp. "You're not in jail. He is. What happened?"

"I'm sorry, Jerry. I'm not embarrassed for myself. It's the kids."

"The kids?"

"Yes. Gaven and I have two children, Duane and Liz."

Karp knew that. He'd seen Melora with them in the neighborhood.

"You see, Jerry, I met Gaven when I was still a medical student at Emory University. He was a dentist in Atlanta." Her voice took on a dreamy quality. "He was so handsome, so kind. I was a kid. I spent my adolescence focusing on my studies. I'd never dated seriously. He swept me off my feet."

"Why not? He was in practice. You were a student, he had money."

She grinned. "He drove a brand new blue Jaguar, Jerry. He took me out to wonderful restaurants. We went dancing. I felt decadent! It was marvelous."

"What happened?"

Her smile melted away. "What happened was, we had children." She paused. "You see, Gaven is a pedophile."

Karp didn't know what to say.

"I didn't realize it right away. Duane was four. He had nightmares." Her look was intense. "The sleep terrors were awful. He was afraid to go to bed. Petrified. Liz just cried whenever he was near. She was only two. She was a baby."

"He abused his own children?"

Her tone wavered between anger and sorrow. "Constantly. Regularly. Since the time they were infants. I came home from work early one day, and saw him with both kids, in bed. They were all naked. He was making Duane..." She went silent.

"I can guess. It's okay," he said.

In a moment, she regained her composure. "I threw him out of the house immediately. I called the police, pressed charges. He had a very good lawyer. Almost got him off."

"Jesus."

"It was his own arrogance and...passion that did him in. He went berserk when he was on the witness stand. The jury didn't even need an hour to convict him. I divorced him right away. That's partly why we moved here. I didn't want the kids to be near him. Duane is still in therapy."

"And Gaven's in prison now."

She nodded. "At least as far as I know."

"What?"

"He's up for parole. I'm afraid they'll grant it, too. He can be very charismatic when he wants to be. He's also very intelligent. I think he may be out already."

"You don't know?"

She crossed her arms angrily. "It's against the policy of the State of Georgia. They feel that it would violate his rights." She opened her palms toward Karp. "His rights. Can you believe that? My kid is in therapy, and he has rights."

"What makes you think he's out?"

She tried to relax again. "I can't be sure. It's hard for me not to exaggerate." She shook her head. "The phone rings and someone hangs up. I got a card from the Atlanta Visitors' Board, a card I didn't ask for. I think he's trying to send me a message."

"My God, what kind of message?"

216

"That he's out. He's back. He's coming to see his kids."

Karp was incredulous. "You can't be serious. Surely you've got a restraining order."

She nodded.

"Then he knows. He knows that if he gets too close, makes any contact, he'll end up back in prison. Why would he take the chance?"

"Jerry, I think he's obsessed. I honestly believe that he would do anything, risk anything, to be with his children again. He thinks that they love him, and that they want to be with him again." She couldn't hide her revulsion. "He's twisted."

The two sat back in their seats. Karp didn't know how to respond.

"You see, Jerry, I can hardly concentrate on my situation at home and go to work. Add this review to my life, and, well, I may not be able to keep up with it all." She moved forward on the chair, closer to Karp. "Jerry, if he comes here, I'm not completely certain what I'd do."

"Melora. He's going to keep his distance if they let him out. It's got to be a long shot that they'd let him out in the first place, but if he's as intelligent as you say, he's going to stay away."

She reached over to her purse and slipped her hand in. "Just in case, I keep this with me." She extracted an object that looked like a large, black electric shaver. It wasn't a shaver, though. There was no screen or blade cover on it. Instead, the end of it looked like it had antennae. Melora saw Karp's confused look. "It's an electrical stun gun," she said. She pointed at the silver projectiles on the object's nose. "These are electrodes. You touch them against someone and pull the trigger, and it hits them with twenty thousand volts." She pulled the trigger to demonstrate. A sharp blue spark spat across the electrodes at half second intervals.

"It seems like an awfully closeup device. I mean, you have to be right next to the man to use it."

"For Gaven, this will be a good defensive weapon. He's not the kind to carry a gun." She touched her neck gently with her

PRIVILEGES

own fingertips. "He can be violent," she went on, "but he enjoys a hands-on approach." She put her hand down in her lap, and Karp touched her soft skin for a moment. He didn't know what to say, and could only barely imagine the kind of animal who could rape his own children and attack his wife. "I hate him," she continued at last. "I despise what he's done to me and my family."

Karp worked to draw them back to the present. "Melora, I don't think he's going to come here. Concentrate on this business with the hospital. That needs your full attention now."

She sighed. "Yes, it does. If they do to me what they've done to you, my family is going to face new problems indeed."

Rick Leach kept telling Karp he was acting paranoid, but it was too much of a coincidence that all four of the doctors who had been recruited by Hank Greenley were being thrown out of the hospital. "Melora, do you think that there is any special reason for the hospital to do this to you? Do you think that there is someone with a grudge against you?"

"You mean other than the Women's Medical Group?"

"Right."

She thought for a moment. "No. I can't imagine anyone else has an axe to grind."

"Let me ask you this," Karp said quietly. "Was there ever any talk to you of a payment to the hospital that would be made some time in the future?"

She didn't understand. "Do you mean the money that Jane and I owe from the start-up loan?"

"No. Other money. Payments."

"Why, of course not. What reason would there be for that? I pay dues to the hospital, if that's what you mean."

"No. This money might be a sort of a payoff. A means to get referrals, work together, something."

"That's crazy, Jerry. I wouldn't have anything to do with that."

He sighed, disappointed. "I know. But did anyone approach you with that kind of deal?"

218

"No. Never."

He turned and started pacing again. "It was a theory that Bruce Carver had. It turns out that Kilner did this to him, too. He wasn't sure about it. I was hoping you might know something."

"I'm sorry," she shook her head. "I don't. Have you talked to Adam Bullock? He left CMH a few months ago. Maybe he knows about this."

Karp rubbed his cheek nervously. "I haven't yet, but I will now. I think I'll try to locate him tomorrow morning." He chuckled nervously. "Like I said, I've found myself with some time on my hands."

Melora stood up. "Unfortunately, I have a lot of work ahead of me, and not much time. I should probably be going."

"You're going to be busy for a while," Karp agreed.

They walked toward the door. "Let me know if you think of something, anything that ties this thing together."

"I will."

"I mean it, Melora. It may be something that appears unimportant on the surface. You never know. Ask Jane if they've ever approached her about this deal."

She nodded, and took Karp's hand. "Jerry, thanks for talking to me tonight. I can't say I feel any better about what's ahead..."

"But at least you're better informed," he finished for her.

She looked at him with her blue eyes and blinked agreement.

"I wish I could do more to help you," he said.

"I feel the same. I guess it's our nature...as doctors." He grinned sheepishly. He wasn't really a doctor anymore. "Jerry, I'm sorry about your wife. Maybe this will all work out for you."

"Yes, maybe so. In the meantime, let me know if you think of anything."

"I promise."

She left, and each felt a little awkward. They were strangely drawn to each other, united by circumstances that neither controlled. Karp was lonely and alone. His life had changed so much in such a short time. He was scared and angry toward those who had hurt him, and sympathetic for this woman about to experience the same pain. He was confused and frightened, and he was now as certain as ever that some deep, secretive pact was working against him and Melora Peltier. Despite Rick Leach's sentiments to the contrary, it was more than just coincidence to Karp that he and two colleagues had left Compton Memorial Hospital under suspicious pretenses. Now another was to deal with pressure to leave. He was determined to find out what the motive was to crush him and the others. He wanted to discover what secret was more important than the careers and the lives of four young physicians, and just who benefitted from their pain.

Twelve

Karp was plenty annoyed, and the day was only beginning. He'd slept fitfully, mostly catching a few winks from the four beers he'd drunk after Melora left. He missed Val. People were plotting against him. His mind carried on a never ending debate as he tried to convince himself first that he was not paranoid, then that he shouldn't be so naive. His forehead throbbed.

There was half a package of English muffins in the fridge, and he decided that the carbohydrates would make a good breakfast after the beating he'd given his liver the night before. He didn't feel energetic enough to brew a pot of coffee, so he sipped one-percent milk. It was a little thin, and he decided that he'd treat himself to two-percent when this carton was empty. Val wouldn't be there to remind him of his paunch.

Karp spent the rest of the morning on the phone, trying to locate Adam Bullock. The Anesthesia Department at Compton was unnecessarily obstinate. All they would say was that he was no longer with the hospital. He tried the American College of Anesthesiology next, but the only address they had was a post office box in Cincinnati. The Kane County Medical Society didn't even have that. He tried the Ohio State Medical Association, but Bullock wasn't a member. Karp wondered about his long distance phone bill, but since he didn't know how he was going to pay any of his bills, the point was moot. The Ohio State Medical Board, to his great surprise, told him that Bullock was practicing in Clermont County. He had to find an atlas, but Clermont County did include Cincy, so he knew he was on the right track.

Karp went to the Aurora library's reference section which stocked phone books from around the country. He copied phone numbers of every hospital in Cincinnati, then returned home to make more calls. The sixth hospital he contacted, Jewish Hospital of Cincinnati, told him that Adam Bullock was on staff with the Department of Anesthesia. He asked to speak with him, but was told that Bullock was in a case. Karp explained that this was a medical emergency, and promised to hold. That was ten minutes ago and Karp was now on hold listening to the elevator music version of "Goodbye Yellow Brick Road."

"Hello?" The voice startled Karp, who was paying attention only to the violins playing.

"Uh, hi. Is this Adam Bullock?"

"Yes."

"Hi, Adam. Jerry Karp here. How are you doing?"

"Fine." Karp could tell that Bullock didn't know who he was.

"You may not remember me, Adam. I'm an ophthalmologist in Aurora. I'd heard you left Compton Hospital a few months ago."

"That's right." His voice lowered an octave. The very mention of Compton Memorial Hospital was clearly distasteful to him.

"Adam, I've found myself in a difficult position with Compton, and I'd hoped that we might be able to talk about your experience with them. It may prove helpful for me and some others."

"Jerry, I'm not sure I can be any help to you."

"Let me explain. One of the eye docs in Chicago instigated a review of my work which I have reason to believe was not completely objective. I'd heard that Bruce Carver had a similar problem, and last night I found out that Melora Peltier was just starting to contest charges."

Bullock didn't respond right away. "I guess I don't see what that has to do with me."

"Well," Karp continued, "we think it's a coincidence that all four of the docs who began their practices in Aurora during the final year of Hank Greenley's tenure with Compton have found themselves facing expulsion. Three of us--Carver, Peltier, and myself--faced professional censure far out of line with any real deficiency in our work."

There was another pause. "Jerry, I still don't see how I can help you," he said quietly.

"Well," he suggested, "I was wondering if there were any threats made before you left. Did anyone imply that there was a problem with your work? Did you leave under duress?"

Bullock carefully considered his response. "Jerry, I'm not sure I can answer that for you."

That was not enough for Karp. He was sure that Bullock had been pressured out. "I'm sorry?"

"I'd like not to get into it."

Karp, who was walking around the kitchen with the cordless phone, sat down at the table. "I can understand, Adam. I know how embarrassing this can be, believe me. Whatever happened, I don't think you were at fault."

There was silence on the phone line. "Jerry, I can't talk about this. Really. I sympathize with you. I just can't talk about it."

Karp could hear ambivalence in Bullock's voice. "Would that be," he said in a slowly measured voice, "because of some kind of agreement with CMH?"

Silence. Then, "Possibly."

That was it. "So, one might conjecture that in a case similar to this, but not yours in particular, another doctor might have been asked to leave rather than face disciplinary action."

"That might be a reasonable speculation."

"Damn," thought Karp out loud.

"Look, Jerry," Bullock quickly added. "I really do feel sorry for what you guys are going through. You've got to see my position. My wife and I have no kids. We hadn't bought a big home. They wanted me to leave, and I didn't want trouble. I had no roots, no ties to Aurora. I figured I could just work locum tenens for a while and we would settle down somewhere else later. There was no reason to get involved in a fight."

Karp made a few notes. "Okay. I see."

"I hope you do, Jerry. My file was sealed and they prepared a very bland letter stating that I'd worked there, neither supporting my skills nor damaging them. It was hard enough to find work with that kind of lukewarm recommendation, you know."

"I can imagine," he answered. He'd trade for a lukewarm recommendation any day.

"You need to be real clear that I can never, never corroborate your deductions. I can't afford the aggravation."

Karp sighed. "I understand, Adam. What do you suppose the docs at Compton had to gain by your departure? Who benefitted when you left?"

Bullock couldn't imagine. When he left, he didn't care who was taking advantage of it as long as they didn't damage his reputation. "I just presumed that the other anesthesia docs wanted to pay one fewer associate. We never really were overwhelmingly busy. I didn't think there was anything underhanded about it."

"Really?" Karp was surprised. "Then why didn't they just ask you to leave? Why the threat, real or implied?"

"Jerry, it's real unusual for a group to hire on a man then decide right away they don't need him. It's a sign of incompetent planning and administration. It seemed to me that Kilner didn't want to look stupid, and he was prepared to sacrifice me if he had to."

Karp made more notes. "What do you think about all this now?"

"Honestly?"

"Yeah."

"I don't give a shit. I mean, I'm sorry for you and Melora and Bruce, but, I just don't give a shit. I'm past all that, I'm in a new life, and I have no intention of screwing it up just because of some arrogant asshole in Aurora." He stopped for a moment to recompose himself, realizing that it wasn't Karp, after all, who had acted against him. "I'm sure you know now what a mistake it was to become involved with these guys, Jerry. I guess it just doesn't matter to me why this has happened, and I don't want to risk my career."

Bullock had spoken his peace, and Karp could not think of a convincing argument to change his mind. "Adam, thanks for talking with me," he said finally. "I know you didn't have to, and I promise not to violate your confidence."

"It wouldn't matter if you did," Bullock answered quietly. "I would deny whatever you said."

Of that Karp was certain. "If I find out that there is something more to this, Adam, I'll let you know."

"There's no need, Jerry. Good luck in whatever new practice you find yourself in." He hung up.

Karp felt better for a while, but the clanging finality of Bullock's proclamation brought the tenderness of his hangover back. He hung up slowly, then stared at his notes. There was nothing there. His morning was wasted. His life was wasted. He looked at his watch. It was eleven forty, and the day was Wednesday. He realized that the quarterly staff meeting at Compton Memorial Hospital was to begin in twenty minutes. He sniffed, because he knew in twenty minutes, or thereabout, it would be announced to the physicians that Dr. Jerrold Karp was no longer a member of the Active Staff. He still had some documents to retrieve from his mailbox, and there was a spare pair of eyeglasses, some instruments, and his OR shoes in his locker. He couldn't think of a better time to pick up his personal effects than just now, when all of the medical staff would be in the auditorium for the meeting.

His body was leaden as he made his way to the garage. He wasn't sure why he cared about collecting his things, except that it was just...something to do. He breathed in deeply, savoring the rubber scent of the thick Goodyear Eagle tires. He looked over the shining, waxed white paint that covered the smooth lines of the Stealth and drank in the car's pure aerodynamic beauty. He sighed as he walked around the front of the car, just staring at it, because he knew that it would soon be repossessed following his bankruptcy. Somehow it seemed that his little car deserved better. He slid into it, turned the key, and revelled in the engine note. He hoped that the new owner would pay attention to the maintenance schedule as closely as he had.

Karp cruised along Randall Road, then Indian Trail. He sensed anxiety building within him, and knew that his hands were tremulous. He crossed the Fox River, and glanced at the boat dock that was under construction for a riverboat casino. There was a lot of talk about how gambling might revive the downtown area's businesses. He guided the Stealth along the tree lined streets of old Aurora and pulled in to the doctors' parking lot, where he extracted the plastic key card from his pocket, inserted it into the slot, and waited for the gate to lift. When it finally raised up with a wobble, he was the smallest bit surprised. Kilner hadn't had time to contact Security, he thought with a smile. He pointed the car into the lot and sought out a parking space in the crowded area among the Caddies and Bimmers and Benzes.

His heart raced as he neared the heavy electric powered swinging door that opened into the OR suite. It was unlikely that anyone would say a word to him, but he was uneasy nonetheless. Predictably, he received only brief glances from the nurses at the main desk. He walked past them and into the dressing room without incident. There, he quickly dialed in the locker combination, opened the door, and removed his shoes, glasses, a pen, and some papers. He looked around, bidding the place a final farewell, breathing in the sweet and sour scents of the locker room. Unlike the ones he knew from high school and health clubs, this one smelled of volatile antiseptics and clean laundry. He took his things and left.

He went back to the main floor, reasoning that it would now be safe to take the elevators near the doctors' lounge. A glance at his watch showed it was twelve ten, and the docs would be at the staff meeting. He worked his way along the back corridors toward the administrative wing and checked out his mailbox in the lounge. It was overflowing with various papers and folded over manila envelopes. He set down his shoes on a nearby table, stuffed his glasses in his shirt pocket, and extracted the large sheaf of papers from the box.

Most of the documents were of no value to Karp: Meeting schedules, staff change notifications, call schedules, newsletters. These he discarded straight away. Lab reports and admission documents he placed in a separate pile, with plans to drop them off at the office on Paramount Drive. One envelope had his name handwritten on it and was stamped "Personal and Confidential." It was probably from Kilner, and related to the deal in the works between the hospital and himself for withdrawal of his privileges. He opened the envelope and read the letter it contained. "Dear Dr. Karp: This office was notified today by the State Medical Board that your license to practice medicine in the State of Illinois has been suspended. As this represents a violation of the Bylaws of Compton Memorial Hospital, please be advised that your admission privileges in this hospital are hereby suspended until further notice. Please see Vicki Downs in the Administrative Office regarding return of your parking permit, lot entry key, hospital key, and for instructions to complete your outstanding medical records. Sincerely, Daniel Kilner."

Well, he thought, the bastards didn't waste any time. He folded the letter and then glanced at the remaining letters and manila envelopes. Fuck it, he thought, and threw all of it in the trash. He took out his wallet and pulled the doctors' parking lot key card out, then removed the hospital door key, which he had never used, from his key ring. If the bastards want these so badly, they can have them now, he decided.

He gathered up his shoes and stormed out of the lounge. Karp's eyes were fixed in front of him, and he breathed hard as he huffed across the hallway and into the adminstrative suite. The anteroom was deserted. All of the secretaries were at the staff meeting. "Vicki?" he called very loudly. There was no response. "Is anyone here?" he shouted. His anger grew out of proportion to the inconvenience. When no one answered his wail, he looked around, and saw that the door to Kilner's office was ajar. He stormed into the room. "Kilner?" Again, no response.

He stomped to Kilner's desk and looked for a piece of note paper. He wanted to leave a message for the little son of a bitch, telling him that he'd finish the charts when he was good and ready. He found none, but instead saw a file on the desk labeled with Melora Peltier's name. His rage drained; he was again deflated and listless. Staring at Melora's file on Kilner's desk more clearly focused his mind. Karp was thoroughly convinced that he and the others had been censured in order to benefit the practice of another Compton doctor.

Karp looked at his watch. It was twelve twenty. The lunch hour was well underway, but the meeting was probably only five or ten minutes old. They never started on time. Nobody would be coming back to this suite for at least a half an hour, so he put down the shoes and opened Melora's file. Maybe there was something in it that would help.

The front cover was her letter accepting a position at Compton Memorial and requesting an application form for privileges. This was followed by a congratulatory letter from Greenley, and her completed and approved request for privileges. There was a followup report by the chairman of the Ob-gyn Department, and an approved reissue of the initial privileges. Next was a two page letter from Dr. Simons regarding the alleged insufficiencies in Melora's surgery. There were some notes from an administrative meeting, culminating in a recommendation for review as deemed necessary by the QA Committee. The next page was a letter signed by Kip Porchette noting that the QA Committee had reviewed the charges brought up by Dr. Simons. It recommended that a formal independent third party review be performed. Kilner had written on this letter, "Have Hanson," the Ob-gyn chairman, "call MedCo." There were no other documents in the file.

Karp looked at the contract between the hospital and Melora more carefully. As he did, he felt a stab of self-consciousness. He was violating a privacy by invading someone's personal

228

records. He glanced around the room to make sure no one had returned early from the meeting. Satisfied he was still alone, he again snuck a peek at his watch, and then started reading over the contract. It was similar to his own, as he remembered it. The difference between Melora's monthly expenses and the generated paid billing would be borrowed to Melora Peltier as a loan, due in three years from the signing date and payable over a period not to exceed twelve months.

He read through the rest of the contract, and reviewed the last page to see if Melora had signed the deed alone or if Jane Valvano, her partner, was also a signatory. It was Melora alone. At least Jane was not liable if Melora went down the tubes. On the bottom left hand corner of the last page was a small, handwritten notation that read "DF 7/93 500-1000." He recognized the handwriting as being similar to Greenley's signature. He knew that the date referred to the previous month. The rest of it made no sense to him. He looked around the desk, found a pen, and copied the inscription on the sole of his OR shoe.

Karp closed the file and looked around the desk to see if there were any other doctors' documents in the open. There were none. He checked his watch. Twelve thirty five. He walked over to the doorway and peered down the hallway, just to be certain he was alone.

He returned to the desk and sat down in Kilner's chair. He began with the lower left drawer, opening it and looking for files. There were some administrative personnel charts there, but nothing on physicians. The drawer above contained papers on the hospital security and telephone systems. The contents on the right side were of little more help. He looked around again. There was a credenza behind him, so he turned the chair around and began rifling through the drawers in it. Tucked into the back corner of the far right hand side drawer was a file labeled with his own name. He plucked it from the cabinet and began working his way through the papers.

This file was a great deal thicker than Melora's. In addition to the background information, Karp found copies of the formal review and minutes from several QA Committee and MEC meetings. There was also a signed contract between him and Compton Memorial Hospital signed by Hank Greenley. Similar to Melora's, there was a notation at the bottom that read "DF 7/93 1000-1500," although the numbers were crossed out. Underneath it, Greenley had written, "750-1000?" This was apparently added at a later date. Karp copied the message on his shoe, closed the file and carefully replaced it in the same location in the drawer.

He looked through the rest of the drawers, but found no other files. They weren't all stored here, he deduced, so Carver and Bullock's charts had probably been replaced with the rest of the medical staff's once their situations had been resolved to the taste of the MEC. He was getting a little more anxious about the time, and he stole another look at his watch. It was only twelve forty. He examined the desk again, and found nothing that had any obvious bearing on himself or the others. Kilner's briefcase was on the floor, just beside the credenza.

Karp pulled himself, still on the wheeled chair, toward the briefcase. He picked it up and placed it on his lap, hoping that it would be unlocked. He worked the two latches simultaneously, and they snapped to attention. He lifted the cover, and found himself perusing Dan Kilner's personal papers. Tucked in the case along with the papers was also a pair of reading glasses, an appointment book, and a small blue plastic case for transporting computer disks. He opened the case. There were four disks in it. Two were unmarked and had no labels. One was labeled "active data." It was the fourth disk that piqued his curiosity. It was labeled "DF," similar to the notation on his and Melora's contracts. He removed this disk from the case and turned toward Kilner's computer.

He disabled the screen saver and ran a directory of the disk. He clicked the pointer on "Open a File" from the menu, looked at the names of the various files, and settled on `accounts.wks.' He wanted to know what accounts would be tied to the notations on the contracts. A menu popped onto the center of the screen, reading, "Password Please:_____." As Karp could not know Kilner's access code, he instead chose to close the file. He tried several other files on the disk, all of which gave him the same result.

He looked at his watch. It was not quite a quarter to one. He looked first at the desk, then at the credenza, where he found a package of computer disks. He extracted a fresh disk, and then instructed the machine to copy Kilner's disk onto the blank. It took two minutes. Karp quickly returned Kilner's disk to the bottom of the blue plastic carrier in the briefcase, and replaced the case next to the credenza. He slipped the copied disk in his shirt pocket and collected his shoes from atop the desk.

As he left the administrative offices, he realized that his pace was swift. His heart was still pounding after having violated Kilner's private office, and he was certain he had heard someone talking in one of the side offices as he walked by, although he saw no one. He continued quickly through the hospital corridor, and into the warm sunshine, making his way toward the doctors' parking lot. He glanced over his shoulder to see if anyone was following him. He was alone.

Karp found his car keys and briskly started the Stealth with a fluid motion, closing the car door as he switched the ignition. The engine responded smartly. His movement out of the lot was swift, all the time avoiding suspicious tire spinning. Once he was a few blocks from the hospital and convinced that there was no one following him, he relaxed a bit. The drive back home seemed endless, and he stepped quickly out of the car, closing the garage door behind him without stopping. The flashing red light on his answering machine caught his eye. Shit, he thought. Someone saw me. Now they're calling to ask me what I stole from Kilner's office. He approached the machine and pushed the trigger button to replay the call. Fuck them, he thought. I didn't remove anything from the office, only copied data. They'll never know what's missing, and I'm sure as hell not going to tell them.

231

The tape whirred as it rewound, snapped to a stop, and began to replay. Lon's voice came on. "Hey there, Jerry. Sorry I missed you at home. I hope you're all right." He paused for a moment. "Listen, I have some news for you. Give me a call. I'm at home. Bye." The machine clicked off. He wondered what could be happening, so he dialed his friend right away. The phone rang three times, which was unusual because he knew their apartment was awfully small. "Hello?"

"Hi, Lon. It's Jerry. What's up? Take the day off?"

He sighed. "Sort of. I quit."

"Quit? Why?"

"I was afraid this would happen, old man. With you out of the office, Boren decided to cut my hours to twenty per week."

"Damn. No way a man can make it on that."

"That is for sure, amigo. I'm afraid I lost my temper."

Karp felt discouraged once more. "I'm really sorry, Lon."

"Jerry, you have no control over what happens at Boren's office. I don't consider you responsible."

"It's just that...well, we go back a long way. I wish this didn't have to happen."

"Me too, Jerry." Neither man knew what to say for a beat. "Listen, Angie and I thought this might happen. It's why we made plans to leave in the first place."

"I know."

"We're going to go right away. I don't see any reason to hang around here. The movers are coming tomorrow. We don't have much to take. Can we get together tonight? I thought we might have a little sendoff dinner."

Karp found himself fighting back a tear. "You bet, Lon. What's your choice? Mill Race? The Twin Door?"

Morrissey laughed. "Karpy, I don't think either one of us can afford high living just now. How about Harrigan's? Fine cuisine and quality beverages at a working man's price."

Karp grinned. "Or non-working men."

"Right. Seven o'clock."

"I'll be there."

232

He hung up, and wiped his eyes. He was going to miss his best friend. He sat down and just stared out the window for a couple of minutes. There was a bird on the feeder that Val kept filled in the backyard. It was nearly empty, and he knew that he missed Val just as much as that bird did. With Lon pulling out of town, Karp felt completely alone. He'd lost everyone and everything he loved in life. He stood up quickly and marched upstairs to his study.

Karp flicked on the computer and inserted the disk. He tried to access the files on the disk using several computer programs, and even attempted to alter the file attributes within the operating system, but he was unable to open the password protected files. He held his forehead in his hand and thought about what to try next.

All at once, he remembered the computer whiz he'd seen at the clinic the day before. He stood up and walked over to the bedroom. Unable to remember if he'd left the business card in his shirt pocket or if he'd placed it in his desk drawer in Lisle, he checked the dirty clothes hamper. He looked at several shirts, then extracted the blue short sleeve dress shirt he'd worn. There, in the pocket, was a single white business card. "Avery Prater," it read. "Prater Computer Consulting Services, your personal and business computing source." He went back to the study and dialed the number.

After two rings, the phone was answered by a recorded female voice. "Thank you for calling Prater Computer Consulting Services. At the sound of the tone, please leave your name and telephone number so that we may return the call as soon as possible. Thank you for leaving a message."

At the tone, Karp tried to explain his situation. "Uh, hi. This is Dr. Karp. We met yesterday in my office. I have a disk with some password protected files, but I, uh, forgot the password. I was wondering if..." Before he could finish, there was a click.

"Hi, doc. It's me, Avery."

"Mr. Prater. Thanks for taking the call."

"No problem, doc. I was just eating lunch and left the autopilot on for a while. Lost your password, huh?"

"I'm afraid so."

"Well, don't worry. I've got just the program to help out. Can you bring the disk over to my office?"

Karp cruised around the Elgin address that was listed on Prater's card looking for a parking space to put the Stealth. He stopped in front of an open meter a block down the road. It was a marginal neighborhood, but the afternoon sun was full. Karp felt comfortable enough leaving his soon-to-be repossessed car locked while he met with Prater.

He flew up two flights of stairs to Prater's office, too excited to wait for the elevator. The soles of his shoes clicked along the heavy stone flooring, cracked here and there with age. The hallway was lit only by incandescent fixtures that had to be forty years old. The bulbs weren't much newer. It was ironic, he thought, that a high-tech computer consultant chose to house his business in this antiquated building.

At the end of the corridor Karp found a small plaque labeled "Prater Consulting" next to an old wood door. The transom window above the door was open. As he opened the door, the first thing he noticed was the strong scent of cigarette smoke. The lobby was sparsely decorated, with a dingy still life print on one wall and two dark orange occasional chairs surrounding a small end table. There was a door separating the lobby from the remainder of the office, and it was open wide. No one sat behind the glass partition that separated the receptionist from the lobby. Karp walked over to the open doorway and listened. He heard someone inside tapping away at a computer keyboard. "Hello?" he called gently.

"Dr. Karp," answered Prater, as he appeared from one of the doorways beyond the lobby. "Come in, come in."

They went into Prater's inner office. Only a small table lamp lit the room, along with the blue gray glow of a computer screen.

Clearly the center of attention, Prater's machine was large and wired to more peripherals than Karp could identify. The table on which it rested was clean, except for half a dozen computer disks and a well used ashtray. The large desk along the far wall of the windowless room was covered with various papers and magazines.

"So, you forgot your password," said Prater, sizing up Karp, who only now realized how disheveled he looked. Unlike his attire at his own office, he wore khaki colored casual pants and a button down shirt without a tie. He was perspiring a bit, both from his trip up the stairs and from anticipation over the data on the disk. He hadn't shaven that morning, so he wore a scruffy beard.

Karp rubbed the short, brown hair on his chin. "Yes, I did." He plucked the disk from his shirt pocket. "I tried to pull it up and nothing came to me." He handed the disk to Prater.

The computer expert looked at the disk. There was nothing special about the black plastic device.

"I can't believe I forgot my own password," Karp repeated slowly, worried that he wasn't convincing enough.

"Not to worry," said Prater, as he slipped the disk in his computer drive. "It happens all the time." Without a pause, he reached over for a lit Camel, and took a drag. "I shouldn't have a problem here. You know," he continued as the disk drive whirred, "I worked on security system design protocols for the government. They're quite paranoid about having hackers log in to their equipment."

"I guess it's their business to be paranoid."

Prater laughed. "They're assholes," he said. "They don't know a goddamn thing about how computers work, but they're too proud to ask." He took another drag off the Camel, and replaced it in the ashtray just before the long ash fell into his keyboard. "One time they called me when they forgot their passwords." He took his eyes off the computer screen and wagged a finger toward Karp. "Not just the passwords to a few disks, mind you, but to the whole frigging system. Couldn't turn

235

on their computers." He shook his head and returned to the keyboard. "Morons. One day I don't have adequate clearance to work in their offices, the next I'm the only person--civilian or otherwise--who can fix their fuckup."

The computer beeped, and Prater entered a few more characters on the keyboard. It beeped again, spun the floppy disk, then stopped.

"Sorry to run on like that," explained Prater. "I just can't trust those types. That's why I quit working for them, canceled the contracts."

The computer beeped again.

"They keep coming back, though. The U.S. Army intelligence department is now my biggest customer." He smiled, "They even gave me high security clearance." He turned in his seat toward Karp. "Your password protected files now have no password. Want to look at them?"

"Yes," he answered without a pause.

Prater looked at the directory of files. "Spreadsheets, mostly," he observed. "Let's open them up," he added slowly, typing instructions for the machine to follow.

The screen flashed and opened up a grid of data. There was a column containing a list of surnames that Karp recognized as those of the physicians in Aurora. The next column listed numbers, varying from five hundred to fifteen hundred. This was followed by a series of dates. The two men looked closely at the screen as Prater scrolled up and down the list. He peered at Karp for a moment, then opened another of the files. It listed the names of several banks with account numbers and a list of dates, transactions, and balances. The numbers were substantial. They scrolled along the list, and Karp quickly added up several hundred thousand dollars.

Prater looked at Karp, to see if he could read any reaction. Karp just stared at the screen, breathing through his open mouth. "Lot of money here," he concluded. Karp said nothing. "I guess my mom was right. I should have been a doctor."

"Open another file," said Karp, wholly immersed.

"This looks pretty important," said Prater. "As long as the security lock is opened, why don't you go over this on your machine at home?" He closed the file and ejected the disk from his computer. "You do have a computer at home, don't you?"

"Of course," said Karp.

"Doctor, this isn't yours, is it?"

Karp realized that Prater didn't have to be especially intuitive to come up with that. "No, it isn't," he answered quietly.

"It looks to me like somebody is piling up stacks of dough, doc. Are you involved in this?"

"No," said Karp honestly. "Not directly."

Prater plucked his cigarette from the ashtray and turned toward the doctor. "Look, part of my business is knowing when to pay attention to information and when to ignore it. I get the impression that I should ignore what I just saw." He handed the disk to Karp.

"I'd appreciate that." He replaced the disk in his pocket.

Prater exhaled a line of smoke. "Doc, you seem like a nice guy to me. You're sure you're not involved in this, right?"

"Positive."

"So we can't be sure about whose bank accounts we were just looking at, can we?"

"No."

Prater decided that Karp had discovered something he wasn't supposed to. He didn't impress him as someone likely to steal money from others. Karp did look like someone in a shitload of trouble. "Why don't you look at those files some more on your own. If you decide that you need more help, call me."

Karp nodded.

"Maybe sometime I can help you get more information about those files."

"You probably shouldn't," was all that Karp could think to say.

Prater savored the taste of his Camel, then snuffed it out in the ashtray. "Doc, sometimes little guys can get caught up in shit. I told you, I don't trust the fellows in charge."

237

Karp said nothing.

"If that's what's going on, well, I don't mind lending a hand."

"I appreciate that," said Karp, not sure that he should involve anyone else. He'd already stolen the disk, and he couldn't be sure that the spreadsheets it contained weren't legitimate hospital accounts.

"Fair enough. Take your disk home. Keep in touch."

Karp sat in the waiting room at the law offices of Langworth, Otis, Anthony, and Van Oast, its marble floors looking rich and well established. He read a Time magazine article on the mania created by health care reform proposals. He was particularly fascinated by a sidebar article about a pediatrician in Vermont, so fed up by the changes in his practice that he'd quit medicine and opened a pet store. His income had dropped, but his ulcers healed over in only a few weeks, so he never regretted his decision. Karp wondered when he would begin to sleep well at night.

"Dr. Karp," said Leach, emerging from the doorway to the back offices. "How are you doing today?"

"I've been better, Rick. That's for sure."

They convened in a large conference room just inside the doorway. The heavy mahogany table had room to seat at least ten conferees, and the puffy leather chairs reminded him that his legal fees would be considerable. "I can imagine. How are things at home?"

"Quiet," Karp answered. "Very quiet. Val left last night."

"I'm sorry," the attorney said softly.

Karp shrugged. "I can't say that I blame her. We had to put the adoption on hold," he continued, looking at the floor. "The agency wasn't too pleased, but..." He paused for a second to clear his thoughts. "Time is of the essence, Rick. I've got to get back to work, and then put my life back on track."

"Fair enough," said Leach. "I have yet to receive a response from the Medical Board. Unfortunately, we won't be able to do much about your license until we get their files."

"I know."

He crossed his hands on the table top. "Tell me about the information you mentioned. Something about Compton Memorial Hospital?"

Karp nodded. "Right. You know how this all seemed so arbitrary and aggressive on their part."

"I can't argue with that, Jerry."

"Hasn't it struck you as odd, Rick? How often have you seen a hospital go after one of its own as relentlessly as Kilner and Harmon have gone after me?"

"I've never seen anything like this before. I've been involved in malpractice cases, and doctors will frequently turn their backs on a colleague in order to save their own skins when a case looks like it's going to turn bad on them."

"But this is no malpractice case," Karp pointed out.

"That's true."

"And then there's Billy White. Obviously, he stands to benefit with me out of the picture."

"And you think he and Kilner are working together."

"I've felt compelled to link my situation to what happened to Bruce Carver and the others."

"I know. Your conspiracy theory."

Karp reached into the manila file folder he had brought and extracted several papers. He handed the first one over to Leach. It was a table, consisting of the names and numbers that he had first seen on the computer with Avery Prater. "I found this today. It's a list of doctors' names."

Leach examined the form. "Okay. What are the numbers?"

"I'll get to that," Karp answered. He pulled out a second page, identical to the first except that he had added the specialty and the address of each doctor in another column. "What do you notice here?"

He read over the form. "I'm not sure. Tell me."

"See how the addresses are all the same. Look here. There are three otolaryngologists on this list. They work together. There are five orthopedic surgeons. They're in the same office. Three gynecologists. One group."

Leach nodded. He rested his head in his hand. "Um-hmm." He seemed disinterested. Karp was wasting his time. "What about the numbers in the column?"

Karp smiled. "I'll get to that. Look at this." He handed Leach another paper. "This shows the number of inpatients admitted to Compton Memorial Hospital by every doctor on staff, based on a quick walk through the wards that I did today."

Leach looked up at his client. "What were you doing in the hospital?"

"Walking through the wards," he answered with a smile. "Counting admissions."

"Some doctors have admitted a lot more patients than others."

"Exactly. When you compare lists, you'll find that the doctors on the first list have a whole lot more hospital patients than the others."

Leach looked at the numbers again. "By a wide margin, I'd say." He looked across the table at Karp. "Just what does this mean?"

"In a minute." He handed Leach another spreadsheet, with the bank accounts and balances.

"There's a lot of money here," he observed.

"That's right. Here's what I think we're looking at: The first list is a group of doctors who have somehow agreed to network their services and keep their patient referrals within an elite group. That means that there's plenty of work for them, less for outsiders."

"And that explains why some docs have a lot of hospital admissions, and the others don't?"

"Right."

"And the bank accounts?"

"I think that these accounts are hiding large sums of money somehow generated by this little agreement. I think the numbers on the first page are monthly payments. The balances are the accumulated money paid in."

Leach looked at the documents again. He shook his head. "Why? If they just want to funnel referrals, there's no reason to kick in money. Why bother?"

Karp shrugged. "I'm not sure," he admitted. "Maybe it's insurance...that no one will refer out of the network."

Leach shook his head. "That's a lot of money to pay just to buy silence," he said. "It's an interesting theory, Jerry. How does the problem with the State Medical Board tie in?"

"I can't explain that."

Leach grimaced. "Is this all you have?"

"There's one more thing." He extracted from his file the notes he copied from his file and Melora Peltier's. "These notations were on some papers in my file and Dr. Peltier's. See the letters `DF?'"

"Yes."

"The source for the tables I just showed you was labelled `DF.'" He let that sink in for a minute. Leach showed no reaction whatever. "I think that indicates that Melora and I were to have been added to the lists I just showed you. We would have been asked to contribute the dollar amounts you see here. For whatever reason, they changed their minds. I think the same thing happened to Bruce Carver."

Leach nodded. He didn't believe a bit of this. "Where did you get this, Jerry?"

He sat back in his chair. "From a computer disk," he said.

"They gave you this information on a disk?"

"Uh, no. I found it."

"Where did you find this, Jerry?"

"In a briefcase. In Dan Kilner's office."

Leach took hold of the armrests on his chair. "I presume Mr. Kilner doesn't know that you were looking through a briefcase in his office, does he?"

"Not exactly."

Leach sighed deeply and sat forward. "Just what were you planning to do with this?"

"I hoped that it would be sufficient to hand over to the authorities. An agreement to pay money in return for patient referrals would be collusion. It might even be Medicare fraud."

"Jerry, rifling around in someone's personal office is an illegal search and seizure, and probably also breaking and entering. Any investigation that follows an illegal search would yield evidence that can never be heard at trial."

Karp paled, quivered, and looked out the window. He examined the buildings visible from their vantage point on the thirtieth floor of the Midwest Banking Center building and sighed.

Leach read over the documents some more, then set them down. "I've got to be honest with you, Doc. I don't think that the actions against you are justified. At best, a slap on the wrist might be in order, but losing your privileges, your license..." He shook his head. "Excessive. Unnatural. Unwarranted." He set his hand down on the table to emphasize his point. "We are going to set the licensing problem straight within a couple of weeks. Can you hang on that long?"

Karp stared off at the buildings. He nodded vacantly.

"How about your wife. Do you think that situation is salvageable?"

Karp shrugged, closed his eyes. "Hard to tell. I think it really depends on whether or not we'll be able to complete the adoption." He regained eye contact with Leach. "I don't think that's going to be a financial reality, even if I get my license back soon. You know that I filed my Chapter Seven papers."

"I was aware of that."

"Social workers aren't well impressed by bankruptcy. I think that's going to end the adoption. I'll just have to give Val time to get over that."

"I wish I had an easy answer for you," empathized the lawyer.

"I don't expect one," said Karp.

Leach gestured toward the documents, now piled neatly in the middle of the table. "As for these," he said, "I'd forget them. If you had come by this information legally, I would tell you the same thing. Either way, it's not admissible. No officer could follow up based on this."

Karp sighed.

"Forget this, Jerry."

"I'll try."

Leach sat forward. "Try hard. It's in your best interest."

He nodded.

"The last thing you need is to get arrested for breaking and entering. That won't look good before the Medical Board."

He nodded again. "Okay."

"Mr. Peltier." The voice was a cold monotone. The dentist stood and approached the service desk. His ass stung from the hard bench he had been sitting on for over an hour. His back didn't hurt at all, though. It seems there was an advantage to the shitty furnishings in prison after all.

He placed his hands on the desk. "Yes, ma'am."

She reached into a shelf under the desktop and extracted a plain white envelope. Without a word, she folded the paper before her in thirds, then stuffed it gently in the envelope. "Here is the birth certificate copy you requested, sir," she said without even looking at him. She was the consummate civil servant.

He grabbed the envelope and jammed it into his coat pocket. He owed her no further social amenities, so he quickly turned and left the room. He was going to have to hustle to catch the five o'clock Greyhound back to Atlanta. If he missed the bus, he might be looking at an unpleasant meeting with his parole officer.

He walked briskly from the courthouse down Third Street toward the bus depot. He was pleased at how easily he obtained the birth certificate. He simply told the court clerk that his half-brother, Larry Evans, had lost all of his personal papers in a house fire and that he was living in Oregon. In order for him to get copies of his other papers he needed to start with a new certified copy of his birth certificate.

The bus depot in Savannah was a congregating place for some of the town's more unsavory characters. There were three shabby looking individuals sitting on the bench waiting for another bus, and one laying on another bench, asleep. The depot smelled like urine and mold. The scent didn't bother him, though, since he had experienced worse in prison.

The evening had become yet another wet one for Karp and Lon Morrissey. As it began, they were all rather sullen. There wasn't much to talk about. The movers were due in the next morning, and most of the apartment had been packed. Karp felt guilty for having incited Lon's problem; Lon felt sorry to see his friend facing the loss of his career and his family.

As the Leinenkugels and Miller Genuine Drafts flowed, spirits lightened a bit. Ryne Sandberg slugged a three-run homer to put the Cubbies up on the Braves, four to two. It was only the sixth inning, but Cubs fans need little encouragement to cheer. The crowd at Harrigan's was up. The little, dimly lit pub was busy, and Karp and the Morrissey's couldn't fight the sheer pleasure of the moment.

"Here, Jerry, I want you to have this," slurred Lon. He handed Karp the keys to his Citation.

Karp looked at his friend. "What? You want me to drive both cars home?"

They all laughed at the joke. "No, Jerry, seriously. Take the keys for me. The Green Hornet is sure as hell not going to make it to Virginia. I don't even want to risk taking it."

Karp pocketed the keys. "So you just want me to leave it in my driveway to leak oil, is that it?"

Lon smiled. "Whatever you want, buddy. If you can use it, drive it. If not, sell it. As shitty as it runs, I'm not sure you'll get

244

that much for it. If you want, split the money with me." He drank some beer. "It'll cost me more in repairs to drive it east than it's worth."

Karp shook his head and stared at the TV screen. The reality of it all hit him again. He was suddenly depressed. Soon enough, Karp would find his own car repossessed and he would probably make use of the hand-me-down. "I'll take care of it for you," he said.

Lon, light headed from the alcohol, put his arm around his companion's shoulder. "Don't sweat it, pal," he said gently. "This is just a setback for all of us. I'll get over it. You'll get over it."

Karp shrugged. He said nothing.

"Things will get back to normal soon enough," Lon went on. "I know it. For now, just keep going. If you hang on long enough, you'll find yourself in the clear one day." He held up his glass, and Karp did the same. They clinked them, and drank up.

Thirteen

It was a cold, dark Thursday evening in November and Ronald Reagan was well on his way to winning his first presidential election. The wind howled as Karp sat huddled in the front seat of a rusty blue Datsun hatchback. The car got reasonable gas mileage, which was a big help to his marginal cash flow. Unfortunately, it had turned out to be a lemon, needing repairs to the electrical and cooling systems no less than five times in the last four months. Now the seat belt relay was broken so Karp had to lift himself off the seat in order to start the car and the goddamn buzzer went off all the time. He was looking forward to spring, when he planned to find a new beater medical student car. In the meantime, he figured he might try to disable the buzzer when he found the time. He glanced at his watch. It was seven fifteen. They were due in about fifteen minutes. The wind gusted, and he noticed a few light flakes of snow. It was early for it to be this cold, even in Madison.

Karp was parked in front of the apartment shared by two of his friends from high school, Paul Carmody and J. Robert "Bob" Wilson. Paul had worked at various jobs to pay his way through six years of business school at the University of Wisconsin. Bob completed his undergraduate work at Iowa State and returned to Wisconsin to attend the UW Law School. Carmody, Wilson, Karp, and a few others from the Homestead High School debate team were still close friends. Like a bunch of jocks, they got together and relived past victories. Karp was finishing his second year of medical school, Wilson his second year of law school.

Wilson was dating the sister of one of his friends from Iowa State. He always said they weren't serious, but their relationship became very clingy. Soon enough, Susie was with Bob almost daily and slept over at least three days per week. She was four years Wilson's senior, and looked every bit of it. Unlike the men, she smoked. She was also able to keep up with them in the drinking department. She had chosen to forego college; her long term plan had always been to work just hard enough to support herself then marry upwards. Her lifestyle included heavy duty partying and some previous dabbling in recreational drugs. She wore her mousy hair long, and could have benefitted from a more creative approach to the scant makeup she wore over her pale skin. Her voice was gritty and her demeanor rough, and neither Karp nor Carmody found her particularly attractive.

To be sure, Karp really didn't care much about who his friend dated. Paul Carmody had a personal stake in the matter, though, since her near constant presence meant she was his roommate, too. She had her own way of cooking and cleaning, which was more or less to allow Paul and Bob to do all the work while she smoked a butt and watched MTV. After almost a year together, Bob decided that it would be best for him to break it off with Susie. Marriage to her was not in his best interest: She was not politically desirable. He told Paul that he would inform her of his decision. Soon.

That was several weeks before. Wilson seemed to lose his resolve when opportunities arose. Susie still slept over, and she still drank beer and smoked cigarettes in the apartment, all very much to Paul's great distress. She was not blind to her status and to Wilson's aspirations, and she seemed to sense that her time with him was limited. She spoke to Paul even less than ever.

Karp had not yet met Val. He was dating a nursing student he'd met at the VA Center. Jill was bright and young, and she didn't care for Susie, either. She was also an observant medical professional. She noticed that Susie's cheeks were slightly more pink, her clothes just a little tight. Her breasts seemed ever so slightly larger. She couldn't be certain, of course, but she was very suspicious. Susie was pregnant. Everyone presumed that Susie would insist that they get married, as she saw Bob as her meal ticket. They decided that Bob probably did not know of the pregnancy, and that they must tell him. Whatever he and Susie chose to do would be up to them. At the very least, though, Bob ought to be a part of the decision making process.

For that reason, Karp sat on the cold vinyl seat of his B-210 as a light dust of snow blew in the wind. The crappy little car tended to overheat its engine if he let it run while parked, and he didn't dare run the battery down on a cold night like this. He waited, shivering, for his friends to get home from late classes. Paul was nervous about talking to Bob alone, especially since Susie tended to arrive at the apartment shortly after Bob. He didn't want a shouting match with her. They agreed that it would be better for Karp to "happen by." They would step out for a couple of beers, and then, away from Susie, share their observations with Wilson.

At seven twenty five the lights came on in the apartment. About time, thought Karp. His fingertips hurt. He lifted his rump from the car seat and turned the key. The starter whined and the engine fired. He sat down, and the infernal buzzer hummed. Karp snapped on the belt, but the alarm persisted. He cursed, shifted into gear, and drove the car around the block. As soon as the temperature gauge registered above the minimum mark, he flicked on the heat. It felt wonderful as it blew on his feet.

After two orbits of the block, he pulled into a parking space in front of the apartment. Susie's Toyota was already there. He parked his car and made his way up the sidewalk. Karp had quit locking the car door, hoping privately that some thief would relieve him of the aggravation of selling the piece of garbage. He rang the bell.

Susie answered. "Hi," he said. "I was in the neighborhood and thought I might stop by."

She said nothing.

He looked past her toward the kitchen. "Is anyone else home?"

"They're upstairs," she answered. "I'll tell them." She left Karp alone in the living room.

A moment later Paul appeared. His face was pasty. He nodded to Karp in silence. Karp wanted a beer. Wilson padded down the stairs a moment later.

"Hi, Robert," said Karp. Wilson bristled. He disliked the formal name almost as much as he did his first name. "I happened to be in the neighborhood." Actually, he had driven across town to join his friends. "Thought I might stop by and get a free beer."

"We're out," said Paul. "Wanna run down to Rudy's?" Rudy's Farmhouse was a tavern just a mile down the road from the apartment.

"Sounds okay," Bob said nonchalantly. It gave him an excuse to have something to eat without cooking for Susie. He and Paul slipped their jackets back on. Bob's baby face peeked out from the fur lined hood of his parka. He looked like a very tall kid. "Be back in an hour or so," he called over to Susie, who sat on the sofa watching HBO.

"Fine," she said quietly. She figured she'd be able to have a smoke while they were gone.

The three left, taking Paul's Ford Maverick. Nobody wanted to hear Karp's Datsun blast the alarm buzzer all the way to Rudy's.

Once there, they ordered a pitcher of Miller. They considered Pabst too blue-collar, despised Bud, but couldn't afford Michelob. Karp poured all the way around. Paul hid his face in a menu. Bob sipped the beer and sat back in his chair, hanging his arm over the seat back. He stared off for a moment, oblivious to Paul's stress. "What in the world brings you to this side of town?" asked Wilson.

"Christmas shopping," returned Karp quite naturally, just as he'd planned it. "Thought I'd check out Eastgate Shopping Center. I haven't any idea what to get Jill for Christmas."

Paul was unusually quiet. Karp thought for a moment, and decided that Paul would never make a segue into the conversation of choice. There was no reason to dance around the topic all evening. "Bob, Paul and I wanted to talk to you tonight about something important."

"You and Paul?" He sounded a little ganged up on.

"Uh, yeah. That's right."

"It's about Susie," said Karp softly. "Have you noticed any changes in her lately?"

Bob thought. "Not really." Wilson's mind was unmatched in analytical skills. He wasn't a great observer.

"We have. Actually, we have and so has Jill."

"She's been, uh, gaining weight," said Paul.

"And her complexion is a bit pinker."

"So?"

There was an uncomfortable pause. They were about to embark on very personal subject matter now. "Bob, has she missed a period?" asked Karp.

"Why? What is this about?"

"We think she's pregnant." Karp finally said it.

"We're really worried, Bob," Paul opened up. "You need to find out. You need to know."

"We only want to be sure that the two of you can decide together how you want to handle this."

"If she's really pregnant."

"She is," Bob said finally.

"You know that?" said Paul, incredulous that his friend had let him become so anxious.

"Yes. She told me yesterday," he said without a pause. He sipped his beer. "Did one of those pregnancy tests. Came up positive." He paused.

Karp didn't believe this story. There's no way he could be so relaxed about this. He didn't know until just now. "Geez," he said. "How far along is she?"

Wilson shrugged. "Don't know. Not far, we figure. Anyway, she's arranged an abortion."

Now Karp was certain that Wilson hadn't known until just now. He was a natural bullshitter. Karp knew how much Susie had planned to make her relationship with Wilson a permanent thing. She would never, ever agree to an abortion that easily. "Look," said Karp. "I don't think either one of us wants to get into your personal affairs. We just wanted to be certain that you

251

don't get caught..." he searched for a better phrase, and wetted his dry tongue with some beer. "With your pants down."

They laughed, quietly and nervously.

The following week, Susie had an abortion. She was a little past twelve weeks along in the pregnancy. She was pretty sick for awhile, and she and Wilson spent a lot of time together. After that, though, she never returned to his apartment. Paul and Karp never saw her again, and after a few more weeks she stopped seeing Wilson.

Jerry Karp guided the Stealth north along interstate ninety to Madison. Once he neared the Capitol exit, he veered off the freeway and headed into downtown. He hated driving downtown in Madison, although it was by no means as bad as Chicago. He made his way down Washington Street, catching intermittent glimpses of Lake Monona between the trees and the buildings. Soon, the buildings became more frequent and the views of the lake less so. He turned left on Blair. It took some time, but he finally made his way through traffic to find a lot near the Courthouse building. The LaFollette Federal Building was across the street, and there he would find the office of Assistant U.S. Attorney Bob Wilson.

Karp couldn't give up the feeling that there was more to his story than Leach thought. Someone could find the truth, he knew, if only they were interested in doing a little digging. Karp had reached the limit of his ability to do that. Bob Wilson seemed to Karp to be just the person to put on this trail. As a member of the U.S. Department of Justice, he could gain access to tax records and Medicare data. The banks would have to respond to his inquiries. The problem for Karp was, could he convince Wilson that there was just cause? He also had to avoid sharing the information he'd stolen from Kilner's briefcase, which might taint the investigation.

Karp wasn't entirely sure about his relationship with Wilson. They had drifted apart after school. Actually, Karp simply moved away and got really busy during his internship. Wilson, too, became more involved in his work. They sent Christmas cards back and forth, and Karp was invited to Wilson's wedding. He couldn't make it, but he'd sent a gift and his regrets. Wilson never sent a thank-you card for the gift, and they hadn't spoken since.

Karp followed the directory to find Wilson's office. It was part of a quad, surrounded by three associate U.S. attorneys. The quad was tastefully decorated, but subdued. There was a flag in one corner, and beside it portraits of Bill Clinton and Janet Reno, smiling upon Karp. The whole place was abuzz with lawyers and their clients working with the federal attorneys. Karp waited patiently, alone.

A half hour after the time that he and Wilson had agreed upon, he was finally invited into Wilson's office. Unlike the drab outer area, the room was wallpapered in a clean, dark green. The desk was large, but plain, and very cluttered. The furnishings were otherwise simple, green vinyl covered chairs with gray metal frames. The wall behind him was decorated with his degrees and honors. In addition, there were photos of Bob Wilson with politically influential individuals that he had met: Ronald Reagan, George Bush, Newt Gingrich, Bob Dole, Senator Kohl, Governor Thompson, Janet Reno, Bill Clinton. Each visage of Wilson showed a toothy smile and a handshake with the celebrity of the moment.

Wilson sat behind the desk, reading a brief. He wore fine wire framed readers, which he was too young to need physiologically. The specs were part of his costume, chosen to help the young man look older. Indeed, Wilson hadn't changed a bit since school. He still had a boyish face, fair skin and fine blond hair. He'd cut the hair shorter since school, but otherwise maintained the same style. He wore a simple gray suit and contrasting red tie that hung perilously close to being too large on his fine, tall frame. His thin fingers flipped pages in a brief as Karp approached his desk.

"Bob," said Karp, as he neared his old friend. "Thanks for seeing me."

Wilson set down the brief, face down, atop a pile of documents. He stood and extended his hand. "God, it's been a while, Jerry." The two men sat down. "I'd ask how things are going," he flashed his well rehearsed spontaneous grin, "but I gather from your call that things aren't going all that well."

"No, you could say that, Bob."

"Val is back in Detroit?"

"Yes. At least until this mess gets worked out. She's had about as much aggravation as she can take."

"I'm sorry to hear that. Tell me again what's happened."

Karp went through his tale of woe, relating how Compton Memorial Hospital had suspended his privileges to perform cataract surgery. He told of Dr. White's involvement, and the exaggerated evidence he'd provided of Karp's alleged incompetence. Then he went on to tell of the State Medical Board's actions, his loss of licensure.

"And you think that this is not deserved," Wilson concluded.

"That's right, Bob. I'm not saying that my work is perfect. No honest physician could make that claim. I've maintained from the beginning that the rate of vitrectomy needed some improvement. I also demonstrated that it was coming down. It's part of the natural learning curve."

"Um-hmm."

"In addition to that, my patients' visual outcomes were consistent with expected results. That shows that their care was not grossly negligent."

"Okay." He removed his reading glasses with one hand and placed them gently on the desktop upside down without folding the temples. His chair exhaled as he sat back in it. "Where exactly do I fit into this, Jerry? What do you think I can do to help you? The issue of hospital privileges is hardly germane to federal law."

Karp crossed his leg, trying to maintain an air of comfort with his old friend. "Well, the problem goes beyond my personal conflict with the hospital. I've spoken with three other doctors who have faced, or are facing, similar actions. All four of us began practicing in Aurora at the same time."

"Really? Go on."

"The first doctor is a urologist who faced disciplinary action almost identical to mine. He fought them hard, and eventually had to go back to a retraining program. The second is an anesthesiologist who was threatened with action, but chose to resign his position at the hospital rather than face the board."

"They told him that there was evidence of his incompetence and allowed him to immediately resign without commenting in his records or the Databank?"

"That's how I understand it."

Wilson made his first notes on a yellow legal pad. "Go on."

"It seems that there has been an issue of financial competitors being involved in each case. The urologist had been associated with another doctor, a senior partner. He'd overheard statements made by the partner's wife about money being spent on his behalf."

More notes. "Couldn't that have been the usual expenses of a partner physician?"

"It could have. He didn't think it was, though."

"And the others?"

"The anesthesiologist was very uncomfortable about discussing this with me at all. He said that it placed his agreement with the hospital in jeopardy."

"I can imagine."

"He didn't deny that there were financial implications."

"That's not very concrete," observed Wilson.

"I know," Karp explained. "It's the best he could do under the circumstances."

"And the other doctor?"

"She's a gynecologist. She is currently being investigated by the hospital for incompetence based on concerns raised by the other competing ob-gyn practice in town."

"And the references to money in her case?"

If Karp described the notations on his and Melora's contracts or the computer disk, he would then be tainting Wilson's evidence gathering. "I have reason to believe that there is some sort of payback to the hospital. This gynecologist and I haven't yet been invited to become involved in the scheme."

"And the others were?"

"The urologist was kicked out before he had the chance. I think the anesthesiologist may have been involved."

Wilson crossed his arms. "Jerry, I'm not sure any laws have been broken here."

Karp held his hands out. "Let's say, for reason of argument, that there is a tacit agreement to limit or eliminate unfriendly competition among physicians at this hospital. There is a pact to keep referrals local, and this money is used as leverage to support the pact. If this involves Medicare recipients, wouldn't that be fraud?"

Wilson wasn't sure. He'd have to review the law. "Possibly. Is that all you're giving me to work on? The possibility of Medicare fraud?"

Karp shrugged. "If I had the hard evidence, Bob, I wouldn't have to come to you as a friend. My lawyer would sue if there were enough, but I just don't have it."

Wilson frowned. "And how do you think this all ties in with the State Medical Board? Are they associated with the hospital, too?"

"I don't know," said Karp, working hard to mask his embarrassment by Wilson's patronizing tone. "I don't think they are. I'm not sure. They haven't complied with our request for documents yet."

Wilson made another brief note. "Umm. They will," he said absently. He picked up a pencil and tapped his front tooth three times. "Well, Jerry, there isn't much here, you know."

"I do."

He pursed his lips for a moment. "If you were anyone else, I'd tell you that I wouldn't waste my time. I seriously doubt that there's anything here for me to find, and less to prosecute."

Karp didn't answer.

He looked Karp in the eye. It was not a friendly glance. "You're my friend. I don't want to see you go down the toilet, especially if there is evidence of collusion." He clasped his hands together on the desk and sat forward. "I'll check into this for you," he said finally.

"I appreciate it, Bob. You can't know what I'm going through here."

Wilson thought he did know. He dealt with criminals every day of his life. While Karp was no criminal, he was now labelled as a professional miscreant of sorts. His reaction was no different than the lawbreakers he saw in his office every day of the week. Denial. Justification. Minimizing the seriousness of the accusations. Blaming others. Eventually he would either deal the offense down or accept the punishment rendered upon him. His offer to help Karp was indulgence at most. Wilson had nothing to lose. "I guess you're right, Jerry, but I am sorry to see you suffer like this." Unless you deserve it, of course.

"Can I do anything more for you?"

"Do you have all of the names of the players for me? I'm not from Aurora, you know."

"No problem." He reached into his jacket pocket and plucked a card he'd prepared with names and addresses. "Here," he handed it to Wilson, who reviewed the details it contained.

"Okay, Jerry. Give me a few days to look into this. I'll try to be unobtrusive."

Karp stood. "Bob, thanks. Really."

Wilson walked to the front of the desk and led Karp toward the door. "Jerry, don't expect too much from this. I'm just going to check out your story."

"Any help is more than I have now."

"If I find anything, I'll call you. If it's more of a civil nature than a criminal one, you can let me contact your attorney. Okay?"

Karp smiled and shook his old friend's hand. "Thanks again, Bob."

257

Wilson patted Karp's shoulder and watched the doctor make his way out of the office quad. Karp didn't turn around as he ambled toward the elevators. He didn't see Wilson shake his head, arms crossed on his chest, as he leaned in his doorway. "Asshole," he said quietly.

Assistant U.S. Attorney Bob Wilson returned to his desk and looked over the notes before him on the yellow legal pad. He wondered how he could justify the expense to the Agency for a pair of FBI men to waste their time on this. Still, there might be a useful angle for him. He picked up the phone receiver, activated the speed dial option, and waited as the call clicked in. The phone rang twice.

"Grant," was the answer on the phone.

"Rollie, amigo. I'm glad you're out in the field working hard," Wilson responded.

"Hey, man, give me a break. You know how pissed off you get when we don't file all of the reports and papers you need. Back off on the typewriter work and I can spend more time in the field."

"Typewriter my ass," he retorted. "You guys have been on computers for years. You think the city cops got electronics?"

"Ha!" he laughed. "They're lucky they got erasers." Wilson and the FBI agents had a special relationship. Most of the attorneys wasted little time with them. They were professional, but little more. Wilson had plans to get out of this job eventually. He had honed his people skills to a fine level. Besides, most of the agents were fun guys. When they weren't on a case, they partied and drank. Wilson enjoyed being among them. The lawyers were okay, but when he wanted to let his hair down, he got together with the Feebs. "So what do you have for me, Bob? Somebody take your parking space?"

Wilson sat back in his chair and put his feet up on the desk. "Actually, I do have a good one for you. How do you feel about a little trip to the south?"

"On the company? Sure."

"Good. I'd like you to visit a town just outside Chicago, called Aurora, to check on a bunch of doctors down there. They might be involved in some Medicare fraud. Something about restricted referral patterns, collusion, that sort of thing."

"Okay."

"I want you to look very closely at the recent activities of one doctor in particular. Jerrold Karp. An ophthalmologist."

"Got it. What did this Karp guy do?"

"For one thing, he just got his license pulled. I want to know why. If he's involved in this Medicare fraud, I want to know that, too."

"Done. We'll probably need to trip down to Springfield to check with the Medical Board."

"Whatever. Just send me a report." Wilson hung up. He rubbed his chin and considered his plan. He wasn't sure about Karp's story, and he knew that no one ever told the truth. He also didn't trust Karp. If there was something going on in Illinois, it would make good press. The medical profession wasn't especially popular just now, and this case might be an excellent springboard for media attention. He didn't like his old friend, Karp, but the good doctor may have just given his career the little boost it needed.

Fourteen

Memorandum To: Assistant U.S. Attorney J. Robert Wilson
From: F.B.I. Agent Roland Grant
Regarding: Investigation of Medical Practices in Aurora, Illinois, including Jerrold M. Karp, M.D.

Summary of Investigation

Compton Memorial Hospital of Aurora, Illinois lost its accreditation by the Joint Commission of Accreditation of Hospitals in 1983. The deficiencies noted at that review have been corrected, and the JCAH reinstated Compton Memorial in 1986. The hospital instituted a Quality Assurance (QA) program, which identified physicians whose medical results were insufficient. These individuals either chose to leave the hospital voluntarily or were subjected to critical review under protocols established through the hospital bylaws.

The accounting procedures at Compton Memorial Hospital are acceptable according the Internal Revenue Service agent who has reviewed their returns. There have been no violations of tax code noted at two routine audits performed by IRS over the last five years.

Reports from the Health Care Financing Administration show that there have been no major coding infractions on Medicare returns. Spot audits show no miscoding patterns or charges for services not performed. The rate of referrals, the rate of selected surgical procedures, and the incidence of complications based on charges and coding is not excessive. Specific data regarding incidence of complications from eye surgery was not available.

Interview with Dan Kilner, CEO of Compton Memorial Hospital: Mr. Kilner was reluctant to discuss details of Dr.

Karp's problems as the case is currently before the Hospital Board. A review by the QA Committee uncovered an unacceptably high rate of complications and inadequate surgical and medical techniques. The review was performed by a third party with no associations to the hospital, Dr. Karp, or other area physicians. Based on this, the Medical Executive Committee suspended Dr. Karp's privileges. Dr. Karp now has the opportunity to appeal the suspension at a hearing before the Hospital Board. Mr. Kilner confirmed that one other physician faced punitive action by the QA Committee in the past two years. That physician is currently taking a fellowship retraining course. He declined to comment on any ongoing reviews by the committee, however.

Mr. Kilner denied suggestions that the hospital is closed to physicians outside of the community. He provided a list of physicians on staff at the hospital who have satellite offices in Aurora, and many who work primarily in Chicago. He noted that Compton's small size precludes the acquisition of certain high tech equipment. Therefore, many seriously ill patients are routinely referred out.

IRS reports on Mr. Kilner disclosed no conflicts or audit alarms.

Dr. Karp has no outstanding lawsuits or malpractice claims pending. He has no police record. He was working with a clinic called the Heartland Eye Group, based in Chicago, up until the time of his license suspension. His previous practice, Jerrold Karp, M.D. and Associates, is a professional corporation in the state of Illinois. Credit records indicate that the company is heavily indebted. Dr. Karp has guaranteed his corporate credit lines personally. Based on this, and his personal debt, he has filed for bankruptcy protection under Chapter 7 of the bankruptcy code. Following our inquiry, the office of the Department of Justice overseeing this filing will formally investigate the Chapter 7 request.

Dr. Karp has had his license suspended by the Illinois Medical Board, pending a hearing. This decision was based on the evidence presented to the Board by an outside physician. There have been no patient complaints or lawsuits registered against Dr. Karp to the knowledge of the secretary at the State Board.

Full documentation and notes to follow this memorandum.

Agent's Assessment:

1. No evidence of harassment of Dr. Karp by Compton Memorial Hospital or other parties. All actions appear to be supported by the body of evidence presented to inquiring parties.
2. No evidence of financial transgressions, tax fraud or Medicare fraud.
3. Dr. Karp has been cited by his hospital and the Medical Board for professional incompetence.
4. Based on unsubstantiated charges claimed by Dr. Karp, must question this subject's reliability and motives. Consider further evaluation of this subject.

Submitted and signed by Roland Grant, F.B.I.

Avery Prater was reading a copy of P.C. Networks magazine and smoking a Camel. The office was dark, as usual, and he was taking a break from his work developing a network of CAD/CAM stations for an architectural office. It was simple, boring work, actually, but the money was good. He perused an article on updates to SoftComp's wireless network system, and shook his head. Exhaling cigarette smoke, he realized this system's design had so many intrinsic errors that it would be practically obsolete in a year. The Department of Defense had him work on wireless LAN's, but they couldn't pass security requirements. The signal was strong enough to be picked up by eavesdroppers, and no password protection is impenetrable for a good hacker. He proved it himself by breaking in to their best protected files.

The computer beeped three warning tones. That didn't take long at all, he thought, only a few days. He put down the magazine and swiveled his chair toward the machine. From the Windows interface, he clicked on a point in the lower right hand corner of the screen where there was no visible icon. Only Prater would know that a mouse click in that spot would activate the software. He was using a variant of a program he had written for DOD, called Tom, for Peeping Tom. It was designed for snooping on other machines. Tom could give Prater access to the data on another computer by reading its hard drive. Of course, he had to be sure that the other computer was not being used: If someone were sitting in front of it, the screen would flash the same data that Prater was reading. That happened to him at DOD, and it was one of the reasons he wasn't working with them anymore.

Prater was very bothered about Dr. Karp. It was his practice to make spot copies of any disks that came into his possession. He liked to know as much about his customers as possible. Karp's demeanor and dress were hardly professional that day. The other doctors' names and bank accounts encrypted on the disk just didn't sit right with him, so he did a little hacking over at Compton Memorial Hospital and at the banks where the accounts were located.

Prater discovered that the ten bank accounts had been opened over the last thirty five years. Each account received regular deposits on a varying basis, always apparently cash, and always less than fifteen hundred dollars at a time. None of the accounts was in the name of any physician or corporate group. The doctors whose names were on the lists had nothing in common other than being on the medical staff roster at Compton Memorial Hospital.

While Prater was no investigator, he wasn't an idiot. He knew that the first rule in such matters was to follow the money.

He used Tom to hack into the bank systems and list the names on the accounts. He then returned to the hospital's computer, but found no matches in the personnel files. He logged on to the telephone company's billing system and found no matches, either. That was interesting: A dozen people, together worth several hundred thousand dollars, yet none had a telephone.

Prater returned to the hospital logs and accessed the medical records files. He searched for the names on his list and found that they were all former patients of the hospital, all deceased. None was older than age twelve when they died. Dr. Karp had discovered a system involving many of the doctors in Aurora who were apparently depositing large sums of money into accounts named after dead children. Taxes would probably be paid on the interest, but the IRS might not chase down children depositing gifts from relatives. Very interesting.

Karp had been very anxious about that disk. The absence of his name from it signalled that he was probably not involved in the scheme. Prater wasn't sure if Karp had been approached about it or if he had just discovered it. Regardless, Karp was in a lot of trouble, so he snooped around the hospital some more to see if Karp's name came up anywhere. He found in accounting that Karp owed the hospital a fair piece of pocket change, about a hundred fifty thousand dollars. His name also popped up on an administrator named Kilner's computer in association with legal issues stemming from a Quality Assurance review. The hospital's lawyers had been consulted in a memo about Karp's surgical privileges.

So Dr. Karp, who owed Compton Memorial Hospital a substantial sum of money, had uncovered some link between the hospital, several physicians, and a large cache of money. Now he was under investigation for his hospital privileges. The whole thing smacked of impropriety, and if there was one thing that Prater had come to hate, it was the abuse of power. He looked for other documents in Kilner's computer that mentioned Karp's name, and found a memo regarding a site visit and interview from two FBI agents named Grant and Ellison. They had asked questions about Karp and financial matters. It wasn't obvious why the agents had talked to him or whether they were aware of the bank accounts.

Prater's tenure with the Department of Defense had allowed him to learn a great deal about the federal government's computers and security systems. He dialed the DOD link and logged in with a false security code. Next, he accessed the FBI databases and pulled up information on all FBI agents named Grant. There were sixteen. He did the same for Ellison. There were two. Only one pair matched up at the same office, Roland Grant and Frank Ellison of Madison, Wisconsin. After finding no files there with Karp's name, he set Tom to monitor the agents' computers. When the name appeared, the computer in Prater's office beeped its warning.

He flicked the invisible icon to activate Tom, and read over the report filed by Grant to the U.S. Attorney's office. This wasn't good, he thought. They missed the story. Prater took a draw from his Camel, disappointed at his country's law enforcement information gatherers. They weren't able to obtain information as well as a small town doctor and a darn good computer hacker. Prater was particularly troubled about two facts. First, the charges against Karp were trumped up. Second, because the Feebs had stepped in, the Department of Justice was going to fuck up Karp's bankruptcy filing. The last thing Karp deserved was more aggravation from the feds. Avery Prater realized that he had to let Dr. Karp know what was happening at the Madison office of Assistant U.S. Attorney J. Robert Wilson.

Karp sat in the waiting room of the law offices of Langworth, Otis, Anthony, and Van Oast. This time, though, he was not waiting to meet with Rick Leach. He had been summoned to the office by Cameron Gold, who specialized in the branch of law dealing with bankruptcies and financial restructuring. His clients often had particularly difficult cases. They were usually other lawyers who'd overextended themselves or corporate types with multiple personal problems. Karp's case was, for him, quite straightforward. He was bothered by a notice he'd received from the Department of Justice, and he wanted to confront Karp personally. His clients were too often unwilling to open up about all of their assets and legal problems. Some were involved with criminal charges that complicated his job. He feared that this might be the case with Karp.

Gold's thinning hair was combed neatly back over his head. He was thin for his height, and tried to bulk up with twice weekly workouts which he enjoyed little. He was tall, nearly six feet, and dressed in a tailored gray pinstripe suit with conservative pink tie. He wore matching suspenders rather than a belt, looking more like a banker himself than a lawyer. He opened the door to the lobby. "Dr. Karp?" His voice was subdued and to the point.

Karp stood and approached the attorney. He'd shaven this morning, for the first time in several days. He felt that he needed to have a more professional appearance than he had exhibited recently. Leach still had nothing from the Medical Board, and Bob Wilson had no news. He talked to Val the night before, and she was not pleased by the lack of activity in Illinois. She'd been visiting with friends and family, she said. He suspected she was interviewing for a job. There wasn't much for Karp to do these days but to sit around doing crossword puzzles, drink beer, and run the channels on the cable. The money in his bank accounts would not last for long, though, and he could simply not bring himself to think about what he would do when he was broke. "Good morning, Mr. Gold."

Gold opened the file he had already placed on the table in preparation for their meeting. "Doctor, I appreciate your coming to the office this morning. I know how inconvenient this must be."

Karp shrugged. His schedule wasn't exactly full lately. "No problem. What's up?"

"I received this notice," he said, avoiding the direct answer. He showed Karp a letter from the Chicago office of the DOJ which requested a meeting with Karp to review the bankruptcy filing. "This notification came to me as your attorney of record, but a copy will be sent to your home as well."

Karp read the notice. The DOJ logo alone unnerved him. "What's going on?" he asked. "Is there a problem?"

"Probably not," said Gold coolly. "It is a matter of routine for them to review bankruptcy filings. They look for especially large volumes of indebtedness, cases that involve federally guaranteed loans, individuals with criminal backgrounds, and professionals."

"Doctors," said Karp.

"Yes, and lawyers." He gestured to Karp, then himself. "You and I are not supposed to find ourselves in a position to file for bankruptcy protection."

"Okay. So this is common."

"More or less. I was troubled by one point on the letter."

Karp read it again, and seeing nothing that appeared unusual, shook his head.

"You'll notice that there was a copy of this letter sent to an FBI agent named Grant."

Karp saw the reference at the bottom of the page. "CC: FBI Agent Roland Grant."

"Does that mean anything to you, Doctor?"

He shook his head. "No. Should it?"

Gold clasped his hands together and set them on the tabletop. "I'm not sure. You know that I occasionally have clients with peppered backgrounds."

Karp nodded.

"I know a great many of the FBI agents assigned to the Chicago office. I have never heard of Agent Grant."

Karp was confused. "I don't follow you."

Gold leaned forward to study Karp's face. He wanted to see the subtlest sign of a lie. "I called a friend of mine at the Bureau and asked if he knew Agent Grant. Grant is assigned to the Madison office." Karp's face lit up immediately, and Gold knew that Karp was aware of a connection. The son of a bitch had better not lie to me, he thought, or I'll send him out of here in a minute. Leach's client or not.

"Madison," Karp said quietly.

"That means something to you?" Gold observed.

"Yes."

Gold sat back, removing his hands from the tabletop. "As your counsellor, it is important for me to know everything. It is not unusual for DOJ to review bankruptcy filings, but it is unusual for them to notify an out of state FBI Agent." He narrowed his eyelids together. "Tell me what is going on, Doctor."

Karp realized that Gold presumed he had committed a crime of some sort. He sniffed nervously, unsure whether he should be relieved or angry. "It's not what you think," he said in gentle, measured words. "I have a friend who is a U.S. Attorney in Madison."

Gold continued to watch Karp's face for signs of untruth.

"I went to him a few days ago," Karp continued. "I told him about my troubles in Aurora; explained about my privileges and licensure. I told him that I thought there were inconsistencies with my case and coincidences with other doctors who'd had problems with Compton Memorial Hospital."

"Yes?"

"So I asked him to look into it for me."

"To do what?"

"Check it out. See if I was right."

Gold couldn't believe this. "You asked the U.S. Attorney to look into your situation with the hospital? Why would he?"

Karp shook his head. "Because he was my friend." He exhaled hard. "He owed me a favor. He thought there might be evidence of collusion or fraud. If that involved Medicare patients, it would be a federal level offense."

"Medicare fraud."

"That's right."

"Only instead of investigating on your behalf," Gold went on for Karp, "you are apparently the subject of the investigation."

Karp managed a wry smile. "So it would seem."

So far, Gold felt, Karp appeared truthful. A story like that would be too absurd to make up. "Is there any chance, Doctor, that it is you who might be involved in a potentially federal level offense?"

Karp first shook his head, then shrugged his shoulders. "Shit," he said finally. "You and Rick Leach have all the dirt on me. If the State Medical Board has more, you'll have copies of that soon enough. I've maintained that the charges against me are inflated from the outset."

"All of our clients do," said Gold bluntly.

"Is it ever true?"

"Sometimes," he relented. "It's my job to be suspicious."

"It's part of your job," Karp corrected him. "You are actually hired to represent my best interest in this bankruptcy filing. You have all of the facts of my case in your files. All of them. If that's a problem for you," Karp was having an increasingly difficult time hiding his emotions, "just tell me. I'll ask Mr. Leach for another reference to complete the bankruptcy."

Gold held his hands up. "That won't be necessary. I believe you." He spoke honestly. "When we're working with the DOJ, the U.S. Attorney's office, and the FBI, I need to be certain that I have all of the facts. You don't want to lie to these people."

"I haven't, and I haven't lied to you or to Mr. Leach. Or to the goddamn State Board, the QA Committee, or anyone else." His voice crescendoed as he spoke.

"I believe you, Dr. Karp. I do."

"Good," he said more quietly. "When do we meet with these people?"

"I made a tentative appointment for next Tuesday. You'll need to have access to tax returns for the last two years, the Chapter Seven filing, and some basic data referring to your other legal problems. Will that be enough time?"

What else did he have to do? "Yes."

"Then you should have nothing to fear."

"Fine. Are we done then?"

"I think so. Just one thing, Dr. Karp."

"Yes?"

"I'd like to recommend that you avoid discussing this further with your friend in the U.S. Attorney's office. Between you and me, I don't think he's working very hard on your behalf."

Karp could not argue with Gold's assessment. "Agreed."

"Good. If you have anything else that you wish to discuss with the authorities, please run it by me or Mr. Leach first."

"I will."

Karp thought it odd that Prater sounded so concerned on the phone. He wondered what was on his mind, and agreed to meet after he left Gold's office. The drive gave him something to do. There was a place to park right in front of Prater's, so he hoped that his luck was changing. Karp was really pissed off with Bob Wilson. It was unbelievable that his friend investigated him, he thought.

Inside Prater's office, he was greeted with the scent of freshly burnt Camels. Again, there was no receptionist. Karp decided that Prater didn't have one. "Avery?" he called as he walked down the hall to Prater's inner sanctum.

"Dr. Karp," said Prater as he wheeled his chair out of the office without standing. "Come in, come in." He rolled back in and Karp followed.

"What's up? You said that you had something."

Prater reclined in his chair and took a draw from his cigarette. "Doc, I'm kind of embarrassed about this. I mean, I don't want to invade your privacy or anything."

Karp had come to have little privacy left, what with State Medical Board investigators, QA Committee members, and FBI agents all over him. "No offense taken."

"Well, I was kind of fascinated by your computer disk, so I checked out those bank accounts. Did you know that they are all in the names of dead people?"

"What?" Karp leaned forward.

"Dead children, actually." Prater puffed the cigarette again, and blew out blue smoke as he spoke. "It seems that a group of physicians are depositing money in small chunks under assumed names. Do you know anything about this?"

"No. I've heard rumors. Go on."

"I can't be sure why they're doing this but, obviously, it's illegal." Prater watched Karp carefully, trying to read his face. "Again, excuse my snooping, but I understand that you've been having professional problems." There was no response. "I presumed the events were related."

"Count on it." Karp sat back in his chair. "Damn," he said aloud. Billy White was obviously involved in this scheme, too. It was hard to believe, but it was true. "You don't think this is some story, then do you?" he asked, still incredulous that he had found an ally.

Prater shook his head. "You won't believe the crap I've seen. The Department of Defense is full of this kind of shit. Career military hates career politicians, and vice versa. There's more, you know."

"More?"

"Yeah. Only," his voice got soft, "you really can't tell anyone where you got this information."

Karp laughed. "Nobody believes me, anyway. Not my wife, not even my attorneys. I don't know who to talk to anymore." He held up his palm. "You have my word of secrecy."

Prater extracted from a stack of documents the report he had hacked from Grant's computer, and handed it to Karp. "When I saw this," he explained, "I thought I'd better let you know what I'd found."

Karp read the report. The sum total of investigative work that they had done in checking out his story was to look for anomalies in the IRS filings and to ask Kilner if he was involved in illegal activities. "This is incredible," he said finally. He held the paper out toward Prater. "How did you get this? It must be freshly written."

"It is. I can access certain computers. It's, uh, not legal, you know."

Karp grinned. "I know. Your secret's safe with me." He sat back and thought out loud. "What I need is a way to draw attention to what's happening here so that it can be investigated through legitimate channels."

Prater snuffed out the cigarette butt and worked on removing a fresh stick from his pack. "I don't know what to tell you, there, Chief. It seems as if you could walk downtown, pour gasoline on yourself, and," he lit a match for his cigarette as punctuation, "light yourself on fire. From what I gather, nobody wants to believe you."

"God, that's the truth." It occurred to Karp that there was still one uncomfortably loose end. He wasn't sure what the State Medical Board had to gain by screwing him. "Listen, Avery, can you hook up that machine to any other computer?"

"Well, no. It would have to be one connected to a phone line or to a system with access to a phone line."

"Right. But if it were, you could get on?"

"I've yet to fail."

"You know that the State Medical Board fucked me over by pulling my license. I can't figure out why, but I suspect they have ties with this money scam. I wonder if you could find out for me."

"You mean log on and look around their files."

"Yeah, that's it."

He shook his head. "I can, but it would be dangerous to do that by day. I can get in, but they would know I'm there."

"Damn."

"I'll tell you what I can do, though. I can log on and alert the computer to buzz me if a specific word comes up: Your name, whatever. That's how I found the FBI report. I just flagged the machine to beep when your name was typed in. If nothing comes up, I can snoop around after hours. No one will know what I'm doing then."

"Jesus, that would be great. You could call me if you find anything. No need to generate papers."

Prater tapped some ashes into a soda can. "I get the impression that you can use the help, Doc. Consider it done."

The few moments of elation Karp had enjoyed with Avery Prater evaporated when he arrived home. There were two late notices for credit cards in the mail and the bank had called and left a message about the car payment on his answering machine. Waves of despair swept the physician up and carried him away. He sat in his recliner, drank beer and washed down a bag of peanuts while watching a ball game.

Roger Clemens was pitching for the Red Sox, and he was having another brilliant night. Karp marvelled at six innings of no-hit ball. He imagined how Clemens felt up there, throwing with all of his might and weight and cleverness before the eyes of thirty thousand adoring fans at Fenway Park. How friendly and homey the ballpark looked, with its freshly cut grass and seats so near to the diamond. How confident Clemens seemed, at the top of his game. Karp felt very, very small. He drank more Genny, and awaited the mind numbing sensation that accompanied his increasing blood alcohol level.

Clemens struck out his fourth for the evening on a called third strike, ending the seventh inning. Almost on cue, as the Keystone beer commercial started up, the telephone rang. Karp flicked the mute button on the remote control, pushed the footrest on the recliner downward, and walked over to the cordless phone. "Hello?"

"Dr. Karp. It's Avery."

He lit up. The voice of a friend. He flushed for a moment realizing how much he missed Lon, and it had only been a few days. He smiled, realizing he probably missed Morrissey more than he did Val. "Hi, Avery. What's up?"

"I left the line in the water all day," he said, "but I got no bites. So I went exploring on my own."

"Did anything pop up?"

"Yes. Found you in the system. Also some guy named White."

"Mother fuck," he said. "I knew it."

"Turns out that White made a pretty substantial donation to Senator Schilling's campaign. The good senator used his contacts to suggest the kind of attention this matter should receive."

"That's documented?" Karp asked, finding it difficult to believe that bureaucrats would be that sloppy.

"Not in so many words. I filled in some details."

"Well I'll be damned," he said. "Thanks, Avery. I do appreciate it."

"So what are you going to do?" he asked, partly curious and partly worried that the beleaguered doctor might just go to the feds with all of this illegally obtained evidence.

"I'm not sure yet," Karp answered. "I can't just go drop this on someone's desk. It can't be used in court."

Prater found that reassuring.

"I'll just have to figure out some way to get the authorities, on the right track. I have to draw attention to this."

"I agree."

Karp chuckled. "Now all I need to know is how to do that."

"Good luck. I'll keep my eyes and ears open for you."

"Thanks." They hung up. Karp wandered around the kitchen for a while, trying to decide whether he was hungry enough for dinner. He wasn't, so he returned to his seat in the living room and turned off the mute. There was a runner on first, apparently following a base on balls. The count was oh-and-two and Clemens wound up, then fired a heater toward the plate. The batter nailed it dead on, and the camera returned to Clemens as he watched the dinger go into the stands behind left field. Red Sox down, two to one. Karp smiled. At least he wasn't the only one having a bad night. The manager came out of the dugout and signalled for a reliever right away.

275

Karp felt his blue funk grow deeper and deeper. The game broke for commercials while the new pitcher warmed up, and they played a credit card commercial showing a loving young couple vacationing on some beach. He thought about the trip he and Val had taken for their honeymoon, to Aruba. That commercial was quickly followed by a tire ad showing a baby floating around in a well treaded, new tire. The baby giggled and cooed and spun in the rubber ring. Karp thought of the child he would never see or hold or raise, and he felt even more alone.

Between tidal waves of blue, he ran over the events of the day again and again. His mind kept playing over Avery Prater's statement about Karp lighting himself on fire. He wished he could do just that right now, and poured down more beer while pretending to pay attention to the ball game.

Slowly, not all at once, he developed a plan. The fire concept reverberated in his mind, and he kept thinking about tearing apart Kilner's office. First he thought he might just drive the Stealth into the wall and let the firefighters and cops examine the rubble for evidence. That didn't make sense, though, because there would be no reason to search for clues; no foul play. A fire made more sense because there would be an arson investigation.

But, fire might burn up the evidence he wanted them to find. A bomb, though, without the fire, might accomplish just the effect he wanted. There would be an investigation as to why that office had been bombed, who had done it, and what was the motive. If he parked just outside Kilner's office and blew out one wall, the rest of the room would be thoroughly studied. There was a good chance that someone would find his file, Melora's, and maybe even the computer disks.

Under more rational conditions, he would have certainly sworn off the idea as foolish. By the time he passed out on the recliner, he was convinced it was his only option. He'd lost his career, his family, his friends, and his belongings. By sacrificing himself, he could redirect the authorities to the truth and bring an end to his personal pain forever.

Fifteen

Karp found a dingy little bookstore in Chicago that kept a small selection of books on personal protection, martial arts, weapons and explosives. Among the titles was one that caught his eye: Homemade C-4, The Survivalists' Recipe. He quickly flipped through the book and found instructions on the preparation of explosives from ammonium nitrate--fertilizer--and racing fuel. He purchased the book and read it completely in the front seat of his car.

His next stop was the Farmer's Co-op store. The place carried all sorts of fertilizers, animal feeds, tools and implements. "Can I help you?" asked the clerk, a pleasant looking young woman, maybe twenty two or so. She wore jeans and a pale yellow pullover shirt, with a kelly green jacket bearing the Co-op logo.

"I need some high nitrogen fertilizer," said Karp.

"I see. Is this for your lawn?" He didn't look like a farmer.

"Yes."

"Okay. Did you have any particular mixture in mind? We've got a good turf builder on sale. It's 21-44-8," she said, referring to the composition of nitrogen, phosphorous, and potash. "It's only twenty dollars for fifty pounds, and it works well on fescue and rye grasses."

"I don't know," said Karp, rubbing his chin. "I just want to green up the grass for a party I'm having next week. I was thinking of a high nitrogen-only fertilizer for that."

"Well, we've got a urea spread that's 46-0-0, but that's an awfully lot of nitrogen. You could burn out the grass."

"Hmm," he answered. "I don't want that. What else is there?"

"Two choices. There's ammonium sulfate, which measures 21-0-0, and ammonium nitrate at 34-0-0."

Karp shrugged. "I'll try the second one."

"Okay. How much do you need?"

"I'm not sure. How far does it spread?"

She knew the answer without checking a reference. "Fifty pounds should do about twenty thousand square feet."

"Fine. I'll need three bags."

She grabbed a pen, and began writing up the order. "Wow. That's quite a yard you have," she noted.

"Actually," answered Karp, "I'm going to use some on my lawn at the office, too. That way," he added quietly, "I can write the whole thing off on my taxes."

She smiled. "Well, sir, the twenty seven dollars and forty eight cents should go a long way toward reducing your tax burden."

"Gee, it's not very expensive," noted Karp, as he reached for his wallet.

"No, sir. It also won't keep your grass green for more than a couple of weeks. That's why we generally recommend the more balanced compositions."

Karp nodded. "I see."

She took the money, handed him his change, and completed the receipt. "Your name, sir?"

"If you don't mind, please write the name of my business on the slip, would you? For the taxes."

"Sure."

"Chicago Institute of Ophthalmology. Thanks."

It was a battle, but he managed to load the three massive fertilizer bags into the Stealth. He dropped them off at home, then swung over to the Fox Valley Track, a local dirt track and drag strip where the hot rodders hung out. He took along a two gallon gas can and filled it with nitromethane racing fuel. Although he ended up paying close to seventy five bucks, they never even asked him to sign his name. This all seemed too easy.

By mid-afternoon Karp was back home, playing the role of chemist with the fertilizer and gasoline. Once the proper mixture was obtained, he packed the material into one and two foot lengths of PVC pipe, standard plumbing material. Karp worked in the kitchen all day and well into the evening, eventually creating sticks of varying size and shape. Unlike terrorists who might want to blow buildings up, Karp wanted only to make a hole in the hospital's wall. He didn't want to obliterate the evidence he hoped they would find.

By midnight he was quite exhausted, and decided that he'd better not handle the volatile fertilizer mixture anymore. He packed things up and settled down in bed, reading his handbook of instructions. It recommended using industrial grade detonators, but Karp knew of no way to obtain them. Instead, he planned to use light bulbs whose glass ball had been broken, leaving the filament exposed and inserted in the flammable bomb material. When the circuit was closed, the filament would heat and burn, igniting the bomb. He figured that he could make these out of automotive light bulbs to work off the car's own battery.

The next day, Karp built his igniters. He sealed them into caps and cemented them to the end of the pipe bombs. That evening he worked hard to scrub down the kitchen, taking great care to clean the oven and floor thoroughly. He wanted to leave no traces of the ammonium nitrate behind that police might later discover. It was a moot point, of course, because he would be dead. As he lay in bed that night, drifting off to sleep, he realized that the last two nights were the first in months that he had been able to fall asleep without a single drink. It felt good to be actively involved in something again. It occurred to him that he hadn't heard a word from Leach or Gold, and frankly, he didn't care.

The following day he installed the bombs in the Stealth. He incised the leather seats in the front and back, and stuffed the linings full of one and two foot long pipe bombs. He concentrated his efforts on installing the devices in the driver's seat and under the floorboard. If he was going to die to make his point, he wanted to be sure that the job was successful. As a resident, he'd had the misfortune of caring for several patients who'd tried to end their lives for one reason or another, and failed because they'd not overdosed themselves sufficiently, misaimed their firearms, or inaccurately severed their blood vessels. He wanted to make sure that he wasn't one of those pathetic "underdose" cases.

Before he realized it, the time was close to ten. He'd been working all day planting explosives. He'd put some into the steering wheel by removing the airbag. The fuel tank was ringed with bombs at the undercarriage and from the trunk space, promising a fiery sequel to the explosion. Once again, he'd worked himself to exhaustion, and he called it quits after downing a frozen pizza and a beer.

No one had called him now in three days. There was no word from his lawyers, none from his colleagues, and Val seemed to have given up on him. He was now confident that he had made the right decision. The cost would be great, but if it resulted in discovery of the others' misdeeds, it was sufficient for him. Karp crawled up to his bedroom, flicked on Jay Leno, and fell asleep before the monologue was over.

All at once the telephone rang. The television was still on, and Conan O'Brien was interviewing some bimbo actress. He glanced at the digital clock, and saw that it was one thirty. He wondered what idiot was calling him at this hour. The phone buzzed for the third time as he lifted it from its cradle. "Hello?" he answered, in his learned pseudo-wakeful voice.

"Jerry. I'm glad you're home." The voice was female, rushed, and she was breathing hard enough for him to hear it over the phone line. It wasn't Val.

"Who is this?"

"Melora," she breathed. "Melora Peltier. He's here, Jerry. What should I do?"

He rubbed some sand out of his eyes. "Who's there, Melora? What are you talking about?"

"It's Gaven," she heaved out. "My ex-husband. He's here and I shot him."

Sixteen

Karp always kept several hospital scrub suits at home. They were easy to care for and since they were free, he didn't particularly care about getting blood, vomit, or other excrement on them. He threw on a set of scrubs and ran to the garage. Rather than starting up the explosive Stealth, he took the keys for the Green Hornet, Lon's old Citation. The engine fired and the old car blew a puff of blue smoke. He gave it some gas and it wheezed forward.

Melora managed to explain on the phone that she'd shot her ex- with her stun gun. He was now writhing on the floor of her son's bedroom fighting off a convulsion. Karp squealed the tires taking a corner, not so much because of speed as for the lack of tread on them. He bolted up to her front door, which was open. "Melora?" he called.

"I'm here," came her voice from upstairs. She was noticeably less strained than she had seemed on the phone.

Karp took the stairs two at a time and joined Melora and her shivering ex-husband in Duane's room. There was no blood and no apparent head wounds from the fall. He was breathing, though his respirations were rapid and shallow. Karp looked around the room. The bed sheets were askew, but there was no child. "Where's Duane?"

"I told him to take his sister into my bedroom and wait there. He was pretty shaken up. When he saw Gaven, he shrieked. I grabbed the stun gun and came running."

Karp kneeled down and checked the man's pulse. It was rapid but strong. His color was good. "He's going to be fine. He'll also be awake soon. What do you want to do with him?"

Her voice turned icy. "I want him out of my life. I want him to leave my children alone, forever."

Karp looked again at the former dentist. He wasn't sure how Melora could do that. A term in prison hadn't kept him away, and neither had a restraining order. "Can you get the kids out of the house? Whatever happens here, I don't think they need to see their father this way."

"Okay," she answered. "I'll call my neighbor. I think she'll take them overnight."

Karp looked Gaven over. He was fairly muscular and appeared to be in good health. He was about five foot nine, and maybe one hundred sixty pounds. The food in prison must not have been too bad. Karp decided that it would probably be a good idea to restrain him. He went quickly down the stairs and out to the Citation, where he popped the trunk to get a roll of gray duct tape. Lon knew that driving an older, high mileage car without adequate tools and duct tape was unwise. He slammed the trunk, which shook off a few pieces of rust from the quarter panel, and ran back inside. Once upstairs, he tore out several two foot lengths of the tape.

The kids walked by with Melora, both sniffing back tears. "It's okay," she said, and they started down the stairs. "Everything is fine, and Daddy isn't going to hurt you. I want you to go next door for a little while..." Her voice became more distant, and eventually he heard the door slam closed.

Karp swaddled Peltier's arms behind his back and spiraled tape along the forearms to wrap them together. He removed the man's pants and taped up his legs. By the time Karp finished, the dentist was no longer shivering. His breathing had become slow and regular. He smacked his lips a few times, and groaned. Peltier opened his eyes slowly, and looked around the room. "Fuck," he said with a thick tongue. Suddenly, he jerked awake. He looked around his son's bedroom, seeing no one other than Karp. "Who the fuck are you?" he asked quickly.

Karp looked down at the pedophile. "That's no concern of yours," he answered.

Peltier struggled against his bindings. "I didn't do anything," he said. "Let me up."

Karp didn't answer him. He was thinking about their next move. Should they just turn him over to the authorities? What crime did he commit? Breaking and entering, thought Karp.

Violated the restraining order and maybe jumped parole. Big deal.

"Hey, asshole," said Peltier a little louder this time. "Let me up."

"Listen," snapped Karp. "Keep quiet, or I'll tape your goddamn mouth shut."

Peltier lay still for a minute. He tried to shimmy his arms free, but couldn't.

Karp pondered the situation. The first thing we need to do, he thought, is to get this guy out of the kid's room. Downstairs in the basement would be better. That would give us some space. "Would you like to sit in a chair?"

"Fuck you," he spat.

Karp pulled off a strip of tape about eight inches long. Taking care to leave the nostrils open, he tightly wrapped the duct tape over his captive's mouth. "I warned you." Still on one knee, he leaned forward toward Peltier. "I'm going to help you stand up. You'll have to hop down the stairs. Do you understand?"

Peltier nodded.

Karp held up the index finger of his right hand and held it an inch from Peltier's nose. "Mess with me while I'm moving you," he said quietly, "and I'll toss your sorry ass down the stairs. Okay?"

Peltier glared, his eyes narrowed. He nodded again.

Karp got on his feet, then kneeled down and put his hand under Peltier's shoulder. "Up," he said, and heaved the man to his wobbly feet. Allowing the dentist to balance against him, Karp helped Peltier hobble toward the stairs. With some effort, Karp got him all the way to the basement. He brought a kitchen chair down and used more duct tape to secure him in the chair next to a post. Finally, he allowed himself to take a deep breath to give his head time to clear.

This was a big step. A major change. The whole concept of dealing with the police represented a problem for Karp. His plan required that he maintain a low profile until his last moment. He went upstairs and stared out the kitchen window, into the darkness.

"Jerry?" It was Melora. She came in through the front door, alone. She needed to know that Peltier hadn't overpowered Karp. She was still very afraid of him.

"I'm in here," he called calmly from the kitchen. He stood slowly and approached the foyer. "It's all right."

"Where is he?" she asked quickly.

"I moved him downstairs. He's bound, and he's not going anywhere."

She made a sudden, shallow gasp. She desperately wanted the man out of her house. The only way to accomplish the complete banishment of Gaven Peltier from her life and the lives of her children was to see him executed. Unfortunately, the death penalty was not a sentence presented to pedophiles, even repeat offenders. Calling the police would not solve her problem.

"Melora?" Karp interrupted her thought process.

"Yes."

"I'm going upstairs for a minute. I removed his pants to secure his legs, and I want to look through his pockets."

"Why?"

"I just want to see how he got here. See if there are car keys, plane tickets, whatever. You can wait here."

"I'm going with you," she responded. She did not want to be alone.

The two physicians walked slowly up the stairs. Karp entered Duane's room, but Melora waited in the doorway. Karp studied the room. The spent stun gun lay on the floor with the empty pair of pants sprawled next to it. He picked them up and checked the pockets, where he found a wallet and a set of car keys. The keys were the Chrysler style, with the pentastar logo. There was no key fob, just a bare ring. The wallet was simple, brown cowhide. It had forty three dollars in it. No credit cards. There was a driver's license: State of Georgia, in the name of Lawrence J. Evans. The photo was certainly Peltier.

Karp looked toward Melora. Her hands were crossed in front of her. She bit her lip. "Who's Lawrence Evans?" he asked.

She shrugged. "Never heard of him. Why?"

"That's what the driver's license says. Lawrence J. Evans of Atlanta."

She shook her head. "I don't know."

He threw the pants down on the floor and held the keys out in her direction. "I want to find this car."

"Why?" She contorted her face in disgust.

"I need to know what his plans were. What was he going to do when he was done here? For that matter, what was he going to do here?"

She turned. Karp walked over to her, put his hand on her shoulder. "Melora, it's all right. He's not going anywhere."

She faced him and threw her arms around his neck. "I'm sorry," she whispered. "I've been running from him for years. He's frightened me, hurt my children. I changed my practice to try and get away from him." She paused, squeezed Karp's neck.

He felt her breath behind his ear, smelled her scent. It was sweet and warm. He felt her breasts pressed against him, and for a moment he thought...No, not right. It would severely complicate his plans. He was here to help her and get out.

"I've spent years distancing myself from him, using the courts and the police. They've done nothing for me, and now he's just walked back into my home to threaten my children." She stood back from Karp and took his hands in hers. "Thank you for coming here. I need help to get through this. I don't know what to do."

"Neither do I. I'm very, very confused. That's why I want to try to figure out what it was he'd planned to do. It will help you...help us decide what the next step should be."

She nodded, and turned toward the stairs. She held on to Karp's right hand as they walked slowly back to the foyer together.

"Tell me about the kids," said Karp. "How are they doing?"

"They're two doors down at the McKinney's. Duane and their son, Patrick, are good friends. I'd hoped that being with Patrick would help him stay strong. Liz was feeling all right. She didn't see him."

Karp nodded. "Good."

"I called my mother. She lives in St. Louis, and she'll drive up tomorrow morning to take care of them."

"That will help," he said. They stopped in front of the door.

"Is he going to get loose while we're gone?"

Karp shook his head. "No. If you'd like, go ahead and check him. He's just downstairs, tied to the post."

She closed her eyes. "I don't want to see him." A breath, then, "Would you?"

He smiled. "Yes." He squeezed her hand, and she returned the gesture, lifting his hand toward her mouth. Again he felt her breath. He flushed. They parted, and he made his way down to the basement.

Peltier was just where Karp had left him, securely taped to the chair. There was no slack in the tape; the bindings that connected him to the chair were unerringly tight. He returned to the stairway and stepped briskly up to the kitchen. "Get some rest, Gaven," he said, as he clicked the light off.

Karp went to the front door. "He's fine," he said. Melora held out her hand, and he took it.

"Let's go," she said.

They walked into the front yard. The bluish glow of the mercury vapor lamps was filled in by silver white illumination from the nearly full moon. The evening was cool and clear. There were no cars parked on the street other than Lon's rusty, green Citation. Karp and Melora walked toward it, and he hesitated for a beat, embarrassed by the condition of the old car.

"What's wrong?" she asked.

He stifled the urge to ask what wasn't wrong. "This, uh, isn't my car," he explained. "It belongs to a friend."

"He won't mind that we use it, will he?"

Karp smiled. "No. He gave it to me for a while." He pulled the keys from his pocket. "It's a little rough."

She shrugged, and rubbed his hand. Karp opened the passenger door with a rusty squeak, and she slid into the car. He closed the door and entered the driver's side. He started the car, and it responded with a belching backfire. "Sorry," said Karp.

Melora gave a little laugh. It was the first time Karp could remember seeing her smile, and her teeth and lips shined in the moonlight.

He clunked the car into gear, and they started down the street. They drove around the neighborhood for twenty minutes, but found no strange cars. They began to work their way back toward Melora's house, disappointed. As they turned a corner, the headlights reflected back from a "For Sale" sign in the middle of a front yard. Melora knew that the house was vacant and there had been no interested buyers. She noticed, though, that there was a Plymouth Voyager in the driveway, which she pointed out to Karp.

"Let's check it out." He pulled over, shut off the Citation, and walked over to the Voyager. It was dark red, black cherry colored, with gold zig-zag trim painted on the side. The top was elevated to make a conversion camper, and the windows were darkened with shades. He took the key from his pocket and inserted it in the driver's side door lock. It turned.

Karp opened the car door and looked around. There was a folded Illinois highway map on the passenger seat and several empty soda cans on the floor. The rear seats had been removed, and in their place was a folding bed. There was a cooler and a gym bag on the floor. He opened the bag. There were a couple pair of underwear, some socks, and a few shirts. Not much to speak of. On the other side of the bed, closer to the rear hatch, he saw a shopping bag. He crawled toward it, then peered inside. There were several changes of children's clothes, for a boy and a girl.

Next, he checked out the storage bin under the front passenger seat. It was locked, but he was able to open it using the key. Inside he found an envelope containing the Georgia title for the car, registration, and an insurance card with coverage extended for one month. A second envelope contained a notarized and embossed birth certificate in the name of Lawrence Jeffrey Evans. There was also a social security card and a City of Atlanta Metro Library System card in the same name. One more envelope was in the bin, a large manila one. He opened the clasp. Inside were several stacks of hundred dollar bills, banded together. He counted ten stacks of thirty bills. That was a helluva lot of cash. He replaced the money.

Karp walked back to Melora, who still hadn't gotten out of the Citation. She was peering at him through the open window of the car. "Well?"

Karp nodded. "It's his. He was planning on taking the kids."

"Bastard," she hissed.

"There's also some identification papers in that same name, Lawrence Evans, and a great deal of money."

She looked through Karp. "I always knew that he'd hidden some money away before they took him to jail. I could never find it. I don't want it anymore."

"We ought to get this van out of the driveway. Someone may report it to the police and have it towed."

She looked him in the eye. "You don't plan to turn him over to the police, do you?"

"You said you want him out of your life. Do you think turning him in will accomplish that?"

She shook her head. "You have a plan?"

"Maybe. I want to sleep on it. For tonight, I want to put this van in my garage. Can you follow me home?"

She nodded, and slid over to the wheel.

They drove the two vehicles back to Karp's house. He maneuvered the van in next to his Stealth, and returned to Melora in the Green Hornet. Once again in the sputtering Chevrolet, he headed back to her house. "Take me there," she said, gesturing toward the house of Duane's friend. "I need to check on the kids."

Karp nodded and continued the short distance. The car nearly stalled before he could shift into Park. "Wait for me, please," was Melora's request. Karp, transfixed by her eyes, only nodded. She left the car and he watched her until she was inside.

The night was clear and the moon not yet full. The neighborhood was quiet except for the whoosh of a gentle breeze now audible through the open window of the car. He hung his left elbow over the sill, as if he were on a pleasant weekend drive. Karp felt suddenly invisible, unseen by the judging eyes of his neighbors. He'd been scrutinized at work to an infinitesimal degree, his every action dissected under a microscope of peer review. Too many of his neighbors had heard the rumors. Everyone watched him. Everyone knew.

Tonight Karp felt different. He'd reached a new resolve since deciding to create the car bomb. With the Citation's headlights turned off, the scene was illuminated only by the street lights and the moon. The trees cast long shadows on the street. His eyes had become adjusted to the darkness, and Karp saw the fine details of his neighborhood: The criss-crossed patterns in the cut grass, the reflected glint from clean chrome on the parked cars. He missed the calm sense of family and home, and that part of his identity which was linked to his profession. He missed his work, his wife, and his friends. At least creating his car bomb had brought some meaning to his life. He stared into space, then closed his eyes. He breathed in the night air and sighed.

Karp came to a new realization at this moment. He did not want to die.

He did want to leave his checkered past behind. He also needed to somehow shine the light of truth on the actions of Kilner, White, and the others. He knew that the car bomb and his suicide would do that. He looked out the side window. A light breeze flicked through the grass and shuffled the leaves on the trees. A dog barked in the distance. He could run, he decided. It wasn't a good choice, though, since the FBI and the Federal Bankruptcy Court, not to mention his creditors, would be after him. If he set off the bomb and ran, he'd probably spend a decade or two in prison. Even if he weren't caught, Val would be left with nothing but the legacy of an incompetent, indebted arsonist husband. That was hardly fair to her. Running was no answer. Dying was an answer, but not an ideal one.

Karp longed for a second chance at life. He'd trade all the years of school and promises of success in a minute for a clean break and a new start. He hated his life. He hated it just enough to gladly leave it behind, but not quite enough to be comfortable about ending it outright. He felt worthless.

Just then, Melora appeared at the door. The dome light caught Karp by surprise, and he jumped to cover his eyes.

"Sorry to keep you waiting," she said.

"No problem," answered Karp as the door closed with a creaky slam, returning them to veiled darkness. "How are the kids?"

"Liz is sleeping. Duane and Patrick are playing a game. He doesn't want to talk about it."

"He will."

She looked away. "I just wish I knew what to tell him."

"I know."

"Jerry," she said, "what are we going to do with Gaven?"

Karp didn't answer right away. "That depends," he said.

"On what?"

"It depends on what you want to do."

She didn't wait to answer. "If I could do it, I would kill him. It's just that...I'm no killer."

"No. You're not." He thought about his plan to kill himself. "Neither am I." The two looked out the window of the car in silence for a few moments. "Let's just sleep on it tonight, okay?" he said at last. "Gaven's not going anywhere for now."

"Jerry. Can I stay with you? I don't want to go back there. With him."

He nodded. "I understand."

"I don't want to be alone tonight, either."

"It's okay," he said, and he started the car. He paused for a moment, and just watched her. Her features were soft and her scent was heady. He wanted to take her in his arms, to kiss her and tell her he would make things all right. He couldn't make that promise, though. All at once reality blew into the car, carried along with the strong smell of burning oil. He started down the street. As he drove, Melora reached out to him. She took his right hand from the steering wheel, then cupped it gently in her own soft, warm palms. She lifted his hand to her lips and kissed it gently.

PRIVILEGES

Seventeen

Karp set about clearing an adequate area to work on the basement floor. He moved the old boxes and toys out of the way, then scrubbed down the floor with Pine-Sol. He wanted it to be as clean as possible, and Peltier had already pissed on it several times out of spite. He moved a big gooseneck lamp into the area for better lighting, and then ran an extension cord over to the area for his equipment.

Karp and Melora had spent the morning visiting their offices to gather supplies and instruments that they needed for this procedure. Melora also scrounged around the storage areas in the CMH OR suite for materials. He arranged things about him on three trays that he then set on the floor. There was a scalpel, several forceps, some scissors, and suture material. The tubes and lines that they brought in were all lined up on a tray, still covered in sterile packages. Several different sized arterial catheters were there, an intravenous setup, a nasogastric tube which Karp planned to use to feed the man, and a Foley catheter to insert into his bladder so that the floor would no longer be used as a urinal.

He drew up twenty milligrams of Valium and injected it intramuscularly. Peltier grimaced with the needle, then glared at Karp. Karp didn't want to move him to the floor until he was tranquilized. He removed the needle, then tore the tape off of the man's mouth. "I want you to be able to breathe easily," he said, as if he were talking to a patient.

"Pussy," said Peltier.

Karp shook his head, then went upstairs, giving the medicine some time to work.

Melora waited for him in the kitchen. She was looking over the vials that Karp had brought from his office on Paramount Drive. "Oculinum?" she asked, reading the label. "Isn't this used for eye muscles?"

"That's right. I've used it for treating crossed eyes and for blepharospasm. You inject the stuff into the offending muscle to paralyze it."

"Is this going to work?"

"I don't see why not. It's pure botulinum toxin, the poison from botulism bacteria. A large intravascular dose should get enough of the drug to all the muscles. I want to make certain that he can't move his arms or legs. He needs to be breathing on his own."

They waited for half an hour and went downstairs, Karp first. Peltier was sleeping, his head cocked to one side. "Gaven," he said. There was no response. "Gaven. Are you awake?" Nothing. He picked up the needle that he'd used to give the IM injection, uncapped it, and jammed it into Peltier's right shoulder. He groaned and moved gently away, but nothing more. "It's okay. He's out."

Melora came down the last two steps and joined Karp. He took a utility knife and slit away the tape that held Peltier in his chair. The two then laid him down on the hard cement floor over some folded towels. Karp reached up to the prepared IV setup, brought the needle down and inserted the intravenous line into Peltier's left antecubital vein. He taped it in place and opened the IV bottle to let the fluid begin dripping. Melora attached a pulse oximeter to Gaven's left index finger. The machine sprang to life and began beeping in time with his heart rate. His oxygen saturation--a measure of how well he was breathing--shown in the digital readout.

Dr. Jerry Karp took a syringe loaded with Versed and injected two milligrams intravenously. Peltier went into a deep sleep, snoring audibly. Melora opened his mouth and inserted an airway to be sure that he didn't swallow his tongue and choke.

Karp cut his patient's underwear off with a scissors. He gloved up, opened a Betadine swab, and cleaned off the crease of skin where Peltier's leg met his abdomen. He palpated the man's inguinal area and confidently felt the big, pulsating femoral artery. "Just like it says in the book," he said. Karp had never catheterized a femoral artery before.

Melora tore open a package and handed to Karp a catheter loaded on a syringe with a stopcock. He pushed it through the thick skin and into the artery, advanced it a short distance, then opened the stopcock. The syringe quickly began to fill with bright red arterial blood. "Piece of cake." He closed the stopcock and removed the syringe, then took the long catheter from Melora. He eyed the length of the line. Generally, an arterial catheter placed in the femoral artery was intended to go far upstream for angiography of the major blood vessels and of the heart. In this particular case, they wanted only to advance the line past the bifurcation of the two femoral arteries, into the distal aorta. It was a short distance, only a few centimeters.

He opened the stopcock and advanced the line, pushing it slowly into his patient's body. He passed about a foot and a half of the tube without difficulty. "Think that's far enough?" he asked, remembering that his assistant had far more experience doing surgery in this region of the body than he.

"Absolutely." Melora drew up two vials of Oculinum into a syringe, then handed it to Karp. As he worked with it, she prepared another syringe of saline to flush the line. He removed the guide wire, attached the poison to the arterial line, opened the stopcock, and began to slowly inject the paralytic drug. At the same time, Melora wrapped each of Gaven's legs with a rubber strap tourniquet to block off venous return without interfering with arterial flow. Once Karp's syringe was empty, he closed the stopcock and switched syringes, flushing the remaining drug from the line into the artery with saline. As he did so, Gaven Peltier stopped breathing.

The pulse oximeter kept beeping with his heart rate, but the tone of the beep got lower and lower to signify diminishing arterial oxygen saturation. Finally, the alarm buzzer went off. Karp taped his arterial line in place and Melora reached for an ambu bag. She placed the mask firmly over Peltier's nose and mouth and squeezed, filling his lungs with air. The stimulation induced his respiratory reflex, and he began breathing again on his own. His respirations were shallow, slowed, but spontaneous. She removed the ambu bag and set it down. Karp realized that he hadn't breathed himself, and he took a gulp of air. The alarm on the pulse oximeter stopped wailing, and the tone of the beep began to rise once more.

"The tourniquets really should prevent much systemic effect from the Oculinum," said Karp. He knew that the dose of poison they had just given Melora's ex-husband was easily enough to kill him if it reached his diaphragm. Karp glanced at his watch to tick off fifteen minutes with the tourniquets. He wanted to give the medication enough time to interact with Gaven's muscles before he allowed the bloodstream to wash it out.

Peltier moaned and moved his head back and forth gently. Melora picked up a vial of Diprovan and more of the Versed. She injected the narcotics into the IV line, and he immediately went limp again. The pulse oximeter beeped along the seconds, flashing a red LED with each heartbeat.

Finally, Karp released the tourniquets. He reached over for a gauze sponge, and then removed the long catheter and applied pressure to the wound. Melora moved over to her ex-husband's side and took over for Karp, pressing on the catheterization site. Karp moved to Peltier's upper extremities. He palpated his patient's radial artery, a decidedly smaller vessel in the wrist. "This will be a bit more difficult," he predicted as he prepped the wrist with Betadine.

"An ophthalmologist should have no problem with microsurgery," said Melora.

Using a similar though somewhat smaller line, Karp catheterized the right radial artery. Since Melora would be applying pressure to the femoral vessel, he made sure that all of his syringes were prepared in advance, and lined them up next to Peltier's hand. He held the long arterial catheter up next to Peltier's arm and realized that he would have to thread most of this line up the fine arm vessel if he was going to advance it

296

sufficiently to deliver the botulinum toxin to the majority of the muscles in Peltier's arm.

More slowly than he had with the leg, Karp ran the long catheter up the arm. He felt it kink, so he backed it out a few centimeters, then began again. Ever so slowly it moved forward. He came to another kink about two inches from the hub of the line, and decided that this would have to be far enough. He backed the line down about an inch, and removed the guide wire, then secured a tourniquet high up on the arm. With the syringe connected to the line, he flicked the stopcock open and injected its contents. He methodically closed the stopcock, switched the syringes, and flushed the line. This time, he flushed even more slowly than he had for the leg vessel.

The tone of the beep on the oximeter went down, but the man did not have another apneustic spell. They watched, listened, and waited. Finally it came back up. He was breathing, but more shallowly than normal. That was fine for Karp, since Peltier had plenty of narcotics on board along with the paralytic agent. As long as he continued to breathe on his own, he reasoned, the man would live.

Fifteen minutes later, Melora taped a pressure dressing firmly on Peltier's leg as Karp removed the arterial line from his hand. She then took over applying pressure to the wrist vessel to prevent bleeding. Karp scurried over to the other arm to perform a similar procedure on his left radial artery. He did so with alacrity, injecting the fourth vial of Oculinum very, very slowly. Once more the breathing slowed, then returned. The oxygen saturation was in the upper eighties. He'd be fine.

As Karp removed the final arterial line and applied another pressure dressing, Melora finished placing one on Peltier's right wrist. Karp's scrub shirt was wet from perspiration. Fortunately, the most difficult part of the procedure was over. Now he only hoped that it would work.

Karp opened the package with the nasogastric tube, coated the end with sterile lubricating jelly, and inserted it into Peltier's nose. He gently pushed it forward, pressing it down past his oropharynx, into the esophagus, and eventually the stomach. He put his ear to the end of the tube to and heard gurgling bowel sounds from Peltier's stomach. Satisfied that the tube was advanced far enough, he taped it to Peltier's nose.

Finally, he turned his attention to the Foley bladder catheter. Karp hated placing these things, even as a medical student. "Would you like to do the honors?" he asked.

Melora stood up and removed her rubber gloves with a snap. "I do not want to touch that part of him, ever again."

Karp opened the kit and prepped the man's penis with yet another Betadine swab. Then he coated the tip of the catheter with lubricating jelly and began passing it up the urethra. He shuddered as he did so, wanting never to need one of these himself. There was a small amount of resistance as he maneuvered the tube past the prostate gland. Fortunately, Peltier was young and had little enlargement of the prostate. With a modicum of pressure he was able to advance the tube. Finally, it entered the bladder and a gush of golden urine made its way through the catheter. The oximeter beeped rhythmically and steadily.

"I want to go upstairs," said Melora.

"Are you okay?" asked Karp, worried that she had second thoughts about their plan.

She nodded and leaned against him to feel his warmth and strength. "I don't want to see him when he wakes." She stepped away from Karp and made her way to the stairs. "He's finally getting what he deserves," she said with contempt. "Can you take care of everything down here?"

Karp nodded, comfortable that the plan would proceed as they had agreed that morning.

Melora made her way up the stairs as Karp began to collect all the garbage into a dark plastic bag. There was still some blood and Betadine dripped on the basement floor, but he would have to wait until Peltier was moved before he could scrub that down. He checked the IV. It was running a little fast, so he slowed the rate. Peltier tried to breathe deeply, and he gagged on the oral airway.

Karp knelt down beside him. "Take another deep breath." Peltier tried, and gagged wetly. Karp looked at the pulse oximeter. Saturation was ninety one percent, and the pulse rate was a steady seventy four. Not bad. He judged Peltier's attempts to breathe to be reasonably successful so, still gloved, he pulled the airway from his mouth, tossing it into the garbage bag with one quick move. The patient's thick tongue pushed some mucus up. He opened his eyes and dully looked about the room. "How are you feeling?"

"Shitty," he whispered. "What the fuck did you do to me?"

Karp reached down and put his index finger and middle finger into Peltier's right palm. "Squeeze my fingers."

Nothing happened. "Squeeze them," he repeated.

"I can't, you bastard," croaked the dentist. He spat some bloody mucus onto his chin. "What did you do to me?" He tried to project his voice loudly toward Karp, but could only utter a loud whisper. "I can't talk," he said. He tried to look around, moving his neck. His own anxiety helped waken him more quickly.

Karp made a mental note of the good range of motion and apparently normal strength in Peltier's neck. "Get up," he said.

Peltier groaned. There was some flexion in his lower back. His buttocks barely moved, but his legs were motionless. "I can't," he said, even more anxious. "I can't move my legs. What did you do to me?" he cried out breathily.

Karp was pleased with the result in the lower extremities. Peltier wasn't going to run away. He guessed that the diluted systemic dose of Oculinum probably accounted for his hoarseness. Either that, or the N-G tube had scraped his vocal cords. "Get up," he repeated. "You're free to go."

Peltier rolled about the floor on his neck and upper shoulder muscles. His lifeless arms and hands dragged with his upper body. "I can't move, I can't move." The pulse oximeter measured his fear with increasing rapidity of the heart rate. It was ninety five.

"Relax," said Karp. "The effects are usually temporary. The longest I've seen this medication last with full potency is four months. I doubt you'll be down that long."

Rick Leach worked his way through the stack of documents that arrived in the mail from the State Medical Board. It was about eight inches thick; sparse documentation, from a legal point of view. He had many cases that required several drawers in file cabinets for the supportive papers.

He flicked through them quickly the first time, wanting to get a feel for the general direction of the evidence against his client. There was a letter from Dr. White initiating the inquiry, similar to the one he'd mailed to Compton Memorial Hospital. This was followed by a reference to a videotape. Although the video was not included in the documents sent over, he presumed it was identical to the one viewed at the hospital. There was a letter from Dr. Fitch, and several communications back and forth to Dan Kilner, Kip Porchette, and Orville Harmon regarding the actions taken against Karp by the various hospital committees.

There was an inquiry to Karp's malpractice carrier confirming that no cases had been filed against him. Of course, the review by Dr. Porter was there in its entirety. The recommendations of the MEC were there, and the documents supporting the pending hearing before the hospital's Board of Directors. There were also photocopies of the papers that he and Karp had provided in his defense including his review of the cataract cases, his commentary on the Porter review, and the supportive letters from Dr. Keith. Copies of the subpoenas served on Karp for the four patients' records were in the pile, along with the records themselves.

The package was then summarized in a memorandum by the case worker, Dr. James Creighton. He listed many of the documents that argued against Karp's skills, but notably made no reference to any of the supportive documents on Karp's behalf. Leach wrote a memo to that effect on a legal pad. Despite what Leach felt was marginal evidence of risk to life, Dr. Creighton concluded that Karp's continued practice of medicine represented a "significant risk to life and well being in the community as a whole." He recommended that the Board suspend Karp's license to practice medicine "in the best interest of the people of the State of Illinois" pending a formal hearing. This document was countersigned in agreement by Chief Medical Examiner of the State Medical Board of Illinois, Arnold M. Lawson, M.D.

Leach wrote a few notes on his legal pad and smiled, thinking that this was going to be a very easy case to defend. It was illogical to conclude that a cataract surgeon, who had no deaths or hospitalizations in his surgical patient population, could represent a risk to life. Even if he were grossly incompetent, which Leach felt to be an exaggeration, this action against him was excessive. In other cases he'd read about, the reviewers were compelled to at least note that supportive evidence had been presented. In this instance, the Medical Board's review process seemed completely one sided. He wondered if Dr. White might have had some influence after all. He chuckled quietly, and decided that he was starting to think like Dr. Karp.

Leach checked his watch. It was four forty five. He and his wife, Theresa, and their two daughters usually went out to dinner on Friday evenings, and he was running late tonight. He decided that he would dictate a few notes and call Karp on Monday morning to advise him that he'd received the documents from the State Board. That would give him some time over the weekend to go over the paperwork in greater detail. Once he was sure he had all of the facts straight, he could also reassure Karp that this would be a fairly simple hearing, from which he could expect that his license might be quickly restored in at least a limited manner.

Dave Barnes hated the job at Sear's. He found it demeaning, but the pay was good and he was still able to run his small business. He was a carpenter by trade. Work had been slow lately, so he sold tools at the department store on his odd hours to make ends meet. He never enjoyed being away from his wife and son on the weekends, but weekday afternoon shifts were by far the worst because they were so slow. He'd already spent most of the day straightening aisles and updating stock reports. There were a couple of small sales, but his commission bonus would not be impressive. When the couple came in and started looking at garage door openers, he noticed right away. Anything that needed to be plugged in would dramatically increase his sales points today.

"Can I help you?" he asked, trying not to sound too anxious.

"We're looking for a small garage door opener," she said.

They were holding hands and looking at each other all goo-goo eyed. Barnes decided that they must have been recently married. They were younger than he, in their late thirties or young forties. It must be a second marriage, he decided. Nobody married for any length of time would still be so clingy in the tool department at Sear's. "We're having a sale on this model," he said, pointing out the three horsepower number. It was a monster garage door opener, and he made an extra two percentage points as a bonus commission when he sold the high end model.

He rubbed his chin with his free hand. "No, I don't think we need that much garage door opener. It's only a one car garage."

So much for making a decent sale, thought Barnes. They looked cheap, anyway, he decided. They could both use a diet. She was awfully plain. "How about this one, then?" He gestured toward the two horsepower unit. It would open any double-sized door easily. "It's got a five year factory warranty."

"I don't know," he answered. The guy was reading the labels on the box as if this were a major life investment.

"It's our best seller," Barnes prodded.

"This one might do, honey," she said. They looked at the half horsepower model, the smallest opener they kept in stock.

"I think you're right," he decided. "This one should be fine."

Big deal, thought Barnes. A measly seventy five dollars for the pint sized door opener. "Okay," he said as he lifted the box so that the romantics wouldn't have to let go of each other. "Will you be needing installation by our certified technicians?"

"No," he said. "I can manage it."

"All right." Barnes set the big box down on the counter and activated the computerized cash register by entering his associate number. Next he ran the bar code scanner over the box, and the machine registered the sale automatically. "Will that be cash or charge?"

"Sear's charge," he said, and he reached into his pocket to go through his wallet.

"What?" she asked, surprised.

"Yeah, hon, I think we'll put it on plastic."

She was uncomfortably silent.

"Certainly. Can I have your card, please?"

He looked and looked, but came up blank. "I'm sorry," he said with a sheepish grin. "I must have left it at home. Can you just look up my card number on the computer? The name is White. William White."

"Let me see," said Barnes, as he entered the name into the keyboard. Several W. Whites appeared. "Can I have your address, sir?"

"You know what," he said, checking through the wallet again. "Let's just pay cash."

"No problem." Barnes punched several keys on the computer, which retained the name W. White on the record of the sale. "That will be seventy eight dollars and thirty two cents," he said as the receipt printed.

Gaven Peltier lay flat on his back with his hands cuffed over his head. He made several attempts to wriggle loose, but no matter how he tried, his muscles simply would not move. He could arch his back and flex his neck, but his arms and legs were dead. His mood vacillated between helpless acceptance and outright fear. There was nothing more terrifying than being paralyzed.

The blue eggcrate mattress was by far more comfortable than either the chair or the hard floor where he had lain before. He still disliked the tubes in his nose and penis. It felt like he constantly had to take a pee, but he realized there was nothing holding the urine back from the tube. He lay back and tried to sigh. Even that was difficult, as his breathing muscles were still weakened by the drugs.

The door to the kitchen opened, and a beam of light flashed down the stairs. There were footsteps, and he turned his neck to see Karp walking down toward him. Turning his neck was painful, as it put enough traction on the nasogastric tube to induce a gag reflex. "What now?" he rasped.

Karp checked the level of urine in the bag. There was quite a bit there. He decided that Peltier had been rehydrated well enough, so he turned off the infusion and removed the IV, covering the site with another bandage. He then went over to the pile of supplies that remained from the morning's surgery. They had brought along from the hospital several cans of Ensure, a milky nutritional supplement that was used to feed debilitated patients. He opened a can and poured it into a glass, then sucked up the contents into a large syringe. "I'm going to feed you," he told Peltier as he connected the syringe to the end of the NG tube and began injecting the fluid into his stomach. "We want you to keep your strength up, Gav," he said.

It took some time, but Karp was able to give him the entire can. He disconnected the syringe and flushed the line with a little cold water. He then checked the injection sites and saw that all of the pressure dressings were clean and dry. "We'll feed you some more tomorrow," he said as he clicked off the lights and made his way back up the stairs. "Get a good night's rest."

"Fuck you," he responded.

Karp walked back home rather than drive Melora's Jeep. He didn't want to raise any suspicions with his neighbors by having her car in his driveway. In fact, he wanted to make sure as few people as possible knew of a connection between them. The evening air was cool, and there was a gentle breeze that made the trees' shadows flicker from the street lights. The walk was pleasant and calming. Karp was truly in a good mood. For the first time in several months, his life had returned to an odd sort of normalcy. He was working again, practicing medicine in a sense. He was using his skills to perform chemistry and to build things. He breathed the air in deeply and hummed as he walked along.

He entered his house and was greeted with soft jazz from the stereo. The lights were on in the living room, but the place was dark otherwise. "I'm home," he called, smiling.

"I'm upstairs," returned Melora.

He ambled up to the bedroom, and found Melora sitting on the bed, wearing his bathrobe, her bare legs folded underneath her. Karp found himself excited by the appearance of this woman, so enticing on his bed. Her face was young and lovely, and she smiled at him. "Welcome home," she whispered.

Karp felt himself flush. "It's been a long time since I've been welcomed home like this," he said softly.

Melora patted the sheet in front of her. "Come join me," she invited.

Karp moved forward, and made a conscious effort to slow his breathing. It had been a long time, he repeated to himself. He lowered himself onto the bed and pressed himself against Melora's body. He reached his arm around the back of her neck and pulled her close to him, and then he touched her lips with his. Their kiss was gentle and slow at first, but rapidly became enjoined with more and more passion. All at once they were both breathing very hard, locked in a sweet, wet kiss that dripped of heat and hormones and long suppressed desires.

Karp savored the taste of her tongue and her mouth. He drank in the scent of her perfume, which clung to her in a sharp yet provocative cloud. They parted, and he looked longingly into her green eyes. For a moment, they just caught their breath. He found her scent too much to ignore. "You smell so beautiful," he said breathily.

She smiled. "It smells like that all over," she answered, stressing the last two words.

Karp kissed her again, but this time allowed himself the luxury of pulling his arm around to slide it under the robe. He touched her bare back and caressed her as they kissed. His hand ran up and down and finally squeezed her naked ass cheek. His heart raced again, this time spurred on by the growing bulge in his pants.

Melora, stimulated by Karp's kiss and by the warm sensation of his hand on her rump, rubbed herself sensuously against his leg. Karp moaned with pleasure. She ran her own hand up and down his chest, and then worked it between his legs. With the first squeeze, Karp's body twitched. Val had never been so aggressive.

"Are you all right?" asked Melora.

"Yes," he answered. "It's just," he paused, "it's just been a long time."

She closed her eyes and nodded. "For me, too, Jerry. I want this...I want you, so very much."

He kissed her again, this time slowly. He ran his hand along her smooth leg, and then up her thigh. He returned her favor by finally allowing himself the delight of caressing Melora's lips. She was warm and wet and she moaned with wanton pleasure as she worked her pelvis with the motions of his hands. He explored her sweet crevice with his fingers, moving deeper with each pass. She squirmed with delight as he tickled her clitoris. Unable to control herself, she broke from his kiss and moaned loudly.

"Yes, Jerry, yes," she sighed. "That feels so good." She gently bit Karp's chin, which prodded him to increase his attention to her pussy. She felt so hot and so warm. "Mmm, don't stop."

Karp nibbled at her ear as he rubbed between her legs. Melora pressed harder against him. "You are so beautiful," he whispered in her ear. "You saved my life. You are a beautiful and wonderful woman."

She humped against him harder and harder, then moaned in ecstasy. Waves of orgasm worked up through her, from her vagina and into her abdomen. Melora's moans intensified and she pulled Karp tighter against her, calling out as she let the orgasm carry her away.

"Yes, oh God, Jerry, yes," she cried. Finally, she pushed away gently. "That was wonderful," she said with a smile and a deep breath. "Let me return the favor." With that, Melora shimmied quickly toward the foot of the bed. As she went, she kissed Karp's body--first his chest, then his belly, and finally the point just above his penis. As he watched, breathing hard, she took him into her mouth.

Val had never done this, at least since they married. She didn't enjoy it, she said. It had been years for Karp. He couldn't even remember the last time. This was wonderful. Incredible. She worked her tongue and lips over him. She nibbled, ever so gently, then ran her tongue over him again.

He closed his eyes and laid back, then watched some more. She caught his glance and smiled. She stopped, and said, "I love it when you watch."

"Don't stop," said Karp. "You are a wonderful woman. Oh, Yes, Melora, yes. That's it."

She nibbled and sucked and rubbed him with her hand. All the time he watched. She repositioned herself so that he could reach her back, and he rubbed her soft skin. This made her work a little harder. He loved it. He loved her.

Karp felt his own orgasm begin to come. There was something more that he wanted, something that he needed. "Wait," he said, working hard to hold back. "I want to be inside you."

Melora stopped and smiled. She rolled over and spread her legs for him. He pulled himself to his knees and positioned

307

himself over his lover. He took her with one arm and kissed her as he positioned his cock with his other hand. They both moaned as he penetrated her, mixing her juices and her saliva in a wet embrace of love.

"Yes, Jerry, fuck me," she said. "Fuck me so well, yes."

He pumped himself inside of her slowly at first, then increased the pace with her request. "It feels so good," she said. She smiled and matched his pace, humping herself against him.

He kissed her cheek, her earlobe, and ran his nose through her hair. Where it felt as if he were about to explode only a moment ago, he now found himself having more control than he could remember having had in years. He reached around to the small of her back, and then kneaded her ass cheek. He pulled her toward him, helping guide their timing together. "You are so beautiful, Melora, so beautiful," he repeated.

She arched her back and moaned for him. He felt his own orgasm peak. "I'm cumming in you," he said as he let go.

They lay together and kissed and cooed and stared into each others' eyes. Finally, overwhelmed by the day, the two lovers gently fell asleep in each other's arms.

Eighteen

It had rained all weekend, but the forecast was for clearing skies and cool temperatures today. The roads were still wet, which made driving around Chicago even more annoying than usual. There was an accident on the inbound Eisenhower and traffic backed up well to the west of the junction with the East-West Tollway. The Kennedy was under construction, as usual, and looked like a parking lot. A lot of commuters took to the surface streets, and that made Greg Garrity's job that much more difficult. The Chicago Institute of Ophthalmology offered assistance with transportation for patients who were unable or unwilling to drive to the office. This included surgical patients and new patients who could potentially require surgery.

The CIO used four black Cadillac limousines which were purchased from an O'Hare livery service. They all carried the CIO logo on the front doors. Greg had actually retired from his job at the Mercantile Exchange three years before, at the age of sixty one. He decided to take the job at CIO after his successful treatment there by Dr. White.

Greg's first cataract surgery two years before had gone smoothly enough. Over time, though, the vision deteriorated in the operated eye. He saw Dr. White on the advice of his sister in law. He told Garrity that it was a lucky thing for him to have come to CIO. White explained how Dr. Alex Boren had completely botched the first surgery. He demonstrated for Garrity how the posterior capsule, the thin membrane left behind in cataract surgery, had opacified once more. Using a laser, White opened the membrane, clearing Greg's vision. He was so pleased and so relieved that White had been able to save his eye after Boren had damaged it that he had White do the second cataract for him. Since he had little to do to fill his days, he signed on to drive patients for White. That way he could return the favor to White by telling patients what a good doctor he is.

He was running just a little late, and he knew that Dr. White would not be pleased. It was important to keep the patients arriving at CIO on time for their cataract surgery. White was very fast, needing only ten or twenty minutes to do each case. His profit margin depended upon maintaining a high volume of surgery, and he tried to do thirty cases per day on surgery days, twice a week.

He weaved the big car through traffic and pulled up to the CIO office at about nine twenty, ten minutes behind schedule. Greg flew over to the passenger door, and helped out three patients who were scheduled to have surgery. He walked them in to the clinic and signed in at the desk. Once they were settled in the lobby, he headed back to the drivers' office to have a cup of coffee and wait for three postop patients to be readied for the return ride home.

As he stirred the powdered cream into his coffee, the intercom buzzed. "Greg?"

"Yeah, I'm here."

"Greg, did you bring Mrs. Wallace in for surgery?"

"Yes."

"Her daughter drove separately from Winnetka to be with her, and she says that her mom is certain she left her purse in the limo. Can you help her look for it?"

Great, he thought. There goes my coffee break. "Sure. I'll be right there."

No one noticed Melora as she waited patiently in the lobby, watching for the limos to start arriving. She simply walked up to the desk as if she were going to check in and looked over the driver's shoulder as he signed in the surgery patients. She picked a name, went back to her seat, and waited a few more moments before telling the receptionist her story.

Greg Garrity returned from the drivers' office carrying his coffee cup with him, and the receptionist nodded in Melora's direction. "You're with Mrs. Wallace?"

"Yes, thanks." They started through the lobby toward the double glass door entry way. "Mom is so nervous. I'm pretty sure that she left her purse at home, like I told her to do, but, well, you know."

He sipped his coffee as the automatic doors opened with a hiss. "I was there myself a while back. She has nothing to worry about, though. Dr. White is the best cataract surgeon in the country."

Garrity unlocked the car and opened the back door. He stood tall and sipped his coffee as Melora got into the passenger compartment. She looked around on the seat, then leaned down toward the floor of the vehicle. She slipped her hand into a pocket of her denim skirt and pulled out two items. One was a piece of paper, which she flicked under the driver's seat. The other was a small envelope. She looked over her shoulder and saw only the chest of the driver as he drank his coffee. She peeled open the top of the envelope and tapped its contents out on the floor of the car.

"Can you open the trunk for me?" she asked.

Garrity made a face. "Why? We never use the trunk."

Melora smiled sweetly. "I know. But if I don't look in the trunk, Mom will be so upset. If you don't mind."

He shrugged and fished the keys out. They walked over to the massive trunk of the Caddy and Greg popped the lid. "Nothing in there, see?"

Melora leaned into the big, empty trunk, and tore open another envelope. She patted down the edges of the carpeted storage space, spreading powder from the palmed envelope as she went. With a fluid movement, she stood upright and replaced the envelope in her pocket. "I knew it wouldn't be here," she said with an innocent smile. "Thanks anyway."

"No problem," said Garrity as he slammed the trunk closed. "I know how it can be when the folks get older." The two walked back into the clinic.

311

Karp dialed the number out of the phone book. It rang twice, and was answered crisply. "Chicago Institute of Ophthalmology. May I help you?"

"Yes. This is Dr. Karp calling." He knew that a phone call from a civilian had no chance whatever to get through. "I need to talk to Dr. White, please."

"Just a moment, Doctor. I'll connect you to his secretary."

There was a pause, then, "Dr. Karp?"

"Yes."

"I'm sorry. Dr. White is in surgery this morning. May I leave a message for him?"

"No, ma'am. It is critical that I speak to Dr. White this morning. I understand that he's very busy today, and I'll be happy to wait on hold until he comes out between cases. I have some very sensitive information to discuss with him before I meet with the FBI, and I think he'll want to take this call."

"I see. Let me talk to him and I'll be right back."

"Thank you."

"Dr. Karp?" She clicked back on.

"Yes."

"Dr. White said that he'd speak with you, but he's going to be a few moments while he finishes his case."

"I'll wait. I've got plenty of time."

Billy White was absolutely pissed off. He was injecting a folded silicone intraocular lens when the circulator interrupted him about a phone call by that putz, Karp. Some bullshit about the FBI, and she said it out loud so that the patient could hear. He worked hard to steady his hand as he popped the lens out of the forceps and into the capsular bag. The superior haptic shimmied anteriorly, and he shoved it in again with the forceps, nearly tearing the lens capsule in the process.

He quickly reformed the anterior chamber with saline solution and tested the wound to be certain it was adequately watertight. "Mrs. Allyson?" he asked.

"Yes," said the patient from under the sterile blue surgical drape.

"The surgery is over. It was a simple lens implantation." The scrub technician moved the instruments out of the way and removed the eyelid speculum, allowing the patient to close her eyes. Another tech pulled the arm of the microscope away and peeled the sticky drapes off of the patient's face as Dr. White spoke to her. "The girls will get you cleaned off and see to it that you arrive in the recovery room. Do you have any questions for me?"

"No," she said, smacking her dry lips. "Thank you for doing such a good job."

"You're very welcome." He stood and snapped his rubber gloves off, then slam dunked them into the garbage can and stormed out of the room. The techs eyed each other over their masks. None of them looked forward to the next case.

Billy White tore the telephone receiver off of its hook and spat into the speaker. "Karp?"

"Thank you for taking my call, Dr. White. I know that you're very busy."

"What do you want?"

"Doctor, I'd like to meet with you this evening."

He snickered. Not bloody likely, he thought. "I am very busy, Doctor." He stressed the last word in irony. "What is it?"

"I've recently gotten access to documents that prove the physicians in Aurora have colluded together to defraud Medicare. They're pooling money to guarantee referrals. A lot of people at Compton Memorial are involved, and I'm meeting with the FBI tonight to turn these documents over to them."

White paused for a moment to absorb this. "And just what does this have to do with me?" he asked, with the same arrogant tone.

Karp noticed that White's pitch dropped a jot. He grinned. "Well, Doctor, I know that you recently established a link with Compton Memorial Hospital. My lawyer tells me that I shouldn't get involved in this, but, I have to. The way I see it, my career is pretty much over." He wanted to play up to White. "I hope to come back after I finish my retraining. Ophthalmology's image, as a profession, has taken a beating lately and I want to avoid any more harm. You understand, don't you? It doesn't look good for any of us."

"Yes?"

"Well, I don't see how someone of your stature could have gotten involved in this, Dr. White. I want to show you the evidence that I have so that you can stay clear of this problem when it goes public."

"Indeed."

"If any of your CIO docs are involved, you can use the advance notice to do whatever you think is necessary."

White didn't know what to say. "I'm not sure, Karp."

"The FBI is coming tonight at eight. I presume that you have a full schedule today, so let's get together briefly at seven. This really shouldn't take more than fifteen minutes of your time. I do think it's in your best interest to come."

White relented. "All right, Karp. I'll be there at seven."

"I think that's wise, Dr. White. Don't be late. This shouldn't take long."

"Fine. Seven." He hung up the phone and stared at it. "Damn it," he said out loud as he kicked the base of the wall. The techs were pushing a patient past him on a gurney, and everyone turned their faces away. White stormed out of the Surgery Center, and nearly knocked over a patient's daughter as he blew into the corridor leading to his office. He strutted past Colleen, his secretary. "Get me Dan Kilner on the phone," he ordered without making eye contact. He slammed the door shut with so much force that a letter blew off of Colleen's desk.

Melora made certain that she waited long enough for the incident with the limousine to be forgotten, melded into the events of another very busy surgery day. The receptionist she had gone to the first time was on the phone and checking in a patient who had come for laser treatment. She approached the other end of the check-in desk and spoke with someone who was free.

"I'm here to check out Dr. White's pager."

"I'm sorry?"

"I'm Laura Jenkins, with Chicago Cellular. Dr. White's office called about his pager. I'm here to check it out."

"Oh, I see." She signalled one of the blue blazered runners, who showed Melora into the back lane of offices. At the end of the hall, they came to Dr. White's suite. "May I help you?" Colleen asked.

Melora repeated the story about the pager.

"I didn't call about any pager," said Colleen.

"Well, I got the call," demanded Melora. "Perhaps Dr. White noticed the problem and called directly."

"I doubt that," said Colleen quietly.

"Perhaps we could ask him," she persisted, working up more irritation in her voice.

"I'm sorry. Dr. White is on the telephone, and I'm afraid we can't interrupt him. Besides, I have the pager right here." She patted the plastic box which her boss left with her to avoid unnecessary interruptions in the OR.

"Fine. Let's just dial it up, then. If it beeps, we know it's working."

"All right," said Colleen, looking forward to getting this woman away from her. She knew the number without looking it up, and she picked up her phone and dialed it. Melora watched carefully, noting the phone number. There was a brief pause, and the pager activated. Colleen deactivated the alarm by pushing the small button on its side. Her phone number, Dr. White's personal direct number, flashed on the pager's LCD display. "There," she said haughtily, a tone that she'd learned from her boss. "It works perfectly."

Karp had barely hung up the phone when it rang, startling him. There was no room for error in his plan, or the whole thing would fall apart. He snatched the phone from its cradle. "Hello?"

"Hello, Doctor. This is Rick Leach. Did I interrupt something?"

"No, no, Rick. Just hanging around."

"Okay. You sounded a little surprised."

"Yeah. I was just washing the dishes and I almost dropped a glass."

"Sorry to bother you, Doc. I just wanted to call and let you know that I received the documents from the State Medical Board late Friday. I went over them this weekend, and I've got good news for you."

"They changed their minds and gave me back my license?"

"No, sorry." He forgot that Karp's idea of good news might differ from his own. "Not that good, unfortunately. I reviewed their case against you, and it's basically the same evidence used by the hospital."

"And that's good?"

"Yes. Yanking your license implies you're a bad doc. The evidence against you only suggests that your cataract surgery is suboptimal."

"I'm very comforted."

"I'm sorry, Jerry. I know it's hard for you to detach yourself emotionally from all this. It's my job to do just that."

"I understand, Rick."

"Good. The fact is that it's going to be easy to overturn their decision."

"Will that clear my record?"

"Not exactly, no. The National Databank has already been notified. You can report that the decision was overturned at the appeal hearing."

Karp shook his head. "That doesn't exactly set the record straight, does it?"

"It's better than average, Jerry. Take my word for it. How are you getting along?"

He sighed. "Swell, Rick. I'm swell." He decided to take advantage of this unplanned call. "Listen, Rick. I think I've got some followup for you on those papers we discussed last week."

"Oh?" Leach didn't sound too impressed.

"Don't worry, Rick. I haven't been doing any more breaking and entering. I did do some checking over the weekend and I think I have a lead, but I'm still working on it. Can I get back to you in the next few days?"

"Absolutely," said Leach, happy to avoid hearing the paranoid story once more. "I'll be in touch with you anyway, just as soon as I find out from the Medical Board the date of your appellate hearing."

"Good. I should have something concrete by then."

"Hang in there, Jerry."

"I will."

He hung up, then checked his watch. It was almost ten. He picked up the telephone receiver once more and dialed the long distance number that he had copied down from directory assistance the day before. "Federal Bureau of Investigation."

"Can you connect me with Agent Roland Grant, please."

"Just a moment." She transferred the call.

"Agent's offices."

"This is Dr. Jerrold Karp calling for Roland Grant."

"I'll see if he is in, sir."

"Thank you." He was back on hold for only a moment.

"Uh, hello?" The answer was tentative.

"Agent Grant?"

A pause, then, "Yes?"

"This is Jerry Karp calling, sir. I understand that you were in Aurora recently."

He had clearly caught the agent off guard. "That's correct."

"I need to talk to you tonight. Do you think that you could see me?"

"I don't know, Doctor. Why don't you just tell me what you have now?"

"Thanks. I'd rather share this with you face to face. I know that you have some doubts about my veracity."

There was another pause. "What makes you say that?"

"I know, Agent Grant. I know. Listen, I need to meet with you tonight at my house at about seven thirty or eight. My source is coming just before that, a little before seven. You need to have me under surveillance by then, because I want you to see who comes and goes from here. It's very important."

"I'm not sure I can do that, Dr. Karp. What is this about?"

"Agent Grant, this is very important. If you're not here and this information is released to the press rather than to you, it will reflect badly upon your agency. I know that Bob Wilson will be very upset if that happens. You need to be here about six thirty."

This time Karp was certain that the FBI agent was taking notes, because the pause was even longer than the previous ones. "What makes you say that?"

"Rollie. Can I call you Rollie? Please. Call Bob. Believe me, this is going to be very, very big. Collusion. Medicare fraud. I've got all the evidence that you need to make a case. You need to see who my connection is, and he'll be here this evening. When he leaves, just come to my front door. I'll give you everything I've been able to put together. What have you got to lose?"

Another delay; more notes. "I can't promise anything, Doctor."

"Just call Bob Wilson." Karp stressed each word. "He'll want this. Set up surveillance by six thirty. You know where I live, don't you."

"Yes I do."

"Good. I'll see you tonight." He hung up the phone.

Melora was prepared for her last and most important task of the morning. She left the lobby of the CIO and went directly

318

back to her Jeep. There, in the back seat, she opened a small brown paper bag. The first thing she removed from it was a pair of rubber examining gloves. She slipped them on and extracted the second item, a garage door opener. She closed the car door and headed toward the back parking lot of the CIO. There, just as Karp had predicted, was a black Mercedes Benz that belonged to Billy White. She found it right away in the first parking space, with personalized Illinois license plates: DR IOL. With her gloved hand, she pushed the button and the trunk popped open. Karp was right, he was too lazy to lock it.

From her skirt pocket, she removed the last envelope, tore it open, and scattered the powdery contents into the trunk. Then she leaned in and found the pass through door to the back seat. It was used for carrying skiis in the little car. She flicked the door open, her body bent over into the back of the car, one foot touching the ground. She rocked it back and forth, then tossed the garage door opener through the ski door into the car. It struck the back of the front seat and fell to the floor in the passenger compartment. Her pulse quickened: The plan was to get the opener on the front seat, not the back. This would just have to do. She stepped back and closed the trunk lid.

"God damn it, Kilner, I don't know what kind of evidence he has. What's going on here?" Billy White was absolutely out of control.

"Well, I can't figure it out. There's no way that Karp could know about this. It doesn't make sense." Kilner remained cool.

"So. What are you going to do?"

"Not a thing, Dr. White. There isn't anything for me to do. On the other hand, you should meet with him."

"Why? I don't need to talk with that little shit." He spun around in his chair. "Honest to God, Kilner, I don't know why I got involved in this. I could have crushed the little son of a bitch without Compton Memorial Hospital."

"Nonetheless, I think it would be helpful to know what information Dr. Karp has gotten hold of. He doesn't think you're involved, isn't that what he said? Take advantage of it. Find out what he knows."

"I don't see why. It can't change anything."

"It can't? If we know what he's got, we can do damage control. This doesn't have to change our position."

White was too angry. He thought it would be better to let Karp just hand over Kilner and all the other assholes in Aurora. He didn't answer.

"Don't forget, Dr. White, that you are involved in this. You have as much to lose as any of us. If I were you, I'd meet with him. Then call me. Call your lawyer. Do whatever you think is right. You have nothing to lose by learning more about what Karp knows."

This made sense. Knowledge was everything. White had plenty of friends in powerful places, and he knew that he could count on them for a favor in a pinch. "All right. I'll meet with him."

"Good. Call me when you know more. We can decide what needs to be done after that."

"Yeah. Right." He hung up. Billy White stood up and walked to the window in the back of his office. He was trying to contain his temper. He knew that there were still twenty cataract procedures for him to perform, and he needed to calm down. He never noticed the woman walking away from his car. He just stared off into space and fumed.

"He said what?" Bob Wilson was usually calm and well composed.

"He said," repeated Grant, "that he had evidence of collusion and Medicare fraud. He said that the other doctors in Aurora were involved, and he insisted that you would want to know."

Wilson shook his head. "That's insane," he thought aloud. "You wrote in your memo that there was no evidence of fraud."

"That's right. I did." He paused. "How did he know that I was involved in this case? He asked for me by name."

"Damn strange. I don't know."

"You didn't tell him?"

"No."

Grant's partner, Frank Ellison, had been watching and listening. He'd added little to the conversation. He looked closely at his associate, who was staring up toward the ceiling. Ellison grinned. He, too, got along with Wilson and the other attorneys at DOJ, but he didn't trust them. They were on the same side, but too many of the attorneys had political agendas.

"What do you want me to do, then, Bob?"

Wilson ran his hand over his forehead and through his fine, blond hair. "Go," he said finally. "If he's threatened to go to the press," he reasoned, "we'll look like idiots whether it's factual or not. I want to know what Karp is talking about."

"You want us to put his house under surveillance, like he asked?"

Wilson shrugged. "Why not?"

Grant nodded. Ellison crossed his arms over his chest. "That's a hot one," he said to no one in particular. "The suspects call us and tell us when and where to surveil. And we do it, under direction of the U.S. Attorney's office."

Grant held up his palm to quiet his partner.

"Tell Ellison that I want to know exactly what is happening in Aurora," instructed Wilson, returning to his customary even demeanor. "And remind him that this trip might not have been necessary if he'd done a better job with his interviews."

"I'll pass that on," smirked Grant. He loved to put his junior associate in his place.

"One more thing," added Wilson.

"Yes?"

"I don't want you to do a god damn thing down there without checking in with me first. Watch. Listen. Ask questions. Ask good questions," he emphasized the adjective. "But don't do anything more without checking in with me first. Do you understand?"

"Yes, sir," said Grant, slightly condescending.

"I mean it, Grant. I want to know if Jerry Karp farts. Do absolutely nothing without notifying me. We are not dealing with dangerous people here. We need to gather information and evaluate it carefully before we act." Wilson didn't trust Karp, and he didn't like physicians in general. "Is that absolutely clear?"

"Crystal clear."

"You can reach me by pager or cell phone, all day and night."

"I know the numbers."

"I'll be waiting to hear from you."

Grant hung up. "Finish up your report," he told Ellison. "We're taking a little trip to Aurora this afternoon."

"This is bullshit," he said.

"Maybe so, but we're going to be on surveillance for a while. I want to get an early start so we can get something to eat first. I know a great little place to get hand made ice cream."

Nineteen

Jerry Karp used a small scissors to snip off the end of the balloon inflating valve, releasing the air from the cuff that held the Foley catheter in place. With his gloved hands, he pulled the tube out of Gaven Peltier's penis. Peltier began to moan, then let out a lengthy wail crescendoed by a loud "Fuck you!" as Karp removed the last inch of the tube. He then dressed Peltier using clothes that he had brought from his own home. The pants went on easily enough as Karp's waist was decidedly larger than Peltier's. The shoes were another problem. His deck shoes were probably the most forgiving choice, and even they were a tight squeeze on Peltier's big feet.

He unhitched Peltier from the post and placed him into a wheelchair for transport, taking pains to avoid dislodging the NG tube. It took some effort to do it one stair at a time, but he was eventually able to lift the paralyzed man upstairs. Peltier squeezed his eyes closed from the bright sunlight that streamed in through the kitchen windows. Karp wheeled him into the garage, where the fully gassed up green Citation waited. He loaded Peltier into the car, opened the garage door, and drove the three blocks to his house. Karp backed the car into his garage so that Peltier was sitting on the side right next to the Stealth. He turned off the car and closed the garage door.

Karp checked his watch. It was four o'clock, time to start working the alcohol into him. He would feed Peltier several shots of liquor through the NG tube before he removed it, to keep him sleepy, quiet, and still. Melora was waiting in the kitchen, her Jeep parked on the next block over. "How is he?" she asked.

"He's fine. I had a hard time getting the shoes on his big feet, but everything else fit well enough." He drew up about twenty milliliters of Jack Daniel's whiskey into a syringe, then returned to his patient in the car. Karp attached the syringe to the end of the tube and injected its contents into his stomach. "Bottoms up," he said.

"What are you doing?" rasped Peltier. "That burns."

By six o'clock, Peltier was snoring. Karp and Melora lifted him from the passenger seat of the Citation, turned him around, and deposited him backwards on the fully reclined driver's seat of the sportscar. He burped as they heaved him around on the seat until they were satisfied with his position. His head rested squarely on the car's floor, just over several strategically placed sticks of homemade explosive. The car seat, too, was fully stuffed with C-4. His feet rested loosely over the top of the seat, to either side of the headrest. A single stick of explosive stuffed into a three inch diameter, two foot length of pipe dangled under the dashboard. It was held in place by a length of duct tape that had been wrapped around the bomb, then unwound. The idea was to make it look as if it had been placed in the dash, come loose, and partially unwrapped itself. It swung back and forth as Karp and Melora positioned Peltier underneath it. His final location left the pipe bomb hanging just two inches above Peltier's nostrils.

Karp took a thick rubber band and spread it over his fingers. He and Melora grasped Peltier's left hand and wrapped it over the pipe, and Karp transferred the rubber band from his hand to Peltier's. He double twisted it, so that it held the hand firmly on the stick of explosive. Using another rubber band, they repeated this with Peltier's right hand so that he grasped the bomb like a trapeze.

"Aren't you worried about the rubber bands?" asked Melora.

"Why?" asked Karp. "They ought to be vaporized. There'll be no trace." He looked at Peltier who snored and burped again. "I don't think he'll be moving enough to work his hands free."

They stood back to look over their work. Melora, who was wearing rubber gloves to keep from leaving fingerprints, put her arm around Karp's waist. She leaned her head against his shoulder. "I'm going to miss you," she said softly to Karp.

He smiled and leaned against her. They turned to walk back into the house and Karp stopped suddenly. "Jesus," he said. "I almost forgot."

He returned to Peltier and got down on one knee. From his back pocket, Karp removed his wallet. This, he placed into Peltier's left back pants pocket. Karp then inserted his car key into the Stealth's ignition switch, and armed the car bomb by turning the key to the "on" position. He removed his wristwatch and checked the time. It was six fifteen. "I'm going to need a new watch," he muttered as he wrapped the band over Peltier's right wrist. He then worked his wedding band loose from his ring finger and placed it carefully onto Peltier's, taking care not to dislodge his hand from the explosive stick.

Finally, Karp reached into his shirt pocket. He removed his eyeglasses, which he placed there after putting contact lenses in his own eyes. The contacts were tinted dark brown, giving his hazel eyes a deep and distant appearance. He planned to bleach his hair slightly, at least for awhile. He placed the eyeglasses gently onto Gaven Peltier. "There," he said, as he stood and returned to the house with Melora.

They walked to the front window and glanced down the block in either direction. About five houses down, parked on the other side of the street, was a three year old gray Chevy Caprice. Karp saw two men in the car, sitting low in the front seat. "Very cagey, the FBI," he said sarcastically to Melora.

They returned to the kitchen, and Karp picked up the Melora's cellular telephone. It was a handheld model that she carried in her purse. He dialed the phone number to Billy White's pager. It beeped, and a tone followed. Karp then dialed in his own telephone number and hung up. They waited two minutes, and the phone rang.

"Hello?"

"This is White."

"Jerry Karp here. I wanted to make sure you were on your way."

"Yes," he said irritably. "I'm in the car. It'll be about half an hour, depending on traffic."

"Good. I'll see you then."

White hung up on him without another word.

Gaven Peltier began to stir toward wakefulness. He felt groggy, tired, and nauseated. He was instantly short of breath. His respiratory muscles, weakened by the botulinum toxin, were further debilitated by the narcotic effects of the alcohol. He tried to get up, but found himself paralyzed. Immediately, his heart sped up. As his senses heightened with the stimulation, he remembered that he'd been made quadriplegic somehow by that bastard friend of Melora's, whose name he still didn't know. He breathed shallowly and rapidly. He felt a wave of nausea well up. He felt as if he might vomit, and he turned his head weakly to one side and burped. His breath was awful. He moaned, and looked upright again.

It occurred to him that there was a bright light under him, or rather above him. He was on his back again, and his feet were dangling in the air, over his head. His hands ached. Although he was immobilized, he still had full sensation in his limbs. His fingers were strapped to something hanging above his head. With his arms up, the blood had simply run out of them. They were cold and tingly. "Shit," he whispered thickly. He swallowed. He was pleased to realize that the tube had been removed from his nose.

He tried to orient himself, but the visual world was a meaningless blur through Karp's thick glasses. He squinted and squeezed and twitched, but remained unable to make out any details. He didn't realize he was wearing glasses, and he thought that Karp had done something to blind him. Maybe he had given him methanol, wood alcohol, to poison him. Peltier closed his eyes and tried to steady his breathing. The dentist realized that if he were to throw up he would almost certainly choke on his vomitus and die. He wondered where he was, but decided to try and relax. He made an effort to breathe slowly. Eyes closed, he lay back. I got through prison, he thought. I'll get through this.

Karp glanced at the clock in the kitchen every few minutes. At six forty five, he suggested that it was time for them to leave. Melora thought that was a fine idea. She didn't relish being in the house, so close to the bombs, knowing they were armed. "I want to check on Gaven," said Karp.

"I wouldn't," she suggested. "The garage door is open. Someone might see you."

He nodded. That wasn't a good risk. They opened the back door and started across the yard, walking at an angle to avoid a direct line with the gray Chevy across the street. They kept the house next door between them all the way.

It had turned into a lovely summer evening. The sun was still high in the sky, and the suburban neighborhood carried on routinely. A grill was fired up down the block and the scent of cooking meat was in the air. An automatic sprinkler, unfazed by the morning's rain, spurted along two doors down, watering the still moist lawn. A lawnmower was buzzing around the block, and several kids were playing street hockey just near enough to hear their shouting.

They got into the Jeep, and closed the doors. Melora started the car and moved up the block about twenty yards, so they could see the edge of Karp's driveway between the houses. She shut off the engine and they waited.

Billy White exited the freeway and heard the thump again as he came to a stop at the red light. At first he thought that he might need a new shock absorber or strut, but the car was only six months old and that made no sense. He listened more carefully and realized that the sound was coming from the back seat. He looked over his shoulder, and saw nothing. The stop light changed to green, and he continued down Lake Street, into the city of Aurora.

At Sullivan Road he slowed to turn right. He heard the thump again, looked in the back, and saw nothing. He shook his head. There was a stop sign a quarter mile up the road. He slowed and stopped. Ka-thump. "Damn it," he said. "What is that?"

White pulled forward through the intersection and slid the car gently onto the gravel shoulder. As his forward motion ceased, he heard the thump once more. He clicked the gear shift lever into Park and unsnapped his seat belt. Pushing himself up with his left foot, he peered over the seat toward the floor of the passenger section behind him. He saw a small black box on the floor. He reached, but couldn't grab it.

He opened the car door and nearly had it torn off by a red pickup truck. He looked down the block and saw no further traffic. This time, he quickly stepped outside, opened the back door, and plucked the garage door opener from the back seat. How did this get back there, he asked himself. A cookie delivery van pulled up toward him on the two lane road and the driver beeped quickly at White. He waved and jumped back into the driver's seat.

There was something unfamiliar about the garage door opener. It wasn't the right size or shape. He reached up to his sun visor, and felt the plastic box his fingers were accustomed to finding there. He examined the remote control in his hand. It was a Sears Craftsman model. He knew that the opener installed in his garage was a LiftMaster. Out of habit, he pushed the button.

Frank Ellison and Rollie Grant sat in the front seat of the Chevy Caprice on Birch Lane. Ellison hated surveillance work. It was boring. He loved the excitement of the hunt. He enjoyed putting a case together based on evidence left at a crime scene.

Surveillance was a drag. He sat in the passenger seat, scrunched down, his hands crossed on his chest. He fidgeted.

"Goddam it, Frank. Will you sit still?"

"I gotta pee, Rollie."

The senior agent laughed. "I told you not to have a large Coke, you twit. What are you going to do, get out of the car and piss on a mailbox?"

He shifted in his seat. "That's sounding mighty fine to me about now, partner."

Grant reached over to the aftermarket cup holder that hung limply from the driver's side window. He had a cup of icewater there. He tried again to remove the stain on his tie from the butterscotch ripple ice cream he'd ordered at Oberwies Dairy on Lake Street. His wife was going to be mad. He rolled down the window and tossed the water out. "Here, pal," he said, handing his partner the empty cup. "Always be prepared," he grinned.

"You're not serious," said Ellison.

"Fine. Hold it."

He shifted in the seat once more. Ellison adjusted the mirror on the sun visor and looked down the sidewalk behind them to make sure that there were no pedestrians coming. "Fuck it," he said, zipping down his pants.

"Just don't spill any. I'll make you wipe it up before I sit here for another hour smelling it."

Nothing happened. Billy White shook his head. Of course nothing happened. What did he expect? Idiot. Luann must have dropped this, or one of the kids. But where did it come from? It wasn't important. He decided that it would have to wait until later. He leaned over to open the glove box door and tossed the garage door opener into it. He snapped it shut, fastened his seat belt, and continued on his way.

Karp fidgeted in his seat. He leaned over to see the clock on the Jeep's dash. It was six fifty seven. He rubbed his cheek, then leaned over toward the open window. He poked his nose out and craned his neck, as if it would give him a clearer view.

Melora reached over and took his hand in hers. She lifted it to her lips and kissed it. "Relax," she said. "Everything is running on schedule. He'll be there."

Karp nodded and looked at her. Her smile was comforting. And it was inviting. He leaned over and kissed her gently on the mouth. He again filled his nose with her smell and felt himself stir. As anxious as he was at this moment, he could not help but think of touching her body.

She pushed him away and gulped a swallow of air. "It's him," she whispered.

Karp turned and saw the black Mercedes slow and turn into his driveway. He watched the car carefully, carefully. He waited for it to stop. It seemed to creep up the incline forever. Stop, he thought, stop. He willed it to happen. Finally, it did.

Karp picked up the garage door opener which had been resting in his lap. With his right hand, he held it out the window, aiming it at his home. He pushed the button.

Frank Ellison nearly spilled the cup of urine as he set it down on the floor of the car. He watched the black and chrome Mercedes as it passed their Caprice, slowed, and turned into Karp's driveway.

"Nice catch," said Grant without taking his eyes from the car.

"Bite me," said Ellison. "Did you get the plate?"

Grant shook his head and squinted. "Illinois. D-R something. Personalized."

Ellison opened the glove compartment and removed a small pair of binoculars. They were little more than four power opera glasses, but often that was all they needed. "D-R I-O-L," he read

330

the tag. Grant jotted down the license plate number in his notepad. They watched.

Nothing happened. "What the..." thought Karp out loud. He pushed the button again.

White checked the sheet of paper on his passenger seat. The address was eighteen forty Birch Lane. He glanced at the ten inch tall brass numbers affixed to the house over the front door. One eight four oh. This was the place. What was that asshole doing in the car, he wondered. The door of the white Dodge Stealth in the garage was ajar, but he wasn't sure he saw anyone in the car. No one had gotten in or out, and there was no motion in the garage. Was Karp leaving? He was insistent that I meet him here.

Jesus, thought White. He's going to run me down in that car. He tensed up, pushing hard on the brake pedal with his right foot. He waited a moment, but there was no movement. No one came out of the house or the car. He rolled down his window and cocked his head to listen more closely. The engine was not running on the white car. The piece of shit green Citation next to it didn't look as if it ran at all.

Nothing happened. "God damn it," said Karp as he opened the Jeep's door.

"What's wrong," yelled Melora in a whisper, her eyes wide.

"Not sure," said Karp as he hopped out of the Jeep. He took two quick steps toward the house and pushed the button again.

White sat for a few moments and tried to decide what was going on. Nothing moved. No one came from the house. The car didn't budge. Maybe Karp had just left the car door open when he went in the house. He didn't see anyone there. That made sense, he decided. Karp had just left the car door dangling open. Incompetent. He couldn't even close the door to his own car without screwing up.

White pulled on the latch to his car door, and it snicked open. He swung his legs out and slowly stood up, leaning against the window frame of his car door. "Karp?" he called out. He thought he saw something move in the car.

Nothing happened. Karp went over the system in his mind. The batteries were fresh. When he rewired the electrical board from the receiver to create the triggering device, he tested the system, retested it, and checked it out a third time again every time he made a new connection. He must have triggered that receiver fifty times before he'd actually connected it to a stick of explosive. It worked perfectly in all the tests. He'd attached the whole system to the car battery using wires that bypassed the fusebox, so there'd be no chance of blowing a circuit when the power was applied. No, he was confident of the system.

This mental exercise took only two steps as he continued to pace toward the house. He could see that the car door was open on the Mercedes, though he wasn't sure if anyone had gotten out. He pushed the button again. Nothing happened.

Melora opened her car door and ran toward the front of the Jeep. She could see Billy White standing in the driveway, and that meant that he could see her. She wanted to shout to Karp to stop, but she knew that her voice would attract White's attention. Her mouth opened, the words formed, but there was no sound. She froze in front of the passenger side headlight of her Jeep.

Of course, thought Karp. "We're too far away," he said in a normal speaking voice.

Melora could only hear a few of the words. "Too far."

He knew that he could not open the garage door under normal circumstances until he was directly in front of the house. The transmitter was too weak, or the receiver poorly tuned, whatever. The house was made of brick, and the radio waves were partially absorbed by the heavy material. These were less than optimal circumstances. He picked up his pace.

Karp was halfway to the house now. He pushed the button. Nothing happened. He slowed his pace, now, deciding that he was discharging the battery in the transmitter too quickly. He needed to get closer, but he wanted to give the machine a few moments to regain its normal charge.

He was twenty yards from the back door. He pushed the button.

Peltier lay on his back, groggy, but coming to. He thought he'd heard a car pull up, but he wasn't sure. Then he heard someone call out. What did he say? Carp? Cart? Cards? He smacked his lips. "In here," he moaned with his thick, sticky tongue. "In here." He tried to look around, but found his attempts hampered by the goofy glasses he was wearing.

Somewhere behind his head, under the hood of the Stealth, Gaven Peltier heard a muffled click.

"What's he doing?" asked Grant.

Ellison peered through the opera glasses. "Nothing." He squinted through the eyepieces. "He's just standing there, as far as I can see."

The radio signal closed the circuit on the trigger. Karp designed it to split the current into several lines which ran to various areas within the car bomb. This way, if any of the main trunks were not functioning, at least some of the explosives would fire off. He presumed that the explosion itself would probably trigger the other bombs nearby, leaving as few duds as possible.

A turn signal lamp extracted from its glass bulb acted as a detonator for the stick of C-4 that was wrapped to Peltier's hands. As electricity flowed into the filament, it quickly glowed white, burned up, and ignited the explosive fertilizer and fuel mixture surrounding it. An intense flame burned away the skin and most of the fat that made up the fleshy portion of Peltier's fingers. The shock wave that followed fractured and dislocated the bones of his fingers and hands, sending tiny fragments scattering. Most of the bone slivers imbedded in the floor material and seats of the car, although a few were sent toward the soft tissues of his face.

The widening blast tore through the palm of his hand. The carpal bones, more dense than those in his fingers, were fractured and torn free of the ligaments holding them together. The soft tissue, blood vessels and nerves and tendons, were cauterized by the hot flame that hissed away from the pipe bomb. The ends of the bones in his arms, the radius and ulna, shattered, sending chips in several directions. The impact jammed the bones up toward his bent elbows and pushed the joint apart like nails driven through a wooden block. As Karp had predicted, the rubber bands were instantly vaporized. Freed of their attachments by fingers and bands, the arms were thrown away from their location in space along with the advancing shock wave. Even before the power of the detonation reached the shoulders, the strength that was transmitted through the arms dislocated his shoulders.

Karp's eyeglasses were shattered in an instant, emitting shards of sharp plastic toward the eyeballs along with the shock wave. The twisted frames blew and rolled off of his nose and, in pieces, were swept toward the base of the firewall of the car. The fireball instantly singed the eyelashes and brows from Peltier's face. Even though tightly closed, the eyelids provided little protection for him. The flecks of plastic from the spectacle lenses propelled by the explosion penetrated the clear corneas, the ocular lenses, and the vitreous gel of his eyes. The blast lacerated the corneas and the white scleras, and the inner fluids of the eyes splashed out, only to be evaporated by the flame.

334

Peltier's mouth was open, fixed in a silent scream which had only begun but was never finished. The impact of the explosion struck his teeth, smashing the enamel and breaking them into small fragments. The incisors splintered into tiny shards while the short, squat molars cracked into fewer gravel-like pieces. The bones of both jaws were pushed inward and broken. His nose, attacked by heat, fire, and pressure, broke away from his face, deformed by a combination of melting and charring.

Meanwhile, additional explosives under the floorboard ignited simultaneously. They blew the steel undercarriage upward, tearing jagged holes in the car's floor. The force of this broke several cracks into Peltier's skull, initially breaking open the meandering suture lines where the bones joined, and later extending in new directions. As the pressure built, the skull broke into pieces, and the contents of the head were torn free.

The explosives in the base of the seat blew out in a direction that hyperextended his neck. This tore the smaller cervical vertebrae apart, severing the spinal cord. With the supportive bones broken, the head was momentarily attached to his body only by the soft tissues located there, the tracheal breathing tube, the esophagus, and the blood vessels. These structures soon gave way under the pressure, and Peltier's head was catapulted upward, into the area under the dashboard.

The rest of the seat detonated as well, including several explosives that had been placed in the headrest. The latter severed his feet at the ankles, blowing them to either side of the car's interior. His legs were shattered into multiple bony and muscular fragments attached to burned skin. His pelvic bones and vertebral column were blasted inward, causing them to cut through the organs in his abdomen and chest. His lungs collapsed, the liver was lacerated, and his intestines were torn in several places.

The limited space under the hood of the car contained dozens of bombs wedged in place around the engine. As these devices fired off, the hood was first torn from its hinges, then literally split apart by the intense heat. The engine, made of thicker metal, was ripped from its mounts on the frame and impelled toward the ground, shattering there into smaller pieces and splattering motor oil into a huge blot on the garage floor. The radiator and other smaller parts in the front of the car were dislodged and torn to pieces. Screws and bolts and fan blades and hoses flew in every direction.

Bombs in the doors, the back seat, and the hatchback storage area tore the thin steel body panels apart. Welded seams split like pieces of paper, and tight connections only caused further splintering and shrapnel formation. The window glass around the car disintegrated into thousands of tiny knife like pieces that scattered in a mushroom pattern.

Grant jumped backward in his seat, catapulted by the reflex tightening of his leg muscles. His arms flailed forward and he bumped the horn trigger on the steering wheel, although no one heard it because of the roar of the bomb firing. Ellison, who was looking through the opera glasses, saw only the reflection of the flash off of Billy White's face and car. The shock wave pushed him backward, though, and the world shook as it was magnified through the binoculars. He kicked the cup of urine over on the floor of the car.

Billy White, who was standing no more than twenty feet from the bomb, was literally knocked off of his feet. The shock wave blew him backwards down the driveway, where he landed squarely on his ass. The blast of warm air enveloped him like a long sulfury breath, and the bellow of sound deafened him. He was fortunate to have been pushed backward and down, as the blast was followed by a hailstorm of shredded metal, bolts, and windshield glass. Several pieces became imbedded in the soles of his shoes and others penetrated his pants, leaving small cuts on his legs. His torso and head were spared injury, aside from the goose egg he would soon have on his occiput where it struck the pavement. The front of his new black Mercedes E420 was not so fortunate, however, as it was scratched and dented by the shrapnel blown out of the mouth of the blast.

From the passenger side of the Stealth, the bomb buckled the wall that separated the garage from the dining room of the Karps' home. A tall oak hutch occupied that location of the room, containing their fine china and crystal glasses for the holidays. The shock wave blew the cabinet over, spreading broken glass and shattered dishes about the room. The heavy oak dining table was pushed forward two feet, and the light fixture hanging from the ceiling smashed to the tabletop, exploding itself into thousands of tiny glass pieces.

The open driver's door of the Stealth blew off its hinges, and the side panel behind the door blew out. The heat reduced the steel parts to so many little bullets of iron, piercing Lon's old Citation along its passenger side. Its door dented inward, the window glass shattered into the interior. Some of the bits of Stealth ricocheted off of the slab floor of the garage, bouncing back up into the bottom of the Chevy. A dozen or so of these pieces penetrated the green car's fuel tank, and liquid gasoline began to leak to the floor. The gas puddle from the Chevy crept along the floor, and was joined by a similar puddle that emanated from similar leaks from the Stealth.

The glass hatchback of the white sports car was blown out, and the shock wave that hit the back wall of the garage tore through it, blasting inward to the laundry room. Several of the two by four studs that supported the wall were torn in half, causing the ceiling above to fall in. The electrical wires running through the wall severed with a spark, leaving the upstairs bedroom cut off. The natural gas line that fed the clothes dryer also ran through this wall, and a washer that held a structural bolt in place on the Stealth buzzed through the copper pipe like a tiny saw. Methane gas began to hiss from the pipe into the room. The force of the explosion toward the back of the house was so strong that it caused a small hole to be blown through the brick exterior of the house. Bits of broken brick and mortar spat outward into the yard.

Jerry Karp took three more steps toward the house and pushed the button on the garage door opener one more time before he even realized that the bomb had detonated. He was unable to see the flame or the debris thrown out of the front of his garage. When the shock wave from the explosion blew chunks of brick out of the place, though, one of the hard pieces struck the right side of his forehead. He doubled over, dropping the garage door opener, and fell to his knees. Melora saw him fall and ran from the front of the Jeep toward Karp.

Karp had designed the car bomb so that there would be two explosions. The main one destroyed the interior and exterior of the car. The secondary explosion, ignited by a separate set of detonators, included a five second time delay. The bombs connected to this device were attached by duct tape all around the fuel tank of the Stealth. Karp had planned to allow the initial explosion to penetrate the tank and cause the fuel to leak out. With gasoline spilled about the garage floor, the second explosion would act to demolish the tank and send any remaining gasoline up in an airy pattern around the garage. Several of the C-4 sticks he'd made for this had been altered in recipe. He'd added gunpowder to some. To others he tossed in some match heads. He hoped that one recipe or the other would make these devices more incendiary than explosive, igniting the aerated gasoline and puddled fuel-oil mixture on the garage floor.

His plan worked perfectly. Five seconds after the initial explosion, the second set of bombs went off. The fuel tank on the Stealth cracked into large pieces, spraying gasoline into the air. The incendiary bombs ignited a huge red fireball that blew up to the ceiling, out of the garage door, and into the house. The gas dripping from the Citation caught fire, exploded, and engulfed it in a blaze of its own.

Billy White lay on the ground next to his scratched and pockmarked Mercedes. He had barely caught his breath as the second explosion ripped through the garage. Hot air blew around him, up his pants legs, and into his nostrils. He closed his eyes tightly and covered his face with his arms.

"Jesus Christ!" shouted Rollie Grant as the fireball blew out toward the neighborhood. His hands were tightly grasping the steering wheel of the Caprice now, pushing him hard against the seat back. His partner sat, motionless, mouth gaping open stupidly, as he watched the fire curl upward into a smoky pyre.

Melora reached Karp's side just as the second set of bombs went off. The sound of the first explosion was still echoing through the neighborhood, and she was able to feel the second shock wave more intensely than the first. She hugged him tightly and cradled his face to her chest, covering her own face down atop his head.

More debris blew out the hole in the back of Karp's house. Karp feared that the wall might come down and he knew that the neighbors would soon be looking out their windows and milling down the street to see what the noise was all about. He reached up to Melora's arm and squeezed hard. "We have to go, now," he insisted.

They each helped the other to their feet. Karp reached over and retrieved the garage door opener as they stood. Melora saw a trickle of blood meander down Karp's forehead. She gestured toward him to wipe it, but instead, he started back to the Jeep.

"No time, now," he panted. "Let's go."

Billy White lay on his back for about fifteen seconds, covering his face. He waited to be certain there would be no further explosions. Once he felt confident that the worst was over, he pulled himself up. Sitting propped on his arms, he surveyed the scene. The little white sports car was not recognizable. The paint was burning from its surface, splattered with flaming gasoline. Fire spit from the interior, belching out black smoke while burning the plastic and leather. More thick, oily smoke spewed from what once was the engine compartment billowing up and out of the garage. The old green Chevy burned even more actively, spitting, hissing, and popping as it did. The rear tire on the right side of it exploded with a ringing noise as the air inside it expanded from the heat.

White ducked his head for a second when the tire popped. The noise somehow woke him up from his daze. He assembled himself and stood up, grasping the open door of his Mercedes. He looked around nervously and saw no one on the sidewalk. He saw the gray Caprice, but was too anxious to notice the two men sitting in it. As far as he knew, he was alone on Birch Lane.

He threw himself into the Mercedes and scrambled to close the door. He was so excited that he almost fell out again when he reached for the door handle. Once the car was started, he threw it into reverse and spun down the driveway, squealing his tires as he started moving and slamming on the brakes when he got to the street. Then he threw the car in gear and tore off down the block, leaving a puff of blue smoke where he spun the tires on the pavement.

"He blew up the doctor," said Ellison. "He blew him up."

Grant turned the key and started the Caprice. He reached for the gear shift lever and missed, his hands shaking. "I've never seen anything like that," he said as he grasped the chrome knob and put the car into gear."

"Go, go," said Ellison, waving his partner on. "He'll get away." Both men had investigated murder scenes before.

Neither had been material witnesses at one. The car lurched forward as Grant gunned it down the street. The black Mercedes was already halfway down the block.

Karp and Melora dove back into the Jeep. As he closed the passenger door behind him, Karp glanced around the street. He didn't see anyone, so he hoped that their sprint across the yard had gone unnoticed. Since his ears were still ringing from the noise of the explosion, he didn't hear White's Mercedes or the FBI agents' Caprice as they sped away from his home. As soon as the car doors were closed, Karp ducked down in the seat.

"Start the car," he instructed Melora.

She complied. "What are you doing?" she asked him, as she watched him hide himself from the car windows.

"I shouldn't be seen. You still live in the neighborhood. Pick up your cellular phone and dial your home number."

"Why?"

"Do it."

As she dialed the phone, she realized that several of the neighbors had come out of their houses and were walking in their direction.

"Is anybody coming?" asked Karp.

"Yes."

"Look over at the house, then talk on the phone."

Melora understood. He wanted it to look as if she had just been driving by as the house blew up, stopped, and phoned the fire department. She nodded and blabbed into the cellular phone.

"Good," said Karp. "Nod more. Right. Now put the car in gear, and let's go back to your place. Slowly. Don't speed. Stay on the phone."

She complied, and the white Jeep slowly accelerated down the block. Melora looked at the growing number of people milling toward Karp's burning house.

The fire from the burning cars had ignited the ceiling and supportive beams of the garage. Much of the dining room next to the garage and the bedrooms upstairs were also engulfed. Meanwhile, natural gas blew out of the severed pipe in the laundry room. Lighter than air, it billowed up to the ceiling and crept into the adjoining kitchen. The cloud of gas grew and grew as the fire spread through the house. Finally, the amorphous blob of methane made its way into the dining room, where smoky flames flicked up from the carpet and the draperies. A finger of fire connected with the cloud, then spread along its length through most of the first floor of the house.

The gas exploded so violently that the back wall of the house blew well into the next yard. The second floor, robbed of its structural support, fell in, spilling the master and guest rooms' contents into the backyard. The windows in front of the house broke out, and air rushed in to feed the hungry flames.

Still bent down in the Jeep, Jerry Karp's hearing had begun to return. In the distance, he could make out sirens.

"Police," said Melora anxiously.

Karp listened. The sirens wailed. They were different from the blare of police cars. He shook his head. "Fire trucks."

SCOTT RACHELLE

Twenty

Billy White didn't even slow down for stop signs as he flew along the streets of Aurora heading back to the freeway. Grant and Ellison followed, taking great pains to keep the back of the black Mercedes in sight. This was no small effort, as other traffic between them was moving much more slowly. Rollie Grant did not want to wreck the Caprice in a collision. Not only would he end up injuring a civilian and damaging the car, he would lose their suspect and have to explain how that happened to his boss. He would also have to deal with Bob Wilson.

As Grant concentrated on the road, Frank Ellison dialed Wilson's home telephone number into the cellular phone. "Damn it," he announced as he misdialed the number, his finger pointed in an errant direction by a bump in the road. He cleared the number and started again. "Are you sure you want to talk to Wilson first?" he quizzed his partner. Ellison wanted to overtake the bomber and arrest him immediately.

"Look," answered Grant, hitting the brake to avoid tail-ending a rusting Ford Escort in front of him. "Wilson said to call him if, what was it?...If Karp farted, I think he said." Oncoming traffic in the left lane cleared, and the engine roared as Grant opened the throttle full bore. He pulled into the left lane and whistled past the Escort. "I'd say that what happened back there would qualify as slightly more than a fart."

Ellison punched the green Send button and the cell phone beeped to life.

Bob Wilson sat in the living room. The picture window behind him overlooked the tree shaded street of Gardenview Drive in the Shorewood Hills home that he and his wife, Charlene, shared. The evening was cool, with a light breeze blowing in off of Lake Mendota, which was only three blocks to the east. He was reading the newspaper and drinking a Special

343

Export. Charlene, an attorney in private practice, was late coming home from the office. She was preparing a corporate merger that was to be presented the following morning. They planned to stop at Numero Uno's for pizza. Neither of them was much for cooking.

The telephone rang, and Wilson got up to answer it. He expected Charlene to be on the line. She was probably going to be even later, and wanted him to go to the restaurant to pick up the pizza. "Hello?"

"Bob. It's Rollie."

Wilson hadn't expected to hear from the FBI agent until morning. "What's going on?"

"Bob, I'm sorry to tell you this, but I think your friend, Dr. Karp, is dead."

Wilson stood up straight. "What?"

"Sorry. There was some meeting planned, I guess, like he said. We were watching the house. Someone pulled up the driveway and saw Karp getting into his car. There was a bomb in the car, and he blew it up."

"Are you making this up, Rollie?"

"We saw it, Bob. All of it. Frank and I watched the whole thing. We had no idea about the bomb."

Wilson just stared out the picture window. The sky was deep blue through the patchwork of dark green leaves. "I can't believe it."

There was a pause. Grant was waiting for instructions from the Assistant U.S. Attorney. It was important that they not lose the suspect. He waited, then finally reminded him. "We're following the suspect now, Bob. He is fleeing the scene in a black Mercedes at high speed, and we've just pulled onto the interstate highway. He's doing eighty, eighty five, and we're keeping up."

Wilson didn't answer.

"Uh, you told us not to do anything unless you knew first. We think it would be advisable to stop this man and take him to the Chicago office for questioning."

Wilson snapped back. "Who is he? What do you know about him?"

Grant described Billy White. "White male, fifty or so. Five ten, two hundred twenty pounds. Well dressed, gray suit. No, blue. Driving a black Mercedes Benz, late model, Illinois tag David-Robert-Ida-Oscar-Landmark."

Wilson was confused. "Driol?"

"No, sir. It's Doctor IOL, whatever that means. Initials?"

"I don't know. Call the DMV and run the tag. Then follow him. If he tries to escape the area, arrest him and call me. We can hold him till morning as we sort this out. If he doesn't try to flee, just follow him. My guess is he is an otherwise upstanding member of the medical community. I don't think he's going very far for now."

"You don't want us to bring him in?"

"That's right. Find out who the hell he is and call me back. I'll go to the office and get started on the warrants. We have to figure out what's going on here."

"And let the bomber go."

"No, don't let him go. Have him observed and be certain that he doesn't flee. As long as he stays put, use the time to perform an investigation." His voice became angry. "Karp told us something was going on in Aurora and all you guys were able to come up with was that he had filed for bankruptcy. He calls us back, tells us he's got some new evidence, and then gets blown up while some doctor in a Mercedes leaves the scene."

"I understand," said Grant.

"I hope you do. Get someone to watch this guy when he stops moving, and you guys get to work. I want to know what Karp knew that was important enough to make a physician kill him. I want to know by tomorrow when I get to Aurora. Do you understand me?"

"Clearly."

Karp stood in the bathroom and examined the cut on his forehead. It wasn't nearly as bad as it appeared at first. He'd washed away the blood and saw a superficial laceration that extended toward his brow. The bleeding had slowed, but the edges of the wound were a bit ragged. He dabbed at it, hoping that it would not leave a bad looking scar.

"Do you think we should stitch it?" asked Melora.

He shook his head. "Not that deep."

She walked into the room behind him, and put her arms around his waste. Melora hugged him and kissed his neck. Karp was worried that she would be upset about him leaving, and it was essential that he get far away from Aurora as quickly as possible. He turned and kissed her, and he liked it very much.

"I have to get going, you know," he said finally as he looked into her blue eyes.

She nodded once and blinked. "I know. I guess you won't stay the night."

He shook his head and stroked her cheek. "Not that I don't want to."

She smiled and kissed him again. "Still going to cut your hair?"

"I think so."

She ran her hand through it and caressed his head. "What a shame."

Detective Ramon Cardena was talking with the owner of The Corner Grocery, a small food store on Aurora's east side. Ray, as his friends knew him, spent the greatest part of his day dealing with the kids in Aurora's gangs. Most of them lived in this part of town, although they travelled all over. They had begun to recruit younger boys, and now included many nine and ten year olds as their own. Cardena was checking on a group of kids that had been hanging around the store, panhandling customers and maybe selling crack cocaine and crank, methamphetamine.

Cardena had moved up through the ranks of the town's police force quickly. His brother was killed years ago in a bar fight. Ray was only twelve when it happened, but it had a profound impact on the boy. Before that, he was downright lazy in school. He'd gotten into his share of fights and deals. Afterward, though, he straightened up and finished high school. He did a four year hitch with the Army and decided to try out for the Police Academy in his hometown.

As a hispanic cop, Cardena was respected in this part of town. The kids didn't see him as an outsider. The young kids ran away from other cops, and the older ones lied and dissed them. Cardena understood. Although he was a cop, he was also one of them. He could be trusted. The suits downtown put Cardena on the fast track to his detective's shield.

"I tell you, man, you got to do something to get these kids off my sidewalk," said the shop owner. He worked long hours in the old-fashioned grocery store, and he kept the place clean. Competing against the big supermarkets was difficult, but some of the neighborhood people remained loyal to him. He extended credit to good families who needed help. He turned a profit, enough to feed his family; his wife, daughter, and two grandkids. Right now, he didn't need the gangs scaring away his customers.

"Who was it, Teo? What kids?"

The man shrugged. "I don't know. Kids. They hang around all the time."

Cardena shook his head. "Come on, Teo. I can't help you if you don't tell me which ones are here. You know that."

The storekeeper turned away.

Detective Cardena's pager went off. He checked the digital readout, which showed the phone number of the main office downtown, followed by the digits zero and one. That meant it was a number one priority call. There weren't many detectives on Aurora's small police force, so they rotated calls for murders, rapes, and the like. Cardena didn't have time to kill on this gang case if the victim wasn't going to cooperate. He reached into his suit pocket and pulled out a card with his telephone number.

347

"Here." He handed the card to the store manager. "Think about what you want to do, then call me. I can help you, but you have to help me, too. Entiendes?"

Teo looked at the card. "Sí, sí. I'll think about it."

Ramon Cardena returned to his unmarked car. He lifted the radio microphone from its cradle. "Cardena to base."

The radio hissed. "Detective. Proceed to one eight four oh Birch Lane. Fire, possible arson or explosive. One victim."

"Ten four." He started the car and slipped the portable flasher onto the dashboard.

When he arrived at the house, the crime scene had already been marked off. There were five patrol cars there, and yellow tape surrounded the house, or what was left of it. Two fire pumpers were on the scene with firefighters finishing the job of putting the house fire out. The gas company had shut off the main.

The right side of the house, including the garage, had been blown well into the yard. There were two by fours and bits of wall that had only been charred on the edges, indicating that the explosion blew the wall out before the fire took over. The roof of the garage had collapsed down on the cars, then fed the fire. The Stealth and the Citation were little more than blackened frames. Most of the body metal had been melted, crushed, or blown away. The house was severed at the margins of the gas explosion: Half a roof and two thirds of the facade remained, still smoking. The rest of the scene was soaking wet.

Cardena had been to several house fires, but this one was messier. The explosions had left a wide area of destruction. There were papers and furniture and bits of shattered belongings strewn all over. It was even more out of place in this neighborhood, nestled among the trees and upper classers. He lifted the yellow police line tape and crawled underneath, making his way toward the house. He stepped in large greasy puddles of oil stained water and silently cursed what this would do to his shoes. One of the uniformed cops met him halfway up the driveway.

"Bad scene, Detective," said the cop.

"Arson?" asked Cardena.

The uniform shook his head. "Fire says it's a bomb," he answered, referring to the Aurora Fire Department Investigative Team. The two men walked over to the firefighter assigned to the case, Russell "Rusty" French. Unlike the rest of the firefighters on the scene, Rusty wore a suit and tie. The only distinguishing part of his dress was the yellow firefighter's helmet that he kept on his head while on the scene. Although Rusty had been a member of the AFD for thirty years, he no longer worked as a smoke eater. He was an assistant to the chief, spending most of his time working arson and other suspicious cases. He was slight, but had great strength for his size. He was unafraid of hard work, and he was methodical on the site of a fire. Rusty was working his way through the wreckage in the garage, looking for evidence.

"Hi'ya, Rusty," said Cardena.

French shook his head. "Bad one, Ray," he answered, without looking away from the debris.

"The guys tell me that you think this was a bomb."

"Know it," he said. "Look at the blast debris pattern."

This wasn't Cardena's forte. He looked around. It was a mess. "Shit blew up, all right. Couldn't it have just been the gas line?"

"Look," demanded Rusty. "Look at the blast pattern." He pointed toward the outside wall of the garage. "See that? Blown out twenty feet at least." Cardena nodded. "Helluva blast. Now, look at the back wall." There wasn't much left of it. "Blown clean away. Gas welled up for a few minutes before it went up. What set it off? Fire was already burning."

Cardena nodded. "Okay."

"Now look at the inside wall," said French. "See that? It's blown in. Not out. Did the gas line blow through the garage? Doubt it."

"Something in the garage blew out the walls," concluded Cardena.

"Makes sense. Check out the dining room. The furniture against the wall was knocked over. If the same blast that did that back wall had done the inside wall, the furniture would have been disintegrated. Get me?"

"Right. There was an explosion that blew the inside wall into the house."

"And?"

"And a big explosion after that one that knocked out the back wall and brought down the second floor."

French smiled. "Got ya' thinking like a fireman now. Where did the first explosion start?"

Cardena looked around the garage. There were two burnt out hulks that used to be cars. One appeared to have been a ten year old Chevy. The other was reduced to cinders. "There," he said. "In that car."

"Exactly," exclaimed the firefighter, clapping his hands together. "Something took out that car, started a fire, then set off the gas line."

Cardena put his hands on his hips. "Bomb? For sure?"

French shrugged. "More than a simple car fire. Still looking for bomb parts."

"Any fatalities?"

"One. Guess where."

"The shredded car."

French nodded.

"Any ID?"

French shook his head. "Check with your guys," he said. "I think there is, but it's not my interest. I fight fires."

Cardena nodded. "Thanks, Rusty. Let me know what else you find."

"You bet."

Cardena stepped over toward the Stealth, still steaming from the water that had been poured on it. He saw the remains of a body inside the car. "Gloves?" he asked his compatriot. The officer produced a pair of vinyl examining gloves from his pocket, and Cardena donned them. "Has CSU been here?" He referred to the Crime Scene Unit. They collect evidence and photograph the crime scene. He didn't want to move anything until the scene had been appropriately photographed.

"Yes, sir. They've taken photos."

He leaned in and poked about the body in the driver's seat. He found that the head was unattached. "Lovely," he commented. He reached for the head and tried to lift it. The back of the skull was disinserted from the rest of the head, and the two parts fell away. He grimaced. There was no skin on the face, all of the facial bones had been broken or crushed, and none of the teeth were intact. "Well, this should aid identification," he noted.

He replaced the severed head, noting the location of the bent eyeglass frames. He picked them up and examined them. "Helluva blast," he commented.

"I'll say," responded the uniform. "It blew him backwards in his seat."

"Um-hmm," said Cardena. "Unless he was already backward before the explosion. Help me turn the body." The two men tilted the burned corpse to its side. Cardena placed his gloved hand into the back pocket, and removed what was left of the wallet. He opened it, and the ragged, burnt front cover fell away. The plastic laminated Illinois driver's license was half melted. What remained was distorted, but the photo showed a man in his thirties or early forties wearing glasses. He thought he could make out the name as Karp, Jerrold M. Out of habit, he checked to see if there was any money in the wallet. It was scorched around the edges, but there was some there. He didn't bother to count it. This was not a robbery related murder. The uniform had already produced a plastic bag, and Cardena deposited the remains of the wallet into it.

"I presume this car was Mr. Karp's."

"Yes. We found a license plate in the front yard, and ran the number. This was a white Dodge Stealth registered to Jerrold M. Karp at this address."

Cardena glanced at the remains of the Chevy beside him. "And this car? His wife's?"

"No, sir. It's a Chevy Citation registered to Alonzo W. Morrissey of two ten Clark Street."

What was this car doing parked in the garage, nose out, like it belonged there? "Was there anyone in it?"

"No."

"Anyone else in the house?"

"Not that we've found yet. Just this one."

Cardena nodded. "Has anyone contacted Mr. Morrissey?"

"We sent a patrol over to the Clark Street address. Mr. Morrissey moved last week."

"Interesting. Any witnesses?"

The patrolman nodded in the direction of three teen aged boys who were talking with another patrolman just outside the yellow safety line ringing the blast site. "Those kids were out on the street. They might have seen something." He shrugged. "Everyone else came out to watch the fire."

"Thanks." Cardena ambled over toward the young men who were giving their statements to the officer. "I'm Detective Cardena," he introduced himself. "I understand you fellas might have seen something here?"

"I think we saw the bomber leave," said the oldest of the three, perhaps fourteen years old. "Just after the blast, two cars went tearing down the street."

"Yeah," chimed in another of the boys, not older than twelve. He wore baggy pants and a Nike T-shirt, and held his street hockey stick in one hand. "It was a mob hit, for sure."

Cardena wrinkled his brow. Very reliable witnesses, he thought. "Mob hit? Why's that?"

"The car, man, the car," said the boy.

"What kind of car was it?"

"Black Mercedes," answered the older boy.

"Better not say anything," said the youngest. "They'll come back and whack you. The mob don't like no witnesses."

"I doubt that it was organized crime," said Cardena, finally bothered by the young man's persistence. "If this were a mob bombing, they'd have been miles away before it went off." He turned back toward the older one. "This was a fairly new car?"

"Yes. I could tell by the rear end--it had those angled taillights. Couldn't be more than a year old."

"Uh huh. You didn't happen to see the license plate?"

"No. He was going too fast. He was flying, man."

"Okay. How about the second car."

The boy shrugged. "It's hard to remember. It was dark, gray or blue. GM car, a couple years old. He was following the Mercedes."

"You think they were together?"

"They were both going real fast."

The squad car pulled up behind Grant and Ellison. A uniformed city of Chicago officer got out, adjusting his checker-rimmed cap. He leaned into Grant's window. "Officer Sharpton," he said, introducing himself. "I got called in for a little overtime tonight."

"Thanks for coming, officer," said Grant, shaking the man's hand through the open car window. He'd called a friend in the Chicago office and asked if they could get surveillance on William White's home. In the meantime, they would begin the monumental task of investigating this case. "We're interested in the movements of a bombing suspect who lives at this address. William White. Followed him here in a black Mercedes."

Sharpton nodded.

"We don't expect he'll be going anywhere, but we want to keep an eye on him overnight."

"Sounds easy enough. Does he have any priors?"

"None," answered Grant. "Not known to be armed. Still, keep your distance and call us if he moves." He handed the officer a card with their pager and mobile numbers.

"No sweat, sir." He looked at the card then pushed it into his shirt pocket. "Anything else?"

"No. Thanks."

Sharpton stood and winced. He leaned back into the car and took another whiff. "What is that smell?" he asked.

Larry Evans and Melora Peltier stood in the parking lot at O'Hare International Airport. It was there that they had put the Plymouth Voyager several days earlier. Evans had cut his hair short and shaved off the moustache he'd worn for over a decade. With contact lenses and a clean shave, he appeared at least five years younger than Jerrold Karp.

Evans and Melora shared a long, savory kiss. They finally parted, and Evans entered the minivan. "Will you keep in touch, Jerry?" asked Melora.

He smiled gently. "I can't, not right away. We don't want to stir any suspicions." He sighed. "It's bad enough that I have to run away and start a new life. You shouldn't have to as well. You've got to think about your kids."

She looked at the ground. "I know. Duane's going to have to start therapy again after this."

"At least you know Gaven can never come back. He'll never harass you or your children again."

"I'm grateful for that."

Evans started the van.

"Where are you going to go?" she asked.

He shook his head. "You're better off not knowing." Through the open window he took her hand. "Don't worry. I'll keep tabs on what's happening in Aurora."

She took a deep breath. "You've given me a new start on my life."

He touched her cheek and ran his thumb over her lips. "You have done the same for me." He wasn't certain whether she would express any other deeper feelings toward him, but he knew that it would serve no purpose for either one of them.

With his foot on the brake, he shifted the van into reverse. "I should go now," he said quietly. "Take care of your kids, and take care of yourself."

She fought a tear and nodded, letting his hand return to the inside of the van. Slowly, he pulled out of the parking space, put the car into drive, and made his way down the aisle of the lot. She didn't move until he turned toward the exit and out of her view. Dr. Melora Peltier returned to her Jeep and prepared for the lonely drive to Aurora. Tomorrow she would bring the children home from St. Louis.

It was nearly eleven o'clock when Agents Grant and Ellison returned to the scene of the explosion. The fire was out, and the firefighters were packing their hoses and other paraphernalia from the site. Most of the neighbors had returned home long ago. A few curious stragglers stayed behind, watching the police and arson investigators sift through the debris that remained in Dr. Karp's yard.

Grant asked a uniform officer who was in charge of the investigation, and they were referred to Detective Cardena. He was questioning a witness, who, it turned out, had seen nothing. One of the neighbors mentioned that men had been poking around the Karps' house late at night, she thought. She couldn't pinpoint the time, though, and hadn't seen anyone's face. She might have heard a car, but then again, she wasn't sure.

"Detective?" interrupted Grant.

Cardena held his hand up toward the agent. He handed his card to the woman. "If you think of anything else, will you call me?"

"Sure."

"Thanks. If I need anything else, I'll give you a call." He turned toward the FBI agents. "Yes, gentlemen?"

"Detective, I'm Agent Roland Grant, this is my partner, Frank Ellison. We're with the Bureau."

The men shook hands. "Ramon Cardena. Call me Ray. Who called FBI?" He never trusted the feds.

"Fire Department," answered Ellison. "They reported a bombing."

"I see," said Cardena. That would be very unlike Rusty French, who preferred to work alone.

"What have you got?" asked Grant.

Cardena exhaled into the cool night air. Not much, he thought. "A car bomb," he said. "Set in a Dodge Stealth registered to a Dr. Jerrold Karp. Dr. Karp appears to have been in the car at the time of the explosion, and was laying on his back on the driver's seat, his head under the dashboard."

"On his back?" asked Grant. He didn't remember anyone moving around in the garage, although he honestly didn't think they had a very good view from the street.

"That's right. On his back. The driver's side door was open. It was blown forward, off its hinge. I think Dr. Karp had discovered the bomb, or part of it, under the dash. He must have rolled over to check it out. The bomb went off very close to his face. He must have been holding it, because his hands were severed from his wrists. We have yet to find much that resembles fingers, so I doubt that there will be any fingerprints for ID."

"But you've got dental records?"

Cardena shrugged. "Probably dental records somewhere. No teeth. Bomb blew up near his face. Like I said, he gets down to inspect something under his dashboard, and bam."

Grant shook his head. Ellison made a face, unable to hide his disgust. All of this happened while they were watching.

Cardena noticed Ellison's discomfort. "The car bomb severed a natural gas line in the house, which ignited later. That caused the lion's share of the blast damage you see. The rest is fire."

"If you've got no fingerprints and no dental ID, how do you know that this is Dr. Karp?"

Cardena sighed. "I don't know for a fact, Agent Grant. I doubt that there will be a positive ID. There was a driver's license in the man's pocket, and a twisted pair of eyeglasses that may have matched the photo. We found a demolished watch, but no other jewelry. Most of his skin is burned, so we can't use tatoos or scars. Frankly, his body is so badly maimed, I doubt that his wife will be able to identify him."

"His wife survived this?" asked Ellison.

"His wife," answered the detective, "was not home. We have yet to locate her."

Grant gestured toward the burned out Citation. "She went somewhere without her car?"

"That is not her car," Cardena pointed out. "We ran the plates and found it registered to Alonzo Morrissey, who moved out of Aurora last week. Forwarded telephone number is somewhere in Virginia. I haven't had the opportunity to call it yet."

Grant made some notes. "Found any pieces of the bomb?" he asked.

"My men are still sifting through the rubble. It's going to be quite a job. Would you care to lend your expert assistance?"

"Thanks," said Grant with a grin. "We're working some other angles in this case. Just tell them to collect anything homemade looking so that I can FedEx it to the lab at the Hoover Building in D.C. Our technicians can go over it there."

"Yes, sir," said Cardena sarcastically. "Are you gentlemen formally taking over this investigation? If so, I'd appreciate knowing now before I waste any more of my time slowing you down."

Ellison bristled, but Grant kept a cool head. He still hadn't forgiven him for spilling the piss in the car. "For now, Detective, we're just here to consult on the case. We want to make sure that this isn't part of a pattern of bombings."

Cardena nodded. "Just exactly what angle of this case are you working?"

Grant gave a sneaky smile. "I'm sorry, we can't get into that just yet. Were there any witnesses to the bombing?"

"Not really. Bunch of neighbors came by after the explosion. A few might have seen a car or two screaming out of

357

here." He decided not to tell the Feds about the Mercedes yet. "It was a sedan, dark color. Black, maybe gray. Nobody recognized anyone. Maybe one passenger, maybe two." He shrugged his shoulders. "Not much help, really."

"So you have no suspects."

"That's right. Any direction you can give me would be a great help. I'd hate to go over the same evidence trail you fellows have been following."

Grant tried to be very friendly. "We haven't much to share on this case. Frankly, we're going to be doing some research tonight. Why don't you see if you can find Mrs. Karp and this Morrissey. They may have some information. We can meet tomorrow afternoon."

Terrific. Cardena never liked the feds. They'd walk in after he had worked on this case for weeks, done all the tough evidence gathering, talked to all the witnesses. Then they'd claim federal jurisdiction, take over the case, and get the collar. He decided that he'd be talking to Captain McKane first thing in the morning. He'd be damned if he was going to do all the legwork for these guys and get no credit. "Sure. That's a great idea."

Lon Morrissey was settling down for the evening with a book. He and Angela were staying with their son and his wife while things settled and Lon worked on finding a job. It was a tight squeeze in their little house but it would be only temporary. His son came into the room. "Phone, Dad. It's the police."

"What?" He picked up the extension. "Hello?"

"Mr. Morrissey. I'm sorry to bother you. This is Detective Cardena with the Aurora Police Department."

"Yes?"

"Sir, are you the owner of a green Chevrolet Citation?"

"Yes."

"Do you know Dr. Jerrold Karp?"

"Yes, I do. Detective, what is this about?"

"I'm sorry, sir. There's been a terrible accident here. Dr. Karp is dead."

Lon was deflated. He almost dropped the phone. There was nothing to say. He only hoped that Karp hadn't gotten drunk and killed himself. Lon didn't want his friend to be remembered as a drunk. "What happened?" he whispered.

"There was a fire at his home, sir. Would you mind if I asked you a few questions?"

A fire? "No. How did this happen? Was it an accident?"

"We don't think so, sir. May I ask why your car was in Dr. Karp's garage?"

Lon sighed. What on earth did Karp get into? "Jerry was having some...problems. He'd filed for bankruptcy. When we moved, I knew my car wouldn't make it. I gave it to him. For after they repossessed his car."

"I see. He was a physician, correct? An ophthalmologist."

"That's right."

"He was having financial trouble?"

Jesus, thought Lon. This guy doesn't know shit about what they'd done to Karp. "Have you talked to Jerry's lawyer?"

"No."

"My God, have you talked to Val?"

"His wife?"

"That's right."

"No. Mrs. Karp isn't at home."

"For God's sake. Val walked out on him last week. You didn't know that, did you?"

"Do you know where I might find her? I would like to talk to her about this."

"Yes, yes. She's staying with her parents in Detroit. I can get you the number. You should also talk to Karp's lawyer, Rick Leach. He's somewhere in Chicago."

"Mr. Morrissey, is there anyone that might have wanted to hurt Dr. Karp? Someone who had something to gain by his death?"

Lon laughed. "Hell, Karp never hurt anyone. You don't know about the hospital, do you? Those people destroyed a good doctor's career, and they did it for nothing. No, Detective, I don't know who would benefit from Jerry Karp's death. They'd already emasculated him. You need to talk to his lawyer. Then check that bastard Dan Kilner at Compton Memorial Hospital. He and Dr. Billy White worked together to ruin Karp's life." He paused for a moment to recompose himself, realizing that his voice had gotten louder as he went on. "I guess it wouldn't surprise me if they were involved in his death. It's just a goddam shame, that's all. It makes no sense."

Twenty One

Cardena's initial theory was that Karp was somehow involved in the drug trade. He was disappointed when there was no evidence of drug paraphernalia found in the wreckage of the house. There was also no sign of ready cash. Karp's belongings really didn't show the trappings of a lavish, luxurious lifestyle. He'd keep working on this theory, though. It was palatable for the violent murder of a physician with ready access to pharmaceuticals. There was evidence that Karp had financial troubles. Cardena's men had found in the blast debris several bills that showed he was heavily indebted, and that his payments were behind schedule. He wondered if Karp owed money to organized crime sources.

Cardena wanted Karp's autopsy to be performed immediately. The corpse had been badly damaged by the fire and he needed to get all the information he could before decomposition caused further deterioration. The pathologist wasn't too pleased about being dragged out of bed, but when Cardena told him that he would be working on one of his colleagues, he softened.

The Coroner's Office was located in the basement of Cottage Hospital, a tiny community infirmary of twenty five beds in Geneva, the county seat. Cottage could hardly compete with Compton Memorial for patient care, but there was no comparison when it came to managing the dead. Their Pathology Department was top notch, simply by having the good fortune of being supported by state funds for its County Coroner. The only instrument they lacked was a scanning electron microscope, which was available in Springfield at the state's crime lab.

Don Chester had held the post of Kane County Coroner for over twenty years. He was also the only pathologist on staff at Cottage Hospital for the past twenty years. The docs at Compton had tried in vain to get the post so that their department could benefit from state funding, but they lost their bid every time because Chester could argue that his proximity to the County Courthouse made testifying that much easier for him. His many years of experience and good relationship with the district attorney's office didn't hurt, either.

Chester was a colorful sort. His hair was white, as was his long, flowing beard. He wore thick glasses in dark frames, and could pass for Colonel Sanders' brother. His tall stature and big frame combined with a booming baritone voice to give his courtroom testimony great credence. There, and in his path lab, he was all business. The cops referred to him privately as Dr. Death, though none dared use the name to his face.

"Good morning, Detective Cardena," thundered Chester as the policeman entered his grand office in the hospital basement.

"'Morning, Doc," answered Cardena. "What have you got for me on this Karp?"

Chester grinned. "Not much. There wasn't much left of Karp." The pathologist referred to his notes. "The body suffered blast injury and severe burns. My best guess is that it was a male, thirty to forty five years of age. He had been decapitated and there was a great deal of facial soft tissue and bony damage from the blast. He had both hands blown off at the wrists, and both feet at the ankles. His pelvis was shattered, and his spine suffered multiple fractures. There was a great deal of damage to the abdominal organs."

"He was blown up," Cardena stated the obvious.

"That's a reasonable conclusion."

"Was he alive at the time of the blast? Could he have been shot or beaten and dumped in the car?"

"Based on hydration, liver temperature, and lividity, I'd have to conclude that he was alive when the bomb went off. There was a great deal of burn artifact, however, and I can't be certain. Besides, why would a killer bother to place him head down in the car? Based on injuries to his legs, I'd say there was plenty of explosive to have killed him if he had been sitting upright."

Cardena nodded. "Our working theory is that Karp had gotten in the car, seen or suspected the bomb, then flipped over to look under the dashboard when he set the bomb off."

Chester shook his head. "He was in no shape to be screwing around with bombs," he said.

"How so?"

"His blood alcohol was at least .020." This was well over the legal limit.

Morrissey had mentioned that Karp had been drinking heavily. They found a bottle of Jack Daniel's that was left out in the kitchen before the explosion. Morrissey mentioned that Karp's beverage of choice was beer. He had apparently moved up a rung in his liquor consumption. "Any other drugs?"

"No. Nothing else showed up on the chromatograph, legal or otherwise."

"Um-hmm. How about ID? Were you able to get dental records?"

Chester laughed. "Didn't bother. There wasn't much of a face left after that explosion, let alone a single tooth. We found a few fragments, but I've nothing to match with the records. Don't bother to ask about fingerprints, either." He held up his hands and wiggled his fingers. "All gone."

"There wasn't anything to help ID?"

"I can give you more next time if you have more body for me to examine. This one was char-broiled, Ray." He glanced again at his notes on the desk . "Blood type was B-positive. That should narrow it down to a few hundred thousand people. No evidence of healed bony fractures, no major surgeries evident. Cause of death was multiple trauma from explosive injury and extensive burns post-mortem."

"Thanks, Doctor. I'll see what else I can find."

Ellison and Grant waited for Dr. White outside his personal office. It was time for them to have an initial interview with the man who was their prime suspect for the bombing. Finally,

White opened the door to his examining room, and he bade farewell to an elderly woman who needed a walker to move around. Her eye was red as she had undergone cataract surgery the week before.

"Don't worry, Mrs. Nelson," said White as he patted her shoulder. "The redness will go away in about a week. You can come back here in three weeks."

"Thank you, Dr. White," squeaked the old woman.

Colleen met the two at the doorway and whispered to White that there were two men from the FBI to see him. He paled for a moment, but quickly recomposed himself and nodded to her.

"Gentlemen." White acknowledged the agents and motioned them in to his private office.

"Thank you," said Grant as they sat in front of White's massive mahogany desk.

"Not at all. What can I do for you?"

"You may be aware that one of your colleagues died last night."

"Yes. Dr. Karp in Aurora." He shook his head. "I heard about it this morning. Dreadful thing, dreadful."

"Dr. White, did you know Dr. Karp?"

He shrugged his shoulders. "Only professionally. Even a city as large as Chicago has only so many ophthalmologists. We tend to know each other."

"I understand. You're very well known among your colleagues, I must say."

"Thank you. I am considered one of the nation's experts in techniques of cataract surgery. But what brings you here today?"

Grant sat forward in his seat. Ellison didn't move. "Are you aware of the violent nature of Dr. Karp's death, sir?"

"I understand that there was a bombing. At least, that's the rumor."

"That's right. The FBI routinely investigates bombings. It's a federal crime."

"Okay."

"Doctor, how well did you know Dr. Karp?"

364

"We never met personally, if that's what you mean."

"Uh huh." The agent just maintained eye contact. He wanted more information, but he'd let White go on without prompting if he could.

"Dr. Karp and I...shared certain patients."

"I see. He sent patients to you."

"Not exactly."

Without blinking, Grant folded his hands together on his lap. "Well, sir, what exactly was the relationship, then?"

Billy White sighed and moved closer in his chair toward his guests. "This is difficult for me, Mr. Grant. You know, it's not in my nature to spread bad stories about my colleagues."

"Yes, sir."

"Dr. Karp was not a very good surgeon. I had the opportunity to see several patients on whom he'd done cataract surgery. The results were terrible."

"I see."

"The man was a butcher." He leaned back once more, comfortable that the secret was out. "I don't know how he stayed in practice."

"So you'd discussed that with him."

"No. We never talked about the subject."

Grant smiled stupidly. "I'm sorry, I don't follow you. You knew Karp, you saw his patients, and you felt he wasn't a very good doctor. But you never discussed this with him?"

"That's right. We were competitors, in a sense. CIO is opening a satellite office in Aurora."

"So, what did you do?"

He thought for a moment, then answered. "Dr. Karp was a menace. I had no choice but to report his incompetence to the hospital where he operated. They needed to review his work. I knew that there would be no way he could pass muster and that he would end up suspended from the hospital."

"I see."

"Please, gentlemen, understand that this pained me a great deal. I felt that I had to act in the best interest of the community. I had no choice."

"So you reported Dr. Karp to the hospital."

"That's right."

"And you and Dr. Karp never talked about this."

"No."

"That's all you did. Talked to the hospital."

"Well, I did provide them with some evidence of his incompetence. I sent information and records on his former patients. Pictures and such."

"I see. And what action did they take?"

White knew, but he decided that he'd better not divulge that. "I understand that he did lose his privileges, but I wouldn't know for a fact. You should probably talk about this with Dan Kilner at Compton Hospital."

"They never told you what happened?"

He shrugged. "It's none of my business, and the activities of the peer review committees are confidential."

"I see. So that was your only interaction with Karp."

"Right."

"And the two of you have had no other dealings?"

"That's right."

"And you're not aware of any other problems that Dr. Karp had? Any rumors? There wasn't anyone who had a grudge with him?"

"Not that I know of, gentlemen." A grand smile took over White's face. "I'm certain he had a few patients that might carry a grudge, but I suspect that they would have sued him rather than doing this."

"I would imagine so. Well, then, I guess that about covers it. Was there anything I left out, Frank?" asked Grant of his partner, who had remained silent through most of this interview.

"Not that I can think, of Rollie."

The two men stood. "We'll let you get back to work."

White lifted himself to his feet and offered his right hand to the agents. "I'm sorry I don't have much to tell you. If something comes up, just let me know."

"Oh, yes. There is one other thing," added Ellison, shaking his suspect's hand.

"Yes?"

"I understand that the State Medical Board had taken some action against Dr. Karp. You wouldn't know anything about that, would you?"

"Why would I?"

"Their report," he filled in, "sounded a lot like what you told us you'd said to the hospital: Patient reports, records, videotapes. You wouldn't have turned Dr. Karp in to the State Board as well as the hospital, would you?"

"I understand that the State Board's activities are privileged information," he answered slowly.

"They are. It just seems quite a coincidence."

"Yes, I imagine it does." He decided that they'd already made up their minds. "Yes, it was me. Like I said, I was concerned for the best interests of the community."

"I see," said Ellison.

"Did Dr. Karp know about your satellite office in Aurora?"

White decided that the agents might have already talked to Kilner. "I imagine so. It wasn't a secret."

"So you stood to gain a great deal by seeing Dr. Karp out of business."

"Gentlemen, whether or not the hospital or the Medical Board took actions against Karp, the CIO's competition would have closed him down within a year. My actions were in the best interests of the community and to maintain the standards of my profession. Nothing more."

"Of course," said Grant. "I understand."

"Is there anything else?"

"No." Grant hated a liar. "Not just now."

Val Karp was dressed simply. She wore a loose pastel blue blouse and khaki pants with tennis shoes. Her face was puffy from crying, and her eye makeup had long been cleared away. She was traveling with Carolyn Masters, a friend of hers from high school who wouldn't let her make the trip alone. The two women sat together in the small, plain waiting room at the Aurora Police Department.

"Mrs. Karp? I am Detective Ramon Cardena. I am sorry to have kept you waiting."

"It's all right," she said, mustering her strength.

"I hope you didn't go by the house already."

She nodded. "I did. I couldn't help myself."

"I'm sorry, Mrs. Karp. I know that this is very difficult. Will you join me in our conference room?"

The three stood. Cardena looked askance at Carolyn. "I hope you don't mind if my friend, Carolyn joins us. I think I need the support."

"Of course."

The conference room was little more than a large side office with a table and four chairs. There was a cabinet with a sink and an old Mr. Coffee along one wall under a corkboard with memos posted on it. There was a two way mirror along the other wall and the ceiling was wired with microphones as the detectives used this place for questioning suspects. The room was stark, to say the least. The table had been graffitized many times and the scent of ancient cigarettes lingered in the place. The floor tiles could use replacement.

"Thank you for coming in this morning, Mrs. Karp," said Cardena as they sat at the table. "We can go to the house together after our work here is through. Unfortunately, you won't be able to remove any property as it is all considered evidence for now."

Val nodded.

"As you know," continued the detective, "your husband was the victim of a bombing and fire. There was a great deal of damage from the explosion. I'm sorry to say that we have had a difficult time identifying the body."

Val said nothing. She didn't want to start crying again.

"I would like to show you some personal affects that we were able to collect from the scene. Do you think that you could look them over and tell me if they belonged to your husband?"

"Yes," was all she said.

"Thank you," said Cardena as he stood. "They are just next door on my desk. Can I get you a cup of coffee or a cold drink?"

"No, thank you."

Cardena left the room for a moment. Carolyn took Val by the arm. "It will be all right. I'm right here."

She nodded. "Thanks."

The detective returned with a manila envelope and a small black plastic bag. He sat down at the table and poured the contents of the envelope on the table. It contained the twisted eyeglass frames that he'd found on the floor of the Stealth and the charred remains of the wallet. There was also a bent and burned gold wedding band. Val looked at the eyeglasses first and began to cry. She hugged Carolyn and just sobbed for a few moments.

Cardena hated this. Having the victim's family identify remains was never, ever pleasant. He'd never dealt with a death as violent as this.

Val took a moment and wiped her red eyes with a tissue. She took a deep breath and looked next at the wallet. She saw the mutilated driver's license and a charred photo of the two of them taken at a Christmas dance four years before, in Oklahoma. She put that down quickly and looked at the wedding band. Even without looking at the inscription, "To J with love, V," she knew that it was the wedding band that Jerry Karp wore. "This is his," she said finally. She breathed hard and asked, "Can I see him?"

"In a few moments, ma'am. Would you mind looking at some clothing he was wearing? It's all part of the identification process."

"Okay. Fine."

He opened the plastic bag and removed a very burned shoe. There was also a scrap of the shirt that the victim of the bombing

369

had been wearing. Val looked over both. "I can't be sure; I think they're his."

"Okay. Thanks." He replaced the objects in the bag and the envelope. "I need to ask you a few questions, Mrs. Karp. Is there anyone who might have wanted to kill your husband? Anyone with whom he'd been fighting recently?"

She gave a small, ironic laugh. "You've got to be kidding. You know that the hospital had revoked his privileges to do surgery."

"Can you tell me about that?"

She shook her head. "I thought everyone in the world already knew. The administrator at Compton Memorial and the medical staff voted to remove his privileges. There was some question about complications from cataract surgery, but it was all exaggerated out of proportion."

"Was your husband being sued?"

"No. He'd never been sued for malpractice."

"I find that hard to believe."

"Why don't you ask Jerry's lawyer, Rick Leach. He can fill you in on what was happening professionally."

Cardena noted the name. It was the same one that Lon Morrissey had mentioned the night before. "But certainly," he continued, "there'd be no reason for anyone at the hospital to kill him."

"I guess not," she answered. "I know I'd like to kill that bastard Kilner."

"Kilner?"

"Dan Kilner. The administrator at the hospital. Jerry told me that there were several doctors who'd been discharged like this since he came on board. The two faced little weasel teamed up with Billy White and together they ruined Jerry's career."

"Who is Billy White?"

Val's face turned to ice. "Dr. Billy White is with the Chicago Institute of Ophthalmology. He used to do a lot of cataract surgery on patients who live in Aurora. Jerry believed that White and Kilner had some sort of mutual agenda, and that damaging Jerry's reputation was part of this plan. His lawyer told him it was silly, that the entire medical staff wouldn't be going along with it."

"Did Dr. White ever threaten your husband?"

"No. As far as I know, they never spoke."

"You were in Detroit, Mrs. Karp. Why was that?"

She looked down. "I left Jerry. He lost his license to practice medicine, and he lost his job. We had no money. He filed for bankruptcy. I was angry, and I needed to be away from him. I left him last week."

"I see. Was there any violence between the two of you?"

"Do you mean that I might kill him? Why? If I wanted to be away from him, I was away. I'd left. I was thinking of divorce, not murder."

"I'm sorry, ma'am. I have to ask."

Grant piloted the gray Chevy along Mannheim Road, and into the lot of Jacobsen Buick and Mercedes. A row of neatly aligned Mercedes Benz cars faced the street. Ellison pointed out the entrance to the body shop, which was around the corner of the building. It wasn't hard to find White's car, as the agents figured he'd not send his brand new vehicle to any place but a certified Benz dealer. It only took three phone calls.

They parked the car and entered the body shop, which was as clean and brightly lit as a new car showroom. They were met by a neatly dressed service manager. "May I help you?"

Grant showed his ID. "I'm Agent Grant, this is Agent Ellison. We phoned earlier about a car belonging to Dr. White."

"Yes, sir?" responded the manager.

Ellison produced a court order signed by a judge earlier that morning when Bob Wilson arrived in Aurora. "This is a search warrant," explained Ellison. "We'd like to look over the vehicle."

The manager looked at the form. He'd never seen one before. "How do I know this is real?" he asked slowly. "This is very unusual, you understand."

"Yes, sir," Grant said with a smile. "I do understand. This is real. I'm sorry to interfere with your work. It is very important that we get a chance to look over the car. You can join us if you like."

He went over the document again. "All right. I guess I can take you to the car."

"Thank you." The agents followed him around the counter and into the service area, past a number of cars in various states of disrepair. Some had been given new body parts, others had masking tape and primer. Others still had wrinkled fenders and bumpers from their collisions. In the back corner bay was a black Mercedes Benz E420 with a personalized license plate, DR IOL.

Grant walked in front of the car and squatted down on the balls of his feet. He and Ellison took rubber gloves out of their jacket pockets and put them on. Grant looked at the damage done to the front of the Benz by the bomb. The smooth chrome brightwork of the ornamental radiator cowl was cratered and scraped by shrapnel. The Mercedes Benz logo tag on the center of the shroud had been knocked off, and deep scratches gouged the previously glassy smooth black paint. Long chips had been ripped out of the hood. He stood and walked toward the driver's door. The windshield glass was scratched as if it had been washed with steel wool. "Some damage," he noted.

Ellison pointed out the driver's door panel. It was pitted and pock marked like the front of the car. Behind it, the back door was pristine and shiny. "Pretty interesting pattern of damage," added Ellison.

"Better get the video and still cameras."

Ellison nodded and walked back toward the front of the shop.

"Is it locked?"

"No, sir."

372

Grant opened the door with a gentle lift of the perfectly balanced handle. The car seat was tan leather, smooth, clean, and fresh smelling. He poked a hand under the seat back and felt around. There was nothing there but the latch for the seat belt. He hadn't really expected to find anything. Next he reached toward the floor. The mat was tightly woven but plush, in the same color as the leather seats. The tri-star Mercedes logo was dark brown, just visible in the weave. It was meticulously clean. He lifted the mat to look at the carpeted floor. Nothing was out of place. He found only a few pebbles that had been missed at the last detailing. He slapped the edge of the carpet back in place.

Grant ran his hand along the smooth lower fascia of the dashboard. There was no place to hide bags of crack under the dash in this car. He opened the ashtray. He could have guessed the result, though. It was clean, never seen a lit cigarette. He looked around the driver's seat and glanced at the roof of the car, the seat back, the dashboard. Nothing was out of place or unusual. Inside, the car looked brand new.

Rollie Grant stood and walked slowly around the front of the car. He kept looking at it the whole time. He'd examined cars that had been in crime scenes hundreds of times. He'd looked over vehicles that had been shot from and shot at. This one struck him as different somehow. He felt...attached to it. He'd never witnessed a murder before, and this car was a tool of the murderer. He wanted to know it intimately. He knew he would one day be testifying about this car.

Grant opened the passenger side door and started the routine again. He first ran his hand through the crease between the seat and the back, finding nothing. Next he went over the floor, under the mat, looked under the seat. Nothing. Still kneeling outside the car door, he flicked open the glove box door. It was a marvelous door. The wood was real, not plastic. And this guy needs to kill another doctor. He looked in the glove box. There was a cassette tape; Mozart. A Chicago map. The car's registration. A silver pen. A garage door opener. Nothing. He sat back and closed the glove box door. He kneeled back and ran his hand along the base of the dashboard fascia. It was smooth and clean. There wasn't a scuff mark on it. He looked up. Everything was perfect. There was the sun visor, the dome light, the reading lights. He glanced at the driver's side once more. The reading lights, the dome light, the sun visor. Clipped on the sun visor was a garage door opener.

He stopped and squeezed his eyebrows together. He went back to that beautiful wood covered glove box door and gently opened it. He reached in and extracted it. A second remote control garage door opener. The murder weapon. He looked at it. It hadn't been altered or opened or changed in any way. It was clean and its edges sharp. It was new. He knew that it was the receiver, not the transmitter, that had been altered.

Frank Ellison returned with a plain blue gym bag. In it he carried a hand held VHS camcorder and an automatic camera with flash. There were also several plastic bags for evidence and a mini-vac for collecting samples of dirt, dust, fibers, and drug residue. He set the bag down on the clean, painted gray floor of the shop just in front of the black Benz.

"Frank," called Grant from the passenger side of the car. "Bring me a baggie." He stood up straight and displayed the garage door opener in his gloved hand.

"A garage door opener?" asked Ellison. "How do you know that's what he used? Even I have one of those."

"Yes, Frank, I know. But Dr. White has two. And they're different from each other."

"Come in, Detective," offered Dan Kilner. As usual, he was smartly dressed and his hair was neatly sculpted on his head. He smelled of just a bit too much Drakkar, noted Cardena. He wasn't sure what that meant.

"Thank you," he replied as he entered Kilner's private office.

"Can I get you a cup of coffee?"

"If you don't mind," he answered. "Black."

374

Kilner poured from his personal coffeemaker into a cup with the Compton Memorial Hospital logo and the phrase, "Fifty years of Excellence."

"I hope you don't mind decaf," he apologized. "Caffeine really bothers my stomach."

"Decaf is fine, thanks." He sipped the hot liquid. "I'm sure you know why I'm here."

Kilner sat down behind his desk. "I presume it's about Dr. Karp."

"Yes."

Kilner shook his head slowly, and took a measured sip of his own coffee. "It's a sad, sad thing. We'll miss Dr. Karp." He set the coffee cup down. "Is it true what I'd heard, that he'd been killed by a bomb?"

"Yes, sir. It is."

He sighed a fast breath. "I hope he wasn't mixed up with the wrong kind of people," said Kilner, making a thinly veiled reference to the drug trade. "That happens in this business from time to time."

If what Val Karp had told him about Karp's relationship with the hospital were true, Cardena thought that Karp might have, in fact, been mixed up with the wrong people. "Has that been a problem with other members of your staff?"

"Oh, no. No," Kilner responded quickly. "I just thought that this kind of killing, with a bomb...I thought it implied organized crime."

Cardena decided that he'd had enough of this bullshit. "Was Dr. Karp getting along all right here at the hospital?"

"As far as I know, he had quite a few friends among the staff doctors."

"And professionally?"

Kilner needed to be cautious. The QA issues and MEC actions were privileged information, not available to the public. He clasped his hands together and leaned forward. "This is difficult for me, Detective. There were some problems with Dr. Karp's work. Much of that matter is confidential, though. I don't want you to think I'm being uncooperative, but I can't discuss this in great detail."

"I understand your dilemma," said Cardena, trying to sound sympathetic. "I surely don't want to get you in legal trouble."

"I appreciate that."

"Dr. Karp's wife suggested that you specifically seemed to have it out for her husband. She said that you'd been involved in some action against him."

Kilner sat back once more. "That's one of the problems I have to deal with in my position as chief administrator," he explained. "Because I represent the best interest of the hospital, I sometimes need to take the role of the heavy. I have to act as the inquisitor and judge, so to speak, to get the Quality Assurance team to do their job. When there are patient complaints, I'm the one they come to."

"Were there patient complaints?"

"Yes. It seems that his surgical skills and medical decision making wasn't exactly up to par."

"So you instigated a review of his performance."

"I had no choice. That's the way the system is designed. It's called Quality Assurance, and that's just what we do. We review a physician's work to assure the hospital and the community that the doctor's results are of adequate quality."

"All right," continued Cardena. "I need to know about a Dr. White. Mrs. Karp said that this man also had a role to play in the process."

"I'm afraid I can't discuss that. It's confidential."

Cardena sat forward. "Mr. Kilner, I am conducting an investigation of the brutal and violent murder of one of your staff physicians. His wife intimated that his death may have been related to activities at this hospital. I can obtain a court order and take possession of your records. Please, sir," he said slowly and clearly, "do your best to assist me here."

Kilner nodded. "I'm sorry, Detective." He looked down. "Dr. White did play a role in instigating the review process. This is all supposed to be confidential." He looked down.

"Thank you. Can you elaborate on that for me?"

"The four patients who called to complain about Dr. Karp had also seen Dr. White. He provided us with detailed information about their condition. His input was a vital part of Dr. Karp's case."

"Okay. I understand that White and Karp were competitors."

"Of a sort. They practiced the same specialty."

"Mrs. Karp suggested that there was more to it than that."

"That could be," answered Kilner. White was a bastard and he had powerful friends. He had treated Karp most viciously. Maybe he did have something to do with his death. "He was planning to open a satellite office in Aurora." He decided to push the detective in White's direction. "I think he considered Karp a real threat."

Cardena took some notes. "I'm not sure I understand that," he said. "If Karp wasn't any good, why wouldn't patients flock to White's new office and leave Karp?"

"I don't know. You'd have to ask that of Dr. White."

Cardena rubbed his chin. "I will. There was a suggestion that your people and Dr. White worked in concert against Dr. Karp."

Kilner straightened. "Detective Cardena," he said softly in order to sound most sincere, "Compton Memorial Hospital has nothing to gain by implicating one of our staff physicians as being incompetent. There is no pleasure for any of us in taking this kind of action. The only thing that we gain is the knowledge that we are providing the highest level of care for our patients."

"I see."

"As I said, this was very painful to me. I am sorry that Dr. Karp had this trouble, and I am sorry that he met with violence. I can assure you that it had nothing to do with me or anyone at Compton Memorial Hospital."

"Of course. Mr. Kilner, did you and Dr. White speak together in the last few days? Have you discussed this situation with him?"

Kilner decided that it would be better for now to distance himself from White personally. "No, we haven't spoken in some time. The situation with Dr. Karp was, as I've said, confidential."

Grant and Ellison returned to their suite at the Aurora Hilton, one of two hotels Aurora offered visitors on the Lake Street exit from the interstate. They took the suite so that there was extra room to spread out documents for review. This would be their office for the next few days. Grant opened the door and found Bob Wilson poring over one of several long computer printouts. Wilson had already obtained a warrant and copies of financial reports, bank statements, and IRS records for Dan Kilner. He'd spent most of the morning reviewing similar records for Billy White and the CIO. White's dealings were numerous and confusing.

"Was our information from Dr. White sufficient?" asked Grant quickly as the two agents returned to the room. "Did you get the warrant?"

"Yes," answered Wilson slowly. There were stacks of paperwork in every corner of the room: On the desks, the beds, the dressers, and piled on the floor along the far wall. Wilson peered through his reading glasses, and held up a tax report, as if lifting it from the table top would make it more sensible.

"Well," asked Ellison. "Is there anything there?"

Wilson just stared at the paper without answering right away. "Hard to say," he said finally, then set the form down. He removed the glasses with a sweep of one hand. "Dr. White's company is a multi-multi-million dollar a year enterprise, and they do pay their share of taxes. The accounting seems reasonably clean, although a good tax audit might help to cover the expense account you gentlemen have generated by your trips to Aurora."

"But nothing to tie large sums of unaccounted money to this guy," noted Grant.

"Billy White and CIO make such large incomes legitimately that they don't really need to hide money anywhere. I've seen organized crime rackets that have smaller cash flows than these guys." He slapped his hand on a stack of documents on the table. "Mr. Kilner," he said, "is a different story. It seems that he had been chugging along on a reasonable income at his prior job. A few years ago he came to Aurora to run this hospital with an awful reputation, and he now makes a comfortable income. He struggled to get a home mortgage with a minimum down payment. A short time later, he's paying off the mortgage in advance, and he is somehow able to buy himself a new Lexus."

"The guy is quite a money manager," said Grant suspiciously.

"Quite a money manager, indeed," answered Wilson. "He's made all of these payments in cash."

"So you think White has been paying off Kilner?" asked Ellison.

Wilson shook his head. "No. If he had, Karp would never have been recruited in the first place. Kilner and White have only been in bed together a short time, as long as they've been harassing Karp." He stared off into space. "No, I think that Mr. Kilner has had other dealings. I need to find out where he's getting the money." He changed the subject. "How was your morning? What did you find out?"

Ellison sat down at the table and began to peer over the telephone records that they had obtained for Karp and White.

"Pretty good, actually," said Grant. "We talked to White. He denied everything, of course."

"Of course."

"He said that his only dealings with Karp were to have turned him over for review of his work. It was all in the best interest of the community."

Wilson huffed. "My ass."

"Toss me the phone book," instructed Ellison.

"Did you find something?" asked his partner as Wilson reached into the nightstand shelf and extracted a thin combination volume of the Aurora white and yellow pages.

"I think so." He flipped through the book and ran his finger down the page. "Jesus," he said. "This is too easy."

"What?" asked Wilson.

He looked up. "White said that he'd had no contact with Karp, right?"

"Right."

"Well, right here at ten-oh-five on the morning of Karp's murder, Karp called the main number of the CIO. The call lasted thirty three minutes."

"So?" asked Wilson.

"So," answered Grant, "you don't think he was just calling for an appointment to get new glasses, do you? He talked to White."

"Wait," said Ellison, "wait. It gets better."

"Yeah?"

"At ten forty there's a call from CIO to Compton Memorial Hospital."

"White to Kilner?"

"Makes sense."

"And that night," concluded Grant, "Karp gets whacked."

"The last call Karp received, maybe ten minutes before the explosion," prompted Ellison.

"White?"

"A cellular phone registered to the good doctor. He probably needed to get Karp into the car somehow."

"Then I'd say it's time to begin questioning Dr. White seriously," suggested Grant. "Maybe he'll turn evidence on Kilner to save himself on the murder charge."

Wilson stood up and walked over to Grant, looking him directly in the eye. "I want to get to the bottom of this collusion situation in Aurora. It will expose a large number of dishonest doctors who've been bilking taxpayers. I want Kilner in jail and the rest of those bastard doctors to pay, too. But," he stressed the word and continued very slowly, "I will not let a murderer go free to do that. I think we need to visit with the detective handling the murder case to see what they have on Dr. White. I want to scare him first. Then, he'll talk to us."

Rick Leach was shocked when Cardena told him of Karp's death. He made time in his schedule to meet with the detective right away. "How can I help you?" the lawyer asked quietly.

"Well, sir, I am trying to put this tragedy into perspective. You see, Dr. Karp had no criminal record and no apparent dealings in criminal activities. Frankly, I'm trying to find some reasonable suspects for this case."

"I see."

"His wife said you knew some details."

"Dr. Karp's case is most unusual," began Leach. "He has never been charged with malpractice. Until recently, there have never been any charges of professional misconduct made against him. He was a young, struggling eye surgeon."

"Okay."

"Several months ago Dr. Billy White, a competing physician in Chicago, sent a letter accompanied by a videotape to the administrator of Compton Memorial Hospital charging Karp with surgical incompetence. He also informed several patients that Karp had ruined their eyes. This incited a formal review process."

Cardena noted the story.

"Simultaneously, White made plans to open an office himself in Aurora, in direct competition with Dr. Karp. Two of his practice associates applied for privileges at the hospital."

"A conflict of interest."

"I think so. The peer review nature of medicine makes that and restraint of trade issues difficult to prove. However, the evidence against Dr. Karp was marginal and the sanctions taken against him were harsh. He lost his privileges to operate in the hospital. Dr. White also incited a review by the State Medical

Board which resulted in the suspension of Karp's license. He lost his job and filed for bankruptcy."

"So Dr. White had it out for Karp."

"Without a doubt. The problem," he said with a grimace, "is that Dr. White could not have done this alone. The hospital and the medical board had to work with him."

"So you're saying Karp wasn't incompetent."

"Karp may not have been the finest surgeon that ever practiced, but he was not a bad doctor. I think that Dr. Karp was doing his level best. This was not nearly as good as an average day's surgery for Billy White, but was by no means below the standard of care for the community."

"So he was unfairly treated."

"That's my opinion. I felt very certain that we could defend the charges against Karp before the State Medical Board and then deal down the suspension at the hospital."

"How did Karp feel about that?"

He shook his head. "He kept after this theory that there was a conspiracy at the hospital involving the medical staff. He was obsessed by the fact that several other doctors he knew had lost their positions there."

"Was there any evidence of this conspiracy?"

Leach did not want to tell Cardena about the computer disk that Karp had obtained illegally, as it might taint the investigation. "Karp thought he had some evidence, but I never got to evaluate it. I'm not sure where it came from. He suggested to me that there was some intricate financial network that linked the physicians and the hospital."

"What kind of evidence was this?"

"I can't say. You'll have to dig a little on your own, I'm afraid. I can tell you this: If Karp was right, and if he found proof of some conspiracy, there would be a great many people who might be angry with him."

Cardena leaned forward. "Do you believe this conspiracy theory, Mr. Leach?"

He smiled. "Two days ago, Detective, no. Today..." He held both hands up before him. "I'd sure like to see that evidence."

Ray Cardena strode into the station house and was greeted by the Officer of the Day, a uniformed sergeant. He worked his way into the squad room and passed the two telephone operators. "Message for you," said Grace as he passed by. She was forty three and divorced, and had a great crush on Cardena despite the fact that he was a married man. "He said it was no emergency and you could call back any time today."

"Thanks, Grace," he said in his usual professional tone as he glanced at the pink slip. It was from Rusty French. Cardena walked over to his desk and dialed the number as he sat down.

"Illinois Bureau of Investigation Crime Lab."

"This is Detective Cardena returning a call from Rusty French."

"Yes, Detective. I'll connect you."

French must have found something.

"Ray. How's the murder investigation?"

"Murky. What have you got down there?"

"Ray, we collected everything that looked even marginally electronic out of that burnt up pile last night and I raced it all down to the lab here before those federal boys could get to it. You know what I mean?"

"I do. Thanks."

"Found a lot of junk there. Junk. Bits of radio and electronic fuel injection system and like that. Not much help."

It sometimes took Rusty a while to get to the point, but it was always worth the wait. "I'm with you."

"Good. We found most of what we think was the control system for the bomb. It was very amateur, Ray. Not at all a professional job, get me?"

"Right. You don't think this was an organized crime hit."

"No. Couldn't be. The work was very sloppy, very amateur."

"What did you find?"

"The control module was wired into the car ignition to power the bombs. The actual trigger mechanism looks like it was patched into the taillights. The bomb was supposed to go off when Karp hit the brake pedal."

"So that he had to be in the car, in the driver's seat when it went off."

"Right. But it was real sloppy. The patch cord from the taillight was soldered so bad that it broke off."

"So," Cardena completed the thought for him, "the bomb didn't detonate as planned."

"That's the idea, Ray. That's the idea. The bomber was sloppy. But he wasn't stupid, Ray. He put in an alternative trigger. A backup, get me?"

"Some kind of remote control?"

"Exactly. A remote control. Matter of fact, that's just what he used. A commercial remote control. It was off a garage door opener."

"Okay," Cardena put it all together for Rusty. "The bomber wasn't a pro, so he designed a trigger mechanism but built it so badly that it never worked. Instead, he had to use his backup mechanism from a garage door opener remote control."

"You're with me, now, Ray. What does that tell you?"

"First of all," he deduced, "the killer had to be real close to Karp when he set off the bomb."

"Exactly. There are two reasons for that. For one thing, the range on this remote wasn't too impressive. He needed to be nearby."

"And second, he needed to be certain that Karp was in the car."

"So your killer was either watching Karp or made arrangements to get him in the car. Does that help you, Ray?"

Cardena cradled the phone against his ear with his shoulder. "Some, Rusty," he said as he rubbed his eyes. "If I can establish which of my suspects was close enough to Karp that evening, I'll find my killer."

"Right. Then I'll have my bomber."

"Any leads on what kind of garage door opener I'm looking for?"

"Not sure yet, Ray. We've got it narrowed down to a couple of makes. A lot of guys use the same guts in these things, right? We think it's probably a late model Sear's or maybe a Stanley. We're checking. The board was pretty melted by the fire."

"Thanks, Rusty. You've been a big help."

"Any time, pal. Any time. I'll stay in touch if I find out anything more."

"Ray?" It was his boss, Captain McKane. He had walked up on Cardena while he was on the phone.

"Yes, sir."

"Ray, can you join me in my office? The FBI guys working on your case are here, and they've brought along someone from the U.S. Attorney's office in Madison."

Cardena looked at his watch. It was three thirty. "They're early," he said.

"I know. They have some information that ought to help with your investigation."

"Damn it, Captain. You know they're just going to take over this case after we've done the legwork and then share nothing with us. I thought..."

"Ray," he interrupted quietly. "They have information for you. Join me?"

"Detective, I think you know Agents Grant and Ellison." The former was seated along with Bob Wilson, the latter was standing. "This is J. Robert Wilson of the U.S. Attorney's office." He and Cardena shook hands as McKane took his seat at the desk.

"Call me Bob."

"Ray Cardena."

"Agents Grant and Ellison have some useful information for you, Ray. It seems there was a material witness to the bombing. Two, as a matter of fact."

"Really? I canvassed the entire neighborhood. Nobody saw a thing."

"You missed the witnesses, Ray," said McKane. "They left the scene. Agents?"

"We saw the bombing," said Grant.

There was a pause. Finally, just containing himself, Cardena said, "You what?"

"We saw the bombing," Grant repeated. "We were there, just down the block."

"I don't believe this," said Cardena, the veins on his neck standing out. "Two FBI agents are witnesses at a murder scene and they flee without giving a statement? This is absurd. This is obstruction."

"Ray, relax. That's why they've come here today. You need to know what's going on in this case."

"Detective," said Wilson with the calmness of a conversation over dinner, "no one wants to see Dr. Karp's killer brought to justice more than I. He and I went to high school together. I've known him for twenty years. That's why the agents were there."

Cardena was breathing hard. "Go on."

"Dr. Karp had some professional and personal problems of late."

"I'm aware of that. Lost his hospital privileges and his license."

"Right. He suspected some sort of conspiracy and he asked me to investigate. I assigned Agents Grant and Ellison to look into the matter."

"Karp had us watching the house last night while he had a meeting," continued Grant. "We were supposed to see his informant then retrieve the evidence. Instead, the informant blew him up."

"Why did you leave, then?"

"The agents were in communication with me at all times," explained Wilson. "We are conducting an investigation into a ring of collusion and Medicare fraud involving a number of physicians and Compton Memorial Hospital. I instructed them to follow the suspect and make certain that he did not leave the area. Our evidence gathering for the collusion and fraud cases is not yet complete, and I don't want to tip off the others."

Cardena shook his head. "I'll be goddamned. What else do you know?"

"We followed a lone man driving a black Mercedes, Illinois license DR-IOL. The car is registered to Dr. William White. We followed him to his home, where he stayed the night."

"Dr. White," repeated Cardena.

"You know him?" asked Wilson.

"This may come as a surprise to you, but I have been investigating this case, too."

"I'm sorry," he said quietly.

"Obviously, you know the connection between Dr. Karp and Dr. White. Karp's phone records show that he had spoken to White on the day of his murder. Immediately following this call, White talked to someone at Compton Memorial, probably Dan Kilner. Of course, White denied this."

"We have reason to believe that White and Kilner were working in concert to Dr. Karp's detriment," Wilson added.

"Detective?" prompted McKane.

He nodded. "As you know, the body was in very bad shape from the explosion and fire," started Cardena. "Karp's wife walked out on him last week. She was in Michigan at the time of the bombing, and corroborated the connections to White and Kilner. She identified the body based on his personal affects and clothing." The agents and Wilson nodded agreement. "I talked with Karp's lawyer, Rick Leach. He told me that Karp had some conspiracy theory which involves the professional censure of himself and three other doctors at Compton. Two are gone, one is still in practice."

"What did you find out about the bomb?" asked Grant.

"The crime lab found a radio receiver in the debris of the Stealth. It was a garage door opener of some kind."

"I agree," said Grant.

"You do?"

"Yes. Frank and I have the triggering device."

"What?" Cardena was beside himself.

"We found it in White's car this morning on a search warrant."

"Jesus, mighty. Have you arrested White?"

"Not yet," answered Wilson.

"What on God's earth are you waiting for? He'll try to get away if he finds out..."

"We've got Chicago P.D. tailing him full time," assured Wilson. "Billy White isn't going anywhere because he doesn't know we've got the trigger. We've still got work to do."

"Captain?" Cardena was looking for support.

"Hang on, Ray. Listen to the man."

"Agents Grant and Ellison have come this afternoon with all of the documents that we've gathered on White, Kilner, and Karp. We've got financials, phone records, most of the bloody review. I want them to give you copies and I want copies of everything you have. That way we can all go over the documents together."

Cardena stood and faced his superior. "Captain, I have no intention of wasting my time sifting through papers so these guys can collar my murderer. I will not..."

"Ray, sit down," said McKane evenly. "There's more."

"Detective," said Wilson, holding his palms up, "I don't want the murder case. Like I told you, Karp and I were friends. That will give the defense an edge. I want to see White put away for this. You get the murder case. It can be tried in Kane County. You can even have him on the bombing beef if you want."

"And what do you want?"

"I want Kilner and the other doctors on Medicare fraud. I think this thing is huge. I just don't have enough evidence yet. I want to know what Karp found out."

Cardena put it all together. "So we work on the same case from different angles. I've got opportunity, eyewitnesses, and physical evidence for the murder case. I just haven't found a strong enough motive yet for White."

"When you find your motive, Detective, I'll have my fraud case."

PRIVILEGES

Twenty Two

Billy White was in the middle of his third case of the day. It was only eight o'clock, and he felt as if he was behind schedule. He was so much more irritable on surgery days lately that the staff had begun to dread them. They'd rather work with any of the other doctors, including the retina docs. Their cases took hours to complete, but by nature they tended to be more calm and methodical. Dr. White was always concerned about turnaround time, volume of surgery done, and the most efficient use of materials. He wasted nothing and he wanted none of the staff to "stand around on company time." He was much crankier than anyone could remember.

The capsulorrhexis tear in the lens capsule was smooth and quick. He removed the capsule with a flick of his wrist and returned the instrument to the scrub tech. Without saying a word or removing his glance from the microscope, he mechanically held his hand open waiting for the irrigating cannula. The three seconds that it took for the scrub tech to set down the capsulorrhexis forceps and hand him the irrigator seemed an eternity.

There was some noise outside, shuffling and voices. It subsided, and White returned to his work. He removed the irrigator and, silently once more, waited to be handed the phacoemulsifier. There was more shuffling. Someone was shouting. Footsteps, maybe a scuffle, and then quiet once more. White pushed on the foot pedal and began to remove the lens nucleus. "Darla," he asked for the circulating nurse. "Would you kindly go out there and remind them that we're doing delicate work in here." His words and tone were measured, calm. His patient was awake, and he did not wish to alarm her. Darla knew that he was angry enough that he might fire someone.

"Yes, sir."

"Thank you." He continued to work, splitting the nucleus with a central groove and pushing the two pieces apart.

"You can't go in there," demanded the nurse. "There is surgery going on and it is a sterile room."

"What about the other room, then," demanded the police officer. "There isn't any surgery going on in there."

"The patient is being prepared for the next case," the nurse insisted.

"Ma'am, this is a search warrant. You cannot refuse the search. The case that is going on may be completed, but the next case is canceled unless it is a medical emergency to continue. Is that the situation in there?"

"No, but Dr. White..."

"Whether Dr. White wants to or not, that room will be searched. End of discussion."

"Wanda," Darla approached the group. "What's going on out here? Dr. White is having a cow about the noise."

"That's not all he's going to have a cow about this morning."

Detective Ramon Cardena was leafing through the various papers and files on Dr. Billy White's desk. He had four other officers assigned to his detail this morning. He instructed one pair to begin searching all of the CIO vehicles for evidence. Another pair would do a room to room search, and they were to begin with whatever room Dr. White was in so that he did not have the opportunity to discard or remove anything. He himself would take charge of White's personal office. A copy of the search warrant had been sent to the Forest Hills police department, who would send a team to White's home.

Cardena evaluated every document on the desk. There were no fewer than three dozen patient records. Although he did not fully understand the medical histories of the patients, he was looking for any reference to Dr. Karp, the city of Aurora, or Compton Memorial Hospital. There were some medical journals on the desk, some purchase orders for intraocular lenses, and various letters to referring doctors awaiting signatures. Nothing of interest to this case.

He methodically went through all of the drawers in the desk. He found documents pertaining to the furniture and equipment in the building, the vehicles owned by CIO, and some contracts with intraocular lens manufacturers. There were financial documents for the corporation and contracts for the CIO's physicians.

The next drawer held some financial reports for the CIO. The papers showed the numbers of patients seen and surgical procedures performed on a monthly basis for the last two years, and on an annual basis for the last five years. White's business manager had prepared the reports which included graphs showing sawtoothed lines representing the practice's activities.

He continued making his way through the desk drawers and found nothing else of importance. He turned his attention to a large horizontal filing cabinet along another wall. It was locked, and he called Colleen into the room from her desk just outside the door.

"I'm sorry, officer, I'm not allowed to open that without Dr. White's permission," she answered when Cardena instructed her to unlock it.

"That's fine," he said. "I'll just have to use a pry bar to rip it open, then."

She threw him a dirty look, then returned to her own desk drawer for the key.

Inside the file cabinet, Cardena found employee reports and payroll statements, tax forms, and medical records on White and his family. Another drawer held a series of copied medical records, each of which had on the cover sheet a statement about the patient having been operated upon by Dr. Karp in Aurora. Cardena read all of the patient histories, still understanding very little of the detailed course of their medical progress. It appeared that each of the patients had undergone cataract surgery by Karp, and all of them had been referred to White by a Dr. Demmel.

Each of the patients underwent some kind of surgical procedure at CIO. There was little that connected the cases other than Aurora addresses, Dr. Karp, and Dr. Demmel.

Following the patient histories was a copy of a letter sent to Dan Kilner at Compton Memorial Hospital. The letter reflected very poorly upon Dr. Karp's surgical skills and medical judgement and outlined briefly the cases that Cardena had just read. There was also a similar letter to the Illinois State Medical Board. After these were some reports about case volume at CIO. They showed that the number of cases being referred to CIO from Aurora had declined over the past two years, punctuated by a printout of referrals from individual Aurora optometrists, including Dr. Demmel.

Billy White blew into his office and was surprised to see Cardena reviewing his personal papers. "Who in the hell are you?" demanded White.

Cardena rose to meet his host. "I am Detective Ramon Cardena of the Aurora Police Department, Dr. White. I have been assigned to investigate the murder of Jerrold Karp. I'm sorry to have to meet you in this way, but I do have a warrant to search the premises of your home, your office, your vehicles, and those that belong to the Chicago Institute of Ophthalmology."

White's face was crimson. "I don't give a damn who you are, get out of my desk."

"Dr. White," repeated Cardena in a calm, even tone. "I have a search warrant. I assure you that the warrant does, indeed, give me the authority to do this."

White took three quick, deep breaths. He wasn't sure just what to do. "I spoke to the two officers about this the other day," he said finally.

Cardena looked up from the documents on White's desk. "Yes, sir. The gentlemen who visited you are with the FBI. They are assisting me with my investigation."

"What does this have to do with me?"

Cardena stood and walked around White's desk toward the center of the office. "Dr. White, perhaps you may want to call your attorney. I do have some questions for you."

Cardena had cordoned off White in one of the examination rooms that the uniformed officers had already searched. They were waiting for White's attorney, Michael Hande, to arrive. In the meantime, he decided to interview White's employees. "How long have you been with Dr. White?" he asked.

"Five years," answered Wanda. "I am the Surgery Center Supervisor."

"You like working for your boss?"

She shrugged. "Dr. White is very particular about how things need to be. He doesn't tolerate any deviation from his protocols, and he doesn't tolerate professional incompetence. He can be demanding."

"Hard to get along with?"

"Not as long as you do things his way. I've learned to predict his moves. I try to know what he will ask for five minutes before he asks for it."

"So you haven't had any problems with him personally."

"Not really."

"Not really?" echoed Cardena.

"Well, no. He's been a little moody lately."

"How so?"

"He's just a little more on edge. More temperamental."

"Can you think of any reason why that might be?"

With a sigh, she finally answered, "I think it's because of this business with Dr. Karp." There was no attempt to hide the disdain in her voice when she mentioned his name.

"What business did Dr. White have with Dr. Karp?"

"You're kidding me, aren't you?"

"Indulge me."

She sighed again. "Dr. White was very busy lately correcting Dr. Karp's screw-ups. He wasn't a very good surgeon."

"I see. Did Dr. White discuss this with Dr. Karp?"

"No. At least, not until that last day," she said thoughtlessly.

"Last day?"

"I'm sorry," she looked down. "The day that Dr. Karp died."

"The day he was killed," Cardena reminded her.

"Yes."

"Dr. White spoke with Dr. Karp that day?"

"Yes. Dr. Karp called in the middle of Dr. White's OR day. He interrupted him between cases. Dr. White was very angry after that."

"Really? What did they talk about?"

"I don't know. All I know is that he stormed out of here for half an hour and threw the schedule off."

Colleen McKenna was not at all happy about talking to the detective. She fidgeted in her chair, unable to get comfortable. The phone rang, but the telephones had all been forwarded to the answering service. She was told that no one would be allowed to place or accept telephone calls during the search, and this irritated her because she knew that the patients would suffer from this decision. Dr. White was too incensed by the search itself to pay attention to this indignity. She decided that it was better he not know.

Dr. White had always been good to Colleen. She'd worked for another medical practice before, but they paid her so poorly she didn't stay there after her second year. The pay at CIO was good, and even though he could be terse, Dr. White was never mean to her. She always got a generous Christmas bonus, and that was a welcome change that made the difficult times worth the extra effort.

"I just want to ask you a few questions about Dr. White's activities in recent weeks," explained Cardena.

"Fine." Colleen once overheard a conference between White and one of the other doctors before he was to be deposed for a lawsuit. She remembered the instructions and figured this was as good a time as any to follow them. Answer the questions with one word, yes or no. Don't offer more information than that which is asked for. Don't elaborate on your answers. Tell the truth.

"All right, then." Cardena tried to make himself comfortable. He sipped at his styrofoam cup of cold coffee. "Did Dr. White have any contact with Dr. Karp recently?"

"Do you mean a meeting?"

"Yes. Or a conversation."

"They never met, as far as I know."

"How about a conversation? Did they speak together?"

She paused to consider her answer, and realized that the delay was as good as a verbal response. "Yes," she said.

"When was that?"

"Monday."

"Monday," repeated Cardena, hoping that this would stimulate Colleen to offer more.

"Yes. Monday." No more.

"Okay. What did they talk about?"

"I don't know."

"You don't?"

"No. I didn't hear the conversation."

"Then, how do you know they spoke?"

"Dr. Karp called the office. I transferred the call to Dr. White in the OR suite. Afterward, he came back here and made another call."

"I see. Who did he call after Dr. Karp?"

"Mr. Kilner."

"And do you know what they discussed?"

"No."

"Any thoughts?"

She shrugged. "I didn't hear the conversation."

"Did he mention Dr. Karp, perhaps?"

She had, in fact, overheard most of the conversation. White was practically screaming, he was so angry. "Perhaps."

"So you did hear some of the conversation."

"Some of it."

"How was that?"

She sighed. "Dr. White was upset. He was...loud."

"So when Dr. White spoke with Mr. Kilner, they discussed Dr. Karp's call."

"I guess so."

"Do you remember anything else about their conversation?"

"No. I don't eavesdrop."

"Of course not. Still, Dr. White was awfully loud. Certainly you overheard something."

"Nothing in particular that I can remember. They talked about Dr. Karp, and Dr. White was pretty angry. That's about it."

Cardena decided that she wasn't going to be any more forthcoming. He swirled the cold coffee in the white cup and watched a few grounds stick to the edges of the styrofoam wall. "Did Dr. White have any other conversations with Dr. Karp before this?"

"No. Not that I know of."

"Did Dr. White ever mention Dr. Karp before?"

"To me?"

"To anyone. On the phone, in a letter. Did he ever mention Karp before?"

"Dr. White wrote some letters about Dr. Karp."

"And you typed them?"

"That's right."

"Who did he send those letters to? Do you remember?"

"That's privileged information, isn't it?"

"It would depend upon what was in the letter, I guess. It would probably be up to a judge to decide that. This is a murder investigation. Who did he send the letters to?"

"One went to Mr. Kilner. The other to the State Medical Board. Dr. Karp was incompetent."

"So Dr. White was, sort of, out to get Dr. Karp? Because he was incompetent."

"He wasn't out to get him. This was nothing unusual for Dr. White."

Cardena swirled the coffee cup again and tried not to look too piqued by the answer. "Not unusual? How?"

"He'd written letters like that before."

He paused a beat. "He'd written letters about Dr. Karp before?"

"No, letters about other doctors."

"Letters about other doctors' incompetence?"

"Right."

"What other doctors?"

She had to think for a minute. "There was Dr. Bookner," she answered. "He was defrauding Medicare."

Cardena remembered something about that case. It was in the newspapers a few years back. He also vaguely remembered that the doctor was acquitted, perhaps. White was involved?

"And there was Dr. SanFelipo. He was like Dr. Karp, a butcher."

Cardena saw that this was a pattern for White. He had a penchant for harming other physicians' reputations. Other competing physicians.

Michael Hande was fifty years old, bald, and overweight. He still refused to wear glasses all the time despite the fact that he could barely pass his driver's test without them. He managed to pull a few strings in Springfield to eke by. He did use thick half-frame readers. He wore them now as he read over the search warrant one more time at the request of his client, Billy White.

"Billy," said Hande finally, "it's a valid search warrant. There's nothing you can do to stop this."

"It's outrageous," White bellowed. "I won't have it."

"You can't stop it, Billy, so relax. You have to be very careful about this." White had finally told Hande that he was present when Karp was killed. He insisted that he'd had nothing to do with the bombing, and Hande believed him. White was an arrogant asshole, not a killer. Hande was more concerned that his client's all too predictable ill temper would get him in trouble. He was also bothered by the fact that White had lied to the FBI about his presence, as this would be viewed as an attempt to cover up involvement. "I want you to be completely honest with this cop when he questions you, do you understand me?"

"Yes."

"I don't know why you're a suspect in this killing, but we'll find out shortly. As long as you have done nothing wrong, you'll have nothing to fear."

"We've been over it. Karp was a pest and I got rid of him." White hadn't mentioned the Development Fund at Compton Memorial Hospital. It wasn't important.

"I'm certain you did, Billy," said Hande. "You have a special skill for that." Hande had advised White before that his strong arm tactics might one day cause him pain. "I'll tell the cop you're ready to talk to him. Remember, answer questions slowly so that I can stop you if they're out of line."

"I'll remember."

Hande lifted his substantial body from the chair and the two men walked together into White's own office. There, Detective Cardena was seated in the guest's chair in front of White's desk, poring over White's papers on his desk. He was looking over files that White had kept on Karp, Bookner, and SanFelipo. As the ophthalmologist and his attorney entered, Cardena ignored them to finish the page he was reading.

"Detective?" said Hande.

Cardena didn't respond verbally, holding up the palm of one hand so that he could finish reading the letter. Satisfied, he closed the manila file folder and stood. "Dr. White," he greeted them finally. "Please," he motioned toward White's chair behind the desk. "Sit down."

400

Without hesitation, White took his seat. Hande flushed noticeably, as he was now separated from his client.

"Dr. White, Mr. Hande," Cardena addressed each of the men, "I appreciate the opportunity to speak with you."

Neither man commented. It wasn't as if there were a choice.

"This is just an informal questioning, you understand. No one is in custody here, all right?"

"Yes," answered Hande.

"Still, you are aware that I am investigating a murder." He turned to Hande. "Your client is aware of his rights, I presume. He knows that he does not have to answer any of my questions. Obviously, he has exercised his right to have an attorney present."

Hande nodded.

He turned toward White. "As this is an investigation, the answers you give may be used as evidence in court."

"I understand."

"You're satisfied that your client knows and understands his rights, Mr. Hande?"

"I am."

"Dr. White, you are aware that a bomb killed Dr. Karp, correct?"

"Yes. What does that have to do with me?"

Hande shifted in his chair. He wanted to signal to White that he was being too arrogant. He had also violated the rule of answering questions with yes or no answers only.

"I gather that you didn't much care for Dr. Karp," Cardena observed.

"Karp was incompetent," answered White.

Cardena nodded. "You certainly thought so."

"So did others. I understand that Dr. Karp failed an impartial review of his work."

Cardena ignored the comment. "You stood to benefit from Dr. Karp's failure, Dr. White, didn't you?"

White considered his answer. "The entire community benefitted when he was relieved of his privileges to operate."

401

Cardena glared at White. "You are opening a satellite office in Aurora, isn't that right."

"Yes."

"And the documents that I found here show that your business from there was declining over the last few years."

"Are you suggesting that I had something to do with Dr. Karp's death?"

"Billy..." interrupted Hande.

Cardena ignored the lawyer. "You did stand to benefit by his dismissal, didn't you?"

White grinned. "The Chicago Institute of Ophthalmology treats tens of thousands of patients per year. Our doctors perform several thousand cataract procedures annually. I don't think that the few procedures Dr. Karp did made much of a dent in our patient volume."

Cardena raised his eyebrows. "Your own notes demonstrate that you had quite an interest in Dr. Karp long before you began seeing any evidence of his surgical skills."

White sighed. "There was no reason for me to kill Dr. Karp, Detective." Hande glared icily at White. "I had nothing to do with Dr. Karp's death," White said.

Cardena nodded once more. "Tell me, Dr. White, are you on staff at Compton Memorial Hospital?"

"No."

"Applied for privileges?"

"No."

"But you do know Dan Kilner at Compton, do you not?"

"Yes. I contacted him about my concerns with Karp's surgery."

"Have you spoken to Mr. Kilner recently?"

"No."

"Anyone at the hospital?"

"No."

"I see." White did not respond. Cardena wrote some notes. He loved to do that so that a suspect knew he had been caught in a lie.

"Dr. White, have you ever acted in a similar manner with other physicians?"

"What kind of manner do you mean?"

"I mean, Doctor, have you ever written letters about the skills or actions of any of your other colleagues?"

Practically everyone in Illinois had heard of Ben Bookner's trial. Cardena probably knew the answer to that question. "Yes," he said finally.

"Can you tell me about that?"

This time Hande interrupted before White could answer. "Detective, I think those situations are confidential between Dr. White and the individuals to whom he sent the letters. I'm afraid that I have to advise my client not to answer that question."

White smiled.

"Very well," said Cardena. "Is it safe for me, then, to presume that this is common between professionals?"

"What do you mean?" asked White.

"Discussing your colleagues' shortcomings with others. Is that a common practice among doctors?"

White considered for a moment, then answered, "Probably not. Most physicians don't want to get involved in any potential lawsuits."

"Like malpractice, or that sort of thing?"

"Right."

"But you're not afraid of that."

"If one of my colleagues is inept, I have a duty to protect the community."

"Especially if you stand to benefit financially."

"Don't answer," warned Hande.

Cardena wrote more notes. "Doctor, did any money change hands between you and anyone from Compton Memorial Hospital?"

Kilner had sworn to him that no one would ever know about the Development Fund. There was no way to find it and no way to track it. "No," he lied.

403

"How about anyone else at the Chicago Institute of Ophthalmology?"

"Not that I know of."

There was a knock on the door. "Come in," said Cardena. Officer Phil Smoltz entered the room. He and his partner had been out searching the CIO vehicles. He approached Cardena and handed him a small plastic bag with a slip of white paper in it. Smoltz leaned forward so that he could speak quietly into Cardena's ear.

"We found this in the back seat of one of the limos, Ray," said Smoltz. "I thought you might want to see it right away."

Cardena looked at the paper through the clear plastic bag. Smoltz stood up. "Thanks, Phil." He made a note in his book. "Good work."

Smoltz nodded and took his cue to leave the room, closing the door behind him.

Cardena handed the bag with its contents to Michael Hande and allowed him to examine it. Hande arched his eyebrows and passed the bag back to Cardena, who slid it across the table toward Billy White.

"Dr. White," asked the detective, "do you know anything about this?"

White looked through the plastic bag and saw a receipt from the Farmer's Co-op for the purchase of three fifty pound bags of ammonium nitrate by the Chicago Institute of Ophthalmology dated eight days earlier. His jaw dropped. "No," he stammered, "I don't...What is this?" he spat.

Michael Hande stood. "Detective, I think I'll have to ask you to end this interview," he said gently.

Cardena stood as well. He walked around White's desk, avoiding Hande. As he did, he reached into his jacket pocket and removed a thick, folded packet of paper. He tossed it on the desk gently in Hande's direction. Then he reached into the case clipped on his belt and extracted a pair of handcuffs. "I agree, Mr. Hande," he said. "Will you stand up, please?" he asked White.

"What is this?" White snapped, now pale.

Hande reviewed the document that Cardena had given him. It was an arrest warrant for his client, William White.

"Stand up," repeated Cardena.

"Mike?" demanded White.

Hande was still looking over the paper. "Do it," he said calmly.

"What?"

"Stand up," insisted Cardena. Finally, White complied. "Turn around, hands behind your back."

White stared at his attorney. "He can't do this," he yelled, waiting for support from Hande.

Hande flipped the page and read on. "Yes, Billy," he said in an even tone, "he can."

"William White," intoned Cardena, "I am placing you under arrest for the murder of Jerrold M. Karp. You have the right to remain silent..."

PRIVILEGES

Twenty Three

Michael Hande circled the block for the second time, looking for a place to park. The visitor lot for the Courthouse complex was filled, and Hande was not familiar with Madison's downtown streets. He craned his neck as he looked for another parking lot. His passenger, Dr. Billy White, rubbed his eyes then stared heavenward for divine intervention. The brown Cadillac DeVille screeched to a halt, its nose bouncing twice, as Hande braked hard to avoid hitting a stalled car that he didn't notice while peering around a corner.

"Jesus," said White, exasperated. "I hope you handle this D.A. better than you can drive."

"He's not a D.A.," corrected Hande as he started the car moving forward once more. "He's a U.S. Attorney. He's not handling the murder charge, but I'm afraid that the feds are going to come down on you because of the explosives that killed Karp. It's a federal offense when you bomb someone."

"I didn't bomb anyone and I didn't kill Jerry Karp," said White through lightly clenched teeth. "I would hope that you believe me, Michael, or I'll have to find another law firm."

Hande was the senior partner of Hande, Davidson, Hande, and Brady, a prestigious Chicago firm with its main office on Michigan Avenue. He'd built the practice up from ground zero, and now he spent most of his time enjoying a tremendous view of Lake Michigan from his office window as he reviewed the briefs and documents prepared by his younger colleagues. Billy White was one of his early clients. He'd drafted the papers that gave White control of the CIO. Criminal law was not Hande's specialty, and he'd arranged to have a criminal specialist assist him with the trial. White balked at that, refusing to have one of the less tenured partners take his case. Today he insisted that only Hande accompany him to see Assistant U.S. Attorney J. Robert Wilson. "Billy," he said to his long time client with a friendly smile, "if you think another attorney will take this case, don't let me stand in your way. Of course I know you're innocent of these charges."

White sat back in the car seat, reassured by his attorney's remark.

"Everyone knows, Billy," said Hande as he stopped in traffic, waiting for a delivery van to pull out of a space, "that you're an arrogant bastard, but you're not a murderer."

White snorted. If that comment had come from anyone else, he'd have been pissed off. For that matter, he had begun to recognize his own arrogance over the six weeks that had passed since his arrest. Those intervening weeks had been hard on him as the volume of patients coming to CIO dropped precipitously. No one referred patients to him personally anymore. Only his established patients still came, primarily because they believed that Billy White was empowered by God himself. Most of them had already had their cataracts removed, though, and were of minimal financial value to the practice.

The CIO had developed a very bad reputation in the wake of Billy White's arrest. The devious practices that White used became public knowledge. Now that they felt protected from White, other ophthalmologists in Chicago were all too happy to share their stories of White's professional abuse. The local news channels, the Trib and the Sun Times all ran reports detailing Billy White's evil methods. Of course, not all of the CIO docs operated in this way, but they were guilty by association. It did not take long for White to realize that his practice, only as financially stable as the next week's surgical referrals, was now in an untenable position. He agreed to step down as the Medical Director and Chairman of CIO and offered to see only his established patients. Other CIO docs would manage all the new referrals. This did little to strengthen their position as more and more of the lurid details surrounding Jerry Karp's death were made available to the public.

Nothing bothered White as much as the fact that all of his cronies had distanced themselves from him. At one time he was the Chairman of the Ophthalmology Division at St. Vincent's

Hospital and Catholic Medical Center in Chicago. Now, none of the physicians there returned his calls. He needed character references for his defense, and no one unassociated with CIO was willing to step forward on his behalf. He called his political associates: city councilmen, state senators, even the federal representatives from Chicago, all of whom he'd made significant contributions to support. None were able or willing to exert any meaningful pressure that would aid Billy White. He found himself a man outcast by his community; a community that he, for the most part, had defined only weeks before.

To Billy White, J. Robert Wilson's office was small, if neat. He kept a short stack of files pertaining to the cases he planned to work on in a given day on his desk. Amid the files and books and photos sat Bob Wilson, reviewing the evidence on the Aurora physicians' case he planned to prosecute. There was a good amount of documentation on referral patterns of the physicians he suspected to be involved in the scam. There was also plenty of evidence that Dan Kilner had prospered beyond his reported payroll. Finally, while the hospital had been growing steadily over the previous two decades, there became evident a source of hospital income aside from usual payors. Even the reported donations were not enough to balance the books.

Wilson was concerned that his evidence was more or less circumstantial. He needed a witness to testify against the doctors enjoined in this conspiracy, and it would be difficult for him to find one. For that reason, he had arranged to meet this day with Dr. Billy White, who had been arraigned for first degree murder in the killing of his competitor, Jerry Karp. By history, it was apparent that White was more than willing to testify against his colleagues.

"Dr. White," said Wilson, eager to get to the point. "I want to talk to you and your attorney about another case I am working on."

"This isn't about the murder charge?" asked White, barely hiding his irritation.

"No, sir," answered Wilson. "It's not."

"What exactly is this about, Mr. Wilson?" asked Hande.

Wilson crossed his hands on the desktop. "For the last several months I have been investigating Medicare fraud and collusion among the physicians in the city of Aurora. You may realize," he nodded toward Hande, knowing that he had seen the FBI agents' reports, "that this was the reason Agents Grant and Ellison had Dr. Karp's home under surveillance on the evening of the bombing."

Hande nodded.

"I was hoping, Dr. White," continued Wilson, "that you might be willing to assist me with this case in return for some assistance with your legal problems."

"You mean a deal on the murder charge."

Wilson closed his eyes and shook his head slowly. "No, sir, I do not mean the murder charge. I do have reason to believe that you were involved, or about to become involved in this collusion scheme. I believe that you might find it preferable to help us with this case than to face charges in it."

"Are you out of your mind?" blurted White.

Hande reached over to White's arm, and patted him, reminding him to stay calm. "I'm not sure I follow you, Bob. You think that my client knows something about this collusion situation? He didn't even have an office in Aurora. He couldn't be a part of it, as far as I see."

"Mr. Hande, my friends call me Bob. I might remind you that Dr. Karp was one of my friends. We went to school together."

Hande nodded.

"Let's not waste each other's time," Wilson continued. "We both know that your client didn't care for Dr. Karp. We know that they spoke together on the day of his death, and we know that he talked with Dan Kilner afterward. Dr. White lied about that to the police, and as far as I can see he lied about a lot other

410

things, too. He was very upset, several of his employees will testify to that."

Neither Hande nor White responded.

"Dr. White and Mr. Kilner had some kind of interaction. I think it revolved around this collusion scheme."

Still no response.

"Dr. White, I am willing to offer you immunity on the collusion charge and on the Medicare fraud charge. You do realize that the latter is a federal offense? All you have to do is tell me about the referral agreement, the cost, and so on, and testify in court about the scheme. You will not be charged and we will not remove your Medicare provider eligibility status."

White began to respond, moving forward in his chair. Hande held him back.

"Dr. White, you are in a great deal of trouble. I understand that the State Penitentiary facility in Joliet is a very unpleasant place." He tipped his chin down to look over the edge of his reading glasses. "I assure you that the federal prison system is much more onerous. Do yourself a favor."

The ophthalmologist and his attorney discussed the offer quietly between themselves. White shook his head.

"Don't forget, sir," added Wilson, "that Dr. Karp was killed by a bomb. Bombings are a federal offense, and I see no reason to prosecute that if you show good faith in your effort to assist us with this case."

This time Hande could not restrain the doctor. "I did not kill Jerry Karp."

Wilson held his temper. He calmly removed his glasses and set them down on the desk. He stood and walked over to the small window looking out over Blair Street traffic. He held his hands behind his back.

"Dr. White," said Wilson, looking out the window at the cars and buses moving slowly up the block. "We know from the telephone records that Dr. Karp made several calls to your office in the days leading to his death, and that you and he had a long conversation that morning." He turned, keeping his hands held behind his back, and walked across the floor. White and Hande turned in their seats to follow him. "Our lab found traces of ammonium nitrate, the chemical used to make the bomb that killed Dr. Karp, in the trunk of your Mercedes. They found traces of the completed explosive mixture in one of your clinic's cars. There is also a sales reciept for the fertilizer found in that car. Then, of course, there is the remote control transmitter in your glove compartment, which just happens to match the make of the device that was used to detonate the bomb. Your fingerprints were on that transmitter, including a single print of your thumb on the trigger button." He turned and glared at White. "There is a great deal of physical evidence that links you to this bombing."

White looked away from Wilson. He knew that the garage door opener was planted in his car, he just didn't know who'd planted it there. Karp's murderer, of course, but who was it? He and Hande had discussed that, but they remained at a loss.

Wilson stood behind his chair and placed his hands on it. He leaned forward a bit. "Then we have eyewitnesses of impeachable character that can place your black Mercedes, damaged from blast shrapnel, and you personally at the scene of the bombing. Your license plate was identified and you were followed in flight to your home."

White clenched his fists in his lap. He was there. He ran. He was frightened. He didn't know what to do.

Wilson sat down. "Means. Motive. Opportunity. Physical evidence. Eyewitnesses. I'd say the case against you is pretty strong, Doctor." Calmed by his own words, he summarized his deal. "Gentlemen, I can offer you immunity in the fraud case, and I am willing to drop the bombing charge. I cannot and will not offer a plea bargain on the murder case, as I am not trying it. I do have some friends in Illinois, and I can make an effort to request that you are placed in a medium security facility to begin with rather than a high security location."

Hande looked at his client. White looked at the floor. He didn't care for this deal. "If my client helps you with this," said

Hande, buying time for White, "he will be adding fuel to the fire of the murder case. It will strengthen the arguments supporting his motive for Karp's death."

Wilson shrugged. "I think the motive for that case is already strongly established. Frankly, I've prosecuted dozens of murder cases with far less. I have nothing more to offer you, and you have nothing more for which you can ask. You need to make a decision."

Hande looked at his client again. There wasn't much to discuss.

Wilson's phone rang. Who in the hell could that be, he thought. Not now. "Yes?"

"Bob. Rollie Grant. Sorry to interrupt. Maggie told me who you're interviewing, but there's someone in my office that I think you should meet."

"Now?"

"Now."

Hank Greenley stood six foot two, and cut a classic stance. His grayed hair was neatly coiffed, combed lusciously full atop his head. The lenses in his wire framed glasses were the kind that get dark when exposed to sunlight, and they hadn't yet fully lightened in the muted blue fluorescent light of the office. His falcon nose supported them regally, his head held high. The gray suit he wore looked as if it were tailored, although it wasn't. It rested comfortably on his lean body, accented nicely by the gold Rolex on his left wrist and a heavy man's bracelet on the right.

Greenley had the countenance of success, but his confident appearance masked the fact that he had been working odd hours selling refrigerators and stoves in Waukegan following the blood letting that cost him his job at Compton Memorial Hospital. He'd found that at fifty four years of age, it was difficult to wrest a meaningful job in the executive market with the kind of bad paper that dogged him. Fortunately, he'd managed to save enough over the years so that he and his wife could get by.

413

PRIVILEGES

He sat alone, now, in the interrogation room. There was a single small window to one side of the room, looking out onto a building some five feet away that was not yet there when this one had been constructed. The other wall had a mirror, obviously two-way, so that others could observe the questioning process. There was an ashtray on the table, but nothing else. No pens, no papers, no machines, no telephone. Greenley sat and waited.

Eventually, Grant and Ellison returned with a tall, thin man. "This is J. Robert Wilson," said Grant. "He is the Assistant U.S. Attorney." They all sat down around the table. "I'd like you to tell him what you just told me."

Greenley, a moment earlier the scene of strength and confidence, glanced nervously around the room. The seriousness of his actions this day finally got the better of him.

"It's all right, Hank," said Ellison. "This is the right thing to do."

"Okay," he said tentatively. "You're right." He took a deep breath and began. "Mr. Wilson, do you know who I am?"

Wilson nodded. "You used to be the chief administrator at Compton Memorial Hospital in Aurora." He sat forward in his chair, his eyes wide open. He looked ready to pounce, to prevent any of Greenley's words from escaping the room without his attention.

"That's right. I ran the hospital for five years. The doctors there decided...they didn't want me there anymore. I was discharged a couple years ago."

"It was pretty acrimonious as I understand it."

"You could say that. I can't even get a lukewarm job recommendation, and that was a pretty important part of my career. I've...not done so well of late."

"I understand." Get to it, get on, he thought.

"I spoke with Detective Cardena in Aurora. He says he knows you and that you were working on the Karp killing with him."

"That's correct," answered Wilson.

414

"I heard about what happened to him." He hung his head. "It was awful." He looked at Wilson. "They ruined my life, Mr. Wilson. I'd heard they'd ruined his, too. Neither of us deserved it."

"I'm sure of that. Jerry Karp was my friend, Mr. Greenley."

He looked at the floor once more. "I didn't know. I'm sorry. It's just that...that they seem to have made a practice out of ruining people."

"The doctors."

"Yes, and the hospital administration. I mean," he looked Wilson unflinchingly in the eye, "look at what they did to me. I was one of them. Understand?"

"I think I do. Whatever is going on there, they think they can act without fear of recourse."

"Right," he said with a gleam in his eye. Someone understood. "When I heard about Jerry, I..." He paused, organized his thoughts. "When I heard about Jerry, I couldn't stay silent any longer. They castrated me professionally. Karp must have fought back, and they killed him. He must have found out, and they killed him so that he couldn't tell anyone else."

"Tell them what, Mr. Greenley?"

Greenley breathed hard, and sighed. Once the story was out there would be no turning back. For weeks he'd been unable to sleep more than a fitful few hours, waking in a sweat. He couldn't eat, and was uncomfortable at work, even irritable. That bastard, Billy White, had been arrested for Karp's murder, and what he'd read in the newspapers supported the charge. Still, what he knew about Compton Memorial Hospital implicated the others in the murder as well. It didn't seem right that White might bear the blame by himself. That lizard Kilner needed to be punished, too. Hank Greenley didn't care anymore what his own consequences might be, as long as Kilner and those other dicks with ice water for blood, Orville Harmon and Kip Porchette, were punished right alongside him.

"The doctors at Compton Memorial Hospital developed an informal society several decades ago. It was a small hospital, and the doctors closed ranks. They wanted to keep all of their patients in Aurora."

"Okay."

"They agreed to pool some money together to help recruit other doctors and develop inadequate departments within the hospital. They called this the Development Fund."

Wilson nodded.

"The lawyers told us that the fund and the agreement to limit referrals represented Medicare fraud and collusion. They recommended that the Development Fund be disbanded."

"But it wasn't."

"No. The doctors continued to pay money, and it was agreed that the chief administrator would oversee how it was spent. Anything that benefitted the system was pretty much acceptable, as long as the hospital grew bigger and better and stronger."

"And you took some money from the Fund, too?"

"Yes."

"That's why they fired you?"

"No, not really. The political milieu just kept changing. I kept trying to predict the direction that the government was going, and I wasn't accurate enough. The doctors didn't like my decisions. They wanted me to leave."

"And you resisted?"

"No." His voice became quiet, and deadly serious. "They never gave me a chance. They simply destroyed my reputation and cut me loose to drift. I am not a young man. I couldn't get a decent job. I had a hard time finding any job at all."

Wilson nodded. "But they are still paying money to extort referrals and buying silence with growth of the hospital."

"As far as I know, yes. It certainly seems that they are most enamored with this Kilner fellow. His methods are...more like their own. Together, Kilner and the medical staff can really trash people who threaten them. This Billy White is the same. They're all made for each other."

Wilson needed to get Greenley back to the Development Fund. "If they all know that this Development Fund is illegal, how are they hiding the money?"

"They keep a list of names of pediatric patients who die in the hospital. If the kid hasn't gotten a social security number, the administrator applies for one as if he were the parent. I did it. Once you have a social security number, the money can be deposited in bank accounts opened under that name. By keeping deposits small and paying taxes on the interest, the authorities don't have to be alerted."

Wilson sat back in his chair and crossed his leg, clasping his hands comfortably around his knee. His heart raced. "Do you have any evidence of this, Mr. Greenley," he asked coolly.

He nodded. "Yes. I kept copies of the names and bank account numbers that I used. When they got rid of me," he looked at his shoes, "I decided that I might get back at them some day. I decided not to until now, because I knew that what I did was wrong. Now, though, after Karp's murder, I can't keep the secret any longer."

"And you're willing to testify about what you know?"

"It would ease my conscience, but I was hoping we might be able to make a deal about my own involvement. My life is already ruined."

"I think we can work something out," said Wilson.

They returned to Wilson's office, where Michael Hande and Billy White had agreed to take the deal. White would put the hospital people away, and so would Greenley. Cardena and the Kane County D.A. would lock up White. Only Greenley would walk, and his life was ruined anyway. By adding the suspended sentence to the man's record, he was condemned to a career in the periphery.

Wilson explained to White that Agent Grant would be taking his statement, and that together they would review the result with Hande.

"There's one thing I want you to know," said White meekly. "For what it's worth, I did not kill Jerry Karp."

"That's not for me to decide, Dr. White," said Wilson without a speck of emotion. As much as he had carried on about how he and Karp were friends, that they'd been school chums, he didn't miss the physician a bit. "I do have a question for you, doctor. Off the record." His curiosity had gotten the better of him.

"Yes?"

"Why Jerry Karp? I mean, even if he was grossly incompetent, your superior skills and new office would have minimized his effect on you as a competitor. We looked at the numbers, and you could have bought and sold that guy's little practice ten times over."

"So?"

"So, why? Why bother screwing him over the way you did? What did it accomplish?"

White crossed his arms over his chest and leaned forward. He paused for a moment, then answered. "It was the letter."

"Letter? You mean Karp wrote a letter complaining about you?"

"No, no. He wrote a letter to the editor. Of a journal."

"I don't follow you."

"Two years ago, maybe three, I wrote an article with my partners, Drs. Genello and Stutz, on the incidence of complications related to anesthesia for cataract surgery. In our hands, these complications did not require that surgery be canceled even though that was the classical thinking. The reason is that we are better cataract surgeons, of course."

"And Jerry Karp wrote a letter to the editor questioning those conclusions."

"Right. The little prick suggested that the incidence of our complications was unacceptably high and inferred that we were proceeding with surgery only for financial gain. He implied that if we were more careful with the anesthesia, took more time, that our patients would have simpler surgeries and equally uneventful postoperative courses. You see, we delegate the anesthesia to our technicians in order to save time and money."

"So you went after Karp because this letter was published."

He uncrossed his arms and slapped his palms on the table top. "Not on your life. I squashed it right away. I know the editor of the journal. He wouldn't publish that letter."

"So no one else knew what Karp wrote?"

"Well," he said slowly, "the journal received about a dozen letters saying basically the same thing. They printed two of them."

"But not Karp's."

"Absolutely."

"But others felt the same way."

"Presumably."

"And that is why you went out of your way to disgrace Jerry Karp professionally. Because he wrote a letter to the editor that was never published." He didn't fully comprehend this until he actually said the words.

"That's right. He had the balls to imply that I was not acting in my patients' best interest, but rather that I was cutting corners in order to save money."

"But you were. You just admitted it."

"Yes. But he had no right to point it out in that way. He was a punk. He needed to be shown what can happen to a smart-ass kid who doesn't respect his rival, particularly one who has been around for as long as I have."

"Did you mention this letter to anyone else? Any of the reviewers or examiners who you'd set out to attack Karp?"

"Of course not. Why should I?"

Wilson rose and pushed his chair in. "I see," he said quietly. "Agent Grant will take your statement. I'll be in touch with Mr. Hande." With that, Bob Wilson left the room.

The heels of his shoes clicked on the linoleum floor as Wilson made his way through the brightly lit hallway. People moved quickly around him in the busy office. The place was alive with lawyers, secretaries, suspects and police. Bob Wilson barely noticed them just now.   His case against the administrators and physicians of Compton Memorial Hospital in Aurora, Illinois would be air tight, insured by the testimony that his two witnesses would provide. He smiled. Then the smile ran away from his face. Bob Wilson knew that one of his star witnesses was a murderer.

No murderer ever committed the crime for a good reason. There were jilted lovers, drunken friends, greedy business associates, and career crooks like the mobsters who killed for intimidation as well as personal gain. Billy White was a special kind of murderer though. Before he ended Karp's physical life, he had already squeezed out the man's self respect. He was more than just a murderer, this Dr. White. He had elevated character assassination to an art. The justification haunted Wilson. He'd killed Karp because of an unpublished letter to a medical journal that would never have caused its subject more than a moment of professional embarrassment. Embarrassment that, in fact, he still suffered because someone else had published a similar letter. Despite that, White's practice suffered absolutely no ill effects from the whole affair. Karp was dead because of written words that spoke the truth to no one.

Epilogue

Morrissey could hardly believe at first that he'd even received a response. He'd attended the Academy meetings, the annual conference for the American Academy of Ophthalmology, thinking that his old friend might show up to stay in touch with his profession. He should have known how fruitless this would be, since Karp would hardly take the chance of being spotted by an old colleague. Lon simply could not accept the fact that Jerry Karp was dead. These doctors were not murderers. They were happy instead to inflict nonlethal wounds to the soul, amputating a man's reputation as they might cut off a leg or resect a tumor. Their actions were manipulative and well orchestrated, but they were not the stuff of killers.

They had never positively identified the burnt corpse that was removed from the shell of Karp's old Stealth. Val had looked at the body, but it was disfigured and blackened beyond any recognition. There was blood sent to a crime lab, but they had no reference from Karp to compare against. Lon was forever skeptical.

He'd done some research and called several of Karp's best friends from medical school. There had been five residents altogether when Karp trained at Detroit General. He'd even managed to get Karp's old high school yearbook. He found the telephone number of every individual who'd signed it and called them, thinking Karp might look up an old girlfriend or school pal. There was not a single person who had heard from the late Jerrold Karp. Most hadn't heard from him for years when he was alive, and only a very few even knew that he was dead.

At one point during Billy White's trial, Detective Cardena had called him. He'd gotten wind of Lon's attempts to find Karp. "Is there a particular reason that you believe Dr. Karp is still alive?" he asked.

"You mean do I have any evidence? Did Karp contact me? No."

"Did he ever talk about running away?"

"No."

"If Dr. Karp is still alive," he asked, "who is it that you think we found in his car? You know, you are linked to this killing, Mr. Morrissey."

He laughed. "Why? Because you found my old piece of shit car burned up next to Karp's?" He belly laughed. "I lent the man my car. No," he corrected himself, "I gave it to him. They were about to repossess his. We were friends." That was the whole point, after all. "I just can't accept the fact that he's dead. I certainly don't know who else that might have been in his car."

If Karp were still alive, he would have avoided medicine, Lon decided. Karp was intelligent. He was creative. He was visually oriented. He could work with his hands. Lon thought he might have become an architect or designer of some sort, but Karp had had plenty of formal schooling. He could have been a writer, but the pay for that kind of work tended to be spotty. Lon thought Karp might want a regular paycheck at this time in his life. Perhaps he had gotten into some sort of creative job for a larger company as an ad exec or artist or such. That was possible, and he might even be able to bullshit his way into an entry level position without formal training. Lon contacted several magazines for writers, advertisers, and graphic artists, and placed ads in their personals. There was no response.

Angie was worried about Lon's obsession with his dead friend. She argued with him to let Karp's memory rest peacefully. He was dead and nothing could bring him back. He agreed eventually, but asked her to indulge him in one last attempt to reach the man. She consented, but only with Lon's solemn promise that this would be the last time.

Morrisey learned of Karp's association with Avery Prater, and convinced him to have a personal message sent out on the Internet. It was a photo of Karp and Lon taken in happier times. Prater posted it on a missing persons website, and they added the text: Have you seen me? A post office box number followed for response..

There was no answer. Lon continued to receive mail at the box, bills and junk and the like, but no reply came from the late Dr. Karp. Two months later, though, when Lon had finally accepted the death of his friend as a matter of fact, there was a personal letter in the box.

There was no return address on the letter, and the postmark was from Denver, Colorado. Lon knew well enough that if Karp had sent the letter, he would have taken care not to mail it anywhere near where he was living. The letter inside was brief: "Lon; meet me at the Cheers Bar in Boston's Logan Airport, September 7, eleven a.m. BE ALONE, or I will leave. The Green Hornet." Only close friends knew the nickname for the old car.

Lon managed to get the day off from work and used cash to buy the airline ticket to Boston. Karp would be very cautious about the meeting and Lon wanted to avoid any unnecessary paper trail. To be sure, he wasn't altogether convinced that the meeting hadn't been dreamt up by Detective Cardena to test him. He barely slept for two nights leading up to the appointed day.

Now Lon Morrissey sat conspicuously at the bar, sipping a beer and nervously munching on a plate of nachos. He glanced around the pub every few minutes, seeing only airline passengers reading, watching CNN on the TV, smoking cigarettes and drinking expensive beer. There was no familiar face, no mustachioed ophthalmologist.

He drank a second beer slowly, as it was still before noon. Glancing at his watch for the fourth time in as many minutes, Lon began to wonder who had sent the note. Karp was always punctual, he remembered. Now he was nearly an hour late. He sighed, ate a chip, and looked up at the TV.

"In Chicago," claimed the news anchor, "the first guilty verdict was handed down in the series of Compton trials, so named for the hospital involved in Medicare fraud, collusion, and money laundering. The former administrative executive of the hospital, Daniel Kilner, was sentenced to ten years in prison for his central role in the case which was tied to the death of a local physician. Assistant U.S. Attorney J. Robert Wilson called the case evidence of efforts to reform health care gone awry."

The video image cut to film of Bob Wilson speaking to reporters, half a dozen microphones held toward him, standing outside the federal courthouse. His fine blonde hair blew slightly in the gentle breeze. "Our best efforts were put forward to attempt reform of the health care industry," said Wilson to the crowd. "Despite this, the result was not so much managed competition as it was hyper-competition, an attempt to lock out others as providers. We need to rethink our position on health care reform in order to provide the less fortunate with the care they deserve without rebuilding our entire medical delivery infrastructure."

"Spoken like a true politician," said Lon to no one in particular.

"Asshole. The Compton scam had been going on for nearly forty years. That was nothing but politics." There was a pause and a slurp of beer. "I always knew that shithead would run for office. He'll win, too."

The voice was familiar, if quieter than he remembered it. His heart ran and his breath became short. It wasn't often that a man talked with a ghost. Lon turned and looked at the man who had been seated next to him for almost ten minutes. He was clean shaven and had long, sandy hair tied back in a pony tail. He wore no glasses; his eyes were dark brown. There was a small diamond earring in his earlobe. He shifted the simple striped tie that accompanied the fine off white long sleeve shirt and navy blue suit. He sat straight in the chair, never removing his gaze from the television yet still watching for sudden movement elsewhere in the bar.

Karp had lost at least fifteen pounds since Lon had seen him last. That and the hair were the greatest changes in his appearance. He reached for him, slowly at first, then hugged the well known stranger. "Jerry," was all he could squeak.

Karp returned the emotional display, himself drawn to his old best friend. He had planned to avoid any such show, but found himself disarmed by the man. "I'm pleased to meet you, Mr. Morrissey. I am Glen. Glen Houston."

Still hugging his friend, Lon smiled, "Glen it is, then." Finally they let each other go. "How in the hell are you?" he asked, still finding it hard to believe that they were together.

"I'm doing very well, Lon, as you can see." He poured down the Sam Adams with a huge gulp. "I am a little uncomfortable just sitting around here. Care to join me for lunch?" The two men rose. "I know a brewpub just a few blocks away from Boston Gardens, and they've got pretty good food." Karp dropped a twenty on the bar.

"Jerry, uh, Glen, I just can't tell you how great it is to see you. Honest to God, I didn't recognize you and you were sitting right next to me."

Karp smiled. "That was the idea, Lon."

"I knew you were alive," said Lon finally. "I just had the feeling."

"God knows," answered Karp, "I hope you're the only one. I thought I'd done a pretty damn good job disappearing."

"You did. I got a call from that detective in Aurora. He thought that I knew where you were. I told him I was just acting out a hunch, that I couldn't accept your death."

Karp never stopped watching the crowd ahead, never broke his pace. "He doesn't know you're here, right?"

"I haven't talked to him in months," Lon reassured. "He seemed pretty comfortable with the outcome of his case."

"Good. I want to see that bastard White stay in prison for many years to come. It would be...disappointing if they discovered he hadn't killed me."

"You gave up ophthalmology?" Lon changed the subject.

"It's a small community, eye doctors. I have to depend on being anyone other than Jerrold Karp. I couldn't take the chance." The afternoon sun was warm as they stepped out of the terminal to catch the shuttle over to the subway station. "And frankly, I don't miss medicine or ophthalmology. I was ready for a change."

Lon rubbed his neck as they sat down on the old bus used as a shuttle. "Subway, huh? Very different from the past. I'd have expected you to rent a car."

"No, pal, not today. I want to keep transportation very public. Very open. Better chance to duck out in case someone's following us."

"Hey, listen, Glen," said Lon, a bit irritated. "I promised to come alone and I did. I wouldn't rat you out."

"Easy, Lon. I know. I can trust you, but I don't dare trust anyone else. Even if the cops are satisfied that this case is closed, our friend Dr. White isn't. I wouldn't put it past him to hire a private detective to follow you around, just in case."

Lon nodded agreement. He had been trying very hard to forget that Karp's presence here meant that he had, in fact, killed another man in his place. The pause was uncomfortable, and he couldn't help himself. "Glen. Who was in the Stealth that day?"

"You never heard about any missing persons, did you?"

"No."

"No family crying that Daddy never came home? No stories about some guy who ran off and left the bills unpaid?"

"No."

"None of the other doctors in town disappeared?"

"No."

Karp nodded. The shuttle bus stopped and they disembarked, walking toward the subway station. He reached into his pocket and removed three subway tokens. He handed two to Lon: One for the trip out, one for the trip back. He kept the other for himself. "It's better that you not know who was in the Stealth subbing for me, Lon. That would make you an accessory to murder. Meeting me here today is dangerous enough. Trust me, the world is a better place without that individual."

Lon nodded. "And White?"

Glen grinned eerily. "That bastard, Billy White, killed Jerry Karp as sure as you and I are standing here," he said. "As God is my witness, he got what he deserves."

426

They each slipped a token in the turnstile slot and passed through, then down the stairs. A train screeched to a stop and its doors fell open, flinging a half dozen passengers lazily onto the walkway. This was not a busy time for the airport stop on the subway loop. Karp and Morrissey boarded the train along with a young woman dressed in a business suit, two chattering teens, and a lone black man wearing a running outfit. The woman carried her briefcase in one hand and a small suitcase in the other. The two teens each had large backpacks, and the black man carried a gym bag. Karp hoped that they were all legitimate travellers and not undercover cops. He recognized none of them from the bar. "I had hoped, Lon, that by meeting you I might be able to get you to promise me that you'll let your old friend, Karp, stay dead. Let me get in touch with you next time."

"You have my word."

"Thanks."

They rode the train silently for a while, neither quite sure what to say next. Finally Lon broke the silence. "I'm sorry, Glen, I just have a hard time with the guy in the Stealth. I mean, you were a doctor. You made a career saving lives. I don't know how you could kill a man."

Houston thought for a moment, then answered. "There is death, Lon, and then there is death. Think about it. You know how some patients came to us, still alive yet nearly dead."

"You mean the sick ones?"

"No, I mean the ones that were more than just sick. The moribund ones whose lives had been taken from them. The ones who were old and debilitated, unable to walk. The ones who'd had a stroke, or maybe three. The ones who could barely breathe, who couldn't control their bowels or bladders."

"Okay. But you never killed any of them."

"No. How about the ones who'd lost their minds. The ones with Alzheimer's Disease or other problems, who couldn't recognize their own family."

"Right. I know the kind. You never killed any of them, either."

"Nope. Never took a knife and stabbed them, never took a gun and shot them."

"And yet you did it to this guy."

"Sure, Lon," continued Houston. "But I did sometimes hasten death for these sad individuals. Some of them were made `no codes,' where we agreed along with the patient or the family that we would not go to heroic means to resuscitate them. For others, we'd agreed to withhold antibiotics in cases of infection. That certainly killed them."

"Sure, Glen. But that's different than killing a man."

"Yes it is. No it isn't. Sometimes death is welcome, and sometimes it is a relief of suffering." He paused to make certain that Lon was following him. "For some of these unfortunates, death was the only relief that could come for their physical or mental pain."

Lon nodded. "That's still not murder."

"No," said Glen. "It's not. It's not even mercy killing, per se. However, along with the family, I was involved in making life-and-death decisions. Sometimes, allowing someone to die is the kindest thing you can do. It allows others to live better. It relieves the pain of the family."

"Okay."

"Lon, I relieved the pain of the family of a raping pedophile. He terrorized his own children. He terrorized his ex-wife. He'd escaped from prison, jumped parole."

Lon said nothing.

"The man I killed hadn't done anything useful for society or himself in years, and he had plans for his kids that are inconceivable for a decent human. Lon, he was an evil human. He was sadder than any poor old stroked out coot we ever took care of. He didn't deserve to live, not for what he wanted to do to his children. Society has no place for his kind, and there was no chance to change him. On the other hand, when he took my place for that car bomb, he gave me a new life. He gave his kids a new life. He gave his ex-wife a new life."

Lon nodded, but said nothing.

"This was much, much more than a mercy killing," Karp concluded. "Alive, all this man offered his family was fear. He was a threat to those around him, and there was no means of rehabilitation. He frightened his children. He cost all of us to watch over him. By killing him, I saved the lives of two children. Do you understand, Lon, that this wasn't cold blooded murder? It was calculated, but it was an opportunity that happened along at the right time. I didn't hunt him down. I was just there to intervene. Everyone was a winner."

"Except for him."

Houston shrugged. "Maybe he was, too. He had an uncontrollable compulsion. He couldn't change himself. You have to wonder if, given the facts in an objective manner, he might not have agreed to this end as an alternative. Do you think he would have preferred a life of incarceration? Do you know how they treat child molestors in prison? He wasn't a very popular fellow there."

"Maybe so," said Lon. "At least, I see your point. I mean, you never lied to me before."

"I have no reason to lie now, Lon. You either believe me or not. He was evil. Billy White is evil. The two of them were made for their storybook endings. Either way, I have no remorse. In the end, everyone got what they really deserved."

Lon decided to change the subject. "What are you doing, now that you're out of medicine? I'm curious."

"I started working with an old laptop computer that I bought used, doing some freelance writing and then taking odd jobs for companies. I did some technical manuals, corporate newsletters and the like. Eventually, one of my clients needed some maintenance work on their system. They asked if I could do it, and I said I could." He laughed. "Of course, I'd never tried to fix a network before, and man, I need to tell you, they had really fucked it up good. Took a week. I got it to sing. They hired me as a full time computer consultant. It's a good job, even if the pay sucks. I got no debt and no need to live in a big house anymore. I'm happy."

"Don't you ever miss your old friends?" asked Lon quietly. "Val?"

"Of course I do," he answered seriously. "I think of Val a lot. As far as friends, well, you're the only one who made any effort to find out about me." He shrugged. The train stopped at a station. "But I do follow up on Val," he continued. "I know that she got paid off by my life insurance company, so she's pretty well set for a few years. I also know that she's filed an application for adoption with our old agency, this time as a single parent."

Lon steadied himself on the seat in front of them as the train lurched forward. "She did," he said. "You're right."

"Everyone got what they really wanted," he observed. "I got out of an impossible jam. Val got a child. It would have been nice if we could have managed to do both together." He shrugged. "It wasn't meant to be."

"It just seems such a waste," said Lon. "A waste of your life, your training. A waste of your skills."

"That's just the way it had to be," Karp repeated.

The subway train stopped. Karp nodded to Lon to get up. They walked off the train and up the stairway that led to Boston Gardens. The sun was bright and the air was clean. "Great town," said Karp as he pointed down the block, showing Lon the way to the restaurant.

"But don't you miss medicine?" asked Lon, returning to the subject at hand. "You had a future. Karp was a good doctor. Even the Illinois State Medical Board returned your license after an independent review."

"Posthumously," grinned Karp. "That was little more than public relations." He shook his head. "Jerry Karp was deep in debt. I could never have made it without a big chunk of money from somewhere. No. Thanks. Medicine doesn't miss me, and I don't miss medicine. We weren't meant for each other. Hi, darlin'," he said to the waitress greeting customers for lunch at the door of the Commonwealth Brewpub. She smiled a young, toothy smile at the two men.

"Good afternoon, Mr. Houston, Mr. Morrissey. Your table is right this way."

"Thanks."

"She knows you?"

"Of course." He smiled slyly. "Glen Houston is well known here. You don't think I'd have a power lunch with my old friend someplace where they didn't know me."

Lon was in a dream world as they took their seats. "You're full of surprises for me today, old friend. I don't know what to expect next."

"As long as you have no surprises for me, Lonnie." He turned back to the hostess. "Could you have someone get me a pale ale, and a weiss beer for my friend, please?"

"Of course, sir."

"Thanks."

Morrissey looked over the menu, trying to find something good for lunch. He'd been looking forward to a good bowl of New England clam chowder at the very least. "What," he finally asked, "made you choose Boston for our meeting?"

"Simple," said Karp. "It's a long way away from where I live, so I could change planes a couple of times."

Lon figured that was part of the plan, though he presumed that Karp might also live only a few miles away and this was just an excuse to throw him off the trail.

"I'd hoped that you and I might be able to catch a Red Sox game. I've never been to Fenway. Then came the damn strike." He shrugged. "I knew that we could get Sam Adams on tap at the airport," he gestured around the room, "and incredibly good microbrew here." He leaned toward Lon, putting his elbows on the tabletop. "I may not love medicine, but I still love a good beer," he said. The two men laughed like schoolboys.

Karp-Houston and Lon Morrissey drank quite a few good beers that afternoon. Satisfied that Karp had done what he'd done for good reason and comforted that he'd made sure his wife was well provided for in her new life, Lon settled back and enjoyed the afternoon with his friend. They talked about the baseball strike and cars and computers and flying and women and beer. Before they realized it, Karp saw that it was six o'clock. It was still light out, but the dinner crowd was already beginning to wander into the pub. He was happy and flushed. He was also feeling...full. He stood and put his hand sloppily on Lon's shoulder. "Got to hit the head," he said.

"Don't be long," slurred Lon.

"Hey, where would I be going?" said Karp too loud. He teetered off toward the restroom.

Before ten minutes had passed, Lon knew well enough that Karp had gone. He wasn't sure if his friend had chosen to do without an emotional goodbye or if he'd been spooked. He kept an eye on the door to the can, but Karp never showed.

"Here's your change, sir." The waitress left a receipt and nearly a hundred dollars in change.

Lon held up his hand. "I didn't pay yet," he said.

"Yes, sir. Mr. Houston handed me the cash, but he left too much. He asked me to leave the change with you, sir."

"Did he leave?"

"I wouldn't know. I don't think so." She left to wait on another table.

Karp had left him dinner money, cab fare, whatever. He didn't see him go, but he knew. He'd changed his clothes, his hair, something. Maybe it was the UPS man he watched leave the bar. Maybe he was with the group of students who went home a few minutes earlier. He wasn't sure how Karp had gotten out unnoticed, but he had.

Lon thought that if he hurried, he might be able to catch a cab to the airport to say goodbye to Jerry Karp. He then sat back in his chair and sipped a beer. He'd probably never recognize Karp, and he couldn't be certain that he would leave via the airport, let alone whether he was leaving that night.

He toasted the invisible man in the empty seat in front of him, a good man he once knew. "God bless you, Jerry Karp," he said quietly. Or Glen Houston, or whoever you are. He knew that he must let Karp go. Karp had promised to stay in touch,

432

and Lon knew that he was good to his word. He drank down the beer because he knew, too, that Karp hated to see a glass left unfinished.

About the Author

Scott Rachelle is an ophthalmologist who has been in practice for fifteen years. After working as a general ophthalmologist in the midwest, he returned to complete a fellowship in vitreoretinal surgery. He now devotes his career to this medical and surgical subspecialty. He is the Regional Medical Director of a large private practice of ophthalmology and the Chairman of the Department of Surgery at his local hospital. He has presented papers at several national and international conferences and has published various research projects in peer-reviewed journals. He is a Fellow of the American Academy of Ophthalmology, a member of the Association for Research in Vision and Ophthalmology, the American Society of Cataract and Refractive Surgery, the American Diabetes Association, and the American College of Physician Executives.

Privileges is the first novel by this author, who relies on his experiences as a practicing physician and knowledge of the politics of the medical profession to weave a tale of conspiracy and greed that takes place in the setting of a modern medical facility. The character, Dr. Jerrold Karp, lives in a frightening world where patients have become a commodity, and the mutual respect of colleagues is discarded in return for promises of riches. It is a microcosm that could occur anywhere and anytime, except for the practice of medicine by professionals with high moral and ethical caliber.